I DID WARN HER

I DID WARN HER

A NOVEL

SIAN GILBERT

WILLIAM MORROW

An Imprint of HarperCollins*Publishers*

I DID WARN HER. Copyright © 2025 by Sian Gilbert. All rights reserved. Printed in the United States of America. No part of this book may be used or reproduced in any manner whatsoever without written permission except in the case of brief quotations embodied in critical articles and reviews. For information, address HarperCollins Publishers, 195 Broadway, New York, NY 10007.

HarperCollins books may be purchased for educational, business, or sales promotional use. For information, please email the Special Markets Department at SPsales@harpercollins.com.

FIRST EDITION

Interior text design by Diahann Sturge-Campbell

Yacht photo © Alexey Seafarer/Stock.Adobe.com
Hand lettering on page pages 190 and 197 by Patrick Barry

Library of Congress Cataloging-in-Publication Data

Names: Gilbert, Sian, author.
Title: I did warn her : a novel / Sian Gilbert.
Description: First edition. | New York, NY : William Morrow, 2025. |
Identifiers: LCCN 2024021167 | ISBN 9780063388505 (paperback) | ISBN 9780063388512 (ebook)
Subjects: LCGFT: Novels.
Classification: LCC PR6107.I417 I35 2025 | DDC 823/.92—dc23/eng/20240506
LC record available at https://lccn.loc.gov/2024021167

ISBN 978-0-06-338850-5
ISBN 978-0-06-343663-3 (simultaneous hardcover edition)

25 26 27 28 29 LBC 5 4 3 2 1

For Mum and Dad, my number one fans and the best parents in the world. Thank you for everything you do.

And for Toby, who always meant home, and who I miss very much.

PROLOGUE

The body lies face down in the water, blonde hair fanning outward. The backs of her arms and legs are visible. Barely, I can make out the glittering silver of her nail varnish.

She's still wearing the coat. Once red and fluffy, it is now sodden and limp, the collar stained dark with blood. The back of her head must have been sticky and wet with it, because a large area has now dried and become encrusted with the stuff.

Was death instant, or a slow suffering? A struggle to breathe as water gathered in her lungs and drowned her?

It is better this way, no matter how much I wanted to see the life leave her eyes.

Well. We have our confirmation now, don't we? The bitch is definitely dead.

I did warn her.

PART ONE

CHAPTER ONE

SASHA

I don't deserve it: the sparkling sea lapping against the pier, the smell of salt and petrol, the freedom that awaits me. I don't deserve any of it.

But I'm here now, and I'm not looking back.

The name, *Ophelia*, is the first thing I see, spread across the sixty-meter superyacht in huge letters. White and sleek, the bow sharpens to a point and gives the entire vessel a predatory, sharklike quality. A strip of black across the port side makes the white sparkle, each window placed to maximize aesthetics above all else. Even though there are other boats close by in the marina, they don't compare. If the name wasn't displayed so proudly, I'd be sure I was stepping onto the wrong one.

My greatest example of luxury travel is the time I got upgraded to a first-class train ticket back in the UK. I've never even flown extended legroom.

How the other half live. Except this is more like the other 0.1 percent.

It's a baking-hot morning, the sky a clear blue. Even though I'm wearing shorts and a tank top, dragging my suitcase straight from my flight on barely any sleep has meant I'm both exhausted and sweating buckets. Any makeup that was once on has long since melted away. Hopefully, I'm still as presentable as always. *Ophelia* and I have that in common: I stand out in a crowd too.

Not that I should be thinking about that. My looks are what got me in trouble before.

This is what I need. Something entirely unlike the life I left behind. Even if Dr. Martin did give me the idea to do this in the first place.

For a second I'm back there, the memory hitting like the heat and salty air. It's that moment. The one I keep trying to forget—I'm crying, holding my hands out, gasping at the blood.

"Sasha Quill?"

Everything comes back into focus. A woman is standing on the gangplank between the yacht and quay, arms folded.

She's obscured by the shadow of the boat, so I step forward and offer my hand for her to shake. "That's me."

I'm not sure what I'm expecting. Eagerness, perhaps? Maybe even for her to be impressed. I'd have thought someone like me would be an asset to a boat like this.

Instead, she merely looks me up and down. "I'm Jade. Chief stewardess and your boss. Is it true this is your first charter?"

"Yes," I say, cringing when she gives a disappointed sigh. "But I'm here to make a change, and I'm good with—"

To my astonishment, she raises a finger to silence me. "I don't require your life story. We needed someone to fill in on this last charter, and a newbie like you is the best we could get on such short notice. You're at least aware that your hair should be tied into a neat bun?"

I touch my hair, conscious of it hanging in a low ponytail, scraped back more out of necessity due to the heat than anything else. Normally, my hair is my best asset. It has a shininess to it only otherwise achieved in hair adverts. People reach out and run their fingers through it of their own accord, as if they can't help it, and tell me they wish it was theirs. "Yes. I knew that. I thought, because I was arriving when there weren't any guests—"

"It's better to be prepared, isn't it?" Jade says. "I haven't come and greeted you looking like I rolled out of bed, have I?"

She hasn't. It's at this point, finally, that she steps back and allows me onto the yacht, and I get my first proper look at her.

And now I can see why she wasn't bowled over by me.

Jade is intimidatingly pretty, and this is coming from someone who rates herself an easy nine out of ten. I think my scales have been off. She's model tall like I am and looks like one, wispy blonde hair pulled into the most perfect high bun I've ever seen, not a single strand out of place, a pen tucked behind her ear. Her figure is incredible, like a dancer's. She stands with the same poise and posture as one too, shoulders back and chin up as if she could take off at any moment into a spin.

It's unnerving. We could be sisters.

But Jade doesn't have the same disconcerted reaction.

"At least you're on time," she concedes, checking her watch. "Even if your overall appearance leaves much to be desired. You'll see soon enough that sloppy standards won't cut it on this boat. Leave your suitcase by the entrance. I'll give you a tour of *Ophelia*."

Overall appearance leaves much to be desired? I have the desperate urge to check a mirror, but refrain from dipping my fingers into my handbag and focus on trying to make small talk instead.

"Bit of an unlucky name, isn't it?" I say, thinking of *Hamlet*.

"It is the owner's mother's name. Another thing you'll learn—keep your mouth shut unless you've got something worthwhile to say."

I'm not a stranger to biting, bitchy remarks. I got enough of them in my last job. But at least then the nurses had the sense to whisper behind my back and I wasn't meant to hear. Jade is direct.

I head through the entrance, stepping over the precipice between land and sea, shoes off at Jade's command, and take in a marble spiral staircase. A crystal chandelier hangs from the ceiling, and all around are mirrors and expensive-looking paintings.

"Incredible, isn't it?" she says. "We won't be using the toys on this charter, so I won't bother taking you down into the water garage, but we have several items that the guests enjoy. The Jet Skis, the slide, and we have two sets of inflatables too. One large enough for eight people, the other for five."

It's wild what being rich affords someone.

"We'll start at the top," Jade pronounces, and we go up two flights, feet sinking into the plush cream carpet. Gorgeous wood banisters snake their way up and around to an open-plan living area. "This is the sky lounge." She begins pointing things out, but I'm too dazed by everything to take it in. "This whole level is for guest leisure."

The lounge is enormous, sweeping at least a quarter of the length of the boat, light pouring in from windows on either side. A bar sits tucked in one corner, plush stools a grey velvet to match the grey-painted walls. In front is a pool table—"designed by Porsche," Jade informs me—and in the corner a grand piano. A huge flat-screen television rests against a metallic pillar, and there are even drinks stored within the sofas, as Jade bends down to demonstrate. In the opposite corner to the bar is a dining area. Outside is a swimming pool, hot tub, and cabin. The cabin, Jade explains, is the sauna.

Of course. Heaven forbid we are on a yacht without a sauna!

Moving back past the stairs reveals a large gym with state-of-the-art equipment I'm not sure even professional athletes could afford. There are iPads hooked up to everything, in case the gorgeous view outside isn't enough.

There is still one more floor above, but Jade takes us down again, shaking her head. "The owner's suite is upstairs. No one is allowed there while they aren't on board. Even *I* haven't met them."

She moves swiftly, not giving me a chance to process it all, and brings me to the main salon, where a huge table with twelve chairs takes up most of the room. Another bar area leads out to a terrace, with more dining space.

"This is where the guests eat," Jade explains. "If the weather is bad, they eat inside. Back across the hall is the galley."

It's almost as big as the salon, with a huge array of cabinets and appliances. A door at the back must lead to a pantry of some kind, because it swings open and a woman walks through carrying leeks. Her dark hair is pinned into a similar high bun, thick eyebrows her best feature, but she keeps twisting her mouth and making her face pinched as a result.

"Yes, Your Majesty?" she growls, attention focused on Jade. "What could possibly be wrong now?"

Jade narrows her eyes. "Sasha, this is Runa, the chef. Runa, this is Sasha. She's our new stewardess. Have you packed away the provisions we brought up?"

"No, I thought I'd kick them into the sea, one by one." Runa steps forward, dropping the vegetables on the counter, then wraps me in an embrace, kissing both cheeks. I'm not sure if this is a friendly gesture or a territorial one. "Jade thinks she is head chef," she explains when she releases me. "She thinks she can order me about like you dear little stewardesses."

I chuckle nervously, but neither laugh with me.

"Anything to get work done on time," Jade mutters.

"Darling, it is not your job to worry about me." Runa's voice is light, but there's something about the way she says it that puts me on edge. "You are the one who has lost a stewardess and had to replace her. And after what happened last year as well, my, my. Worry about your own role."

Jade folds her arms. "Come on, Sasha. You'll be seeing the galley enough times."

"What happened to the stewardess before me?" I ask once we leave. "The agency said I was lucky to get a position so late. They said they couldn't give any details."

Nor would I give the agency any details about why I, on the other hand, was even trying so late in the season. I just gave them the same spiel I tried to give Jade: *I want a change. I want to see the world.* It's not technically a lie.

It's just not the whole truth either.

"Well, neither can I," Jade snaps. "What have I told you about speaking out of turn?"

Even when the other nurses turned against me, in their jealousy, they still wouldn't have dreamed of talking to me this way. Who does she think she is?

We pass by the front entrance again and head down a corridor. "These are the guest cabins. You'll be here a lot. Cleaning, preparing the beds."

The guest rooms are as I expect, an endless array of luxurious white marble bathrooms and king-size beds staring at flat-screen televisions. There are four in total, each in its own style and theme to not look like clones of one another. I can't help finding this ironic when Jade and I look the same.

Across the lobby (I am *never* going to remember this layout), where Jade points out an office and even a massage parlor, we come to a short hallway that leads to another row of doors. Someone is heading out as we come in, a man in a deckhand uniform, the red shirt a contrast to all the muted colors.

"Is this the new stewardess, then?" He's quite short, but broad-shouldered and smiling, with shining eyes and freckled cheeks. He offers me his hand. "Drew. Nice to meet you."

I shake it; his skin is rough, calluses grown in the grooves of his palm. "Sasha."

He's eyeing me appreciatively enough, but again I feel wrong-footed, like I'm missing something.

"She can meet you later," Jade says. "You've got things to be getting on with. I think Chief was looking for you."

"Yeah, yeah, on my way." He walks past, but when Jade's back is turned, looks round at me and pulls a funny face, miming slitting his throat. It makes me grin as widely as he is.

"This is the bridge deck," Jade says, with a deep sigh, as if the thirty-second inconvenience has ruined her day. "The captain's quarters are through that door. There is also Chief's quarters, but she brings us her linen and doesn't like us going in her room. Which suits me fine, as it's one less item on the list. And through that door at the end is the bridge, where you'll speak to the captain."

"The captain?" I echo, mouth dry, as we head toward the bridge.

Jade knocks on the door. "He's expecting you. I'll wait here. You can go straight in."

"Is he not too busy to see me?"

"Probably." She sighs again. "You'll have to do. Though really, could you not have freshened up after your flight?" I'm about to open my mouth to protest when she carries on. "This trip is very important to him. It's Captain Howard's last charter. Now, hurry up, I haven't got all day to be standing around. You haven't even met the other steward-esses yet."

I haven't even had the chance to *breathe* since arriving.

There's no point arguing with her, though, so I go inside while she impatiently waits outside the door.

"You must be Sasha Quill!"

Captain Howard Asteridge looks to be in his late fifties. He re-minds me of men from the fifties too—very upright, military and old-fashioned, especially in his pristine uniform and hat. But there are wrinkles around his eyes, signs of smiling too much, and he greets me warmly, shaking my hand and clapping me on the back. There's no lingering touch on my shoulder, no kisses on the cheek just to get close. He's a consummate professional. He returns to his desk, gather-ing some papers together—a file on one of the stewardesses (squint-ing gives me the name Euphemia Brentwood, a name I'm pretty sure should only exist in Victorian novels)—and, catching me staring, quickly puts them all in a drawer.

He's nothing like Dr. Martin. I can relax somewhat, take in my sur-roundings.

The bridge, the navigational command center, is impressive. I need to try and remember all the technical terms for everything. The marble theme continues here, sleek grey across the ceiling with dark wooden panels that lead down the walls and showcase the huge windows. A door to the left exits onto the terrace, and I can see a couple more deckhands. Beneath the windows are a row of six screens, each displaying a different tracking system. Two comfortable leather swivel chairs sit behind them.

"Interested?" Captain Howard asks. "There's lots to keep track of. GPS, engine parameters, communications, observations. It isn't all serving drinks and looking pretty."

His patronizing tone makes my smile strained. When you're blonde and beautiful, you're assumed to be an idiot.

"The owner will be pleased with you," he says. "Once you've cleaned yourself up."

I ignore the implied insult. "Will they be on board?"

"Not this time."

"Well, thank you for the job," I say. "I'm aware the stewardess I'm replacing had to leave unexpectedly."

The captain shrugs. "These things happen. We run a tight ship, as the saying goes. I'm just glad you're here and the charter can continue as planned."

There's a knock at the exterior door, and a man wearing the red uniform comes in. He looks as if he's stepped straight from the pages of a magazine: all muscle, bleached hair, and tanned skin. He towers over us both, even the captain, who must be at least six feet, and winks when he sees me, making me blush. I've never seen a man so attractive, not since . . .

"You must be the new girl," he says, in the most stereotypical American accent I've ever heard. "I'm Axel."

Axel? This guy can't be serious.

"Axel is our bosun," the captain says. "Axel, this is Sasha, junior stewardess. Why don't you take her down to the crew mess so she can get settled in?"

"Jade is waiting for me outside." I open the interior door, but Jade has disappeared.

Axel laughs. "As if our chief stew would ever wait around. Let's go, Junior."

"Welcome aboard, Sasha," Captain Howard calls after us as we leave. "I'm sure you'll be very happy here."

Once we're back out in the corridor, Axel grabs my arm so we're linked and leans in close while we walk. "So who have you seen so far, then? Have you met our chief officer and engineer Melinda yet?" he asks. "She's a character. Dying for Captain Howard's job."

She must be the "Chief" Jade was referring to. I shake my head. "Just Jade, the chef, someone called Drew, and the captain. And now you."

"Drew's met you! Trying to get in there before me, I see."

"He was nice," I say.

"Oh, he's *very* nice. Be careful with that one."

More like be careful with you, I think.

He insists on carrying my suitcase, which has remained languishing by the front entrance, and I finally get to see where I'll be sleeping. Axel explains the lowest level of the yacht contains the engine rooms, but the penultimate one is our crew mess.

The decoration budget has run out. Plain white walls and a linoleum floor greet me, with basic cupboards, a couple of small fridges, a microwave, and a sink. Over one wall is a pinboard, covered with various notes and shift patterns. Half of the room is taken up with a Formica table, reminding me of an American diner, and a long bench has been built into the wall. Three women are eating lunch.

"I bring you your new stew, girls," Axel says to them. "This is Sasha."

They move in eerie unison, three blonde heads turning toward me. Three pairs of eyes, narrowing to take in my every feature. Three mouths, pink and glossy, stretching into easy smiles—or smirks. Three women, and they look exactly the same. Not just the uniform, though that exaggerates it. Crisp white shirts, buttons strained at their chests, cinched at their waists. But also their hair in the same style. Their nails painted the same baby blue. Their actions too, assuming the same inquisitive expressions, straightening their posture (for me or for Axel, I'm not sure), turning in the same way to face me.

When I say they look exactly the same, I mean *exactly* the same.

And now I know why Jade, why Drew and the captain and Axel, weren't taken aback at my appearance. Normally I walk into a room and I'm the one being looked at.

I walk into this room and it's like walking into a house of mirrors.

Because they don't just all look like each other. They all look like *me*.

I could handle Jade. It's a coincidence, but two similar-looking blonde women working on a superyacht? It's hardly stretching the realms of the imagination.

But *five* stewardesses? *All* of us?

We're *identical*.

All blonde, all tanned skin, all high cheekbones. Same height, practically the same weight. It's disorienting. Put us in a lineup and turn us around, and I'm not sure our own mothers could tell us apart.

What's worse, they can see it in my face: my discomfort, my shock. They're prepared for this—whatever the hell this is. They knew I would be another one of them. They knew I would be like a lamb fed to the wolves.

And like prey, there's a primal urge in me to run. Get out. These women feast on me, one by one, wearing the same grin, the same gleeful expression, and I've never felt so exposed and unremarkable all at once.

This was meant to be my escape. Getting away from what happened before.

Not another nightmare.

CHAPTER TWO

⌒

JADE

The first thing you have to understand is the rules.

I've worked on many boats, and all have their own ways of doing things. Some are more relaxed. Some are incredibly strict. I prefer the latter. I like knowing exactly what's expected of me, and how then to direct the stewardesses I'm in charge of. There's not an official rule-book, per se, beyond the formal qualifications required and health and safety training. But there is an *unofficial* one.

Rule Number One: Discretion. What happens on superyachts stays on superyachts (and perhaps a trip to the pharmacist afterward). You walk in with eyes that cannot see and ears that cannot hear. You might have perfectly well-behaved guests. You also might be a unicorn. The odds are about as likely.

Which brings me to Rule Number Two: You don't have any kind of relationship with guests. No touching, no kissing, certainly no sleeping with. We are staff. We are here to please and cater to their every whim, but not *that* one. Guests can be very insistent. Very persuasive. I know a stewardess who was offered a nose job and a holiday to a destination of her choosing if she joined a guest in his room for the night.

What if it is the owner of the yacht asking? An A-list celebrity? Well. Perhaps that is a judgment call. Sometimes there are very *special* guests. But you won't catch me doing it.

Rule Number Three: Smile, darlings. You're going to be happy for the entire charter. Whether a guest is yelling at you for daring to bring out the red wine instead of the white, whether a storm is raging, whether you've been awake for twenty-five hours straight and you think you're going to scream, that smile never drops. Your mouth will ache. Its muscles will twitch in agony, begging for a release. But in front of guests, you are charm. You are grace. You are the perfectly amiable personal assistant and no task is too big or too much for you. In fact, you are positively *delighted* to agree.

I sleep with a mouth guard at night because I grind my teeth so much they're wearing down, tiny little holes in each molar. During the day I can feel myself gritting my teeth hard to avoid saying something I'll regret. But you can bet those teeth are bearing a gorgeous grin.

Rule Number Four: The primary comes first. Every guest is important, but the primary is on top, because they're the one who's going to tip you at the end of it.

And, of course, Rule Number Five: Be beautiful. Not passable. Not pretty. *B-e-a-u-t-i-f-u-l* with a capital *B*. Some women are fortunate enough to be born that way, although even with plastic surgery there has to be something to begin with that just needs elevating. You can't look too manufactured or too fake. Even with all our pristinely applied makeup it has to have a fresh, dewy quality, like you've just woken up to a kiss from a prince after one hundred years. Natural. Effortless.

Of course, it is anything but. The uniforms are tailored specifically to our measurements, meaning it is wise to add an inch all round for some space to breathe. White shirt, washed and ironed every morning, buttons just high enough to avoid flashing our bras but low enough to show our cleavage to its maximum potential. Epaulettes on the shoulders depicting rank. Thin black tights that show off our legs more than hide them. No shoes allowed, so even though we wear tights our feet must be immaculate. Clean, no bunions or dry skin, nails trimmed and painted a bright color so guests can see our toes if they peer closely enough (and if they're making the effort to do that, there's a reason).

Skirt so short it just covers us decently, meaning we have to bend awkwardly with a straight back to fetch something that has fallen on the floor. Hair pulled into a tight bun, stud earrings in each ear. No visible tattoos. False eyelashes. Pale pink lipstick with a gloss over the top. No glasses—contact lenses only. Physically fit, but not too muscular. Soft. Approachable.

And then, even with all this, you must fit the particular yacht's requirements. On this yacht, beautiful means one thing only: tall, slender blondes with big breasts and plump, pouty mouths that beg for a smooch. Beg for, but never receive. No touching, remember? Rule Number Two.

Sasha, it seems, is just discovering she no longer stands out from the crowd. I enter the crew mess carrying sheets that should have been dealt with hours ago and discover her staring, appalled, at the other three stewardesses, who are by contrast finding her reaction rather amusing. Axel is between them, oblivious as ever to the atmosphere in the room. I think I am the only woman immune to his charms; I overheard him call me Miss Trunchbull once and that turned me off for good.

Euphemia, seated on the left, rolls her eyes. "What a surprise. Another blonde."

Imogen points her fork, lettuce leaf dangling, at Axel. "You've been avoiding me all day."

Axel shrugs. "I'll see you tonight, won't I?" He turns to Sasha. "We're all heading out for a meal and drink before the last charter tomorrow. It's mandatory that you attend."

Of course he's trying to get with Sasha already. She's pathetically thrilled too, enjoying being squeezed into a hug as Imogen stares daggers at her. She's picked the wrong enemy to make there.

Axel is Captain Howard's favorite. Scratch that, he is *everyone's* favorite. The man can clear his throat and the captain will proclaim it genius while my stewardesses swoon. The other day I suggested changing how they organize the life jackets. Axel added a small point about what tool to use to hang them, and not ten minutes later Captain

Howard was announcing an innovative new strategy by the bosun that he was going to implement. Axel got his job as he knew Captain Howard before—pure nepotism. Meanwhile I spent four years at university studying international relations with specialisms in Mandarin and Russian. I lived in China and Russia, learning Italian on the side, and then worked as a stewardess on yachts for years before joining this one, taking courses in medical training, computer science, accounting, and etiquette along the way so I'd be the best of the best. I'm at the top of my game and Captain Howard still calls me sweetheart and thinks my grandest achievement is how well I can make a porn-star martini.

Thank goodness for our Hollywood-hero-can-do-no-wrong bosun. The yacht would truly fall apart without him.

Still. At least Captain Howard hired me again after what happened last year. I was terrified he wouldn't, even after all I've done for him. But he said as long as I kept quiet about it things could go back to normal.

"Prick," Imogen says as Axel heads back up the stairs. She turns to Sasha. "You seem to have made yourself comfortable already. Not even opened your suitcase yet and you're ready to open your legs."

Typical Imogen diatribe. Sasha's face falls.

"Imogen," I snap. Euphemia and Lola, on either side of her, can't hide their smiles.

My stewardesses—infuriating at the best of times. Euphemia, second stewardess, only in this position because she fluttered her stupidly long eyelashes at the captain and has modeled in the past. She prefers to be called Effie; that's not my problem. Let me be clear: I could have been a model, but I'd never empty my brain with something so vapid. Euphemia is definitely after my job. She can't stand me. And if I were anything but a professional, I'd admit I can't stand her either. Imogen, third stewardess, unfriendly to the core but at least she's useful as she can speak French. Shame about her Geordie twang and resting bitch face. And then Lola, fourth stewardess, too young to take seriously and a tragic drip of a thing, constantly coming to me with issues about the other two that could be settled by her developing a spine.

What will Sasha be like? She's not as young as Lola, thankfully, but seems equally as stupid. Her CV said she was a nurse, which I find hard to believe. Why on earth is she here if that's the case?

I focus my venom on her first. "There you are, Sasha. I was beginning to think you'd got lost. Why didn't you wait for me by the bridge?" She opens her mouth to reply, but I look past her. "And ladies, why were these sheets left in a pile upstairs and not brought straight down? They could have been washing while you were eating your lunch. Oh, before I forget." I reach behind and detach a radio from my belt, handing it to Sasha. "Your radio. It's already switched on. Please respond any and every time I call you. You've met the other stewardesses? Euphemia is the second stew, Imogen the third, and Lola the fourth. You listen to them in that order."

"Wait—Euphemia is . . . who is who? We all look the same."

"Like cards in a pack." Imogen grins. "Some better than others."

Is that some insecurity I see behind the new girl's eyes, as they flick from one of us to the other? No doubt she's trying to compare, weigh us up, make some kind of judgment that means she still comes out on top. I remember my first day as a stewardess. I'd lived my whole life being told how beautiful I was, and all of a sudden there I was on a boat with other gorgeous women.

But this yacht is particular in its tastes. Where before you could rationalize it with oh, she's a redhead, she's curvier, therefore different enough from me—this is a direct contest. We're all beautiful in the same way. So who's the best?

One thing you don't want to do is tell a woman she's stunning her whole life then stick her with a bunch of women who look like the upgraded version. That will never do for her self-esteem.

Nor for building friendships.

I'm used to it now. Though I did ask Captain Howard if the owner's tastes had changed at all after what happened last season and was told no. It wasn't great meeting Euphemia, Imogen, Zara, and Lola and seeing *her* in each of their faces. And now Sasha probably looks like her most of all.

If I'm being strictly truthful, Euphemia is probably the best-looking. Not that I'd ever let her know that. The first time I met her I made sure to give her whitening toothpaste and a pair of tweezers and said in warm tones, "You'll be sorted soon enough."

I'm old, by stewardess standards. Thirty-three, soon to be thirty-four. I lie about my age to guests. I have frown lines between my brows and around my mouth, and no amount of coverage will hide them. I've never wanted to admit I might need Botox, but I think it could be time if I want to stay in this industry. Sometimes I look at Lola with her youthful, rounded cheeks and want to tear them from her face to add to my own.

"The owner likes us this way," I explain to Sasha now, as though it's not bizarre at all to conform to the beauty standard of someone we've never met.

"As ridiculous as it is," Euphemia mutters. "Isn't variety the spice of life and all that?"

"Not on this boat," Imogen says. "Identical quintuplets only."

Sasha shakes her head in disbelief. "But—we're *so* similar. It's not just like we're all blonde. It's everything. Is it not . . . strange?"

"Oh, definitely," Imogen says. "When we all look the same, it's easy to think certain men might be interested in you too when they're *not*."

She's getting protective of Axel already. That took all of two minutes.

"You need to go and put your uniform on," I say to Sasha, because I haven't got time for this. "Come on, I'll show you your cabin."

We head down the corridor, past the laundry room ("room" being a generous word for the tiny space with three washing machines in a line, three dryers stacked on top, and two ironing boards opposite) to where Sasha will be sleeping. She peers quickly in the bathroom, face falling as she learns about crew-level luxury. It's a tiny wet room with an emergency hatch above the showerhead that means anyone taller than about five ten has to crouch down to use it properly. In the corner mold is growing, and when she turns on the light the extractor fan buzzes, a sound that will definitely be loud enough to wake her up from right next door. It's precisely why I'm as far away from the bathroom as possible, and can't help feeling a little smug every time I need to use the toilet at night and keep it on for a long time.

There is a free bed on the top bunk in her cabin (again—think less *cabin* and more *cupboard* with a bunk bed, wall mirror, drawers, and bedside table), made obvious by the fresh new uniforms set out for her by myself. Treating her rather like a kid at school, but when I have stewardesses like Lola, who asked me on her first day what detergent was, I can't be too careful. Euphemia, who Sasha is rooming with, has no sense of sharing the space. Her clothes are scattered across her bunk and half the floor, spilling out the drawers and bedside table too. In a row under her bed are her shoes, dozens of them squished beneath. A big fluffy red coat hangs on the door. Being the same size as one another has its advantage in one sense: we're forever borrowing each other's things, our clothes flung from one cabin to another. I spy my favorite top crumpled on the floor, borrowed without asking.

"I'll give you five minutes to get changed," I tell Sasha.

"Right." She looks desperate to have a shower. That will have to come later. Perhaps I should be more sympathetic, but I'm not her babysitter, I'm her boss. "Thanks."

"And Sasha?"

"Yes?"

"Some makeup wouldn't go amiss. And tie that hair up properly."

The others are gossiping about her when I return to the crew mess.

"She's actually weird-looking when you focus on her face," Imogen says. "Eyes too close together. What a shame."

"I think she'll be nice," Lola chimes in, which earns her a look of disgust from Imogen and a cackle from Euphemia.

"Of course you would, Mouse," Euphemia says. "Anyone would be an improvement."

I should get them to stop calling Lola "Mouse," but the girl needs to grow a backbone and tell them herself. Like I said, not a babysitter.

Sasha emerges from her cabin, and instantly she is one of us. We are truly matching now. Her shirt is a little tight; she keeps tugging at it over her chest, fingers anxiously checking she hasn't missed a button. She hasn't; the buttons really do stop there. I'll need to tell her that if she gets a run in her tights I'll dock the replacement cost from her tips, but I can save that for later. Right now, she is presentable. She is transformed: a stewardess of *Ophelia*, just like the rest of us.

The others appraise her. I am sure they see what I do—her ears are asymmetrical, she chews her fingernails (a habit I will have to break her out of), her eyes really are a little close together, yet she is as breathtaking as we are. *Exactly* as breathtaking as we are. It will never not be unsettling, however much we pretend we are okay with it.

"Good enough," I tell her curtly. Compliments never come naturally; they are reserved for guests, when lies drip off my tongue as easily as money falls from their trees. "We have work to do. The guests are arriving *tomorrow*."

Sasha nods, eager to please, while the others huff, but rise from their seats.

Here we are, then: five stewardesses, all identical, all ready for the final charter, and I have them under my control. If I can get through last year, I can get through this.

I know how they all see me: past it, dictatorial, difficult. They can think what they want. Sasha can join them. They're hardly the first set of stewardesses to hate me, and I've proven I can handle them.

I've been through lines and lines of these bitches and I always come out on top.

CHAPTER THREE

LOLA

She looks like the rest of us, of course. I'm pretty sure my parents wouldn't be able to tell the difference if one of those four rocked up in Melbourne claiming she was their daughter. They'd tell her that was nice and when was she planning on leaving again, darling?

Sasha was shocked. Still is, taking glances at us when she thinks we aren't looking, then peering at herself in the mirror with a worried expression. Comparing. Looking at herself and thinking—if I just had Imogen's lips, Effie's eyebrows . . .

I've been there. Before I came on this yacht I at least thought I was pretty. Maybe not stunningly gorgeous, but passable enough. Now it's like my every flaw is on display. My hands are dry, and I have to rub cream into them every night to stop developing rough skin on my palms from all this manual labor. Meanwhile Jade's hands are dainty and smooth no matter what she does. I had acne as a teenager, and if you look close enough you can still see it on my chin. Effie sometimes forgets to take her makeup off before she goes to sleep and still wakes up spot-free, not even a pimple. And Imogen's body is so insane I can hardly bear to look at her sometimes. Zara was just as beautiful as the rest of them, and her replacement, Sasha, isn't a step-down. With the short notice they had to find someone, they still managed another supermodel. They're all so much older and more glamorous than me. I feel like a kid playing dress-up next to them.

At least Sasha arriving has meant I'm no longer the junior steward-ess, however younger I am. It also means Jade has put her on laundry duty, the doomed task.

She is puzzling over where to start when I walk in. The clothes swamp the tiny area, and there's a strong smell of detergent and damp-ness, but of course no windows to let in fresh air. I feel a stab of pity. This is the worst job. Jade relishes making sure anyone but she does it. She's "too busy," but all she ever does is delegate. I stare at Sasha's perfect profile, beautiful even with her brow furrowed, and I know she's going to be just like the others.

"Let me guess," I say. "Jade pointed out which ones were the wash-ing machines and which ones were the tumble dryers?"

Sasha grins. "I'd have been lost otherwise. You're . . . Euphemia, right?"

"Lola," I correct her. Oh, if only I was Effie! I don't tell her that's what she prefers to be called, or that the others call me Mouse. She'll be calling me that in no time as it is. "That might have been my fault, Jade being so finicky," I admit. "Secret confession, being on this yacht was the first time I'd ever done laundry, and I made some mistakes that sent Jade raving mad. I went to boarding school! Everything was done for me."

I chose working on yachts because I could still travel, but it's a lot of work. I thought we'd have weekends off where we could enjoy the facilities.

"And after school?" Sasha says. "No washing machines then?"

"Well, I went traveling, duh," I say lightly. "I had the hotel staff sort my clothes. And—look at all this. You can see why I avoided it."

"If you hate all this so much, how come you're working as a steward-ess?" Sasha asks, gathering the clothes into piles.

"Because I have to." I fiddle with the sleeve of a jumper, considering what to tell her. "My mum and dad said I was spending too much of my allowance, that because I hadn't gone to university or got a real job

I'd have to learn the value of money. I mean, of course I know the value of money."

Sasha smirks, and my stomach twists. She's going to poke fun too.

"I hate being bossed about, especially by Jade. Well, I won't be for much longer. My parents told me I had to stick this job out for at least a year if I wanted to carry on being supported by them, but I don't need them, you'll see."

Oops. Change the subject!

"Why don't we get started on the washing?" I suggest, eager to move the conversation on. I take in the various, haphazard piles that have been created, some of them bleeding into one another. "Let me help you."

I grab hold of certain pieces and group them together.

"Thanks, Lola," Sasha says. "I really appreciate it."

"It's quicker if you wash on a higher temperature too," I say. "Hotter the temperature, better the stain removal, which is good for those bedsheets. They see some things."

We both laugh.

"And obviously"—I finish one pile, taking care with what I'm doing—"it's important not to mix colors and whites."

"I know that!"

I shrug. "I'm just saying. These big industrial washers. All it would take is one piece of clothing—like my red scarf, for example—and the whites would be ruined."

"I think I can handle that," Sasha says. "Thanks, though."

"Well, I'll leave you to it. I've got my own work to do." I give her a wave and head upstairs, knowing Jade will kill me if I have an idle moment. I don't see her, but Imogen and Effie are unloading provisions for the bar in the main salon, griping at each other about whether Effie stole Imogen's mascara.

"Why would I use your gunky old shit?" Effie says. "I have Armani and Chanel, thank you very much, not your dollar store crap."

"I'm not saying you're *using* it," Imogen retorts, though she flushes at Effie's words. "I'm saying you took it just to fuck with me."

As a matter of fact, my mascara ran out so I grabbed Imogen's this morning and forgot to return it. I'm not going to admit that, though. Nor the fact that I'm wearing Effie's spare tights because mine have a hole in them and Jade will dock my tips if she finds out.

You'd think Imogen and Effie would be a joined force, but instead there's this competitive element to them that means they won't ever be friends. Both believe they're the prettiest, the sexiest, the funniest, the smartest. If only I had their confidence. Effie is gossipy, preferring her stupid nicknames and nasty little comments, while Imogen is direct— she'll tell you straight if she doesn't like you, and she doesn't like anyone except Axel. Sometimes this is good. Effie might back me up or Imogen might have a go if she's annoyed at Effie's remarks. Other times I'm between a rock and a hard place.

"Maybe Mouse stole it," Effie says when she spots me. "Hey, Mouse, did you take Imogen's mascara?"

"No!" I protest. It comes out as squeaky as my nickname and they howl with laughter.

"I don't think she even knows what mascara is," Imogen says. "Can you say *ma-sca-ra*, Mouse?"

One of their favorite running jokes is that I'm dumb. All because I couldn't work the washing machines and struggled to open the cabinets when they were childproofed once.

And I'm going to "misplace" Imogen's mascara now, so she can shove it.

But I don't bite back. "I'll go see if Runa needs any help."

"You do that." As soon as my back is turned they burst out laughing again.

Ignore them.

Runa is in the galley, cleaning the stovetops, earphones in, but takes them out when I knock on the counter behind her to get her attention.

I know she's still on edge after everything that happened with Zara. Runa's not the only one who's glad she's gone.

"They're being horrible again," I say, by way of greeting. I don't need to explain who *they* are.

She shrugs, unsympathetic. "You know what they're like."

Not quite the comforting response I'm after. "They make me so frustrated. It's like they go out of their way to . . ." I shake my head. "Whatever. Have you met the new girl yet?"

Runa nods, pressing her lips together. "She seems fine."

"Zara left without much protest. That's good. I was expecting a bit more of a fight from her, considering."

"Lola." She lowers her voice, eyes darting to the empty doorway. "Not here. You promised."

Our radios sound. It's Jade, demanding I come to the laundry room.

"Saved by the bell," I say. "Later, then?"

"Later," Runa agrees, the relief in her face evident. She turns back to the stovetops, slotting her earphones in, and tunes me out.

I know it's bad news when I get to the laundry room and find not only Jade and Sasha but Melinda too. Melinda Fall: chief officer, chief engineer, and chief of butting in. One of her eyes is green and the other blue, and a scar separates her top lip into two. She's blazingly angry, practically yelling at Jade. "I thought Sasha *was* Lola at first, with her back turned. Did no one ever tell these girls not to mix whites and colors? How is this the second stewardess I've had to tell off for laundry-related purposes?"

One of the washing machines is open, the culprit lying on the floor.

It's my red scarf.

Melinda pulls out a sodden long-sleeved white top stained with pink, and screeches. "Your new stewardess has ruined an entire set of uniforms—and *look* at my shirt!" Melinda flails it dramatically. "It is unacceptable! What did you think you were doing, Sasha?"

Sasha shakes her head. She is standing with her back to the wall, piles of clothes still around her, crowded in by the rest of us. "This wasn't my fault, like I told you!"

Melinda cuts across her. "This is why you need to command your stewardesses, Jade."

"I'm well aware of what I need to do, Chief," Jade says through gritted teeth. "But thank you for your input."

"It's Lola's scarf!" Sasha says. "She was organizing some of the piles, and that included one of the white ones. I'm sure she slipped it in then."

Melinda scoffs. "And now you're trying to pass on the blame! I mean, really."

My eyes widen. Is this why Jade called me down? "I would never do that! Why would I want to ruin all of these clothes?"

"To make me look like an idiot!" Sasha says. "I don't know why, but it's obvious. You even mentioned your red scarf had the potential to mess up an entire wash—"

"I was warning you!" I say. "I knew it was with the rest of the clothes to be washed. It must have accidentally been put in there."

"It was stuffed within a bedsheet," Sasha says. "It looked deliberate."

"I don't know what you want me to tell you." I turn to Jade and Melinda, appeal to their better judgment. "This had nothing to do with me."

Melinda nods. Her ire, thank God, is focused on Sasha. "It is only because this is your first day that I am not going to take this any further. But perhaps in the future I'll have to involve Captain Howard." She raises an eyebrow at Jade, then leans closer to her, murmuring something I'm only just able to hear. "We had a conversation at the beginning of this season about expectations after what happened last year. So far I have not been impressed."

Jade turns bright red. She's not usually so flustered. Melinda brings it out in her.

"And Sasha?" Melinda says.

She bites her lip. "Yes?"

"Let's hope our second meeting is under better circumstances."

After she's gone, Jade exhales deeply, rubbing at her temples. There's an awful moment where I think she's going to shout at me too, like I'm some unruly child, but in the end she focuses on Sasha. She believes me.

"You'll redo all this. And I'll show you every little step no matter how patronizing you consider me to be, do you understand? And for Christ's sake, be on your best behavior around Chief."

Sasha wants to argue, but wisely keeps her mouth shut.

"Lola," Jade says. "Back upstairs and vacuuming."

I leave, but I can't help looking at Sasha. She fixes me with a challenging stare, and I turn away quickly, unnerved.

I'm going to have to watch my back.

CHAPTER FOUR

EFFIE

B less her. This new girl is going to be eaten alive.

I'll be nice, though. Promise.

I'm half in, half out of my dress for the crew night out when she comes into our cabin, so I decide to throw her a bone. "Help me with this, will you?"

"You're my roommate?" she says as she zips the dress up. "I thought it would be Imogen or Lola. Shouldn't you be sharing with Jade?"

Her Majesty couldn't wait to get rid of me when Zara left. She moved herself in with Runa instead. We don't do well together. She's a stuck-up bitch who thinks the sun shines out of her saggy old ass, and I'm the hot understudy who should be doing her job. She's jealous, barely disguised envy hidden under petty wins like calling me by my full name and making me do the early shifts. I have my own ways of getting at her, though: telling her she has a hair out of place or lipstick on her teeth when she's pristine as always.

"Sorry to disappoint, babe," I say.

"Oh! No, I didn't mean it like that. I thought . . ."

Thank goodness I've decided to take her under my wing. "Relax. It made sense to do a bit of a switch after Zara was ousted. Jade went with Runa, Zara's old cabinmate, and I agreed to have the mysterious new girl. Lucky me, eh?"

"Well, thank you," she says. She's fresh from her shower (last in the pecking order and therefore last in the queue, no doubt realizing how disgusting it becomes unless you break the rules and get in there fast), but she still looks tired. First days are always rough. I wonder why she's here.

Let's ease her in. "Feel free to wear anything of mine tonight. We always borrow each other's clothes. I hope you have something better than the outfit you were wearing earlier to offer in return, though. Take a look through my things."

When I say we always borrow each other's clothes, I mainly mean everyone borrows mine. The others are like magpies, always wanting my pretty things. I let them because they can't pull them off like I can, even if they come back with tears that weren't there before and I'm met with pleas of innocence. I'm the one with the best outfits, courtesy of being an ex-model. Jade has some decent things, like that white leather skirt that shows off my legs a treat, but she has no sense of style, and most of it is all blazers and trousers, as if she can't bear the idea of allowing her clothes to loosen up any more than she does. It's annoying Zara is gone, because she had great clothes. Mouse doesn't like us taking her things, insisting they'd be too big for us, which doesn't make any sense when we're all about the same size. As for Imogen, the less said the better. Not a designer label in sight.

Sasha looks through my clothes, and I take advantage of the distraction to study her.

She *is* pretty, I suppose, if you're more into the girl-next-door type. Which I guess men are, so no doubt she's spent her whole life being told she's gorgeous when really she's a seven at best, an eight if I'm generous. The stewardesses all love getting told we look similar because that means they look remotely like me.

"I love your red coat," Sasha admits, stroking one of the sleeves. It is hanging on the door, long and fluffy and as vibrant as a fire hydrant. "Although it's too hot to wear today."

"It was actually Jade's," I tell her. "She said she didn't wear it that much and I could have it."

Thankfully Jade hadn't decided she hated me yet on that first day. She said red wasn't her color. Well, it's definitely mine. The coat swamps me because I'm still ultra-slender from my modeling days, but in that stylish way that makes your legs look fantastic. I love it.

Sasha has the coloring of a sickly orphan child, poor thing, but I'm being kind so I say, "Try it on!"

She pulls it around her and poses in the mirror. I daub some red lipstick on her lips and she smiles. She rather looks like Imogen. Which isn't a compliment.

"People borrow that coat all the time," I say. "One of the only things not from when I was a model."

"That must have been cool," Sasha says.

I don't want to actually get into all that. "Come on, let's dress you up, babe. This is our last crew night out of the season! It's going to be wild. Fancy your chances with anyone?"

"Er—not really!"

Bingo. "Man trouble's what's brought you here, then?"

"It's . . . complicated."

"Honey, isn't it always?"

She grabs a random halter-neck dress. "I'll borrow this, thanks."

Her diversion tactic only works long enough for me to finish my hair, tying it into a high ponytail that shows off my fantastic cheekbones and jaw. I pull Sasha's hair back into the same style, even though her side profile is much less flattering, the bump on her nose all the more prominent.

If people want to compare us and claim we look the same, let's give them a fair judgment is all I'm saying, alright?

While we apply makeup—Imogen coming in to return a jacket I definitely didn't let her borrow as it's one of my favorites and then scarpering fast when she sees my expression—I press Sasha for the real reason why she left her last job. She's frustratingly vague, giving me some spiel about how she trained to be a nurse and decided it wasn't for her, but her hands shake. She's hiding something.

Warming her up with some gossip might help.

"Imogen got all touchy about you with Axel earlier because he's her latest," I inform her. "They don't call her Put-It-In-Imogen for nothing."

I came up with that name—one of my finer moments, I have to say. Imogen goes mad whenever she hears it. But really, don't behave like the local bike if you don't want a reputation. No class, that girl.

"And I heard you had a bit of a run-in with Chief earlier," I say. "Courtesy of Mouse."

She flushes, making her splotchy. "It's sorted now. And why do you call her that?"

"Nothing is ever sorted with Chief," I warn her. "She holds grudges like there's no tomorrow. As for Mouse, we call her that because she's so shy, duh."

Another one of my nicknames.

"And she kind of looks like one," I add, snickering.

Sasha doesn't laugh.

Yawn. I hope she's not going to be some do-gooder. Still, I have to work with what I have.

"Let's be friends, you and me," I whisper, linking my pinkie finger with her own as if we're schoolgirls. "I have a feeling we're going to get along."

She considers it, eyebrow raised. She's not as hotheaded as Imogen or as dumb as Mouse. She's weighing up her options, deciding if I'm the lesser of all these evils.

"Friends," she whispers back convincingly, but I'm sure she's lying.

By the time we're done, the rest of the crew are waiting for us on the dock. Drew waves us over, so Sasha and I end up walking to the restaurant with him and my lap dog—as much as I'd love to go and barrel between Axel and Imogen and get on her last nerve.

Drew, predictably pleasant, does the introductions between Sasha and my number one fan. "This is Noah. Noah, this is Sasha. He's a fellow deckhand."

"Um, hi, Sasha," Noah says quietly. He's taller than Drew, though not as towering as Axel, and very pale, with ginger hair that reaches his shoulders. You wouldn't know it, though, from the way he stands, head bowed and shoulders hunched. He focuses on Sasha but steals glances at me while I pretend not to notice. "How are you finding it?"

Sasha hesitates, chewing her lip.

Drew gives her an encouraging smile. "It gets easier, I promise."

Typical Drew. Ever the gentleman.

"She should be used to stressful conditions," I say.

Drew is immediately interested. "How come?"

"I was a nurse," Sasha mumbles.

"I was an accountant," Noah butts in, to my irritation. "My parents weren't pleased when I became a deckhand instead. But my father agreed it would be good for me to toughen up."

"You're certainly *shaping* up," I say, placing a hand on his bicep and squeezing.

The man practically melts, going bright red. He's gagging for me, so I give him these small moments to keep him believing something might happen.

Not a chance. Especially when there are men like Axel on board. Still, men are delusional, aren't they? Let Noah believe someone like him could succeed. It's useful on nights out like this when he buys me drinks.

Up ahead, Axel laughs at something Imogen says (she's wearing these huge gold hoop earrings and a skintight white dress that is practically see-through, so desperate I could almost pity her—almost), and Noah's face darkens, transforming him entirely. Drew notices too, because he places his hand on Noah's other arm.

Noah shakes him off. "I'm *fine*. Don't make a big deal out of it."

"You need to stop making it so obvious."

"I work with the man every day, don't I?"

"Still." Drew sighs. "Sorry, ladies. Deckhand drama."

"That's one way of putting it," Noah mutters.

He and Axel don't get along (jealousy, in my opinion), but it's never been as bad as this. What's happened?

We reach the restaurant, a lovely tapas place where we order large batches of almost everything even though we stewardesses will have to merely pick at the food. You don't get bodies like ours by eating whatever you want. There's an awkward moment when Axel wants to order sangria for the table and Sasha confesses she doesn't drink, the absolute bore, which prompts Imogen to ask if she's an alcoholic and Drew to suggest everyone get their own. Noah still buys mine, of course. I'm seated at the end of the table, opposite Runa and next to Sasha, because I'm still pretending we're the best of friends.

"We didn't really talk earlier," Sasha says to Runa. "Nice to meet you."

Runa is unenthused. "Yes, yes. New girl. Another mouth to feed."

"Er, right, sorry," Sasha says. "You're Italian, right?"

This question seems to irritate her. What doesn't with Runa, frankly. "*Si. Sono di Milano.* I was a fashion model there."

Runa *claims* she was a fashion model. What she means is she did a bit of runway for some barely designer shows and thinks that means we're in any way comparable. Who's the one with her face on magazine covers? Oh, right. That's me.

"How is it being a chef on an incredible yacht like this?" Bless Sasha, she's trying. "The guests must love your food."

"The guests are spoiled brats," Runa says crisply. "They love my food, but they are always wanting more. Nothing is ever good enough when one has everything, no?"

We all hate the guests, but Runa takes that to another level. Their very presence seems to irritate her. Apparently she wasn't always like this—she used to adore cooking their meals and coming up with special recipes tailored to them. I think years of being complained about when everything is perfect has its toll. Now she mainly rants and raves about them, but chefs are a hot-tempered bunch; it goes with the territory.

In perfect timing, Noah arrives with my drink and the one I asked him to get Sasha.

"Cheers?" I say, holding my glass up.

Noah holds up his drink, and I laugh and shake my head at him.

"Not you, silly." I nod at Sasha. "My new bestie."

She smiles cautiously and clinks her glass with my own, then takes a sip—and has to spit the contents straight back out.

I made Noah order her a whiskey Coke so strong I wouldn't be surprised if her mouth is burning off.

"I don't drink," Sasha says. "I just told everyone."

Noah splutters. "I didn't know, Effie gave me your order—"

"Noah," I gasp. "I said a Coke and make sure there is no alcohol in it. *Zero.*"

He stares at me, knowing as well as I do that is not what I said.

But he'll play along, like he always does.

"You're right," he mumbles. "I'm so sorry, Sasha. I made a mistake."

I put my arm around her. "Let me go get you another drink."

Sasha shakes her head. "Don't worry about it. Thank you for the gesture, anyway."

"No, I insist!" I make a great show of getting her one, so she can do nothing but act grateful and swallow it down. Runa, watching all this, snorts in derision.

When the food arrives, I decide to fill Sasha in on the crew. "Let me tell you about everyone. I'm the best stewardess, obviously, but there's more to know than that."

"Okay," Sasha says, finally relaxing.

I lower my voice, leaning close. "You get used to Runa. She's pretty full-on, and kind of intense, but she *can* be funny. She does great impressions. In fact, listen." I tap the table to get Runa's attention. "Hey, Runa, do your impression of Jade."

Runa smirks, checking to see Jade hasn't overheard. She's sitting at the opposite end of the table, having some kind of heated debate with Axel, and doesn't even look our way.

"I must tell you," Runa says, in a dead-on Jade voice. She even does her face—that cold look of disappointment that could kill. "It is inappropriate what you are doing. Do you see *me* behaving in such a manner? No? Then learn to reflect that."

Sasha and I burst into laughter and even Noah chuckles. She's uncanny.

"That's amazing!" Sasha says. "Can you do anyone else?"

"I can do everyone," Runa says. "Get me drunk enough and I'll start doing Captain Howard." She turns back to Noah. "Now, where was I?"

I grin at Sasha. "What did I tell you?"

"You were right," she admits. "You all seem to know each other so well."

I shrug. "When you have to spend twenty-four hours a day, seven days a week together, it feels like you've known each other far longer than you actually have."

For better or worse.

"So you've all only known each other this season?"

"Well, Captain Howard and Melinda are regulars on this yacht. They've done several seasons together. And this is Jade's second on here."

"Did something happen last year?" Sasha asks. "Runa mentioned something about it, but Jade wouldn't tell me anything."

Last year. We've all heard the rumors, of course. Different stories that filtered through about that charter, stirred up mainly because the crew were suspiciously silent about the whole thing, which never happens in yachting. Juicy gossip spreads like wildfire in this industry, so even a whiff of something going wrong creates a ripple effect, and soon enough there are all sorts of crazy tales. Jade, Captain Howard, and Melinda are frustratingly closed off about even mentioning it.

But there's at least what started it all. "Something happened to one of the stewardesses. She went missing."

"Missing?" Sasha echoes, choking on her new drink. "She was never found?"

I shake my head. "She likely fell overboard. It happens."

"How awful," Sasha whispers.

"You'd be surprised how common accidents are on yachts," I say, taking pleasure in the fear that flits across her face. "But trust me, you won't get anything out of Jade about how it all went down."

"Maybe she washed up somewhere and she's okay."

"Sure."

And maybe I'm secretly a fucking princess.

I don't want to put a downer on the night, so I move on. "Imogen and I have worked together before on a different yacht. Runa too. Otherwise the rest of us met for the first time, though when you work in yachting, gossip spreads fast."

This clearly fills her with dread. "Is there a lot of drama, then?"

"There are tensions, like in any group of people."

"Such as?"

"Axel," I murmur. "He and Imogen have this thing where he sleeps with her and she pretends it'll be different every time, except . . ."

"Except?"

I raise my eyebrow. "She's too easy for him. He doesn't just have eyes for her."

"I'm sure he has eyes for everyone," Sasha mutters.

"Noah too," I continue. "Especially for me, though."

Sasha glances at Noah, who is deep in conversation with Runa. "Noah is into you?"

"Oh, honey, don't tell me you can't see that." I giggle. "Noah is like a lovesick puppy. Obsessed with me. But then, he was crazy about Zara before she left as well."

Zara. Sasha has replaced her, and I'm rattled by the way everyone is pretending Zara never existed. Even Noah in transferring his affections. Not that they weren't always there—he just clearly thought he had a better shot with her. One minute she was here, the next she was gone, and Captain Howard refuses to talk about it. Something big must have happened.

"Now you know the deal with everyone else," I say, "what's the deal with you? Come on. You were far too quiet when we were getting ready."

Again, there's that fear. *Definitely* hiding something. But she's saved. Axel downs the rest of his drink and stands up, addressing the group. "Are we all done? Let's pay the bill and head to a bar."

The bar he chooses is loud and crowded with barely enough room to move. Noah manages to push through and secure us a small table and a couple of chairs, but most people are happy to go and dance, myself included. I'm being spun around by some hot Spanish guy when I catch sight of Sasha at the bar and Axel making a beeline for her.

"There you are, Junior!" Axel slides into a nonexistent gap next to her, so close they're touching.

I leave sexy Spanish man behind and stand just close enough to hear what they're saying as they shout above the music.

"My name is Sasha, you know." Sasha isn't totally bewitched by him, which is interesting. In fact, she seems positively on edge.

Maybe I was closer on the money than I thought teasing her about man trouble.

Axel doesn't seem to notice. I don't think it would ever cross his mind that a woman wouldn't be into him. "I'm teasing you. Let me buy you a drink."

"I've already got one." The barman arrives with what must be a beer for someone else (she is *definitely* too sweet) and juice for her, and she fumbles in her bag for her wallet.

Is she being deliberately slow? Axel hands his debit card over. "I've got this."

"Oh—thanks." I think she's playing him.

"Can't have you buying me a drink on the first night."

"It's for Noah," she says. "He got us all a table."

Oh, yuck. Pass me the sick bucket.

"How very Noah of him," Axel says. He takes a sip of her orange juice without permission. "You really don't drink?"

Her hand shoots out and grabs the glass from him. I really don't get her problem.

"Hey," Axel says, tone changed. "Sorry. None of my business, right?"

"Where are you from?" she asks, as they force their way out of the crowd. I follow behind, ignoring a guy trying to grab my waist and pull me in for a dance.

"California. And you?"

"London."

"Ah, a city girl. Just my type."

Sasha murmurs something I can't quite catch, but Axel misses it too. "What was that?"

"I said I think everyone is your type."

He leans in closer, mouth brushing against her ear. If she turned, he would kiss her. I can feel him waiting, wanting her to be the one to make the first move. Sasha doesn't look happy about it. I spot Imogen across the room, clutching what looks like water. That's not like her. It must be straight vodka.

She frowns when I approach. "What do you want?"

"Thought you'd be interested in that little display over there," I say, pointing to Sasha and Axel. "That's all."

Imogen's face is a picture. She's ugly when she scowls like that, nose scrunched. Certainly not how I'd march up to Axel if I wanted to re-mind him who was better. Oh well. Her problem. It's amusing watch-ing Axel scarper before she reaches them, seeing Sasha grab her arm and try to apologize.

"You're just the shiny new toy," Imogen snaps.

Sasha ignores the insult. "I'm sorry. Effie told me the two of you had some kind of . . . thing going on. I wasn't doing anything. He came up to me."

Great, drag my name into it.

"Thing?" Imogen throws her head back to glare at me, and it's time I make like Axel and disappear. "Is that what she called it? You ought to be careful trusting what comes out of her mouth."

She's one to talk.

"I don't want us starting on the wrong foot!" Sasha appeals as I head back to the dance floor.

Imogen's retort is the last thing I hear as a different guy locks eyes with me. "You've been after him since you got here, you lying cow. And please—you're the bargain bin version of me, so don't even think you're going to get anywhere."

Before I can agree to dance with this admittedly rather attractive man, we're interrupted by loud voices coming from the other side of the room, and then a crash.

The music cuts, leaving an awkward silence, and then Axel's voice filters across the bar. "What the fuck are you doing, mate?"

I hurry to the scene. The small table Noah secured for us has been tipped over, beer emptied across the floor. Axel and Noah stand facing one another. Noah's hands are balled into fists.

The others have come running too, Runa and Mouse together, wob-bling drunk on their heels. When did they become such good friends? Drew steps between Axel and Noah, palms raised. Security arrives.

"Let's end this here, guys," Drew says.

"I'm not your mate," Noah shouts at Axel. Did he drink a lot at the restaurant? He seems drunk, the alcohol giving him a confidence he would never otherwise have. He makes to come toward Axel, and Drew grabs him and pulls him back. "You're a liar!"

"I haven't got a clue what you're talking about!" Axel says. "Don't come at me as if you're going to do anything either. We both know I could flatten you with one hand."

I can't wait to find out what's caused all this.

Noah tries to shake Drew off. "Let me go!"

"Not until you calm down," Drew says. "Axel, get out of here."

"Don't know what his problem is anyway."

Security follow Axel to make sure he leaves.

Another bouncer tells Noah and Drew they have to go too.

"Right," Drew says. "Party's over. Come on, everyone."

"I told you," I mutter to Sasha as we head out, giggling at her shocked expression. "Tensions. You wouldn't believe some of the things that happen aboard this yacht."

CHAPTER FIVE

~

IMOGEN

S ome exciting news for those of you not yet in the know. This charter is transatlantic. Destination: New York."

Captain Howard announces this with a flourish, spreading his hands wide. We're all sitting in the main salon for our final pre-charter briefing, recovering from the night before. I feel dangerously sick, breathing slowly to avoid throwing up. Drew is between Axel and Noah, Effie rubs at her forehead, and the new girl keeps glancing at me. We each have a champagne flute in front of us filled to the brim, and I watch carefully to see if she'll drink hers.

I've never been to America. Hell, before a few years ago, I had never been abroad. I grew up in Newcastle and barely left it, other than the occasional outreach trips my school used to run to introduce working-class kids like me to things like trains, beaches, and the countryside. I knew as soon as I finished school I wanted to get out of England, finding a job as a nanny to a French family and picking up the language along the way. I've always been good with kids. I looked after my younger brother all the time while my parents were working hard, practically helped raise him. It was only when the French family's mother asked if I'd ever considered working on superyachts, as she had a friend who was looking for a nanny, that I was introduced to this world. Finding out I could work on superyachts—although not as a nanny (the requirements were insane)—and travel the world and get paid for it seemed like a dream.

The work is shit, I'm not going to lie. The people are hardly any better. But it is still a dream. There are unexpected perks, like a certain bosun and the fact I can wear Effie's designer clothes and pretend they're mine. And then there are the times we dock in a brand-new country and I take my first steps off the yacht, breathe in the air and feel like I'm doing something worthwhile with my life.

New York is the culmination of all this. Me, in New York!

"New York is so overrated," Mouse says. She would say that. Spoiled child. She moans about her parents cutting her off and doesn't realize how lucky she was to get that kind of head start. After my brother died, Mum stopped working and things got tight. She's doing better now. Well, as better as she can do anyway. I still worry about her, still feel guilty that I got away as quick as I could when I turned eighteen, even with Dad there to look after her. I'm pretty sure the earrings Mouse has in are worth more than a month's rent.

My earrings have gone missing. The gold hoops I wore last night have vanished, and no one is owning up to taking them, just like the mascara. I bet it's the new girl trying to fuck with me after her pathetic attempt at flirting with Axel yesterday.

Not that she'd have a chance with him. We may all look the same but I'm easily the best-looking. And that's because I work at it. Every morning I do yoga and weight lifting for an hour to keep myself toned. Then I shower and shave my entire body—yes, *every* morning. I can't let Axel see me with stubble; the one time I forgot he rubbed a hand against my shin and asked how long it had been since I last took care of myself. I use two different cleansers, toner, and then a collagen-boosting serum followed by moisturizer to keep me looking young. Sun cream next, even though I'm interior, and a primer before applying makeup. All in all it takes me over two hours to get ready. No one is this beautiful without effort, and if they pretend they are they're lying. I won't have some new bitch on my turf thinking she's all that.

I need to talk to Axel. Tell him what I'm hiding. But every time I think I'm going to something interrupts us and now that Sasha's here I just can't do it.

They all think I'm a grumpy cow but you try being surrounded by a bunch of overprivileged stuck-ups whose biggest problems are whether or not their tips are going to stretch to a holiday in the Maldives. Sasha will be just the same.

I'm watching her now for her reaction to Captain Howard's words, and enjoy how terrified she is at the prospect of her first charter being an Atlantic crossing. No doubt she expected an easy cruise around the Mediterranean, plenty of stops in Greek or Italian towns. Not miles of sea as our only company, land a distant memory.

"You're of course aware this will be my last charter," Captain Howard continues, pausing as a couple of people whoop and cheer, which starts up an applause I have to half-heartedly join in with. "Thank you. It's about time I retired."

This prompts some polite laughter. Not from me. I'm no suck-up. Unless it's for a very big tip.

"Our clients are my dear friends Benjamin Edmondson and Digby Johnson," the captain says. "Mr. Edmondson is a financial advisor and Mr. Johnson is a business owner, both from the UK. I went to Eton with them when we were boys, and they take annual charters on this yacht. It was their idea to go to New York. I want them treated as extra-special VIPs."

Jade nods. I can picture her taking mental notes, her fingers absentmindedly reaching for the pen behind her ear even though she has no paper.

"They are bringing two ladies, and they will be treated with as much respect."

Escorts for sure. Certainly not the first we've had on board.

"And what is our motto with guests?" Captain Howard asks.

Our cue to be a rehearsed chorus: "We always say yes."

"That's right. Nothing is too much or too good for them."

I'm too good for them. If they put their crusty old fingers on me I'll break them off.

"Preference sheets came through," Runa says. "They'll be stuck up in the galley and I'll put spare copies in the crew mess."

I wish I had a preference sheet. I'd demand only the highest-quality ingredients, try food I've seen Runa serve but never tasted myself. Although if we're going the whole hog and having wishes, I'd rather like the ability to eat carbs without gaining weight and millions in the bank, thank you very much.

That, and for what I'm worried about to disappear.

"I know you'll all do a fantastic job and make me proud," Captain Howard says. "Having something like this to go out on gives me so much joy. And oh!" He claps his hands together. "You all met her yesterday, no doubt, but let me formally introduce our newest crew member, Sasha Quill."

Ha. She's practically an afterthought. She stands up and gives a tentative wave.

I lean over and whisper in Effie's ear. "She's overplucked her eyebrows."

Effie smirks, and I catch Sasha biting her lip at us. Good. Feel insecure. That's what you get. I glance at Axel, but he's not even looking at her, off in his own world with a sexy frown I'd love to iron out with a kiss.

"And you know our motto now," Captain Howard says to her.

"We always say yes to guests," Sasha says, desperate to please.

"They should be here at eleven, so let's get changed into our whites and meet on the dock in twenty minutes." Captain Howard lifts his glass. "To a fantastic charter. Be prepared for choppy waters!"

We all stand and toast, and Sasha pretends to sip her champagne while everyone else downs their glasses. I should tell her that's bad luck, but then I'd be guilty too. My glass remains as full as hers.

We head to our cabins to change, and Mouse won't stop blabbering on about how happy she is that this is the last charter. It's alright for her. She'll swan off to some five-star resort and blow all the cash she's made. Some of us—hello, me—have to actually save our wages. You know, for real-life things that are impossible to afford if you don't have the Bank of Mum and Dad. Especially because we haven't had many tips this season what with all the *issues*. I can't stand sharing a room with her (and I've made sure to tell everyone, especially Axel since I caught him checking out her ass last week, that she snores like a trumpet) but Queen Jade wouldn't listen to me when I asked about a swap. Even though *she* moved quite happily into Runa's cabin after Zara left.

"I'm sorry to hear about your earrings," Mouse says, retouching her makeup in the mirror. "I hope you find them soon."

She can't apply eyeliner to save her life, that one. Thick as two short planks.

"Still, at least they were cheap, right?" she says, then claps a hand to her mouth. "Oh my God, that was rude, I'm so sorry. Here!" She reaches in her things, takes a pair of earrings out, and places them in my palm. "You can have these. I don't like them anyway."

They're a decent pair. Probably not as expensive as the ones currently in her ears, but more than I could ever afford.

I drop them on the bedside cabinet, disgusted. "I don't need your charity, thanks."

She sighs. "Oh, Imogen, you're impossible sometimes."

"Oh, Mouse," I mimic. "You're *fucking irritating* sometimes."

She wisely chooses not to respond.

Jade is waiting in the crew mess, immaculate and staring impatiently at her watch. She appraises us, nodding to show we fit her exact standards. Effie and Sasha emerge, Sasha looking hassled, and Effie comes to my side.

"Her epaulettes are missing," she murmurs. "I might have told her to go without, that she didn't need any."

Despite myself, I grin. Effie is a scheming cow, but she can be funny.

Jade homes in on Sasha immediately. "Where are your epaulettes? Put them on."

"I didn't have any in my room," Sasha bleats. "They weren't with my uniform."

Jade stares at her as if she's grown a second head. "I laid out your uniforms before you arrived, and I most certainly did put your epaulettes with your whites, so if you've lost them, that is your own fault. You were a nurse before this, no? How was that possible with this continuing incompetence?"

This is barely Jade Anger Level 2, so it's surprising to see Sasha react as if she's been punched.

"We have spares in our cabin," I say, because I need this first meeting to run smoothly. I need a good tip. "Some of us take pride in our job."

I lead Sasha to my and Mouse's cabin and take out the epaulettes, looking at the silver crescent moon and single stripe stitched onto black cotton.

"These?" Sasha says. "Are they definitely for me?"

"Yes," I say. "One stripe. Like me and Mouse. Undeservedly."

"Thanks." She doesn't put them on, instead heading out while I redo my hair.

I return to find Jade snapping at her. "Of course those are right. For goodness' sake, put them on."

"So you didn't trust me, eh?" I say.

Sasha turns, flushed, to find me behind her. "I'm sorry. I wanted to make sure."

"I'm professional," I say. "Unlike some."

Stuck-up bitch, just like I thought. Jade shows us the preference sheets, making us take notes on what the guests look like and their names. Sasha stays far away from me. Probably a sensible decision.

"Let's go," Jade says when we're done.

We line up on the harborside. In order of rank, which means I'm toward the end with Mouse and Sasha. Fortunately, the weather is perfect: less hot than yesterday but still dazzlingly sunny with a soft breeze. I look gorgeous and I know it. There's a line of blondes here and you'd pick me out of them all.

"Here we go," Effie whispers from my other side, and I lean forward to see the guests heading our way.

Benjamin Edmondson is our primary, which means he's the one paying. Whatever he wants, he gets. Digby Johnson walks alongside him, dark hair and intense eyes. They're both in their late fifties but look well for it, which I suppose should be the case when you're able to afford holidays on a superyacht. Two women wearing tight dresses and stilettos follow behind, both blonde, both clearly selected to be as similar as the five of us. More confusion to add to the mix. More women to compare ourselves to.

"Mr. Edmondson, what a pleasure it is to have you on board," Captain Howard says, shaking his hand. *Mr. Edmondson?* I thought the captain said these men were his *dear friends* or whatever. Why the formality? It's not like I'm going to follow his lead and clap Benjamin on the back and call him Benny-Boy. "Welcome back to *Ophelia*. You remember our chief stewardess, Jade. She will give you a tour of the vessel and go over our safety regulations, and then we can set off and enjoy ourselves."

"Not those blasted safety regulations again," Benjamin says. "As if I haven't heard them a thousand times!"

Digby shakes the captain's hand next, rather vigorously, muttering something in the captain's ear that makes them both laugh.

Melinda is eager. "It's wonderful to have you back on board. I'm—"

"You're the chief officer! I remember." Benjamin laughs. "How did you swing that one, love?"

Melinda's smile strains. "I can assure you I am fully qualified."

People give Melinda a hard time, but to be honest, if I was that qualified and had to serve directly under an oaf like Captain Howard I'd have thrown him overboard and declared myself the new captain by now.

"Well, that's fantastic." It's obvious Benjamin doesn't care. "You ladies can't all be supermodels, I suppose."

I'm yet to meet a guest with even the slightest degree of self-awareness.

"Melinda is my best chief officer in years," Captain Howard says smoothly. "I haven't done nearly half the courses she has. She's a credit to the team."

"I'm sure she is," Digby says, and he and Melinda exchange a smile.

Benjamin passes me easily enough, though he insists on kissing my cheek, but when he reaches Sasha he holds her hand tight and leans close. "You must be the junior, standing at the end of the line like this."

"Yes, Mr. Edmondson," she says. "I'm Sasha."

"Is this your first season?" he asks.

"Yes, sir. My first charter, in fact."

"Good luck, darling. You're going to need it!" And then he roars with laughter, and we all have to join in, even though it wasn't remotely funny. "I'm afraid I have rather high standards. I like to have pretty women at my beck and call."

Yuck. But I'll grin and bear it. If it means a bigger tip, I'm going to go as far as I can without slipping on some stilettos and becoming an escort.

I'd fit in with them too—Digby shakes my hand without incident, and then the first escort steps in front of me, another clone of us stewardesses. So is the second one. The first has a gap in her teeth and the second is too skinny. She needs to build some tone.

"Welcome, Jasmine," I say to the first one, and she wrinkles her nose at me.

"Eva," she says. "Get it right next time."

I'll say your name every single time I speak to you now, *Eva*. Just to piss you off.

The real Jasmine is friendlier. "Nice to meet you."

"I'm Imogen. Happy to be on board?"

She looks up ahead at Benjamin and Digby, a strange expression on her face. "Oh, yes, very happy to be here."

Introductions done, Jade takes charge. "Let me show you around now," she says, bringing them across the gangplank. "If you don't mind taking your shoes off, we can head straight inside."

This is my and Sasha's cue to hurry on board. Effie has prepped a champagne bucket of Héloïse Lloris, and I pour it into four champagne flutes on a silver tray while Sasha grabs hot towels. It has to be done in less than two minutes but we manage it, standing together with bright smiles when Jade and the guests arrive. We've even gone to the trouble of adding a strawberry to the rim of each glass, and a handful of blueberries on the tray.

"This is our main salon," Jade says, nodding at us both to come forward.

"Champagne, Mr. Edmondson?" I ask. Time to blend in; northern accent vanished.

"And would you care for a towel?" Sasha adds.

"I wouldn't expect anything less," Benjamin says, popping a couple of blueberries in his mouth. "Is this the champagne I requested?"

"*Oui*, it is the Blanc de Blancs Tête de Cuvée," I reply. "We hope it is to your taste."

"It's fantastic," he says. "Eva, Jasmine—have a glass. Enjoy yourselves."

Jade indicates that Sasha and I can leave, then continues explaining the features of the main salon.

Melinda and Drew pass us on the stairs in the midst of conversation, but Drew calls out to us as they go by. "Suitcases are in their bedrooms."

"Thanks, Drew." Sasha can't help watching him walk away, though he and Melinda don't look back. So it's not just Axel she's after. Talk about the yacht tramp. And Effie likes to claim that *I'm* bad.

We reach the master suite and I start with Benjamin's suits, arranging them carefully. "Put clothes in the wardrobe, anything else in the drawers."

One of Benjamin's suitcases contains a pair of red fluffy handcuffs and stockings and garters, and Sasha waves them at me. "Check this out."

Does she think we're going to bond over some handcuffs? Ironic. But I play along. "Hey, whatever floats his boat. If you excuse the pun."

We're able to work in companionable silence, occasionally commenting on some ostentatious piece of clothing and making sure for the thousandth time everything is spotless. We move on to Digby's cabin, then take each escort's room separately. The one I am sorting has stuck a note to her suitcase requesting it not be opened, which strikes me as odd (trust me, I've seen my fair share of sex toys and God knows what in these people's things), but I shrug and tuck it under the bed so it's out of sight. I send Sasha to report to Jade as I complete the finishing touches and she obliges happily enough, stupid girl, thinking we're the best of friends now.

Jade is already having a go at her when I come up. She slams mixers down on the bar and starts preparing cocktails, practically spitting her words. "The primary always comes first. Always. Rule Number Four."

Oh God, Jade and all her rules. She never stops banging on about them.

"I'm sorry." Sasha sounds nervous. "He asked me to make him an espresso martini, and the escorts wanted piña coladas. I thought I'd just make the piña coladas first—"

Uh-oh. Big mistake. Huge.

Jade places a hand to her forehead for a moment. "*The primary always comes first.*"

I think it's time to kick her while she's down. I make my grand entrance, fix a forlorn expression to my face, and call across the room: "Sasha, how could you leave me to do the bedrooms all by myself?"

She turns, startled. Jade finishes the cocktails and frowns.

I pout. "I think Sasha thought she only had to do the one room. I've had to do the rest while she swanned back up here."

Sasha opens her mouth to protest, then catches sight of my triumphant grin and closes it again. She knows now. Of course I haven't forgiven her for what happened with Axel last night. I was biding my time until the right moment to strike.

"This is unacceptable," Jade says. "First the laundry, then the drinks, now this."

"But—"

I smirk. "Looks like you have a lot to learn, *Junior.*" I shrug at Jade. "What are you going to do with inexperienced staff, eh? I'm off to set the table for lunch. Sasha should probably go downstairs and do the laundry with Mouse."

"You're right," Jade says. "Sasha, leave my sight for the rest of the day."

Sasha follows me out, furious. "Why did you do that? Is this about Axel? Nothing even happened! Or is it the epaulettes? I said I was sorry!"

I smile innocently. "I don't know what you mean."

"You're crazy," she says.

If only she knew. "I'm the least crazy one around here. Why do you think I've had to resort to such tactics? You're new, so here's some advice. Don't trust anyone on this yacht."

She can't say I haven't warned her. She leaves without another word, knowing there's nothing she can do about it. Not my problem. It's better she learns now.

Runa is nowhere to be seen when I get to the galley, but I carry on regardless, setting out the plates and getting more drinks ready.

"Oh!" I turn at Runa's voice. "You are here."

She seems flushed, no doubt embarrassed she's been caught out not being where she should. "Where were you?" I ask, determined to make her as uncomfortable as possible.

"Nowhere," she says quickly, then realizes that can't be true. "Toilet."

I don't really care. I care about getting the clients on our side, and that dunce Sasha has already fucked up with the cocktails. "We have hors d'oeuvres to prepare."

After we're finished, I take the opportunity to go down to the crew mess to check my phone and see if Mum got the last check I sent her, and end up overhearing Mouse and Sasha in the laundry room.

Sasha is pouring her dear little heart out. "I shouldn't have trusted her, not when she was so rude to me last night. But I felt bad after she was right about the epaulettes."

I'm the topic of the day, naturally.

"She was rude to you?" Mouse replies. "Not a surprise."

A bit of mouth from Mouse. Interesting.

Sasha tells her the whole story, my apparent complete misunderstanding about her and Axel (funny how I see it in a different—and the correct—way), and Mouse giggles. "You are daft, you know that, right?"

"What's Imogen's deal, anyway?"

"Imogen is, like, povvo." My gut twists. "I think she's jealous of us."

My stupid eyes sting and I blink to stop them watering. Not crying. I wouldn't cry over something as pathetic as that.

"*Povvo?*"

"Poor." Mouse laughs. "She pretends she's proud of where she's from, but then why hide her accent? She takes this job so seriously. And she's such a desperado about Axel. Like he'd ever stay with someone from her background!"

"I wish she wasn't so nasty," Sasha says.

I'm the nasty one? That's funny. Who is currently being raked over the coals here?

"You'll get her back. That's what we do around here," Mouse says. "Get even."

Oh, is it now?

Well, then.

Game on.

CHAPTER SIX

⌒

SASHA

Get even, Lola said. *That's what we do around here.*

Her words reverberate in my brain as I make my way outside for some fresh air. I've already made a fool of myself, already trusted Imogen too much. These women know how to play whatever game this is better than I do. I wanted to get away from drama, not end up right in the middle of more.

The captain comes over the radio, telling the deck crew to prepare for embarking, and my heart starts pounding. If I'm going to make a break for it, run away again, this is the last opportunity. The yacht is going to pull away from the harbor, this glorious marina with its paved walkways and palm trees and hustle and bustle of people, and take us into the great blue beyond, with only each other's company for weeks. No stops, no breaks, no escape.

But isn't this what I wanted? Total isolation, something completely different from what I left behind?

I can't leave. I haven't even properly started yet.

I find myself at the stern, gripping the handrail. Drew and Noah fasten fenders on either side of the yacht while Axel takes in the mooring ropes, Melinda barking instructions over the radio as she engages the engines. A low rumble starts up, the calm water underneath the boat beginning to stir, and then Axel makes a signal with his hand to someone in the harbor, who gives a thumbs-up back to him. After a few moments, we finally begin to pull away, drifting softly backward out of our position and leaving dry land behind. Drew spots me looking at him and gives me a wave.

No turning back now.

The thought is a mixture of exhilarating and terrifying.

The man on the dock has moved on, walking toward a different yacht. There are other vessels in the water nearby—a couple of fishing boats, a large freighter. People stop and stare as we go past. How could they not? *Ophelia* makes everything else seem so tiny in comparison, so unimportant. Excitement finally begins to swirl in my stomach; I'm part of this yacht. And yet the nerves don't disappear, my fingers don't loosen their grip.

The deck crew don't waste time. Drew and Noah bring the fenders back on board, Axel is checking the anchor, making a note of something, and Melinda fires off a brief weather report over the radio.

Overhead, a seagull flies past, probably the last animal I'll see for a while. It gives a great screech before soaring in the direction of the marina, which is growing smaller and smaller, a hazy blur of dots that were once boats, a dark shape that was once the Rock of Gibraltar. I suck in a salty ocean breath, my first proper one, and feel very far from home already. It's another gorgeous day, but just as I think of returning to work before Jade starts asking where I've got to, a single cloud passes over the sun, casting a shadow across the deck. The sudden shade chills me, a surprisingly bitter coldness that makes me shiver.

"*Our voyage begins*," Captain Howard's booming voice announces over the radio. "*Welcome to paradise.*"

CHAPTER SEVEN

~

JASMINE

I'm here. It's been a year in the making, but *I am here*.

The first day done, the first night with Benjamin, the yacht long gone from Gibraltar and heading toward New York City with nothing in between. I'm going to let us travel for a couple more days, make sure there are no last-minute changes, no chance of turning back. But I'm just being cautious. Everything has gone exactly as it should. I've slept in a plush guest bed, I've eaten ridiculous meals (well, bites of them at least—I have a new figure to maintain), and now I'm sitting in this ridiculous hot tub, champagne on the side, Benjamin's eyes on me, pretending to laugh at one of Digby's jokes.

It's funny, really. All the careful planning, and I have blended in with relative ease. I am the same girl I was before, but now I am what men consider beautiful: the slender frame, the blonde hair, the blue eyes. Markers of beauty, rather than the finer details. If they cared to look closely, they could spot the differences between every one of us, but that's not what matters. We're not *individuals* to them, and that's why I've been able to slip in without trouble. I fit their ideal, a tick box of qualities.

That's what I did, Hallie. Every point they wanted: tick, tick, tick.
I did it!

Sure, if this bikini doesn't give me thrush by the end of the day it will be nothing short of a miracle. I think I'd be better off wrapping myself in dental floss. But sometimes you have to suffer to get what you want. And I have suffered far worse than this.

That's the whole reason I'm here.

Bubbles are at full power in the hot tub as the yacht takes us across the open water, sun beating down warm on my back. There's enough room to stretch out our legs, but Digby has pulled Eva onto his lap while Benjamin rubs his foot up and down my thigh in a gesture I think is meant to be enticing.

I survived my first night with him. I thought it would be harder than it was, but it's incredible what you're prepared to do when necessary. Thankfully, he seems to be easing me in. There was nothing weird, nothing like the horror stories I've heard from conversations in the past. Anyone who thinks escorting is being nothing but a pretty ornament is living in a fantasy. It's still odd, though, the way he looks at me. The way everyone looks at me now. I'm not used to being beautiful. I miss how I used to be.

I hope Eva won't make things difficult. I don't think she was pleased one bit when I rocked up to the harbor yesterday, nor Digby for that matter. She's been cold, not chatting to me during dinner last night but preferring to hang on to Benjamin's and Digby's every word, laughing in this high-pitched giggle before glaring at me when no one else was looking.

A couple of stewardesses are hanging around on the terrace, laying the table for dinner later. They're able to hear our conversation, not that the others care. Stewardesses are just the staff. Not worth wasting a thought on. It's still a shock to see them all: blonde, beautiful, thin. Just like me now.

Just like Hallie.

Digby nuzzles his face into Eva's neck. "You smell gorgeous."

"Thank you," she breathes, a terrible Marilyn Monroe impression. The men enjoy it, though, so I'll adopt something similar myself. "It's the fragrance you gifted me yesterday."

"I can get you anything you want, you know," Benjamin says to me.

"Ooh," I say, just as deliciously breathless, curling my body closer to him. If Eva dials it up to ten, I need to crank it to eleven. "How exciting."

Anything I want? If only. I'm not sure he'd be so courteous if he knew what I was really after.

Digby checks his watch, an expensive brand of some kind, then eases Eva off his lap. "We'll continue this later. Benjamin, we're meeting Howard in ten."

"Right." Benjamin stands up, and we're gifted with the full display of his sagging body in tiny swim trunks. I have to say, I'm impressed by the way Eva stares at him as if he's some kind of Greek god reborn. I match her expression, reach my hand to graze his hairy leg.

"We'll miss you!" Eva declares, sitting herself up on the hot tub's edge to wave them off. Her body is angled so her bum sticks out. It's a master class in posing if I've ever seen one. She pouts, pointing to her lips for a kiss, and Digby obliges.

I have to force myself not to gag when Benjamin plants his own sloppy mouth on mine, forcing his tongue inside. When we break apart a line of his spit lands on my chin, but I hold my hands firm until he leaves, then wipe it away with a shudder.

"Bye!" Eva calls, all sweetness and light. The second the door closes behind them and we're alone she rights her posture and raises a disapproving eyebrow at me. "This is your first time, isn't it?"

Her voice is different. Deeper, far less enthusiastic. She's playing a game. She no doubt—mistakenly—thinks I'm doing the same.

"Being an escort?" I say. "Yeah."

"You're *not* an escort," she snaps. "You haven't got a clue what it takes to get to my position. I didn't rock up and decide to do this on a whim."

If only I could tell her. I may not be an escort usually, but it's not a foreign concept to me. Nor have I rocked up on a whim. The exact opposite. Getting to this point has taken months of planning, an entire *year* of preparation.

For the truth. For Hallie.

But Eva doesn't need to know this. So I lie. "Fine, I'm new to this in general."

"I thought so. This isn't just a bit of fun. Has Mr. Edmondson eased you in so far because you were invited, not hired? That won't last long."

I think of yesterday, his groping fingers and hot breath. The rather vanilla night that followed. Eva assumes I do not know how these men are. I do not correct her, fixing a faux-bemused expression on my face. Let her believe I'm an innocent, if it keeps her underestimating me.

"Darling, you didn't think this was going to be a free holiday, did you?" She pulls her hair away from her neck, revealing a small line of purple love bites. It's obvious she intends for me to be horrified, but I don't give her the satisfaction of a response.

I've seen far worse.

But then she leans over and grabs her phone, showing me her lock screen. There's a photo of a young girl with freckles and hair in two bunches, wearing a checkered red dress for school.

"Cute," I say, because this is what I'm meant to say, but also because it's true.

Eva takes a sip of her drink, clutching her phone to her chest with her other hand. "I'm doing this for her, you understand? I worked hard to get to where I am. You may look down on me for it, but I don't care. What I do care about is that you don't mess this up for me."

She thinks I look *down* on her? That couldn't be further from the truth. I suspected before, but I know now for sure, the kind of crap women like her have to put up with. She has her own motivations for doing this. I can respect that. She's worried. I wish I could tell her otherwise, that out of the two of us I'm far wiser to the goings-on of superyachts than she could ever be.

In fact, I wish I could tell everyone. The stewardesses, the damn stewardesses who look so much like Hallie. I wish I could tell them to run.

"Come on." Eva starts pulling me out of the hot tub. I have no choice but to follow.

She leads me to her room, taking out one of her large carry-on bags and thrusting it onto the bed. I don't say a word as she unzips it, then tips the entire thing upside down so the contents spill out onto the satin quilt. There are dozens of condoms, bottles of lube, costumes (one of them a stewardess uniform not unlike the real ones on board), and toys. She grabs another bag and empties that too, revealing books about the yachting industry, about different types of wine, even a travel guide to New York.

"How prepared are you for this trip?" Eva says finally, stepping back so I can view everything in its entirety. "Because this is the tip of the iceberg. You need to find out what makes them tick—and more importantly, what doesn't. These aren't normal men. Not when they've had their every whim catered to their entire lives. They can be . . . dangerous."

She's desperate for a reaction. Does she want me to flee? Fall to my knees and beg for her sage advice, oh wise one?

"As much as *we* must uphold the strictest levels of privacy, don't be surprised if one of them brags to you about some conquest or another." Eva sits on the bed. "You know what Mr. Edmondson was saying to me last night over dinner, before I went off with Mr. Johnson? Last year they did a Mediterranean charter, and even some of the crew were enamored with them."

The hairs on the back of my neck stand up. "Last year? The crew?"

She sucks her teeth in disgust. "Oh, you know what he was suggesting. Like any woman would have a choice. These are the kind of men you're dealing with, Jasmine. That's why it's better they're left to professionals like me, not naive freeloaders like yourself. I tried to move the topic on but he got quite agitated. Said that was the only positive memory of that trip because there was some nonsense afterward. I have no idea what he was talking about."

Nonsense afterward. My hands curl into fists.

Eva mistakes my reaction. "See? You haven't got a clue what you're getting into."

I could tell her what I really think. That she's the one who hasn't got any idea what she's getting into. That in fact, I know exactly what Benjamin and Digby are like, because that *nonsense afterward*, I was part of it. That in my room is a stash of items that far exceed the display she currently has on show, because I truly am willing to do whatever it takes to get the information I need.

Instead, I play up to her. I bite my lip, shake my head. "I guess I don't."

An easy lie. And not the first I've told on this charter.

How prepared am I for this trip? I should have laughed in her face.

No one on board has any idea what's coming next.

CHAPTER EIGHT

SASHA

*T*he other nurses are unable to hide their glee. They hold themselves higher than me, a superior I'm-better-than-you-because-it-didn't-happen-to-me *that they lord over me in their offers of helping to gather my things and bring them outside. I don't even have a car. I will have to take my overfilled backpack, my fit-to-burst handbag, and the cardboard box containing my files and a cactus, and sit on the Tube and then the bus and have everyone around me assume I've been fired.*

"Better she goes," my line manager says, the same line manager who told me to call her if I needed a reference "anytime" when I handed in my access card earlier.

"No one's going to miss her."

"Not even him."

He doesn't say goodbye, of course. After what happened, he has walked by me as if I don't exist. There are no more conversations. No more laughter in his office. But he steps into the corridor just as I'm making my final journey out, and I catch his eye and want to scream to the world about what we did.

If only.

If only I wasn't such a coward.

"Sasha!"

I wake with a jolt to Effie shaking me in bed. The sheets are hot and sticking to me, so I sit up and throw them off. My heart is pounding, my breath in gasps.

"You were having a nightmare," Effie says. The room is dark, and she switches on the bedside lamp, making my eyes strain. She is still in her uniform, though it must be the middle of the night. Where has she been? "Thrashing about and mumbling. Are you alright?"

I try to take a deep breath, but find the action impossible. "Sorry. I don't know what must have come over me. I'm fine."

"Are you sure?"

"Yes," I lie.

"You're not going to be like this every night, are you?" she says. "That would be a right pain to sleep next to."

I promise her I'm not.

"Well, in any case, you'll be too tired soon enough to have any dreams."

I can't tell her how much I hope that will be true.

She frowns, obviously still concerned. "I'd offer you a sleeping pill, but that probably wouldn't be a good idea, right? What with, you know . . ."

Am I still dazed from being asleep? I have no idea what she's referring to, but I'm not going to end up depending on some pills to get me through the night, so I shake my head at her and apologize for the disruption, and she starts getting ready for bed happily enough.

I thought I was safe. The first couple of nights passed by in a busy blur, my head hitting the pillow and waking up the next day with no memory of anything. I thought the change of scenery had cracked it.

But it hasn't.

The nightmares about what happened. They've followed me here.

CHAPTER NINE

LOLA

I know something is wrong before Jade even speaks, because her face is like thunder.

"Where is the Héloïse Lloris?" she asks.

"Champagne for breakfast?" I say, then balk at her unamused expression. "Shouldn't it be in the bucket and ice in the fridge?"

Two nights into this trip, and we're heading toward the Azores, long abandoning mainland Europe and surrounded by nothing but ocean. Yesterday I sat out on the stern, staring at the world we were leaving behind. Gibraltar was very far away. My home even farther. Not that I ever want to go back.

"Yes, that's where it *should* be." Jade opens the fridge. "So why is the bucket here and not the bottle?"

Sasha, standing across from me, frowns. She moves around the bar and looks too, opening the other fridge and investigating the cupboards. She's been on her best behavior for two reasons: one, to win Jade over, which is a futile mission. Jade is only happy when we do mess up, because that gives her some sense of superiority over us. And two, to win *me* over. Ever since the laundry fiasco she's been determined to be nice to me, clearly coming round to the idea it was an accident.

"You put it back in here, right?" Jade says to her. "After using it for the arrival?"

"Imogen put the champagne away," Sasha says. There she goes, blaming someone else again. "Unless someone else got it out to give to the guests?"

Jade shakes her head. "Lola, go and get the spare from the other bar. Thank God I ordered two."

But I come back empty-handed. "It's not there."

"What do you mean, it's not there?" She runs to check herself, returning panicked with Runa in tow. Runa makes a face at me I pretend to not see. "If someone is trying to make me scared, congratulations, it's working. Now put them back."

My expression matches Sasha's: confused, concerned.

Runa has her own bone to pick. "It is happening again. I have already complained to Captain Howard that my favorite knife is missing."

"What do you mean?" Sasha says. "What is happening again?"

I decide to answer. "We've had stuff go missing these past few weeks. Hundreds of canapés. Preference sheets. Even the captain's binoculars."

Whoever it is keeps messing up Jade's precious schedule, getting Effie and Imogen in trouble, and sparking Runa's temper. It would be unwise to admit, but I don't feel particularly bad about it. Jade treats me like I'm an idiot. Effie and Imogen are actively mean. And Runa might be being nicer to me at the moment, but I'm *not* stupid, whatever everyone thinks. I know why she's being sweet to me, and it has nothing to do with sincerity. None of them want to be my friend.

I lower my voice, leaning toward Sasha. "And that's not including all the things that were stolen from guests."

"*Lola*," Runa says in a warning tone.

"Sasha doesn't need to hear this," Jade says.

"Especially not with her delicate emotions," Runa says.

Sasha frowns. "My delicate emotions? What do you mean? What was being stolen?"

"Women's jewelry, mainly," I explain. "Necklaces, bracelets . . . the whole shebang. It's been costing us our tips. Noah outright accused Drew of all people of being the thief. Drew, being a nice guy, forgave him pretty quickly, but that was an awkward day."

It was me who told Noah I saw Drew going into a guest cabin when no one was around. I didn't expect Noah to react so strongly to it—he instantly went to Captain Howard, took the matter seriously. When it turned out Drew hadn't taken anything, Noah was devastated with himself for believing the worst.

"If you ask me," I say, "Imogen has been acting weird about it. You know she said her earrings have gone missing? Those gold hoop ones? I mean, no offense, but they're cheap ones from somewhere like ASOS. I bet she's trying to throw the scent off because it was her."

"Why are you ladies standing around gossiping?" Melinda appears in the doorway. "The guests are unattended, without fresh drinks."

Does she hang about waiting for the perfect moment to strike?

"I'm sorry, Chief," Jade says immediately. "There was a small issue with the champagne, but it's been sorted now."

"An issue?" Melinda of course focuses on the one detail Jade tries to rush over. The woman scares me. She's more intense than Jade, and these past two days she's been checking over all our work and fussing over the guests, even giving Digby a tour of the engine rooms.

"Not an issue anymore." Jade smiles sweetly, but her teeth are clenched together.

"Hop to it, then," Melinda says.

"Gagging to be captain," I whisper to Sasha after Melinda leaves, Runa in tow, though Runa mouths at me to meet her later in the galley. Jade shouts at us to get a new champagne bottle to bring to the guests while she checks on breakfast, and we grab two different options from the fridge to be safe.

"I can see that," Sasha says.

"She thinks she's something special. Looks down on the rest of us like we're nothing." I touch her arm, sympathetic. "Are you sure we're okay after the laundry mishap? I forgive you. There are no bad feelings on my part."

Sasha nods. "Of course. I'm sorry I got the wrong end of the stick."

"So have you and Axel hooked up yet?" I ask as we head out onto the terrace. "Apparently you were getting cozy in the club on the night out."

"Who said that?" She panics so easily. "We were *not*."

"Sure, sure," I say. "Relax. Effie told me. And don't think I haven't noticed you making eyes at Drew either."

It's a flippant comment, but her cheeks flame, so I must be onto something. We reach the two escorts, sat for breakfast, Benjamin and Digby absent. The table decorations are incredible, definitely how I would like to dine every day. Golden place mats are under each plate, and rose-gold cutlery frames the edges. Delicate champagne flutes and wineglasses are on either side, and each guest has a white napkin. The center of the table is covered in soft pink sand, seashells, and gold glitter. A huge white vase of roses is in the very middle, guarded by white candles in gold cases.

"Champagne, ladies?"

"Oh, fabulous," Eva says.

I'm able to tell the escorts apart through small details (Eva has a gap in her front teeth and thick dark eyebrows, while Jasmine is ridiculously thin, even by our standards), but stick a stewardess uniform on either of them and they'd blend right in with us.

While Sasha chats with Eva, Jasmine notices me staring. I offer up an apologetic smile.

"Sorry," I say. "I was wondering if there was anything I can get you while we wait for Mr. Edmondson and Mr. Johnson to arrive for breakfast."

"You can fetch me their heads," she says, then smiles at my reaction. "Kidding."

Huh. There's more to this one than first appears.

Kind of like me, I suppose. Poor little Mouse is hiding more than people think.

CHAPTER TEN

JADE

When you're the chief stewardess, it's your job to ensure everything is running smoothly. Any mishap, any mistake, any negative whatsoever to the guests' experience and you get the blame. The other stewardesses get to work shifts; I work twenty-four hours a day. Even when I'm sleeping, I can never quite fully let myself go. I wake up to the tiniest of sounds or movements. Runa goes to the toilet at night all the time, and I'm forever listening to her shifting in and out of the covers as she sneaks to and fro, thinking she's being quiet and failing. My mind is constantly on. I have to prepare for every scenario. No wonder my frown lines are worse than ever.

All I want is for Captain Howard's final season to go perfectly. Not for entirely selfless reasons—his glowing reference is what I need to ensure I stay doing the job I love for as long as possible. With Benjamin and Digby closing out the season again, this charter in particular needs to be perfect.

I always strive for perfection. And most of the time, I achieve it. There are only a few notable exceptions.

Zara was meant to be the one stealing guest items, the one who ruined excursions and hid the captain's binoculars. I got mistakenly cocky, assured I was right. But now it has started up again. The champagne. Runa's knife. A copycat? I have to find out who is doing this and make them stop.

There are other concerns plaguing me too. An odd one—the new escort, Jasmine, reminds me of someone. I can't quite pin her down yet, but I'll get there. She's also been avoiding me, dodging me whenever I come near. Definitely suspicious. I'm going to keep an eye on her. But right now I'm more concerned by the fact that Euphemia and Imogen should be working and I can't find either of them.

"*Euphemia*," I speak into my radio, aware of my ever-increasing impatience. "*Imogen. Do you copy?*"

I round the corridor that leads toward the guest cabins, and to my surprise find Euphemia down here. A place she has no right being when she was meant to be helping with breakfast and I had to get Sasha to do it instead. I open my mouth to scold her when I spot Benjamin in his doorway, reaching his hand out and grabbing her by the hip. He has an odd, wired energy about him.

Off his head, no doubt. Superyachts are hardly renowned for being law-abiding vessels.

"Ah, Euphemia, there you are!"

I march down the corridor, putting myself smartly between them in a way that requires him to let go of her.

"She's needed, I'm afraid," I say. "Now hop to it, Euphemia! And Mr. Edmondson, your companions are at the breakfast table."

Without waiting for a response, I grab her by the arm and escort her away.

When she doesn't immediately thank me, my tone is cold. "Rule Number Two, Euphemia. You should know how to handle something like that. Don't put yourself in those situations to begin with."

Euphemia shakes herself free of my grasp, and for the first time I notice how flushed she is. It is not like Euphemia to look out of sorts. She's the exact kind of woman everyone hates—she can be hot and sweaty and still be fabulous. But she's practically bright pink, from excitement or nervousness I'm not sure.

"Sorry, Jade," she says unexpectedly, and there's a smile behind her words. Something has cheered her immensely, enough for her to actually apologize.

"It's not as simple as 'sorry,'" I tell her, irritated she's looking like the cat that got the cream when she's meant to be in trouble. "You've been how many years in this job? And you wonder why I'm chief stewardess and you're not. What happened there with Benjamin? What did he want?"

"No, forget it," she says. "Guests come first."

She skips away. I choose to ignore her impudence. I find out everything in the end.

"*Imogen,*" I call into the radio. "*Imogen, where are you?*"

There's only one place left she could be. My anger grows as I head down to the crew mess, my suspicions confirmed when I hear giggling and rustling coming from Imogen and Lola's cabin, followed by a male voice. She's been with Axel.

She'll be working an extra hour to make up for it. She can do what she likes on her break—but when it bleeds into *my* time, that's when it's unacceptable. I've already tried putting a stop to their nonsense and predictably Captain Howard didn't listen.

"As long as they're not interrupting their duties, Jade." He chuckled. "Lighten up."

Let me tell you, I'm positively dark.

I bang on her door, not caring how loud I'm being. "Imogen! I've been calling you on your radio. Get out here now!"

She and Axel emerge, both in rumpled uniforms.

"Morning, Jade," Axel says, relaxed as anything. He's the *bosun*, for Christ's sake.

Imogen is at least more bashful, keeping her head down.

"I could report you for sleeping with Imogen when you're meant to be working," I say to him.

"You could," he agrees. "But we both know Captain Howard wouldn't give a shit, so why don't you remove that stick from up your ass for once?"

If I have to stay on this yacht much longer with that arrogant bastard, I might just end up killing him.

CHAPTER ELEVEN

JASMINE

Hallie would think I was crazy if she could see me now.

But she can't. My best friend, my only real family, Hallie Attwood, disappeared on this yacht one year ago, and no one has seen her since.

Hallie and I met due to being placed in emergency foster care. My mum died in a car crash when I was thirteen. She'd crashed into a tree at three o'clock in the morning, and I hadn't seen her for weeks anyway, fending for myself by stealing food from the local shop. All I had left of her was a box of belongings, more than she'd given me alive. Hallie never knew her mum but had a dad more interested in heroin than his daughter. Yet where I was angry, so angry at my lot in the world, Hallie had nothing but positivity. The day we met, me screaming the place down that no one could tell me what to do, I was going to run away and never come back, Hallie introduced herself as my new best friend.

We got a council flat together when we turned eighteen. We were happy then. Barely scraping enough for living, but happy. We never stopped laughing.

Things changed when Hallie caught an episode of *Below Deck*.

"Look at this!" she called. "We could do that easy. I'd be great at being a stewardess."

I was less convinced, watching the crew argue with each other.

"You could be a deckhand." She was my best friend, but even she wasn't flattering enough to suggest I could be a stewardess. "You're good around the flat fixing things."

"I don't know."

"We've always wanted to travel the world. Now we can! And get paid for it too!"

I was about to protest further when the TV showed a sweeping shot of some Italian coastal town. The sea was glittering, the houses multicolored and dotted high into the cliffs. I had never stepped outside of Coventry before, let alone gone somewhere abroad, let alone somewhere as magical as that.

"Let's do it," I said, words I'd regret forever.

She squealed, hugging me tight. "I knew I could count on you."

For the first season, it really was a dream come true. My mum left a notebook with a name and number in that box of belongings, and I was able to track down my father, who gave me the money for our training in exchange for keeping quiet about my existence to his wife and other kids. Hallie was natural at being a stewardess, I was acceptable as a deckhand, and we got to see the world. Even now I look through photos of Hallie and me in certain tourist spots and I have to catch my breath.

The following year was when we joined the *Ophelia*. When Hallie vanished.

The day it happened, I was cleaning the yacht exterior, spending most of my time hanging off the side and hosing it down. Hallie, by contrast, was working a late shift, which meant I only saw her as I headed down to the crew mess for an early night. Looking back, I try to find some hint, some sense that something was wrong. She was a little on edge, and barely laughed at my joke about whether she could steam my uniform while she was at it, but I just thought she was stressed. It was getting to the end of the season; *everyone* was stressed.

"Thailand and Vietnam soon," I told her. We had been talking about using our tip money to pay for this trip the entire time, our way of keeping momentum.

"Can't wait," she replied. "I'm picturing us on a beach with cocktails as we speak, and I haven't had to make them. Eat your heart out, Jade!"

"See you tomorrow, alright?" I said. "Have a good night."

"See you tomorrow, babe!" She smiled then, her effortless smile. She looked tired, but that wasn't unusual.

That was the last time I ever saw her. I woke up the next morning to find her bunk empty. I was confused, but not too concerned yet. But then she wasn't in the crew mess eating breakfast, she wasn't in the galley, and she wasn't anywhere I could find her.

It spiraled from there, becoming quite clear she wasn't on the yacht at all. The yacht that was currently anchored three miles off the coast. Hallie and I learned to swim while we were doing our training, but while I picked it up quite well, she was terrible; there was no way she would swim in the middle of the night alone. Which meant . . .

I panicked. Screamed at everyone to do something. Jade seemed more fussed about looking after the guests than ensuring the safety of one of her stewardesses, but Melinda made sure the yacht was clear while Captain Howard got us deckhands to swim around and look for her. He didn't even arrange a proper set of divers until hours had gone by, and I finally phoned the police without his permission.

There was no sign of her. She must have drifted with the tide, they said. I was removed from the yacht, told it was for my own good because I was so visibly distressed. And then they finished the charter without me. Hallie was missing and the yacht just sailed on away. They didn't have to stay. There was no investigation. The yacht wasn't registered in this country, I was told, and that was that. Hallie must have gone for one of her smokes and fallen overboard.

No crime. Just a missing woman no one seemed to care about.

I begged and cajoled the police, I contacted newspapers local to us back in Coventry, I tried to start a viral campaign online for justice that went nowhere. Hallie didn't have any other family, no one else to fight in her corner. Just me. *I* was her family, she was mine, and I was never going to stop looking for her.

When it became clear the authorities weren't going to do anything else, I had to switch tactics. The answer to Hallie's disappearance was on that yacht. Digby and Benjamin were the guests at that time, and I knew they took these charters on *Ophelia* every year—I just had to figure out how I was going to get back on the boat.

Et voilà, here I am. Not an easy task.

I had two main obstacles in my way: not being recognized by anyone, and how I could get on there if I wasn't going to be a deckhand.

The former wasn't so much of a problem with Benjamin and Digby. They were guests, they were surrounded by beautiful escorts and gorgeous stewardesses all day. I was distinctly not blonde and gorgeous. Easy not to recognize me when I wasn't worthy of a second glance. On a boat with an endless supply of supermodels, who was going to look at me longer than they had to? Being a junior deckhand, I barely interacted with them, was never the one to take them out on the tender for day trips, often only in the background fixing something or cleaning. Plus, when you're the staff, you don't matter. They don't bother with you because you're lesser than them, so I doubt I ever even entered their minds.

Captain Howard, Melinda, and Jade *were* a problem, however. Although Captain Howard largely kept to himself and didn't see us much, he still led our team meetings and had enough conversations with me to know who I was. He wasn't as pally with me as the other deckhands, but he definitely enjoyed the novelty of a female deckhand more than someone living in the twenty-first century should. But Melinda and Jade were worse. Their beady eyes were everywhere, they made everything their business. Melinda ordered us deckhands around enough times she might as well have added bosun to her many titles, while Jade knew Hallie and, therefore by extension, me very well. She was forever telling Hallie off for joking around with me when she was meant to be working.

So there was no chance of swanning in under a different name and hoping that would somehow be acceptable. Especially not after the scene I had made when Hallie disappeared.

Which meant changing my appearance drastically. I didn't have the money for plastic surgery, but I figured I had a year. A lot can change in that time.

The reflection that stares back at me now is a different person. My hair is a harsh, dyed blonde. I wear blue contacts. My eyebrows are grown out and reshaped. My makeup is different. But it's the weight that's the most shocking, the thing that has changed my entire face. I'm thin—stupidly thin. Almost a year of eating little more than five to eight hundred calories a day has got me so skinny my hip bones hurt if I lie on them. Anything to distinguish myself from the girl I was before. I'm "attractive" now, but there's a part of me that looks in the mirror and recoils, because each time I'm expecting to see me and instead find an ethereal stranger.

This will all be worth it.

First obstacle sorted, along with changing my voice and avoiding as much contact with Melinda and Jade as possible. I was terrified when I first arrived that I would be spotted and sussed out and this would all be over.

Benjamin, Digby, Eva, and I gathered outside a restaurant by the harborside to head to the yacht, and Digby was keen to inform me how to behave, less than impressed at seeing me. He had clearly wanted to arrange the girls as usual, and instead here I was.

"As long as you're aware that discretion is the name of the game," he murmured. "You do not speak a word of this to anyone. Do you understand?"

"She understands," Benjamin said, wrapping an arm around my

waist and giving it a squeeze. "She's never been on a superyacht before."

"Well, not many people have." Digby smiled then, all concern forgotten. "I remember my first time. I was a boy, with my family. My mother was thrilled. She had always wanted to be on one. My father made it happen."

Both of them had no clue I'd been right there with them last year. Washed the deck while they had breakfast. Set up the water toys. Saw their *other* activities and looked the other way. But I hadn't expected either of them to recognize me—it was who was lined up on the dock that was the real test. None of the same crew from last year, apart from Captain Howard, Melinda, and Jade. My heart started beating at the sight of the stewardesses in their uniforms, like Hallie was there waiting for me five times over. Her going missing hadn't changed anything. They still all looked the same.

I went last in line as we greeted everyone in the hopes they'd be eager to get it over with. But Captain Howard gripped my hand in a firm shake.

"Welcome aboard," he said.

He hadn't changed in the slightest. The same confident posture. Easy smile.

He didn't recognize me; he wasn't really *looking*. He had his show face on. The same face he used to tell me my time on the yacht was over and I had better go home. I moved down the line to Melinda.

"Good morning," she said. "Jasmine, right? It's a pleasure. I'm Chief Officer and Chief Engineer Melinda Fall. I'm in charge of most of the general running of *Ophelia*, and your welfare and safety."

How much did Melinda know about what happened last year? She wasn't doing such a good job of looking after welfare and safety then.

"Thank you very much."

No recognition from her, but she wasn't really paying attention either, far more enamored with Benjamin and Digby.

Jade, on the other hand, gave me her full focus. She always was the best at customer service. "It is an honor to welcome you on board *Ophelia*, Jasmine. I hope you have a wonderful experience."

"Thank you," I replied. "I love it here already."

Maybe it was something in the way I said it, but she frowned, squinting as she studied me. She's definitely my biggest threat. I was grateful for the sunglasses I had on, an added disguise. I've avoided being one-on-one with her ever since.

The second obstacle, how to get on the yacht again in the first place, complemented how I changed my appearance. How does one get on a superyacht if they can't afford it?

Be an invited guest.

But what if you don't have any rich friends? I'm not friends with Benjamin or Digby. What then?

Be their *escort*.

Benjamin and Digby had them last year, a couple of women who looked just like the stewardesses and were nice enough. But they aren't the only ones. It's an incredibly common occurrence on yachts like this, not just *Ophelia* but the first yacht Hallie and I were on too. To begin with we found it funny, shocking—but eventually it became more surprising to learn guests were coming on board *without* escorts (normally when their wives were reluctantly invited instead).

I needed to be invited onto the yacht by one of these men. I didn't have enough time to get myself into one of the exclusive escorting agencies, nor could I guarantee I'd even be placed with Benjamin or Digby. The odds would have been astronomical. No, I had to put myself in front of one of them and get them to want me so bad they'd bring me with them.

Benjamin was easier to track down, a regular at a jazz club in London on Thursday and Friday nights. It wasn't exclusive, thankfully. Didn't need to be on any guest list, simply fluttered my eyelashes at the bouncers and soon enough they got to know me, asked why I always came alone, one of these days was I going to bring with me some handsome man?

Well, he wasn't handsome, but I did have one man in particular in my sights.

I'd deliberately put myself in Benjamin's way a few times over a couple of weeks—walking past his table to go to the bar, making sure to drop something and bend over to fetch it, smiling as if we were establishing a friendship. Finally, it was time to take action. I asked for the table next to his.

I was in a killer dress. Skintight, plunging neckline, my recently dyed blonde hair falling in curls past my shoulders, baby-pink lip gloss shining. I still wasn't used to seeing my collarbones so pronounced.

Not a flicker of recognition from him. But I doubt he ever so much as glanced my way before. Women don't exist unless they're beautiful. You bet your ass he noticed me now.

That night, when the waitress brought him his drink, I made a great show of waving my own at him, beaming. "Twinsies! I have the same one."

"Why don't you join me?" he suggested, pulling out the chair next to him. "I've seen you around here quite often. Do you like jazz too?"

Bingo. I jumped up eagerly, sitting beside him. "Oh, I *love* jazz. Can't get enough."

I know nothing about jazz.

"Oh—hold on! I am sure I've seen you before," I said, rather pleased with the way I staged a mock-gasp, hand to my mouth. "I was in Santorini last summer and saw a fabulous yacht. I think it was you on the deck sipping a cocktail. It looked magnificent."

"That's right, a *super*yacht," Benjamin said. "I was there with my friend Digby Johnson. The business magnate? You must have heard of him."

"Gosh," I said. "I don't know much about business and all that kind of stuff. It's too complicated for me."

But I know almost every damn thing about that man.

"I have always wanted to go on a superyacht," I said.

"It's an annual thing for us." Benjamin finished his drink, eyes feasting on me. "I'm actually leaving in a few days for another charter with him."

I know, I thought. *That's why I'm here, suffering your hand halfway up my thigh.*

It took the rest of the night, teasing him, playing with his hair, pretending to drink lots so he thought I was wasted. And then, as the last song played, I clutched my phone and told him I had to go.

"Go?" he repeated, stunned. "You can't leave now, darling, we're just getting to know each other. I was going to suggest taking this to my hotel."

"There's been an emergency," I said, as though I was devastated. I leaned in close, mouth open, whispering so my breath tickled his ear. "If only we could see each other again soon, and not just for one night..."

"My superyacht trip," Benjamin said, as desperate for me as I intended. "I don't think Digby will mind if I ask you to tag along. Would you like that?"

Oh, I liked that very much.

Yes, I was going to have to sleep with him. But now that I'm here, and it's been done, I don't feel any different. I was always prepared to do whatever was necessary to get on this boat and find out what happened to Hallie.

As is evident by the fact I'm in Benjamin's cabin after dinner again.

"You're gorgeous," he growls. "Really gorgeous."

The man isn't drunk, but he's not exactly sober. We lie together in his bed after our entanglement, the sheets thrown off for air.

"Thank you so much for bringing me on this trip," I breathe. "I've never experienced anything like it."

His eyes light up; he enjoys me as the poor girl he's introducing to higher culture. "Are you enjoying yourself?"

"It's so magical." As if we're in some Disney kingdom and not this seedy master suite. I want him to talk about what he told Eva, about the "nonsense afterward" he was referring to. What does he know? "I bet you've had a lot of women in this room, haven't you? Not just lucky women like me invited on board, but perhaps . . . crew members too?"

"Oh my . . ." Benjamin purrs. "That would be telling."

So tell me, you bastard. Tell me now.

And then—shit. Knocks on the door, a pounding three times.

"Not now," Benjamin calls. "I'm busy."

"Too bad." It's Digby. "We need to talk. It's important."

He doesn't wait for Benjamin's answer, opening the door and marching in. It's the first time I've seen Digby looking anything but composed. I have to leap up and grab a fluffy dressing gown from the wardrobe. For God's sake. Isn't he meant to be with Eva? What is she doing? After our little chat about expectations, she's been mostly avoiding me.

"Christ, Digby," Benjamin says, scooping up his trousers from the floor. "Alright, alright. Jasmine, we must continue this another time."

I'm stunned at the way Digby seems to have the primary obeying his every word. "Whatever you want." It's said through gritted teeth.

"I'm afraid I need your man," Digby tells me, oozing charm, but there's an urgency beneath his tone. "I'm sorry to disturb you."

Unceremoniously dismissed, I place my ear against the door to listen. Their voices are muffled, hard to understand at first. It sounds like they're arguing.

"I've already told you it's fine." Benjamin. "Does Howard know?"

"No." Digby's voice becomes clear. "It's better if we keep it that way.

You haven't been shooting your mouth off to this woman? I'm still not happy you brought her on board."

"It's fine, Digby. Just having fun with her."

"She's a *civilian*." The word drips with disgust. "If she were to misbehave, or worse, do something that compromises our p—"

"She won't. She's totally enamored with me, and with this yacht. It's cute, honestly."

Even from the other side of the door I can hear Digby sigh, unimpressed. "Don't repeat your behavior from last time, not with her."

Last time?

There's a sudden noise from within and I have to dart away, the rest of the conversation lost.

I'll find out more about this supposed "last time" later. This is the perfect opportunity to check my and Hallie's spot. It's late. The crew will be asleep other than whoever is on watch. I've been thinking about it nonstop, but avoided doing anything in case there was time enough to turn the yacht back around. Now, I think we're far enough in that I can start enacting what I came here to do.

When Hallie and I first arrived on *Ophelia*, we did our own tour of the boat together, running up and down the various corridors in excitement. Hallie was so eager she accidentally bumped into a life jacket case, and the glass door of it swung open.

"Oops!" she gasped, then dissolved into a fit of giggles.

"Hallie! We don't want to get thrown off before we've even unpacked our suitcases!" But I couldn't help laughing too. I laughed a lot back then.

It was only when I got closer that I saw there wasn't a real life jacket at all, just a display, and a lot of empty space behind it.

We swapped notes this way when we were on opposite shifts, our method of updating each other about what was going on. Sometimes they'd be silly—a smiley face, or how good dinner was. Sometimes they'd be full of gossip—did you know Edward slept with Paula last night? And sometimes they'd have a nice message: you're the best friend ever.

When Hallie disappeared, in my stress and anguish at wanting to find out what happened, I didn't think of checking our spot. By the time I thought of it as a possibility, as a hint to what might have happened, I'd already been told to leave. I wasn't even given the opportunity to pack my stuff; I found it dumped on the dock in bags.

It always felt like a missed chance.

My fingers are trembling now as I ease open the glass, still not secured properly. I'm too scared to look, to have it confirmed there's nothing, so I blindly reach my hand inside, feeling to the bottom where our notes used to sit.

And I feel it. A piece of paper.

I bring it out and see Hallie's signature kiss on the front of the fold. There really is something from her left behind.

But then I read what she's written, and I think I'm going to faint.

WE HAVE TO LEAVE TOMORROW.

CHAPTER TWELVE

SASHA

Effie was wrong. No matter how tired I am, the nightmares haven't stopped.

But I'm fully assimilated now, in the routine of standing under the terrible shower and hoping it comes out lukewarm rather than cold, shoveling down some cereal before being shouted at by Jade for being late. Endless piles of laundry, ironing, cleaning, making beds. Over a week of the same routine. Not much interaction with the guests, kept to the lowly tasks the others don't want to do. Benjamin and Digby have been surprisingly okay, though Jade snorted when I told her I thought they were nice enough.

The waves are choppy. I can feel the force of them hitting against the yacht as it powers onward. We passed by the Azores a couple of days ago, small dots of land in the distance, a comforting reminder that there is civilization out there despite the vastness of the ocean. Maybe it's because we're so far out, but my phone hasn't had any signal today. I've been sitting out on a storage box, spending my break watching the horizon.

"Room for one more?"

Drew stands behind me, bottle of water in each hand. I nod for him to join me.

"Things have been so hectic I feel like we haven't had a proper chat since that first night out," Drew says. He sits cross-legged on the same box and offers me one of the water bottles. "How's it all going?"

He's not my normal type, but as men are currently under embargo, this could be good for me. I ponder his question. How *has* it been going?

I thought everyone would automatically love me, like the nurses all did before it went wrong, but the other stewardesses are tricky. I've never been that great at making female friends, I guess. Imogen especially is annoying. I had a headache yesterday and took some of Effie's paracetamol and she made a weird comment about me falling off the wagon and to be careful. I've pretty much decided to ignore whatever she says. It didn't help that Effie burst into laughter.

Not that I should be seeing this as an opportunity to have fun. It's an escape, not a holiday.

"It's good," I decide. "Benjamin and Digby are easy enough to handle, and I know now to check the washing very carefully!"

Drew grins. "That easy, huh? Be careful. Pride comes before a fall."

Well. I certainly know that's true.

"And an Atlantic crossing for your first-ever charter is pretty rough," he says. "The weather's starting to make itself known! Captain Howard told me there's meant to be a big storm later. He's hoping it'll hold off until after the party tonight, but he's insisting on powering through instead of attempting to go around it."

"Jade won't be happy if her party is interrupted."

Jade is throwing a "Silver Soirée" for the guests this evening, and as far as I can tell that means everything is silver—the decorations, the guests' outfits, even the food somehow. Apparently it's an annual event Digby and Benjamin like to have on their charters.

"This is my first proper Atlantic crossing too," Drew says. "I was born in America, but I've never been back. Was brought up in England."

This surprises me. "I figured you guys had done these all the time."

He shakes his head. "Last year on a different vessel I was the newbie like you, but we did France." He lies down, hands clasped behind his head, and I follow suit. "I wish you'd been on it too."

A tiny thrill churns my stomach. I haven't felt this since . . . no. Stop it. He's easy to talk to. We chat for a while, about everything, and it's surprising how nice it is. There's a spark, and I know he can feel it too, but I try to push it down. You need a *friend*, Sasha. Especially after the mess you left behind.

We're on to pasts now, and though I remain somewhat vague and noncommittal with my answers, Drew is an open book.

"Life's been hard for me," he says. "I grew up poor. My family still are. Imagine having five younger siblings. Mum is unwell, no dad. The burden has fallen on me."

He sounds so sad it makes me reach for his hand. "I'm sorry."

"I'd do anything for them," he says. "Hence me taking this job, sending them my paychecks. It's hard, especially when you look around this place and see furniture worth more than your entire house. Hell, some of the guests have *clothes* worth more. My siblings barely have enough food between them and Mum goes hungry. Why do we get that and other people get . . . *this*?"

He gestures around wildly, and from how we're lying down it's as if he's pointing at the sky above. It fits. Some people get the sun, the stars, the whole horizon. Other people are lucky if they get a hot meal and a roof over their head. Dr. Martin seemed so wealthy and successful six months ago, but compared to all this he's a puddle next to the Atlantic Ocean.

"It's sickening," I say, surprised by how much I mean it. I squeeze his hand. "The world is unfair."

"I knew you'd understand," Drew says. "I got the vibe you weren't well-off like Axel or Lola. You're much more down to earth."

"You're a good person," I tell him. "Helping out your family like you do."

His face clouds. "I'm not so sure about that. But I will help them no matter what." He turns to look at me, and we lie face-to-face for a while. I'm still holding his hand. "Like I said, this is tough. You're handling all this well, especially when you consider what happened with your last job."

I sit up so fast I think the head rush is going to drain all the blood from my skull. My vision blurs, as if Drew has thrown me into the freezing water below.

"What—what do you mean?" I manage to whisper.

"Hey, you've gone white." Drew tries to put his arms around me, but I push him away. "I'm sorry, I didn't mean to upset you. A few of us were talking the other day and I happened to mention you—because I'm interested in getting to know you more—and it came out then about your old job."

There's no way anyone could know. The only person who knows is back in London, probably at the hospital, going about his day without a care in the world . . .

"What do you think you know, exactly?" I ask.

Drew looks sheepish. "That you were—uh—well. Fired."

Do you want to get fired, Sasha?

"Fired?" I echo. "For what?"

"I don't think we should talk about this after all . . ."

"Drew. Tell me."

"You had a problem with, um, medication. You were caught stealing it. I'm not judging you. You had a dependency problem. It's why you don't drink. Trust me, I've been through some struggles myself, you have no idea—"

Oh God. Is this what Runa's weird comment was about? Imogen's jibe about falling off the wagon?

"I quit being a nurse," I say shakily. "I wasn't fired. I don't have any problem with medication. I don't drink because . . ." Here, I falter. I've told the truth so far, but now I'm going to have to lie. "My father was an alcoholic."

"Really?" Drew is gobsmacked. "I'm so sorry."

"Who told you this rubbish?" I demand. "Imogen?"

But a piercing shriek interrupts us. We're both on our feet within seconds.

"What was that?" Drew asks.

"We have to go, come on!"

We head to the source, around to one of the side terraces. I'm intently aware of sudden seasickness escalating as the yacht seems to lurch over the increasing waves.

Effie is leaning against the railing while Noah towers over her, one hand gesturing, the other grabbing Effie's wrist.

"Hey!" I shout, and both of them jump.

Noah drops her wrist like it's scalding hot and backs away.

I march over and focus on Effie. "Are you okay?"

She nods, but seems unable to speak. It occurs to me that no one else has come running, that if Drew and I didn't happen to be nearby she would have been left alone. This yacht is huge. If you're far enough away, no one will hear you scream.

I glare at Noah. "What were you playing at, grabbing at her?"

"Grabbing at her!" Noah splutters, horrified. "I wasn't—that's not—tell them, Effie!"

"Don't lie," I say, before Effie can defend him. "I saw you."

"I was *holding* her," Noah protests. "We were talking. Things got heated—"

"So you thought you'd hurt her?"

"Jesus, I'd never hurt Effie!" He sounds wounded. "How could you think that of me?"

"Drew and I heard Effie scream!"

"I'm fine," Effie says. "Leave it now. I didn't mean to cause such a fuss."

"Effie—"

"Alright, I guess we don't know the full story," Drew says. "Why don't I take you down to the crew mess for a cup of tea, Eff?"

"Well, I need to talk to you anyway, Effie," I say, linking my arm with hers. "So why don't we both go do that, and Drew can talk to Noah?"

I throw Drew an apologetic glance as I lead Effie away, but he's focused on Noah, frowning.

Effie and I are barely two steps inside before she wrenches my arm away. "I'm not a baby, I can look after myself."

"Are you going to explain what that was about?" I ask. Thankfully, the corridor is empty, so there's no one to interrupt us.

She sighs. "Nothing. Stop sticking your nose in my business."

Why is she so defensive? Weren't we meant to be friends when we linked our pinkies together, a gesture I recognized then and know now was faker than Axel's veneers? What got heated with Noah, exactly, and why won't she tell me?

It's weird, but she looks so like me that I can recognize in her face that she's hiding something bigger about all this. She has the same telltale signs I do when something is bothering me. No—there's more than that.

That's it. She's scared.

I recognize it because I was just as terrified. Still am. Drew bringing up my old job, this vicious lie that has spread, has brought it all back. I should have just gone along with it. It's better than the truth.

I've been running ever since.

CHAPTER THIRTEEN

IMOGEN

The weather started getting worse this morning while I was trying to enjoy a snooze. I was still able to do my yoga without a worry. Caught Noah checking out my ass when he stormed downstairs all flustered and shouted at him to stop being a pervert, which made me laugh when he went scurrying into his cabin claiming he'd come to fetch something. Uh-huh, sure, buddy. I know I look great in my yoga pants, but this view isn't for you. Even if I did have to run and throw up afterward. I'll blame it on the choppy water making me seasick.

Now the guests are with us all in the sky lounge whining about the lack of internet. That's right, apparently this superyacht can't handle a bit of wind and rain because phone signals and all internet have stopped working. Here comes the tipping point for sure. Guests always have a window. The I'll-be-polite-because-I've-just-got-on-here window. Soon enough, they'll break through and start acting like their true selves. We've had quite a peaceful time with them so far, nothing too outrageous. A pair of boring businessmen who seem keener on drinking, eating, and relaxing (Benjamin) or taking tours with Melinda to the engine rooms and speaking with the deckhands (Digby). But no guest is ever truly decent. You don't get rich being honest, as they say.

It's not like they now have nothing to do. Watch television. Play some pool. Go fuck one of their escorts. If I had a rainy day on here to myself I'd grab Axel and we wouldn't leave the bedroom. Rich people are so boring. Benjamin is futilely trying to access something on his phone. Digby at least seems more composed about it, accepting a coffee from Sasha and even muttering a thank-you.

"I'm so sorry about this inconvenience," Jade says, a raging syco-phant as always. "Our engineer promises she is working on a fix. In the meantime, Sasha and Imogen are here to top up your drinks while I prepare the fabulous party tonight."

This party. Or Silver Soirée, as Jade calls it, because that elevates it to a whole other level apparently. We're all expected to work, even though Benjamin and Digby have insisted on us "joining in the fun" by wearing silver bikinis and getting in the pool. I'll take it.

"If we even have a party tonight," Benjamin says gloomily.

The boat tips, making Eva, who is sitting beside Digby on the sofa, groan. Weirdly, Jasmine has the same balance we stewardesses do. She's watching the weather out of one of the windows and doesn't even flinch, shifting her body with whichever way the boat goes.

"Bravo, Jasmine," Digby says, observing her too. "Natural sea legs."

She startles at this, and then as if to prove Digby wrong stumbles as she turns back to us. "Oh, I don't think so. I feel a bit sick."

"Nonsense! Anyone would think you've been on a yacht before."

A violent lurch to the left sends Sasha careering backward along with the drinks she's carrying. She crashes to the ground, spilling ev-erything. Benjamin roars with laughter. I watch Jasmine, noting how well she handles herself. She's definitely been on a boat before, unlike our newest recruit over here.

"Oh God!" Sasha yelps. "I'm so sorry!"

I can't help laughing too, even as Jade shoots me a dark glare. Sasha just looks so stupid on the floor, struggling to get herself back up with all the rocking. Talk about ungraceful. I *could* help her, but it's far funnier to watch her scramble to her feet and wobble around.

Jade gets to clearing the glass away. "I'll just take this and be back soon."

Eva clears her throat. "Before you leave—I have some jewelry missing."

The thief is at it again. I knew it! No one would believe me before when I said about my gold hoops, but now a guest has had something stolen too.

I lift my chin triumphantly at Jade, but she's on damage control. "What jewelry? I am so sorry about that. We can help you look for it."

"One is just a costume bracelet," Eva says. "I only noticed because I was going to wear it tonight for the silver theme. But I've also lost an amethyst ring that has sentimental value."

"I'm sure we'll find it," Jade says. By which she means good luck ever seeing it again.

Sasha is finally up, leaning against a wall. She looks *terrible*, all sickly and green. She might be pulling this weak, vulnerable act to win some sympathy points but it won't work with me. That's the only reason why Axel was even bothering to make an effort, because he felt bad for her. He's been acting so off ever since she came on board.

Captain Howard enters at this point looking far too cheerful for someone meant to be bringing us out of this storm. "I know there's a bit of a stiff breeze at the moment, but bear with us. Melinda is getting us through it."

"A woman driver!" Benjamin cackles. "No wonder we're rocking like this!"

Someone push him off this yacht, please. Even Digby looks irritated with him.

"I hope you're all looking forward to the party tonight," Captain Howard says.

"The weather won't spoil it?" Digby asks.

"Not at all," he reassures him. "We're forecast a big storm during the night, but the evening is looking fine."

Thankfully, he's right. At five o'clock, weather clear, Melinda tells the deckhands to take over our duties while we get ready for the party.

The crew mess reminds me of my best friend from school's bedroom—clothes strewn everywhere, makeup on every counter, plates with half-eaten toast, and my downloaded music blaring every cringey pop song imaginable. Jade has bought silver bikinis especially for tonight, and even though the color and material are tacky as fuck, I can't deny my ass looks incredible. No wonder Noah was trying to sneak a peek. We have to wear our uniforms over them, but we're allowed to bling them somewhat, which has mainly meant everyone rooting around in Effie's things for accessories.

Mouse has already bagged Effie's gorgeous red coat, keeping it on to avoid anyone taking it for themselves even though it's boiling down here. She's even put on her red scarf, which Sasha keeps frowning at for some reason. Sasha has offered to paint everyone's nails. I think she means it as a way to draw a line under everything, but I mainly agree because I can see from her own nails there isn't a single smudge, and my hands are never that steady.

"To Mouse and Imogen's cabin!" Effie announces, grabbing something from her bedside cabinet and tucking it behind her back.

"Why ours?" I pout.

Effie grins. "Because mine and Sasha's room is *covered* in all my discarded clothes you lot decided weren't good enough to put on! And anyway—I want to borrow something from Mouse tonight! She never shares."

Mouse turns pink. "Oh, I don't have anything. Why don't we just sit in the kitchen for Sasha to do our nails?"

But Effie doesn't listen to her. She marches purposefully into our cabin, and we have no choice but to follow. Sasha sits cross-legged on the floor, bottle of nail varnish in front of her, and I sit opposite and offer her my hand. Mouse comes in last, protesting to Effie that she really doesn't have much.

"You're always bragging about your designer gear," I say pointedly. "It's only fair. You have on Effie's coat."

"What's this?" Effie brings out a fancy-looking tote bag, and I can see the Gucci label from here. I roll my eyes. Typical, materialistic Mouse. But Effie seems to find it amusing, holding it aloft with one hand, the other still behind her back, and then she bursts out laughing. "Mouse, *please* don't tell me you've fallen for one of those street vendors."

"What do you mean?" Mouse whispers, pinker than ever.

"It's a fake!" Effie declares, still giggling. "Look at this stitching— it's all over the place! And oh my God, is that *glue* keeping the logo on the zip? This is too funny. Mouse, you've only gone and bought a fake Gucci tote."

She drops it on the floor beside Sasha and me, and I'm able to get a closer look. If she hadn't pointed it out, I'd have no idea it wasn't real. Let's be honest, this is the closest I've come to a designer handbag. But I laugh anyway, and even Sasha joins in.

"Why on earth wouldn't you buy from a proper store?" Effie says, shaking her head. "Gucci is far too easy to copy. It's why I stick to Hermès and Chanel."

Mouse is trying to laugh along with us, but her smile wavers. "I can't even remember where I got it from."

"I thought you were meant to have money," I say, eyebrows raised. "Are you scavenging for knockoffs? What about those earrings you so kindly offered me before, eh? Are those fake too?"

She turns bright red. Clearly I've hit a nerve, even if she has just been her typical dunce self, mistaking that bag for a real one.

"I was going to lecture you about bringing a designer handbag on a yacht with all the salt air," Effie says, "but I won't need to bother now. This thing is equivalent to Imogen's crap."

"Thanks, Eff," I say. "You're such a sweetheart."

She blows me a kiss. "You'll be calling me a sweetheart for real in a second. Look what I've snuck down here." At last, she produces what she has behind her back. It's a bottle of vodka, already half empty.

"Effie!" Sasha says. "Won't you get into trouble? We're not allowed to drink on shift!"

"It's a *party*," she says. "And anyway, you don't drink, so you're fine. Keep those hands steady for our nails. Mouse? Imogen? You up for it?"

"Yes!" Mouse says instantly, clearly eager to move on from the Gucci bag fiasco.

Effie swigs from the bottle, then passes it to Mouse, who drinks far more than a shot. She passes it to me, and I hesitate. I probably shouldn't, as much as I desperately want to. But then we hear someone from outside, and as they're turned, distracted, I pretend to take a swig and then wipe my mouth as if it was that refreshing.

It's Jade, appearing in the doorway armed with silver glitter and face paint. "To add to our look," she says, before spotting the bottle in my hand. "Imogen! What is that?"

Oh fuck. "It's Effie's!"

Effie blinks, wide-eyed. "Mine? I've never seen it in my life."

This bitch!

But to my surprise Jade joins us in the circle, sitting down with a thump, taking the vodka bottle and resting it in her lap. "I'm confiscating this, but I'll let you all off with a warning for tonight. It's been a long season."

I don't think we've ever sat like this, all together. Sasha finishes my nails and moves on to Mouse, while Effie adds the face paint to us all, silver swirls that frame our cheekbones and dots above our brows. Jade finishes the look by applying glitter to our cheeks. My music blares in the background, and it's the closest we've ever felt to being something resembling friends.

Effie sits back with a sigh when she has finished her handiwork. "This charter has been rough, and I'm not just talking about the weather."

"For some people more than others," Mouse says. Which I consider a bit of a cheek.

"As long as we do a good job, ladies, it will all be worth it," Jade tells us, and she clearly believes her spiel. "New York beckons!"

"I've never been to America," Sasha says. "I think I'd like to move abroad, in the future."

"You've been awfully quiet about where you came from," Effie says. "We hardly know anything about you."

Well, we know one thing, thanks to a certain someone in this circle. But I think Effie is trying to draw it out of Sasha herself, so I keep my mouth shut.

"I don't know anything about you all either," Sasha murmurs.

"Euphemia can dazzle you with her modeling days," Jade says, to Effie's discomfort.

"Don't get her started, she'll be showing you her magazine spreads next," I groan.

"You're just jealous. Hold on." Effie scrambles to her feet, leaving the cabin and returning seconds later with a couple of magazines, opening them up and showing Sasha various pictures of her in dramatic positions. "It was great."

She's beautiful in them, obviously. But looking between her in the photographs and how she is now, a sadness has grown in her eyes.

She seems to sense I'm appraising her, because she snaps the magazines shut.

"Mouse is all the way from Melbourne, if you didn't know," she says, changing the subject. "This is her first real job."

"You act like that's such a bad thing." Mouse pouts. "I'm only twenty-two."

"You must miss your family," Jade says.

Something darkens across Mouse's face at the mention of her family. Is she really that sore about Mummy and Daddy cutting her off for a year? And as if they'd ever actually let her go hungry. She doesn't know the first thing about family problems. Try having a dead brother, a depressed mother, and a father who works too hard trying to hold us all together.

"Sure," Mouse says quietly.

"Being a stewardess is very different from being a nurse," Sasha says. "But things got hard in the end. I had to get away."

To my surprise, Effie leans across and hugs her.

Even Jade, normally so uncaring, offers a sympathetic smile. "You've picked the wrong job to come into if you don't like things getting hard. This job can be . . ." She gestures at us all, sitting here with bikinis under our uniforms and face paint, and doesn't have to articulate what she means. It's ridiculous, all of this. Like some fantasy.

"The *gaze*," Effie says.

"We can never be real," Mouse adds.

My stomach hurts. Is what Axel and I have real?

"The pressure," Jade murmurs, oddly candid.

We're silent for a few minutes, putting the finishing touches on each other, but there's an undercurrent now, an understanding among us. We're all just trying to survive in this fucking weird world.

"Hey," Sasha says. "About before. It's been bothering me—"

But Sasha doesn't get a chance to say whatever it is that's bothering her. Our radios sound, Melinda calling for Jade, telling her we all need to come up now, we've had enough time to get ready.

The illusion is shattered. We're back to being stewardesses again. Jade rises, brushing imaginary dust from her uniform, and nods at us.

"Game faces on, everyone," she says. "Rule Number Three."

S-m-i-l-e.

Now we all stand, take each other in for a moment. Silver, glittering clones. Mouse has on her scarf and Effie's red coat, bangles clink across my arms, Sasha is adorned with stupidly long earrings, but we're the same beneath it all, beneath the face paint. Like dolls. Packaged and produced and ready to please.

Well. At least we're not made of china. Our faces would crack under all this strain.

By midevening, the party is in full swing on the upper deck, after an obscene dinner of oysters and silver-silk straw mushrooms. The guests are flitting from one place to the next, enjoying the extra treats Runa prepared: silver chocolate balls; silver cupcakes; a silver marble cake, which has already been half eaten. Even Eva is eating them, though I notice she takes a bite of each and then leaves the rest wistfully on the side, clearly dying to eat more. It's the first time I've empathized with her. Jasmine steers clear of all the treats, the willpower of a god.

I'm in the pool, pretending to be enthralled when Benjamin tells me all about his financial firm and the famous clients he works with, when I spot Mouse and Axel leaving the pool and heading inside. She's in her bikini, dripping wet, his arm around her as the doors close behind them.

He's not cheating. He's *not*. He just likes to flirt. I can't follow them; I'll look crazy. I endure a painful half hour listening to Benjamin waffle on, entirely focused on the doors. They still haven't come back.

"How about you come to my room later tonight and join me and Jasmine?" Benjamin whispers. He has food in the corner of his mouth and it's taking everything in me to not gag.

"I wish," I say, "but the chief stewardess has me working the late shift. I'm so sorry."

Translation: Get away from me, you dirty old man, before I kick you in the balls. And yes, I can feel your foot trying to jam itself up my crotch.

"In fact, I had better go and check she doesn't need me for anything," I tell him, and before he can protest I'm heaving myself up and walking away. You give these men an inch, you bet they're taking the whole mile.

I don't even bother giving him the illusion that I'm going over to Jade. I grab Effie's coat, cast off by Mouse when she got in the pool, and wrap it around me as I head straight through the double doors to find Axel and Mouse.

Fuck it if I look crazy. That's my man this bitch is trying to steal.

I need to talk to him. I need to stop imagining the worst, that the times he disappears and I can't find him have perfectly innocent explanations, and the moment he hears what I have to say, everything will be different.

I spot them in the corridor through the doors' glass panels. What have they been doing? Mouse is hitching up one of her bikini straps, which has fallen from her shoulder—had she taken it off? Does Axel's hair look disheveled? Why does he seem so intense, frowning, clearly bothered by something? They're close together, and then Mouse throws her head back and laughs. That stupid laugh she has.

She won't be laughing for much longer.

I'm storming over, my hand on the interior door, when I hear what they're saying.

"Did you know she's never been on a plane?" Mouse giggles, and I freeze.

They're talking about me.

"She's never even stayed in a nice hotel. It's like I'm talking to Oliver Twist sometimes."

My heart tightens. I hold my chest, wanting to rip it right out.

"Well, you don't really talk, do you?" Mouse says. "That solves that problem."

"I don't know why the others call you Mouse," Axel says. "You're always very confident when it comes to me."

She leans forward and whispers something in his ear, making him chuckle, and I want to wipe that stupid smile right off her face.

So much for Mouse. Effie should have called her *Cow*.

I open the door with so much force they hear me coming, springing apart like opposing magnets even though it's too late.

"Having a right laugh at my expense, are we?" I say. "No, do carry on. You were going to bring up the fact my mum's on benefits next, right?"

"Relax," Axel says, hands up in surrender. "It was only a joke."

"I'm sorry," Mouse says, all innocence and light. But I've got her measure now.

I put my face close to hers, all too aware I must be red with anger, even redder than Effie's coat. "You need to stay away from him."

She backs off, fearful. Please. She's putting that on for Axel. "Nothing happened." She doesn't even hang about, running back through the main salon and outside again.

"Coward!" I shout after her. Axel tries to pull me into an embrace, and I shake him away. "Don't think you're getting off lightly. What's going on?"

Axel sighs. "Nothing. You're paranoid, babe. We were just talking."

He thinks he can "babe" me right now?

"Fine, then what's going on with *us*?" I ask. "You've been acting weird ever since Sasha came on board. Is it *her*? Is she the one you're screwing around with? Because you've been disappearing, not telling me where or why or who you're with, and we're on a fucking yacht, Axel. There's only so many places you can be. So many people you can be with."

"Imogen," he says, wrapping his arms around me again. This time I let him. He kisses the top of my head, breathes me in. "There's no one else. Let me prove that to you tonight."

"Tonight?"

"Meet me in the pantry after the party. I'll show you how much you mean to me."

He releases me, that infuriating man, and walks away, doing one of his disappearing acts again. I hate the way my stomach flips when he's near me. I hate that he reduces me to this pathetic state. I hate that I believe him.

I should have challenged him about what he said. He *knows* I'm insecure about it. I've lain next to him in my cramped bed, whispering about how different I feel from everyone, like there's a club with all its rules and regulations I'm not privy to and I keep messing up.

I should want to kill him, not forgive him at the drop of a hat.

But I can't. Tonight will be when I tell him. So I have to focus my anger elsewhere. Mouse.

Her, I could kill very easily. Even just thinking about it makes my fists clench, peeking out beneath the fluffy red sleeves of Effie's coat.

She better hope she stays out of my way tonight or she's in for a world of trouble.

CHAPTER FOURTEEN

LOLA

That was a close one.

If Imogen had come to find us even five minutes earlier she'd have discovered me and Axel in the massage parlor hastily putting our clothes back on.

I've always fancied Axel, but I never imagined in a million years he'd actually sleep with me. I thought he saw me as a baby sister. I didn't think I was good enough.

It was my birthday two days ago—not that anyone else knows—and even after giving my parents the benefit of the doubt that the time zone difference might have meant their message was late, they still haven't sent anything. And yes, the internet has been patchy, and I can pretend it's still coming, but who am I kidding? They barely remember they have a daughter *most* days, let alone one day a year. Earlier tonight I took myself off for peace and quiet—and ended up comforting someone else instead to avoid them noticing my own tears.

So maybe I was feeling a little low afterward, and when Axel came over to me in the pool and murmured how fantastic I looked, maybe I just wanted to feel good. I propositioned him myself, as pathetic as that is. And it was good, if a bit underwhelming. He probably felt he didn't have to put as much effort in with me.

Afterward, he told me we had better keep it between us.

"I really like you," he said. "But Imogen has a *huge* crush on me, you know that. If this got out, things could turn sour fast. Let's keep this quiet."

I was already regretting it, to be honest. It wasn't like he was going to kiss me and tell me we should run away together. But his saying this made me mad, like I was an object he could discard. Just Mouse. Not glamorous, feisty Imogen.

So I giggled. "Maybe I will, maybe I won't."

"Seriously, Lola. This was fun. I want to do it again. But don't over-complicate it."

Any illusions I had about him promptly shattered.

I shrugged. "Maybe I like the idea of having something over on you. It gives me the control, doesn't it?"

"Lola," he said quietly. "You don't want to fuck around with me."

"Isn't that what I just did?" But I softened. "Imogen isn't worth it anyway. Did you know she's never been on a plane?"

That's when we came out into the corridor. Axel was still looking hassled, terrified I was going to blurt it all out. And then Imogen came barging over, raving like some buffoon.

Still, she's scary when she wants to be. Rather like a lion in a cage. When the door opens, you have to run.

I'm halfway down the exterior steps when I spot Sasha and Drew together on the bow. It's clear Drew's already had a few. One positive about being known as Mouse? I can sneak around and find out all sorts of things. Drew having a drinking problem is just one tidbit I've learned.

They don't twig I'm behind them, staying around one of the cargo containers.

"I hope you don't mind me drinking," Drew says. "Me and Chief get along. She'll allow it."

Drew and Chief *do* get along. I saw him go into her room once, so I'm not off base to think there's something there. But Drew gets along with everyone, even Imogen, so it doesn't seem likely. And hearing him flirt with Sasha now, it's obvious where his interests lie.

It's not fair. Sasha's been here five minutes. Drew has never spoken to me like this.

Sasha is into him too. "I'm sorry if you thought I was taking Effie's side in that business with Noah. And I'm sorry about our conversation before that too."

Business with Noah?

Drew takes a long sip of his drink. "I know all about pasts you'd rather not discuss."

"You?" Sasha shakes her head. "You're a good guy. Look what you're doing for your siblings and mum. Me, on the other hand . . ."

"Nah." He sounds miserable. "I did something bad. And I paid for it. But I don't want to talk about that."

And then he leans forward and kisses her.

It's a soft, sweet kiss; I bet he tastes of gin and tonic. They kiss for a long time, his hands cupping the back of her head. Axel never kissed me like that.

No one has kissed me like that.

The thought comes unexpectedly, shooting me where I stand. Shut up, Lola. You're not going to have a pity party. Save that for your diary. I'll show everyone anyway. Things are progressing just fine.

Drew pulls back first. "I've been wanting to do that since I first met you."

But ending the kiss stirs something in Sasha. She looks disappointed with herself.

"Who was it, before?" she asks, and Drew understands the mood has shifted, his goofy smile fading. "Who made up that rubbish about me being fired?"

Oh shit. Time to go.

Something wet lands on my arm, and for a second I'm worried someone has spilled their drink on me from above.

But Drew notices it too, opening his palm up. "Rain?"

The sky answers for him, sending more raindrops that spatter across the deck. Up on the terrace, I hear squeals as people realize what's happening.

"Looks like the storm is earlier than anticipated," Drew says.

That's my cue to hurry up the stairs before they do.

The guests are moving inside, Jade at the doorway waving them in like a teacher on a school trip. She shouts at us to start clearing away the food. I can't see Imogen, which is probably a good thing, but I spot Runa wrapping cellophane over the partially eaten buffet.

She's not pleased to see me. "I said we would talk later."

She's so moody. The only time I ever see her crack a smile is when she's drunk, and she clearly hasn't touched a drop tonight. She should be nice to me. It'll pay off in the end.

"I wasn't going to mention it!" I say. "*Relax.* No one knows."

"They will if you won't stop talking about it," she hisses. "I knew this was a mistake."

"Well," I say, frowning, "you didn't have much of a choice bringing me into it, did you? It was your fault for being so careless."

She's acting far too arrogant for someone in my debt.

This is just like Axel and Imogen. Both of them think they can control me, tell me what to do.

"Hey!"

We're interrupted by Sasha, of all people, marching up to us, face matching the roaring thunder. The rain is hammering down hard now, and I'm still in my bikini. It's freezing. I look around for Effie's coat, but spot Effie reclaiming it from Imogen across the pool.

"It was you!" Sasha shouts.

Effie and Imogen turn around, surprised. They've heard Sasha's outburst too.

"What was me?" I ask.

"You're the one who made up this crap about me messing with medications and getting fired!"

Oh, *that*.

Yes, that was me.

When you're the youngest and the least beautiful, you have to do certain things to survive on here. Getting one over on the girls has become almost a sport. I borrow Effie's clothes and give them little tears or stains in places she won't find on first glance then can't blame me for when she does spot them. I nick Imogen's mascara knowing she can't afford a new one so she has to go without. I sleep with Axel to prove she's not better than me. I act dumb in front of Jade so she never gives me the more difficult tasks, so she's always stressed. I have to undermine them wherever I can.

Sasha shouldn't even complain. She comes in all mysterious and refusing to talk about her past, so what does she expect? I gave her an interesting background. It's the least I could do. I'm good at coming up with stories.

"I'm sorry," I say, as Effie and Imogen hurry over. "I thought it was better for everyone to know. I have painkillers in my cabin, and Effie's your cabinmate so I'm sure she does too. I just wanted to look out for you."

Sasha shakes her head, stunned. "*What are you talking about?* I don't have any kind of problem with medication. I wasn't fired. I quit."

"It is okay, you know," Runa tells her. "We all have things in our pasts we would rather not think about."

But Sasha is adamant. "Lola is *lying*. I don't know why she is, but she's a liar. And now that I think more about it, I was right about Lola messing with the laundry at the start of the charter!" She turns to me, venomous. "I saw you wearing that red scarf earlier. I know you must have seen it in the washing and not told me, hoping I'd miss it."

The scarf. I spotted it lying dangerously close to the pile of whites when I was talking to Sasha that day in the laundry room, and couldn't resist stuffing it inside a bedsheet so it would be difficult to find. I did warn her not to mix colors and whites. It's not my fault she didn't go through and check everything carefully after I'd shoved it in there. I wanted to start Sasha off on a low point, make her look an idiot in front of Jade and Melinda.

"I'm so sorry, Sasha." I walk toward her and put my arms around her, then lean in and whisper in her ear so no one else can hear. "But there's nothing you can do about it."

She reels back and pushes me away before slapping me across the cheek. "I knew it!"

It's a proper slap, pain bursting across my face like a red-hot iron has been pressed against it. I didn't think she had something like that in her—I've never been hit before. I clasp my hand to my cheek and take full advantage by starting to cry.

"Sasha!" Effie gasps, grabbing her hand and pulling her back. "What are you playing at? It's only Mouse!"

I choke out a few sobs. "I made a mistake. I was only trying to protect you, Sasha."

"Like hell you were!" she snaps. "She's putting on an act, can't you all see it? She wants you to think she's quiet little Mouse and she's not!"

Imogen frowns at this, gazing at me suspiciously. She's thinking about earlier for sure. I bury my face in my hands for good measure, peeking through my fingers with satisfaction when she turns on Sasha, telling her to leave me alone, I'm not smart enough to come up with something like that. It must have been a miscommunication.

Runa stands in front, shielding me from Sasha. "The guests are only inside there. This needs to stop. Lola, we'll go to the galley, come on."

"You'll regret this!" Sasha shouts after us as Runa hurries me away. My last glance behind is of Sasha, Effie, and Imogen against the backdrop of the growing storm, a dark sky and flashes of lightning, the rain pouring down, but all three still identical. Effie stands out most of all in her red coat, which she takes off now and wraps around Sasha's shoulders, perhaps in an attempt to get her to calm down. They lead her inside via the side terrace; Runa and I take the opposite one.

We arrive at the galley drenched, and Runa grabs me a packet of frozen peas to hold to my face before pouring us a couple of shots of vodka. She downs hers in one, then quickly pours another. I leave mine untouched.

"So that was, as you say, bullshit, no?" Runa leans against a counter, arms crossed.

"What do you mean?" I ask innocently.

"What you told everyone about Sasha. You do not know why she really left her job as a nurse, do you?"

"Sasha slapped me," I say, indicating the frozen bag of vegetables. "*Something* definitely happened for her to be that sensitive."

"We are meant to be keeping a low profile. The guests could have witnessed that display."

"Since when do you care about the guests?" I snap. "You're the one always complaining about them, saying they don't appreciate what they have. And anyway, I was perfectly calm. That would have been Sasha's fault if they saw."

"I know what you are like, remember?"

"Yes." I frown. "So you should remember who owes who here. Or maybe I'll tell everyone about *that*."

Her face flickers with panic, and immediately she's more soothing. "Right. Of course. Forget about that stupid fight. Is your cheek feeling better?"

She isn't really my friend. She's just pretending to be nice because I have something over her.

"We'll see," I say, watching her face fall. "Maybe I'm done playing Mouse. In fact, maybe I should tell everyone about all their little secrets they think I don't know."

I drop the frozen bag on the counter and leave her there, ignoring her calling my name, just wanting to be alone for a while. I hurriedly put my uniform back on, my hair still hanging loose, cheek still sore.

It's been fun in some ways, being the one people least suspect. Always left out of things, always the butt of the joke, made out to be stupid. So unimportant that when I have overheard conversations or witnessed things I shouldn't have, it's like people don't even count me. I've seen Drew's drinking problem, I've seen Noah drooling over Effie when he thinks no one's watching, and I know *exactly* what Effie has been up to. I know Imogen is hiding something, sneaking off, and one of these times I'm going to follow her. I know the *real* reason why Zara had to leave so fast. I know what Runa has been doing, however much she hates it. And now I've slept with Axel and if Imogen found out, this place would erupt into chaos.

So many secrets, so little time.

I don't feel bad. They all think they're so much better than me. They can afford to be knocked down a few pegs. That bonding session before the party was only brought about because Effie was laughing at my fake Gucci bag.

Fuck them all. I don't need anyone. Fuck Sasha and fuck Axel and fuck Imogen and fuck Runa and fuck my parents and fuck *everyone*. I've been Mouse for far too long.

It's time to spill all their precious secrets.

Who's first?

CHAPTER FIFTEEN

SASHA

Effie and Imogen barrel me through a side entrance and into the office near the bridge. Other than during Jade's tour, I don't think I've ever been in here before, but I don't look around. I collapse into one of those typical office chairs that spin around while Effie and Imogen burst out laughing.

How can they *laugh*?

"You should see your face," Imogen splutters. "You're a picture, honestly. I never thought you'd get so het up over Mouse of all people."

"She made it up!" I snap, anger still simmering. "I was a good—"

A good nurse. The words seem to stick in my throat.

Blood on my hands. Her blood. Dr. Martin screaming in my ears.

"Babe," Effie says. "Calm down. It's really not all that."

"So Mouse got it wrong." Imogen shrugs. "She's Mouse, what do you expect? She can barely put socks on."

They still think this was a simple mistake.

I'm about to correct them when Imogen continues. "Jade is going to have a field day with you tomorrow."

"What do you mean?" I ask.

Her eyes glitter, her mouth upturning into a devilish grin. "Well, duh, I'm going to tell her all about your fight with Mouse. Slapping her! Goodness gracious. You're in for a world of trouble."

No! I turn to Effie, appealing to her. "You know it was Lola's fault, don't you, Effie?"

But Effie pulls a face. "All I know is what I saw, I'm afraid. And that was you attacking poor Mouse."

Imogen cackles. "Oh dear, Sasha, you're all alone on this one. I did warn you not to trust us!" She throws me a wink, and I want to scratch her eyes right out. "I'm off to have a little chin-wag with Jade. Ta-ta!"

I don't even know what to think anymore. My head is a mess. There's no point chasing after Imogen. She has had it out for me since day one.

"I tried looking out for you," I say to Effie now we're the only two in the room. "So you should have my back on this. That whole incident with Noah—"

Effie cuts me off sharply. "We're not going to talk about that. It was nothing. Less than nothing."

"Say what you want, but I saw you were scared."

Her reaction is instant; she grabs my wrist, holding tight. I can't shake her off. "I mean it, Sasha. Drop it. Or you'll see I can do far worse than some nonsense about you being fired from your last job."

For someone so beautiful, in this moment she looks downright terrifying.

"I'll drop it," I say. The time for pinkie promises, for pretending we're friends, is over. She releases me, and I rise from the chair and start making my way to the door.

"Sasha?" she calls. "I want my coat back."

I take it off and throw it to her. She doesn't put it on, merely drapes it across her arm. This time I watch her leave. She's heading back in the direction of the main salon; as long as I'm asleep by the time she gets to our cabin, that's fine by me.

Jade will be wondering where I am—I can even hear the guests laughing raucously, clearly intent on continuing the party indoors—but I head down to the crew mess, a pounding headache between my ears and at a loss as to what's just happened. *Lola*, of all of them, spreading those rumors? And not just that, the sheer joy in her face when I confronted her, the smug tone of her voice. She's been messing with everyone behind their backs and I'm the only one who can see through her. I knew I was right about the laundry. She was too helpful, too sweet. But also too good of an actress, and I fell for it.

And the others! Runa, siding with Lola. Effie and Imogen not be-lieving their Mouse could be anything but stupid. Imogen relishing the opportunity to tell Jade about this mess, Effie refusing to back me up despite her promise of friendship. So now Jade will come for me tomorrow, and I'll be punished in some way, and it's not my fault.

Okay, I shouldn't have slapped her.

But I don't regret it. To bring up my job, after everything that hap-pened back then—no. Stop thinking about it.

At first I think the crew mess is empty, everyone still upstairs, when Noah emerges from his cabin. He has a towel around his shoulders to dry his hair from the rain and doesn't notice me at first; he's clutching tissues in one hand and is evidently stressed. He scrunches the tissues up and throws them into a bin, and that's when he spots me, letting out a little gasp of surprise.

"I didn't mean to scare you," I say. I don't particularly want to get into a conversation with him after his altercation with Effie, however much she's irritating me. "I'm just heading to bed."

He nods, though he seems nervous for some reason. "Jade let you off already?"

"Something like that." I shrug. I grab myself a glass from the cup-board and start filling it up with tap water.

"Yeah, I've been dodging Axel," he says, even though I didn't ask. "I should go back to him now." But he doesn't, he stands there watching me fill up the glass.

"What is it, Noah?" I ask resignedly. I don't care if I'm coming across as rude. It's been a shit night.

"Nothing." He bites his lip. "Okay. Maybe something. Drew is my mate, right?"

Drew. To think before everything that happened with Lola, we kissed. What was I playing at? And yet . . . his name automatically brings a smile to my lips. "Right?"

"I think he's really into you. And I saw you talking together earlier. I know you're probably into Axel more, but—"

"I'm not into Axel," I say, and I'm surprised by the truth of these words. Axel is physical perfection. He should be everything I want—he certainly would have been before. Has what happened really changed me that much? I turn off the tap and take a sip of water, the cool liquid soothing my throat after all the shouting.

Noah doesn't believe me; it's obvious in his expression. "*Everyone* likes Axel. Even though he's an asshole."

I'm reminded of their fight. "I remember you calling him a liar when we all went out together. What was that about?"

"You replaced the stewardess that was here before," he says.

"Zara, wasn't it?"

"She was pregnant."

Pregnant? That's why she had to leave? But does Noah mean . . .

"Axel was the father?"

"Who else?"

"Doesn't he care?"

"Axel caring about women?" Noah laughs bitterly. "That would be the day. Men like him get away with murder."

I shiver. Dr. Martin's face flashes in my mind.

"What does this have to do with Drew?" I ask.

Noah sighs. "He's sensitive. I just don't think you should do anything with him."

Who does Noah think he is? "Well, frankly, that's none of your business."

"I'm his *friend*," he says. "I know things about him, alright? Steer clear."

"Steer *clear*?" I repeat, baffled. "What are you talking about? Drew's a good guy."

"Forget it," Noah says. "Forget what I said. I have to go."

He leaves me like this, hurrying up the stairs without so much as a backward glance. Steer clear of Drew? Noah must be jealous. He's the only guy on board who isn't getting any attention, and he's trying to make me doubt Drew. Well, I'm not going to fall for it.

This horrible night is over. I'm just going to go to sleep and deal with the consequences tomorrow.

But sleep is fitful. It takes me forever, and I still don't hear Effie come in. Worse, my mind starts to wander dangerously into the past . . .

Blood. Wailing. Is that me making that sound—or someone else?

"This is your fault as much as it is mine!"

I wake up, gasping.

The nightmares aren't letting up. I touch my face, feeling the wetness of my cheeks. Tears. I've been crying in my sleep again.

What time is it? I check my phone, *4:24* staring back at me. Too early for my shift. Too late to try to get back to sleep, especially in my state. And still no internet or signal.

Careful not to disturb Effie, who must be in the bottom bunk by now, I put on my uniform. I'm desperate for fresh air.

There's no one around as I make my way upstairs, and I'm grateful for the quiet. Alone, I can force myself to think about something other than my bad dreams. And not my fight with Lola either. Drew perhaps. Our kiss.

The sky is in that in-between stage, a pale blue light infiltrating the windows in the main salon, and to my delight I can't see any clouds. The storm must be over. It's freezing and wet beneath my feet when I go outside onto the deck, but the rain has long gone. I head down to the left—port, I need to remember to call it that—side, then pause for a while, leaning on the railing and staring out at the sea.

There's something red in there. Floating near the yacht, seemingly following us along. I squint harder to bring it into focus, and then I feel faint.

I know what that red is. It's Effie's coat.

With a mass of blonde hair above it.

There's a body in the water.

PART TWO

CHAPTER SIXTEEN

⌒

SASHA

Stewardess uniform. Fluffy coat. Blonde hair. Floating face down.

An arm is caught in a loose stern line, tangled up, dragged along with us as we move.

The image blurs, my mind swimming, and I can't help but think of us stewardesses all looking the same. She could be anyone. If I wasn't standing right here people could mistake her for me. My body.

Is she dead?

No. Don't think that. You have to go and get help. Now.

Do what you couldn't before.

My hands fly for my radio, but it's not there. Fuck. There's no choice but to run for the bridge, for whoever's on watch, screaming as I go, feet pounding on the decking, my tights soaking through as I no longer care about avoiding the puddles formed from last night. "Help! Somebody!"

I'm halfway there when I see Drew, thank God, heading out a side door. He doesn't understand, his face breaking into a puzzled smile. "Sasha? What are you doing up?"

There is no time for pleasantries. I collide into him, burying my face in his chest. "There's a—I can't even—someone is in the water! I think it's one of us stewardesses!"

"What?" His tone instantly changes; he pushes me back to look him in the eye. "What are you talking about?"

"She's over there!" The image returns to me, and I clasp a hand to my mouth to stop myself from vomiting. "I don't know what to do. You're on watch, right? What do we do?"

"Man overboard," Drew says, stunned. "I'll get the captain."

"Your radio?" I say.

He shakes his head. He isn't wearing his either. "Stay here. I'll be right back."

It's a blur after this. When Drew returns he tells me to take him to where the body is, and as we move, the engine dies and the boat slows.

"Captain Howard gave the order for Chief to stop the yacht," Drew explains on the way, and I don't question the fact we're holding hands as we run. "He's marked our position, started the man overboard procedure. Axel and Noah have been woken up; they've gone to get the tender launched."

I take him to where the body is, hoping beyond hope that I've made it up, that I'm wasting everyone's time, that it was some tired hallucination and not what I think I saw. But there it is, that red coat, like a spot of blood in a pool, calling out to us. The arm is still entangled in the line, the blonde hair still peeking from above. The body hasn't changed position, and now with the yacht unmoving it bobs in the water, directionless. Drew processes this with a small intake of breath, before calmly reporting the location on the radio he now has. Then he turns to me. "We need to get round to the swim platform."

Jade didn't show me the swim platform on our tour, the day I arrived. Why would she? She knew we were going to New York, that I would never need to see it. Same with the water toys, the Jet Skis and huge inflatables. Nor the tender, a small speedboat used for transporting deliveries or the guests to their excursions.

Not for this journey. You're not going to be using any of these things on the Atlantic Ocean.

Not normally, anyway.

"Does everyone know now?" I whisper.

Drew nods. "Chief will have made sure everyone is coming. We need to . . ." He falters. "We need to account for who may be missing."

"I can't believe this." A sob chokes out of me. I keep thinking about the last time I felt this hopeless.

"It'll be okay," Drew murmurs.

But it won't. Nothing can ever be the same again.

I know that from experience.

Others are already there when we arrive. Captain Howard watches grimly with a pair of binoculars from the front of the swim platform as Axel heads out on the tender with Noah, and we all stare as they work together to untangle whoever it is and lift them out of the water. How freezing it must be, a thousand icy knives at once.

"Position marked," Melinda shouts to the captain, marching down the deck and terrace stairs to reach us on the swim platform. She has her own binoculars too, scanning the water, and a clipboard. "Drift calculated. Everyone line up! Roll call."

I have tried to avoid this woman as much as possible since the laundry fiasco, but now I'm desperate for her controlling behavior. Make it better, Melinda. Please. Have this all be a horrible mistake.

"She's wearing Effie's coat," someone says.

Effie earlier returns to the forefront of my mind. Fast asleep while I got dressed and left. Was she even *there*? Did I look at her sleeping or did I just hurry straight out? I don't know. I remember her with the coat the last I saw her, slung over her arm. Did she put it back on? Did she somehow . . . no. I can't think about it.

"Captain Howard," Melinda calls, even though we can all see him. She will do this properly. He yells back an affirmative response.

But everyone else is scared, talking among themselves as they try and gather into a line. It's not organized, as emergencies never are.

"Did anyone see Effie this morning?"

"Come to think of it, where's Imogen?"

"Has anyone seen Jade?"

Where *is* Jade? Surely she should be here, bossing us about, telling us what to do.

I should be doing something. It's incredible how quickly my nursing instinct has gone.

"Where is the first aid?" I say as Melinda barrels past, calling Jade's name.

"Here, Chief!"

Jade appears behind me, clutching the first-aid kit.

She's here. A huge exhale escapes me, so strong I'm surprised at how much I care. I grab the kit out of her hands and hurry down to the swim platform.

Axel and Noah are pulling the body up and onto the platform. They're out of breath, exhausted with the exertion, faces white with shock. There's no mistaking it now. This is definitely a body, and it's definitely a stewardess.

She must have been in the water since last night. She's soaking wet, and when I kneel down and touch her arm it's stone cold. I have to swallow down the bile that rises in my throat when I see the blood sticking to the back of her head.

Axel and Noah take an arm and leg each and carefully turn her around.

Fingers shaking, I peel away the hair that has covered her face, left-over glitter tracing my fingertips, then sit back.

It's Lola.

Her appearance is peaceful—like she's fallen asleep. Somehow, that makes it so much worse. With her lying here like this, it's much more apparent how young she is. Was. I want to cry.

"That's my coat!" Effie shouts, appearing from nowhere.

Her coat? Her damn coat, that's what she cares about?

Didn't *she* have it? Why is Lola now wearing it?

"Is there anything you can do?" Axel asks me numbly. It comes out sounding strangled, and when I glance up at him, I can see his teeth chattering.

I shake my head. "She's dead. She's been dead for hours."

I'm about to examine her further when Captain Howard approaches, face solemn. He checks for a pulse even though he can see as well as I can that it's pointless.

"We need to radio for emergency services," I say.

"It's not as simple as that," Captain Howard says gently. "We're in the middle of the Atlantic. There are no emergency services."

There are no emergency services.

Of course. I'm so stupid. It's not like the police or paramedics are hanging around on boats on the off chance things go wrong out here.

No, if things go wrong we're utterly alone.

A circle has formed around Lola's body on the swim platform. Melinda is keeping everyone at a sensible distance, Drew whispering something in Melinda's ear. Effie stares in horror, but whether that's for Lola or her coat I'm not sure. Jade is beside her, one hand on her radio, probably for comfort more than anything else. Imogen, finally arriving, seems upset, eyes red like she could cry, while Runa appears horrified, shaking her head over and over. The deckhands aren't any better. Noah has a greenish tinge and Axel's hands are clasped tight, so tight I can see his skin straining.

"There must be someone we can contact," I say. "Another vessel nearby."

"And what good would that do?" Captain Howard asks. "There is no medical emergency here, nothing that requires urgent assistance. Lola is already dead."

The sheer practicality of his words chills me. "Then what option is there?"

"We could divert?" Axel suggests. "Back to the Azores?"

Melinda nods. "Though we're a fair journey beyond them now, if not longer with the wind against us."

Captain Howard frowns. "That would extend this charter by at least a week. We're not turning around."

Not turning around? Even for this?

"What's the next closest island?" I ask. "If we carry on going, where can we stop?"

Melinda presses her lips together, exchanging an awkward look with the captain. "That would be Bermuda. But there wouldn't be any point stopping there—it would mean diverting from our course, and it's only another day of sailing to New York from Bermuda anyway."

My blood turns cold. "You mean to tell me there's—*nothing* between where we are now and our final destination?"

"It's the Atlantic Ocean, Sasha. It's huge."

I knew it would take us weeks to reach New York from Gibraltar. I could tell standing on deck and seeing we were surrounded by nothing but wide, open water that we were far away from everything and everyone. But where that was comforting before, distance between the old me and what I'd left behind, now it feels paradoxically suffocating: too much space, too much time, too much separation from the real world.

Jade steps forward. "Has the signal issue been fixed? How are we going to contact Lola's family?"

Lola's family. Her parents. Didn't she say she was an only child? I can't face another mother and father in tears again.

"Not sorted," Melinda admits. "The storm has done a bit of a number on the system."

Then even if we wanted to, we have no way of contacting anyone who's not already on this boat.

"We'll inform Lola's family at the end of the charter," Captain Howard says. "I think that would be sensible, as there isn't much they can do on the other side of the world."

"What do we think happened?" Axel asks. "How did she . . . end up in the water?"

"She has a head injury," I say.

"A dreadful accident," Captain Howard murmurs. "Slipped on the wet terrace, perhaps, and was too close to the edge."

"And the coat?" I say, directing this at Effie. "How come she's wearing your coat?"

Effie shakes her head. "I don't know. After you— I think I left it in the main salon. She must have put it on to go outside."

But why go outside in that weather? I glance down at Lola, her pale, soaking body, and notice some shadows on her neck. I start peeling back more of her hair to have a closer look.

"We need to take pictures, record everything in the logbook," Axel says.

The shadows are bruises. Huge ones, dark and intimidating.

If she were a patient of mine, I would swear someone had put them there.

Could her death have been *deliberate*?

I'm all too aware of Axel, Noah, and even Drew beside me. Strong, capable deckhands. Great with ropes.

"I'm not sure this was an accident." I rise, shakily. "Look. She's been strangled."

Jade is first to respond. "She can't have. Don't be ridiculous."

Even Drew doesn't seem to want to back me up. "Maybe those bruises are old. Or she got them some other way."

"Lola said she was going to spill everyone's secrets," Runa says.

There's an anxious energy to everyone now, hushed murmurs and terrified faces.

"What do you mean, secrets?" Jade says. "What secrets?"

"What did she tell you?" Axel demands, glaring at Runa.

Runa holds her hands up. "Nothing else! That's all she said. What if..."

"Now hold on a second," Melinda says. "Are you suggesting someone did this?"

You don't get bruises like that from being caught up in a line.

Captain Howard holds both palms up. "I think we need to calm down. This was clearly an accident."

"Who last saw Lola alive?" Jade says. "What time did she go to bed? Imogen?"

Jade doesn't know. Imogen hasn't told her about our fight yet.

Imogen shrugs. "What am I, her babysitter? We spent about an hour cleaning everything up while you were busy with the guests, Jade, then I went to bed around two. All I can tell you is Lola wasn't in our cabin then. But for all I know she came swanning in five minutes later. Ask Runa, she was with her the rest of the night."

Runa speaks quickly. "She was angry. Resentful, I believe. Said she wanted people to know what she had found out, and then left. I did not see her after this. I finished off a couple of meal plans, then went to sleep myself. Whenever that was."

Jade shakes her head. "I didn't bother checking whether you were in the top bunk or not. But I was the last one to leave the main salon. Lola at least wasn't in there, or in the galley, at about twelve. I didn't see her."

"Hang on," Noah says, speaking for the first time. I can't help but wonder what he was doing last night, after he left me in the crew mess. That weird conversation we had. "Imogen, if you said you went straight to bed, why did you go to sleep at two if it only took you an hour to clear away and Jade was the last one in the main salon?"

Imogen turns pink. "I was—uh. I wanted a conversation with Axel. I waited ages, but he didn't come." She looks at Axel sheepishly. "We were meant to—you were supposed to be in the pantry."

In the pantry?

Axel looks panicked, caught unawares by Imogen's comment. "I forgot."

"Plenty of us unaccounted for, then," Runa says.

"Speak for yourself," Drew says. "I was on watch after the party ended."

"I thought you were on watch this morning," I say, frowning. "You were there when I screamed for help?"

"I was on watch," Captain Howard says. "Not Drew."

So why was Drew up that early? But I don't get a chance to ask; everyone is talking and it becomes hard to piece together what is being said.

Noah points at Axel. "What were you doing?"

"And what were *you* doing, Noah? Where do you get off suddenly speaking up?" Axel growls. "I know for a fact where I was; I went up to the gym, I do it most nights, and if you don't believe me you can shove it up your—"

"Axel," Captain Howard interrupts sharply, and to my surprise Axel backs down.

"Why would she go out in that weather?" Jade says after a beat. "It doesn't make any sense. The storm was awful."

"All the more reason to assume she fell overboard," Runa says.

"Oh, that would suit you, wouldn't it?" Imogen mutters.

I don't think she means for Runa to hear but she does. "Excuse me?"

Imogen lifts her chin. "I said that would suit you. You were the last to see her alive."

"None of this is helpful," Captain Howard says. "Lola had an accident. She was out on deck during a storm. The yacht was at the whim of the waves. One lurch in the wrong direction and she could have hit her head. Another and she could have fallen overboard."

"And the bruises on her neck?" I whisper.

"Sasha, what we don't need is a stewardess turned detective."

"I was a nurse," I say. "I've seen injuries like those before and they aren't accidental."

"You may have been a nurse but you weren't a police officer," he tells me. "An investigation will be conducted when we dock. Until then, don't try becoming Poirot."

But what about these secrets Runa mentioned? What did Lola know?

Enough to get her killed?

"You shouldn't be so keen to tell everyone this wasn't an accident, Sasha," Imogen says. "Not when you're the one who got into a fight with her last night."

Shit. Everyone looks appalled, and even Captain Howard raises his eyebrows.

Jade is on me immediately. "What does Imogen mean, a fight?"

"Lola told people I was fired for stealing medication," I say, trying to ignore the shake in my voice. "She said I had a dependency issue. It wasn't true. She's been winding me up since the start of this trip with the washing—"

"Winding you up?" Imogen echoes with a smirk. "So you admit you have a terrible temper? A short fuse? You were ready to blow at any second, weren't you?"

"No! I wanted to confront her."

"I told you," Imogen says triumphantly. "If anyone did Mouse in, it was Sasha. She was crazy, screaming and trying to rip Mouse's hair out."

"That is *not* what happened!" I protest. "Imogen is making it sound far worse than it was."

"You *slapped* her," Effie says. "She was crying and upset! You got so angry over . . . what? Her spreading some fake rumor?"

Did I overreact? Am I so sensitive about my prior job that anything to do with it sends me into emotional turmoil? Everyone is looking at me strangely, even Drew.

Surely they can't think I'd have anything to do with Lola's death. But then, don't I think one of them did? I think they're capable, why wouldn't they think the same about me? The new stewardess, the one they don't know as well. But the one everyone knows had a problem with the dead girl. God. I'd suspect me too.

"You assaulted another crew member?" Captain Howard says, the disappointment evident in his tone. "Normally we have procedures to deal with this, and you would be immediately dismissed." He sighs. "Circumstances being what they are, however—"

Shit. Of course I'd be fired. What was I *thinking*? I'm becoming a different person ever since what happened.

"Captain," Melinda says, preempting what he's about to say.

"I know," Captain Howard says. "But there is not much we can do in this position. The charter is continuing, accidents happen, and that is final. Do we all understand?"

Accidents happen. The words are like gunshot wounds to the chest.

"Accidents happen, Sasha," he says. *"They happen every day and you need to get that around your thick skull before you think about causing any problems."*

"Dr. Martin—"

"I won't spend another second arguing with you. Accidents happen. Repeat after me."

"Accidents happen."

Melinda accepts defeat. "I'll inform the guests and write a full report."

As if on cue, Benjamin and Digby appear on the terrace above. Eva and Jasmine soon follow, and Jasmine lets out a scream. She hurries down the steps, pushes her way onto the swim platform, and collapses to her knees next to Lola's body.

"This can't be happening," she whispers. Only I'm close enough to hear. "Not again."

Not again?

"What's the fuss, Howard?" Benjamin shouts. He, Digby, and Eva haven't deigned to move from their elevated position. "Why is everyone gathered down there?"

Captain Howard calls over to them. "I'm afraid there has been some kind of accident. One of our stewardesses fell overboard and passed away."

I note the language he uses, the blame he shifts to Lola.

"It wasn't an accident," I murmur. Jasmine lifts her head and stares at me.

To my astonishment, Benjamin yawns. He actually yawns.

"Does this mean service will be affected?" he asks, looking down at Lola. "Can we fly another stewardess in?"

Fly another stewardess in? Does Lola's life mean that little to him? Just the staff, someone who exists to please him, and when that is no longer being fulfilled she's cast aside?

Ahead of me, Jasmine's hands curl into fists.

"I will speak to you both shortly," Captain Howard tells them, then turns to Jade. "Get the guests out of here."

Jade nods. "Right. Runa, if you could start making breakfast?"

For once, Runa doesn't snap at Jade for telling her what to do. "Yes, of course."

They both head up the terrace steps quickly, Jade not even looking back at Lola. Doesn't she care? Doesn't *anyone* care?

"Melinda, why don't you get started on the report for the logbook," Captain Howard says. "Axel, Noah, Drew, I'll need you with me to help move the body into the morgue. Everyone else, please go and help Jade and Runa with breakfast."

"You really think this was an accident, Captain?" Effie asks.

"I do," he says. "Now, please, everyone. Leave us to it."

They start walking away, but I hang back to make sure Jasmine follows. She seems lost, her mind elsewhere, and jumps when I nudge her on the shoulder.

"Wait." To my surprise she traces her fingers on Lola's forehead, murmuring something I can't catch. "Okay, I'm ready."

It feels wrong that out of everyone Jasmine is the one to show some care. I kneel down again, and touch Lola's cheek.

"I'm sorry," I whisper. "I'm going to get to the bottom of this, I promise."

Lola doesn't respond, of course.

The sight of her cold, wet body remains in my brain, long after I've gone up the terrace stairs and collapsed onto a bench. Tears prick at my eyes. Why did I have to get into that stupid fight with her?

All my natural instincts for what to do next are useless. Call an ambulance—no. Call the police—not happening. Even my old faithful, the reason why I'm on this yacht to begin with—*run away*—impossible. There is nowhere to run.

My first impulse is to stay out of it. They want to call it an accident, call it an accident.

Accidents happen.

But I did that last time and look where I am now. In some sick twist of fate, I am faced with a similar problem. So what do I do? The captain said not to become Poirot, but what option do I have?

This is a chance to do something. If I can find out what happened to Lola, maybe that will stop the nightmares that haunt me every night, the anxiety that grips my throat whenever someone brings up the past. I can be a good person again.

Someone wanted to stop Lola from spilling their secret and I'm going to find out who.

Jasmine, watching over the railing as the others move Lola's body, finally relents in her dogged focus and sits down next to me. "You're right. This wasn't an accident."

I feel my face growing hot. The muffled voice of the captain below is carried away by the wind, and it's just the two of us up here. "You think?"

"But you need to be careful."

"Careful?"

"Jasmine?" Eva comes out of the main salon and stops when she sees us together. "Are you coming?"

The engine starts up again, roaring to life, and we begin pulling away.

"I'm coming now." Jasmine rises, then leans down and whispers in my ear. "This isn't the first time something like this has happened. Watch your back."

CHAPTER SEVENTEEN

JASMINE

It's déjà vu. Another year, another stewardess, another memorial.

Except this time we have a body.

"I felt it important to hold a memorial service," Captain Howard begins. "What happened earlier was shocking for everyone. Let's take a moment to honor Lola's life."

The only person missing is Melinda on watch. Even Benjamin and Digby are here, sitting with iced teas while the rest of us are gathered toward the front on the main deck. The crew are in their whites, Eva and I in black dresses. Captain Howard is holding a bunch of flowers, wilting and sad after so long at sea. I keep staring at them. I've been through this exact scene before.

"Lola was a fantastic stewardess," Captain Howard declares, speaking loudly because of the wind. "We're all going to miss her very much. A terrible, terrible accident."

Keep saying that all you want, Captain, but it doesn't make it true. That woman was murdered. I saw her injuries. The bruises. The blow to the back of her head. One woman murdered, another missing, on the same boat only a year apart?

Lola's death and Hallie's disappearance are linked, and I'm going to find out why.

The sight of Lola's body returns in full force. The pale skin, the

blonde hair, the stewardess uniform. The red coat that seems so familiar. Lola may as well have been Hallie, she looked so much like her.
Even the silver nail varnish. Hallie didn't go missing the night of the
Silver Soirée, but only a few days later, and she still had the remnants
of silver varnish on her fingernails. For a second, I really thought Lola
was Hallie. I know that's not rational, that if Hallie truly has been in
the sea all this time there won't be anything left of her. But I saw Lola's
body, and I saw Hallie in her place, and I ran to her.

Eva wipes her eyes while the captain talks. Her tissue remains bone
dry, but she's putting on a better show of sympathy than Benjamin and
Digby. "He's much calmer now," she whispers.

It takes a second to realize she's talking to me. "Who is?"

"Captain Howard. He came in this morning to tell Mr. Johnson
what had happened. I was there." She says this last bit smugly, pleased
she's privy to more information than I am. "You're much calmer too.
What on earth was that scene you pulled when we saw the body?"

I ignore her snide comment and focus on the important part. "He
and Mr. Edmondson didn't know about Lola when we all went to the
swim platform."

Eva shrugs. "Mr. Johnson at least definitely did. Captain Howard
came in frantic, saying all sorts."

"What did he say?"

"He said that they should come clean because of the circumstances.
And then he seemed to remember I was in there because he got all
funny and red-faced and told me not to panic about what had happened, even though he was the one panicking."

Come clean? About what exactly? My instincts tell me this can't be
good.

"And what did Mr. Johnson say?" I ask.

"He was annoyed, mainly," Eva continues. "Told Captain Howard
to deal with it, that he wasn't going to come clean about anything."

"Did he tell Mr. Edmondson?"

Eva shakes her head. "That's when Mr. Johnson knocked on his door and told him to get up, and you heard the ruckus and woke up yourself. Were you not with him last night?"

No. I have been every night, and expected no less after the party, but he shook me off, said he was tired, that we would get together the following evening.

Was he actually tired? Or was he after Lola instead?

"Mr. Edmondson's the primary. Why did the captain tell Mr. Johnson and not him?"

"Maybe Captain Howard wanted to protect him," Eva says.

Something about this doesn't feel right.

"Mr. Johnson went missing in the night," she murmurs.

The two of us are standing farther away than everyone else, and the wind is helping, but I whisper all the same. "What? You just said you were with him!"

"I woke up in the middle of the night," she says. "He wasn't next to me or in the bathroom. But when I woke up to the captain banging on the door, he was back again."

"So neither of them can account for their whereabouts," I say.

"I told you, Jasmine. These men can be dangerous. Be on your best behavior."

She sweeps across the deck, sits next to Digby, and offers her hand for him to hold. Benjamin is too focused on his drink to wonder where I am. I don't want to see Captain Howard throw those flowers over the side of the yacht like he did for Hallie. Everyone is occupied. This is the perfect opportunity to look around.

I step backward quietly, trying not to draw attention to myself. Thankfully, everyone has their eyes on the captain. I edge past the chef and another stewardess, who are whispering to one another urgently.

"Tell the truth," the stewardess hisses. "I know you're lying."

"You're acting crazy!" the chef murmurs. "Stop it!"

"This is why I don't trust any of you. You won't get away with it for much longer."

The chef sighs, then moves away from the stewardess. It's tempting to stay and listen for more, but I'm terrified the stewardess will turn any second. So I keep walking, until at last I'm around the corner and can hurry away.

I can pretend it was too upsetting, or that I needed the loo too desperately to wait. Time to move. I know where to start—the captain's cabin.

The bridge is up ahead, and through the closed door Melinda is on watch. The bridge is never left unattended, much to my dismay. Who knows what could be hidden in there?

But I have to make do. There is no lock on the captain's door so I go in.

The captain's quarters are smaller than I expected. Not that I imagined the captain in some luxurious guest-style bedroom, but it's only about three meters from the door to the wall opposite. The room is covered in glossy wood, with built-in cupboards and shelves. The double bed takes up almost all of the space, and there's a television opposite alongside the bridge navigational alarm system. The bed rests up against a wall-to-wall shelf with books on yachting. To the left is an oak desk and at the back is the en suite bathroom.

I haven't got long.

On the desk is a small laptop, and it's the first thing I seize on. I open it up, and straightaway am faced with a password prompt.

Shit.

I try the desk drawers, hoping some scrap of paper will tell me what the password is. Instead, I find various financial documents, kept together with a rubber band. I pore over the pages, but it's all facts, figures, and legalese. There's something about an oil business, Minterne Ltd., which must be one of his investments. In the other drawer are brochures for holiday destinations, with a particular focus on Las Vegas and Monte Carlo. I guess the captain is planning on enjoying his retirement to the full.

But no password.

"Goddamn it," I mutter. I try a couple of guesses, even try Hallie's name, but come up with nothing. I can't risk locking the computer, so I have to leave it.

It's in Captain Howard's bedside drawer that I find a gun.

The case isn't locked. The handgun is unloaded, I think, but the sight of it still makes me shiver. There are bullets too, waiting to kill something.

Or someone.

Why does he have this? Surely he won't be allowed to dock in New York with a weapon on board.

My hands feel slippery even holding it, and I start panicking about things like fingerprints, DNA. If someone was shot with this gun, my evidence would be all over it. It's ridiculous, but I wipe it on my dress before putting it back.

There's nothing here. It's all going to be on that computer, and I haven't got the time to figure out his password. I creep out and eye Melinda's room farther down the corridor.

How long was I in the captain's cabin? Ten minutes, tops? I can do this.

Melinda's room is a carbon copy of the captain's, only smaller. It's messier too, which surprises me when she's so uptight. Her desk is littered with chip packets and candy wrappers, even a couple of empty cans of Coke. The wastepaper bin is overloaded with rubbish too. She has a desktop, not a laptop, but the password-protected screen taunts me as it did in Captain Howard's room.

Calm down. Check the desk drawers.

I'm stunned when they're full of old newspaper clippings. I know I must be running out of time, but I don't care. I pull them all out, and do the same with the second load I find in the other drawer.

Soon the desk has a mountain of articles piled on top, and I study each one.

EX–STAFF MEMBER CLAIMS WORKING CONDITIONS ON SUPERYACHT ARE "HORRIFIC"

JUST HOW SAFE ARE SUPERYACHTS?

SUPERYACHT GUEST OFFERED TO PAY FOR MY NOSE JOB—WHEN I REFUSED HE DEMANDED I BE REMOVED FROM HIS SERVICE

And then I find her.

WOMAN WHO GREW UP IN CARE WANTED BETTER LIFE

STUNNING STEWARDESS DISAPPEARS ON SUPERYACHT

"HALLIE DESERVES TO BE FOUND," BEST FRIEND SAYS

All from my local newspaper. The stories I begged them to run, even though I hated their sensationalist headlines.

What is this? Why does Melinda have these? My heart starts thumping.

What else is in the drawers? A notebook, the pages covered in her neat handwriting, full of rambling half sentences that bring more questions than answers.

How long until New York? Engines at full power?
The jewelry thief is at it again.

Nothing to indicate a password, unless she's disguised it well.

My gaze rests on a framed photograph of her on the bedside table. She's larking about in a captain's uniform. Smiling wide, looking happier than I've ever seen her. I wonder.

It's daft, but I try it anyway, entering the password *CaptainMelinda*.
Wrong.

CaptainMelindaFall.

Bingo. The screen bursts to life. In the corner, the time stares tauntingly. Melinda is in the other room. She could come in any second. I'm playing with fire.

But I don't care. I ignore my trembling hands and click onto her files, muttering a word of thanks under my breath that she's so organized. Everything is categorized, named, dated. It couldn't be clearer. What should I prioritize?

Logically, the answer should be last night—but my hand has a mind of its own as it clicks on a folder labeled "Spring/Summer 2024," the season Hallie disappeared. There are several documents, CVs of members of staff, information sheets on the guests, and then I spy something interesting.

Axel Brody, Bosun.

He's the bosun for *this* year, not last year. So why is he in the 2024 folder? I think it must be a mistake, but when I click on his file I see to my surprise that he was hired the day after the yacht finished its charter season. Less than three weeks after Hallie disappeared.

And then I see something else: *Incident Report–07/09/2024*

A day I know very well.

My throat growing drier by the second, I read.

Hallie Attwood, stewardess of Ophelia, *missing during the night. Believed smoking and fallen overboard, probable death by misadventure. Authorities informed. One crew member disembarked following due to distress. Vessel moved on shortly afterward. CCTV faulty. No further action.*

Underneath, Melinda had annotated: *Is this all Captain Howard did?*

Is this all, indeed? I'm gobsmacked. Half the form isn't even filled in properly. There are no witness statements, only a vague record of the weather conditions and location. No investigation whatsoever was conducted into Hallie's disappearance. I knew it.

Back in the files, Melinda has labeled the CCTV for that night. I ignore the report, click on it, and hope for a miracle.

But there's nothing. In fact, there's worse than nothing. The CCTV had worked for every single night of the charter before that one. It switches off at 10:17 p.m. and never comes on again. I rewind back and find Hallie at 8:56 p.m.

Hallie, serving dinner to Benjamin and Digby out on the sky deck with a couple of other stewardesses, including Jade. I watch her closely, trying to find a sign of something. Anything. But other than Benjamin touching her ass and murmuring something in her ear, there's nothing. She is the same Hallie, and my breath catches in my throat watching her. At 9:34 p.m. she disappears inside, where there aren't any cameras, and that's the last footage caught of her before the feed cuts.

Is that when she wrote the note? I watch again, all possible angles. And again.

I watch Hallie disappear over and over.

I don't realize I'm crying until I see the tears on the keyboard. I need to look at last night. The memorial service will definitely be ending soon.

But last night's footage has the same problem. It also cuts off, at 12:08 a.m.

This can't be a coincidence. Someone has deliberately cut the feed, made sure it wasn't recording. On both occasions. Anyone could have done it if they knew how. The captain would. Melinda. The other deckhands—I remember from when I was one.

I watch the footage that is there, and at least it has caught the party, a full view of the scene. I remember the Silver Soirée last year, Hallie and I painting each other's nails silver.

It's hard to tell the stewardesses apart on the grainy footage. Lola has come out wearing a scarf and the big fluffy coat, the one she was found in, the one I can't shake the feeling I've seen before. There's something so tragic about watching her last movements that I want to reach into the screen and rescue her. She says something to the bosun, then walks away with a smirk, shrugging off the coat. She spends the night among various people. One of the deckhands. The bosun. Jade, who mainly looks like she's barking orders. Without sound, there's no way of knowing whether these conversations mean anything. But Lola looks increasingly stressed as the night goes on.

The coat confusingly does the rounds—worn by practically every stewardess over the course of the night. It's impossible to say who they are when they all look this identical, and even Eva tries it on, blending in. I'm following Lola only by the scarf she's wearing.

I frown at the screen, watching Lola walk out of the sky lounge with a tray of drinks. She still isn't back in the coat, but the scarf has disappeared. Where's that gone? She's taking off her uniform now, getting into the pool, flirting with the bosun. After a while, they head inside together, and another stewardess soon follows suit after them.

Sasha, the junior stewardess, heads to the terrace below with a deckhand. Eva moves into the sauna with Digby. No one has any idea of what's to come.

No, that's not true. One person knows exactly what they're going to do.

When Lola returns she looks hassled, heading down to where Sasha and one of the deckhands went, observing them. At this point, the rain starts to come down, and everyone rushes inside, but not Lola, who goes over to the tables of food and talks to the chef.

Sasha marches toward them. There's a heated exchange, and then to my horror Sasha slaps her, screaming something. The other stewardesses have to hurry over to pull them apart, one of them wearing the red coat, and the chef takes Lola inside before more chaos erupts.

What was *that*? Is this why Sasha looked so horrified this morning? Did I mistake what I thought was genuine care for . . . guilt?

The coat is exchanged a final time, but not to Lola. The stewardess wearing it gives it to Sasha, drapes it around her shoulders, and she is led inside. So when did Lola get it back?

I flick to a different feed and speed through to check other terrace angles. One side has the bosun and a stewardess having a conversation, and then a deckhand pacing up and down later on. The other side yields something more interesting. After the party ends, after the huge fight, that same deckhand is here with Lola's missing scarf.

He is facing the camera straight on, holding it in both hands. He looks around for a second, then puts the scarf in one of the storage boxes tied with cord to the side railing.

My heart is beating as I watch him hurry back inside.

At that moment, everything goes dark. The computer switches off.

Shit. A power cut, at this time? Or Melinda, trying to fix the signal issue?

As suddenly as it happened, the lights come on and the computer reboots.

This isn't good. If it wasn't Melinda, she might come out and check what's going on. I grab the newspaper articles, shoving them back into the drawers, stuffing the notebook underneath. There'll be the computer file history too. I don't know how to get rid of that.

I click back onto last night, wanting to watch the scarf clip again, and let out a gasp.

It's gone. Every file I was viewing has disappeared.

I check the recycle bin to see if they were accidentally deleted, but there's nothing. A mistake from the power cut?

Or someone remotely deleting them on purpose?

I need to get out of here.

But no sooner do I think that when I hear footsteps outside, see the shadow of feet below the door.

Oh fuck. I shut down the computer as fast as possible, look around wildly at this tiny space. What do I do? There's nowhere to hide.

And then the doorknob starts to turn.

CHAPTER EIGHTEEN

EFFIE

My brain is spinning. I don't know what to do.

Captain Howard takes the bunch of drooping chrysanthe-
mums, procured from a vase in Benjamin's cabin, and tosses them over
the side of the yacht. We all watch them land on the water, pale yellow
against the deep blue. For a moment they float on the surface, dancing
with the waves, and then one swallows them whole.

What if what I overheard has something to do with this? With
Mouse? I can't call her that anymore. Lola.

It was the day Benjamin accosted me and tried pulling me into his
cabin. Jade had told me to fetch Digby for breakfast from a conversation he was having with the captain in the bridge, but before I even
got there I spotted a couple of towels out on one of the sunbeds that
Jade would kill me for if I left languishing. So I scooped them up, put
them down in laundry, and then on my way back heard two people
talking. Because of the way they were whispering, I couldn't make
out who exactly they were. All I know for sure is it was a man and a
woman.

But they might know who I am. My body chose the worst time on
earth to sneeze. I was able to hold it mostly in, but a small noise escaped
me, and immediately the other two questioned who was there. I ran.

What else could I do? What they were saying was *outrageous*. The
kind of gossip you can only dream of hearing. I bolted down a corridor,

out a side door. Ended up forgetting about Digby, walked down to the guest cabins and bumped into Benjamin on his way out. That's when Jade found me.

She didn't listen, of course. When does she ever? If it doesn't fit her own narrow-minded view, where everything revolves around her and how well a job can be done, I might as well be talking to her in another language (and not, as she so often reminds me, Mandarin or Russian or Italian, because she can speak those very well). I shouldn't be surprised she cares more about *appearing* competent than actually demonstrating any real interest in her crew. That's what this yacht is all about, isn't it? Appearances.

But now Lola's death has complicated things. What if what I heard wasn't so innocent, not just a salacious bit of tea to store up and spill later?

No. Lola's death was an *accident*. That's what Captain Howard said, what he insisted, and I have to trust him. Sasha was trying to say it was deliberate, but what does she know? She's hardly reliable. Last night she was slapping Lola and screaming at her!

She's already in my bad books from her complete overreaction to what happened between Noah and me. I was perfectly capable of handling that myself—*have* handled that myself since—and she was treating me like I was some damsel in distress. I'll trust the captain's word over hers, thank you very much.

Now Captain Howard finishes his speech and asks anyone if they'd like to say a few words. Jade, definitely because she knows it's expected of her rather than out of any genuine feeling, launches into an account of Lola's time as a stewardess. I can tell it's fake because she waxes lyrical about Lola's work ethic, her positivity, her team spirit. Lola was a lazy sod who hated this job, and the only team spirit she fostered was between me and Imogen in calling her Mouse. Jade is rewriting history, changing things to suit her narrative.

Runa is as unimpressed by her attention-seeking stunt as I am, rolling her eyes, but she's moved as far from me as possible so I don't try and talk to her again.

She's infuriating. Telling me *I'm* the one acting crazy when I know for a fact she's lying. She was quite happy to tell everyone when we found Lola's body that Lola was with her in the galley and that she had no idea what happened after Lola stormed off. Which is funny because around the time she said she was in bed, why did I see her skulking about the corridor next to the guest rooms?

Jade has barely finished her speech, having the gall to wipe a nonexistent tear from her eye, when the lights go dark. It's the early afternoon, so it doesn't make a difference, but it's a surprise all the same. There are a couple of dramatic gasps, which is a bit much, but things like this shouldn't happen on a yacht worth millions of dollars.

Especially not when a stewardess washed up dead this morning.

Digby in particular is aggrieved. Neither he nor Benjamin rose from their seats for the memorial service, but now he stands. "What's this? Don't say the electrics are gone as well."

Captain Howard is as confused as the rest of us, but masks it quickly with a smile. "I'm sure it's Melinda trying to fix the internet issue for you, Digby. Things will be back on momentarily." As if on cue, the lights flicker, then come to life. "There, what did I tell you?"

"Mr. Johnson," Digby says coldly. "Call me Mr. Johnson."

There's a moment where Captain Howard seems like he wants to say something, a flicker of irritation beneath the professional mask. But then he simply nods. "My apologies, Mr. Johnson."

Benjamin checks his phone then returns it to his pocket with a tut. "There still isn't any internet. Nothing will work on this yacht by the end of the journey."

"We can't afford any delays," Digby says.

"Right," Benjamin chips in, voice slurred. He's had one too many already. Nothing like getting drunk at a funeral. "You wouldn't want that, would you, Asteridge, old chap?"

"Of course not," Captain Howard assures them.

Is this why he was so against diverting? Guest comfort apparently takes precedence over crew life. Working on yachts reminds me of modeling sometimes. The models were always expendable—unless you were one of *those* models. The supermodels. Funny. I've moved from one career to another where *super* is the prefix that makes all the difference.

"Thank you, everyone," Captain Howard says. "Normal service can resume."

"About time!" Benjamin says. "I'm gasping for another cocktail."

Lola got what—a half hour? Don't break your backs, guys.

Jade nods at Imogen to start serving him, then makes a beeline for Sasha as the rest of the crew disperse. I take the opportunity to hurry away before she can bark an order at me, and notice the captain marching off as well. Perhaps he's going to find Melinda and demand to know what that power cut was about, because it hasn't fixed anything.

I can't face everyone so I stay outside, sitting on a lower deck, wishing I had a cigarette.

The deck crew pass me by, back in their reds, Axel putting them to work power washing the decks before heading inside to fetch something to fix the loose stern line that captured Lola. He shouts at them, temper flaring, obviously stressed. I watch them for a while, wondering whether any of them could have been that male voice I heard. They seem tired, distracted. Noah even looks upset. Maybe he had a crush on Lola too. It wouldn't surprise me. Men like him only have to see a woman smile at them and they're toast.

I need to get Axel alone, so I wait for him to return some tools and follow. When he sees me, I sense some reluctance on his part to greet me, but it lasts only a second, and we're in each other's arms.

"Hey, babe," he whispers. "How are you doing?"

Look, don't judge me. Put-It-In-Imogen isn't ever going to have a real relationship with a man like Axel. There's the long distance between them for a start, and then the fact they're opposites. He's vivacious, outgoing, rich. She's moody, mean, poor. He's light; she's dark. Let's face it, he will only settle for the best. And that's me.

So he can screw around with her while we're on this yacht, make her think she's special, just for an easy life because she happened to get there first. But secretly, the two of us have been meeting up. It started about a month ago, just before Zara left. He's what I need. Although I have some questions for him too.

We were meant to meet last night after the party. It's why I saw Runa skulking around where she shouldn't have been; I was waiting for Axel. When he eventually showed up, late, he offered no explanation for where he had been. I was sure at the time he'd been with Imogen, but she admitted this morning that she had been waiting for him too, to no avail. Using the gym? That was always his excuse to her when he was seeing *me*. He's lying.

"Today has been crazy," I tell him. "Lola's death . . . it was an accident, right?"

"Of course," he says, but he's distracted, frowning.

"It's just . . ." I hesitate. "I may have heard something—"

But Axel interrupts. "Captain Howard took me off watch. For the foreseeable, he said. *Me*. The *bosun*. And Melinda is taking over my incident report about Lola. I've never heard of a bosun being treated this way."

Why would the captain take Axel off watch? Captain Howard *loves* Axel. The two of them are always cracking some joke or enjoying each other's company. It doesn't make any sense. Unless . . .

No. What am I thinking? Axel has nothing to do with any of this.

"I'm sorry," I say. "Maybe the captain is just trying to sort some things out."

"Maybe," Axel mutters darkly. "We'll see. I'm not accepting it, that's for sure."

There's an intensity to him I haven't seen before. Axel is known for temper tantrums, for flying off the handle occasionally. But this feels controlled, a building rage that he's holding close.

"Sorry," he says with a shake of his head. "What were you saying?"

Suddenly, it doesn't feel right telling him.

So I shrug. "It doesn't matter."

He distracts me with a kiss on the neck, pulling me even closer to him, but now it feels stifling, and I start struggling to break free.

He wasn't where he said he'd be last night. I need answers.

CHAPTER NINETEEN

SASHA

"Sasha," Jade says, keeping her voice low. "I have a rather delicate task for you to undertake."

Her tone is strange, even for her. She brought me into the main salon after the memorial service while everyone else went to change out of their whites, and I thought for sure she was going to shout at me about my fight with Lola. "What do you mean?"

She flips a page in her notepad and ticks something off before responding. "I'm going to need you to pack up Lola's things. There are a couple of boxes in the storage cupboard should you need them, but most should fit in her suitcase. Hers is the neon-pink one."

They're tidying her away already. It's not even been a day.

I don't know whether to laugh or cry. The staff really are just cogs in a wheel. If one malfunctions, a new one is fitted in, problem solved. This kind of anonymity, lack of importance, should be a welcome difference compared to when I worked under Dr. Martin, but it's just as bad. If it had been me who fell overboard, would anyone have bothered with a memorial service? The crew hasn't even known me a fortnight. My things would have gone into the boxes and I'd be a footnote. Remember that new stewardess who joined us for the last charter? What was her name again?

As if she's read my mind, Jade explains, "It's prompt, as Runa has requested her own cabin space now that there is . . . well, now that there is one less person. So I will be moving in with Imogen." She doesn't sound happy about it.

"Why isn't Imogen doing it?" I ask. "I won't know whose stuff is whose."

"Imogen has told me she's too upset to do it," Jade says. "But she says she and Lola kept everything very organized. Lola was the top bunk and left side of the drawers."

More like Imogen plain doesn't want to do it.

"And pack everything away nicely. These items will be returned to Lola's family." She has been stoic until this point, but at the word "family" her voice breaks, and I can see that behind the wall she's built there might be some emotion after all.

I shouldn't judge Jade, even as she gives a satisfied sigh when her instructions are complete. She craves organization and structure, and if her way of dealing with Lola is focusing on normality, that's on her. But I can't help feeling resentful. One of us has died. And she seems content to accept that it was an accident and move on.

But then, I suppose everyone is.

On my way down I spot Drew and Noah, back in their reds, passing by in the corridor with buckets and sponges and not noticing me up ahead.

"No one will ever believe me," Noah says, sounding worried. "Sasha thinks I'm weird enough. And Effie's been acting oddly ever since, which doesn't help."

"I believe you," Drew tells him. "Other people will too, if it comes down to it. You've backed me up, and you've protected my secrets. I'll protect you too, mate."

"You're not mixed up in anything again, are you?"

I frown. What exactly are they talking about?

And then Drew catches sight of me, offering a wave. "I'll catch you up," he says to Noah. We both watch Noah leave before Drew turns back, hesitantly. "How are you doing, Sasha? Sorry, daft question."

"How are *you* doing? You look tired." His eyes are bloodshot, punctuated by heavy, dark bags. His hair is greasy too, like he hasn't had time to shower in days.

"I am," he admits. "I've been kept very busy these past few days. And now . . ."

Lola's death hangs between us. Our kiss feels like a century ago.

"Today has been rough," he says. "But you're the one who found her. Has anyone even checked on you?"

They haven't, but it hadn't occurred to me. What would I expect—Jade to give me a kind word and a hug? Melinda to offer me a cup of tea or the captain to give me the rest of the day off? Of course not; I understand this crew now.

"Come here," Drew says, opening his arms.

It's so comforting that I stay like this, nestled against his chest, listening to his fast heartbeat. He murmurs something and I lift my head up to hear him better. Our faces are close, only a couple of inches apart, but kissing him again is the last thing on my mind. "What was that?"

"I said I understand. This is a mess. But we'll get through this together. You don't still think this could be something more, right?"

"But it *is* something more," I say, breaking apart from the embrace. "This wasn't an accident. Surely you know that."

"What I know is it must be scary because we're alone out here. You're new, so you don't fully understand our procedures, but this is the way things are on a boat. The captain decided diverting wouldn't be appropriate."

I'm gobsmacked, mouth open. Surely *Drew* isn't going along with everyone else? "This isn't about *procedures*. It's about the fact Lola had huge bruises on her neck that everyone seems to be ignoring. You don't get those from falling overboard."

"She was caught in a line," Drew says. "It could have wrapped around her neck."

"You really think that?"

"I listen to Captain Howard," he says. "I wouldn't have the slightest clue—"

"Well, *I* would. I was a nurse, remember? I know what I'm talking about."

"I mean, that's it, isn't it?" Drew bites his lip. "No, forget it."

"What do you mean?"

"You're cut up about your old job, whatever your reasons were for quitting. Are you sure you don't want to jump back into a nursing role again to make up for leaving?"

"I don't—" But my voice fails me, his words stopping me in my tracks. Am I so desperate to prove myself that I've blown this all out of proportion?

That day comes flooding back, the images so real I can see them in front of me.

Janet Lesley clutches at her stomach with both hands, trying to be strong. She's shaking, but she still offers her boyfriend a watery smile of encouragement, because he is currently pacing up and down the corridor looking even more frightened than she does.

"You'll be alright," I tell her, giving her small hand a pat as she holds it across her front. "This will all be over soon and then you'll be right as rain."

"You promise?" she says, blinking her big sad eyes up at me before biting down hard on her bottom lip and making it bleed.

I reach across with a tissue and wipe her mouth; some of her blood leaves its mark on me. "I promise."

She is whisked away, Dr. Martin giving me a thumbs-up to join them, and I'm about to follow when Janet Lesley's partner grabs my arm.

I turn, seeing the fear in his expression, and promise him his girlfriend will see him soon.

"Sasha?" Drew says now.

I close my eyes so I can't see Drew anymore. So I can't see *them*.

"I shouldn't have brought it up. I'm sorry."

"No." I open my eyes. "I'm sorry. I'm struggling with all of this. I have to pack away Lola's things now."

"Oh God, no wonder you're upset. I wish I could help, but Axel will be wondering where I've got to . . ."

"It's fine." My lungs are no longer inhaling enough air to satisfy what's required. I'm going to have a full-blown panic attack if he stays here any longer. "You have work to do too. We'll catch up later."

"You're sure?" He gives my hand a squeeze, reaches out as if to stroke my cheek, then thinks better of it and heads outside.

As soon as he's gone I rush to my room, pulling off my oppressive shirt and chucking it on the bed before collapsing to my knees to take gulps of air.

Calm down. *Calm down.*

Inhale for four, hold for two, out for six.

Then repeat, for as long as it takes.

When my breathing steadies, I splash my face with water, put on my normal uniform, and head into Imogen and Lola's cabin. It doesn't mean anything, but I carefully fold each and every piece of Lola's clothing, putting them delicately into her suitcase. They don't look as fabulous up close like this, some of the stitching trailing, loose threads catching in my nails. Hems are frayed, labels cut off. I find the bag Effie gleefully declared was fake, and wonder about the rest of her outfits. Surely they can't all be too? Lola was wealthy. She went to boarding school, she was supported by her parents until this year.

Well, what would I know? I've never had anything designer in my life beyond a pair of Versace sunglasses I found in a charity shop. They could be fakes too. And what does it matter now anyway? She's dead. She won't be wearing any of this ever again.

Two cardboard boxes are enough for the rest of her things. Her makeup is first. I'm unable to cram it all into her toiletry bag so I have to put it in the box loose, some of it barely used. She has a tiny teddy bear key chain with no key attached, a couple of Jodi Picoult books, and a phone charger. Her phone is missing, probably fallen into the sea. The final cardboard box is for her shoes, and again I lay them out carefully, taking my time so they don't scuff one another. I'm not sure what for. For her family when they get her things back? Or maybe that doesn't matter when your daughter is dead.

I wonder if *they* had to go through this same ritual. Unlike Lola's family, they would have had to do it themselves, pack away their daughter's life piece by piece and know it could never be whole again. The thought makes me feel sick.

It shouldn't upset me, seeing Lola's space in her cabin bare. People move about all the time. Hell, Jade is going to be in here by the end of the day. It's not like this has been Lola's room for years. It's not even been a full season. But somehow I have to keep blinking so I don't cry.

I do a final sweep of the cabin, then strip the bedsheets to put in the wash, the last remnants of Lola disappearing. Under the pillow, tucked toward the top, is a battered-looking pink notebook.

No, not just a notebook. I open it up. It's a *diary*.

My heart starts thudding again.

I grab the rest of the sheets and chuck them in the washing machine, then sit by Lola's things, leaning against the wall, and read. I keep skipping through until I reach her time on *Ophelia*, when my heart breaks at one small passage.

It was my birthday yesterday. No one sent me a message, not even Mum and Dad. I called them today and left a voicemail asking them to call me back, and they never did. I didn't tell the others because they'd only laugh and call me Mouse.

She was *lonely*.

And clearly took her anger about her parents out on us. She has several catty comments about Jade—*the Chief Stewardess looks like if I went around constipated all the time*; Effie—*and the Second Stewardess is some washed-up has-been who thinks she was Gigi Hadid when she's more like a contestant on America's Next Top Model;* and later on, even me: *New girl is a bit of a weirdo, definitely going to fuck with her for shits and giggles.* It's an endless array of one-liners, complaints about the work in between how much she wants to get out of here, but there are signs of something more.

She's careful, hiding it within passages about other things. But it's there.

Mum and Dad and those bitches won't be the ones laughing anymore when they see what I've done.

If this plan works, I'll be out of here. Living the life they all think I do.

I glance again at the clothes, remembering Lola's embarrassed face. I remember how skillfully she could lie.

Was her whole life a lie too? A conjuring, a facade, to make her look better than she was?

I can't exactly judge her for that. Look at me.

There are only a few blank pages, the diary almost full to the brim, but on the last page is a hastily scribbled note.

After the Silver Soirée. Midnight. Starboard deck.

Oh my God.

She was meeting someone. Outside.

"Sasha?"

Jade's sudden voice makes me jump, almost dropping the diary. "What are you doing? Have you finished packing away Lola's things?"

"Yes—they're all here. Look at this. Lola had a diary."

"Well, you shouldn't be reading it, then, should you?"

"No, you don't understand. She was meeting someone after the party. *Look.*"

She scans the page, a flicker of interest crossing her face, but then resumes her usual bored expression. "That could mean anything. Perhaps after the party at midnight she wanted to sneak some cake."

"Oh, come on, Jade! On the starboard deck?" She glares at me. "Sorry. Do you think I should take it to the captain?"

She sighs. "*I'll* do it. Give it here."

I hesitate, the notebook still in my hands. "I found it. I should be the one to go."

"This isn't finders keepers, Sasha," Jade snaps. "I'll deliver it. Now hand it over." She snatches the diary from me when I don't give in immediately. "I want you on laundry duty while I sort this. And don't look so glum. I'll do as you've asked."

Will she?

She tries a smile, but it's unnatural on her and comes across more like a grimace. "You can trust me, Sasha. I'm your chief stewardess."

Maybe that's the problem, I want to say. I trusted authority before, and it was the biggest mistake of my life.

CHAPTER TWENTY

JADE

None of this, I want to be clear, is my fault.

The missing knife and canapés. The jewelry. Zara. And now Lola's death.

It's not a reflection on me as chief stewardess. It's bad luck.

A deckhand went overboard in my second year of yachting in similar circumstances. There had been a party, the crew had got drunk (even the chief stewardess, certainly not appropriate), and he fell in the water. The yacht was anchored a few miles off an Italian coastal town, but luckily for him, we all saw him walk along the edge of the boat like an idiot and the chief officer was able to dive in and rescue him.

Axel is a pain, but he's a stickler for rules and regulations when it comes to safety at least. So hearing him argue with the captain before the memorial service that things weren't being done to the letter gave me pause. Is the captain insisting Lola's death was an accident because he doesn't want to face the idea he might be culpable in some way? I know if Melinda was captain instead, like she's always wanted to be, we'd be on our way to the Azores right now and filling out statements.

The captain is in the bridge with Benjamin and Digby, but when I knock and enter they don't even register me, continuing their conversation.

"I expected your engineer to be in here," Digby says to the captain. "I wanted a word."

"She has just gone on her break, but I will speak to her about the signal problem," Captain Howard promises. "Rest assured, the remainder of this charter will run smoothly."

"You had better hope so, Asteridge," Digby says. "For your own sake."

The two of them walk past me as though I am a ghost. Benjamin seems anxious, which is strange, casting glances at Digby as though he wants to say something. Captain Howard sighs once they're gone, all energy leaving him. He looks shattered. The feeling is mutual.

"Captain," I say, bringing Lola's diary to my chest. "There's something I need to sh—"

"Not now, I'm afraid, Jade," he says brusquely. "I need to speak to Melinda."

"It won't be a moment, sir," I say, but he waves me away.

"I am aware this is all very stressful," he tells me, as though I might not have figured that out. "Things will get back to normal now, you'll see."

He is so patronizing. I am fully capable of handling things like he wouldn't believe. But I hold my tongue, watching him all flustered, shoving different documents back in his drawers. He's a man panicked, not someone fitting the brief for assuring me all will be fine.

"I have to go," he says, and I decide to let him, lowering the diary back to my side.

It's for the best. I have other things on my mind.

Like that escort, Jasmine. She thinks she was so slick sneaking off during the memorial service, but I saw her.

Her counterpart, Eva, greets me warmly as I head back out to the terrace. She is lying out on a sunbed, black dress stripped off and flung over the other lounger like a towel, bikini back on display.

"Where is your friend?" I ask, keeping my voice light.

Eva lowers her sunglasses to study me for a second, then shrugs. "She wasn't feeling well during the memorial service and went for a lie down."

"Oh dear." Interesting. Eva is lying to protect her. I hadn't thought they were particularly close. "I'd better go and see to her."

"No need," Eva says quickly, defending her fellow escort. "She'll be back soon."

"If you're sure . . ." I fasten a smile to my face, knowing the edges of my mouth are trembling with the strain of maintaining it.

If I go to Jasmine's cabin, she won't be there. I can almost bet on it. Whatever it is she's up to, it won't be a secret for long. I've thought there was something odd about her since the start of the charter.

I have a choice: seek out Jasmine, wherever she is, or deal with this diary. I pick the latter. I can sort out Jasmine later.

I reach the bow within minutes, no one else around, and lean forward onto the railing. I don't look out at the horizon but instead down at the ocean. Waves are churning and crashing against the yacht as we power ahead, leaving them behind to crest and fall into nothing. We are far away from anyone out here. Lola has died and the world doesn't know.

I take the diary and hover it over the edge.

Someone has to hold this place together, and it looks like that will have to be me. I can't risk my job, everything I've built up over the past ten years, my perfect reputation as chief stewardess, being ruined. Not after all that I've done to get here.

I'm prepared to do anything to stay on top.

CHAPTER TWENTY-ONE

JASMINE

It's dusty as hell under here. Cramped. I'm painfully lying on my front, focused on Melinda's feet in their black socks. I clamp a hand to my mouth, and stay as still as possible.

I had no other option. The door was opening, I was panicking, and the only hiding place was under the bed.

There's an awful moment where Melinda stops, and I'm sure it's because I've left something out. I watch her feet, convinced at any second she's going to find me.

But then she sighs and slumps down on the bed. I feel the mattress strain, digging into my back. I never thought I was claustrophobic until now.

She swings her feet up, and to my horror a packet of tissues falls to the ground. Right next to me.

Her hand reaches down, feeling around blindly. She's so close. One attempt too far under the bed, and she'll know I'm here. Her fingers stop less than an inch from my forehead. I freeze. I can't move backward. I'm trapped.

And then—mercy. She finds the tissues, grabs the packet, and lifts it away.

It's only now that I'm calmer that I hear gulps of air, sniffs, her nose blowing.

Is Melinda *crying*?

She leaps up, moving to her desk and opening the drawers. I hold my breath, waiting for her to see things have been moved around, but thankfully she seems more focused on whatever she's looking for, because she shoves the newspaper articles out of the way, bringing out the notebook. She sits, writing furiously, then starts up her computer.

A minute in this position feels like an hour.

We both jump when there's a knock on the door. "Melinda, are you in there? It's Howard."

Shit. What does he want? I can't seriously be stuck under the bed with the captain *and* the chief officer in the same room.

No one knows I'm here. I could be made to vanish, as easily as Hallie.

I could end up like Lola, floating in the ocean.

My legs are starting to tremble.

Melinda shuts her computer down, and I hear the rustling of the tissue packet. She must be drying her eyes. "What is it, Howard?" she calls. "I've barely started my break."

"I need to talk." He opens the door, coming straight in and closing it behind him. "I'm sorry to disturb you."

"Well, you're here now," Melinda observes. I can't help admiring how easily she's put her professional facade back on. No one would ever believe that two minutes earlier she'd been wiping tears from her cheeks. "How was the memorial service? I was sad to miss it."

"Yes, my apologies for that," Captain Howard says. "With all of us occupied, it was important to have someone capable of managing a situation alone on watch. Axel, as you're aware, isn't allowed on watch from this point on."

My ears prick up. The bosun not allowed on watch? That has to be the weirdest thing I've ever heard. What has he done? Is it anything to do with Lola?

"Were they all okay?"

"That's what I wanted to discuss. It's important we emphasize this was an accident, present a united front. We don't want the guests in a panic or the crew not at their best."

"Do you want me to speak to anyone?" Melinda asks. "Perhaps someone saw something. We should be collecting statements, at any rate, on everyone's whereabouts. Some people do think differently about what happened. Maybe we should be allowing them to come and talk to a designated person about their concerns. I could volunteer."

I think of Captain Howard's incident report for Hallie. Melinda's own comment, expressing surprise at how little was filled in, how little he did to investigate.

He won't want that. Her sticking her nose in.

"That won't be necessary, thank you, Mel," he says.

"Sasha's assault? You're really going to let it go?"

"What choice do I have? We're already a stewardess down. There's nowhere for her to dock."

"We won't be diverting to the Azores, then?"

"Absolutely not."

Of course.

"While I'm here," Captain Howard says, "a warning before restarting the electrics would be useful. We were at the end of the memorial service when the power cut out."

"That wasn't me," Melinda says. "I thought it was a brief blip."

"I'm aware you're on your break, but perhaps you had better try sorting that out now and rest later." He says this in a tone that implies Melinda doesn't have much of a choice.

"Of course, sir," she says, and follows him out of the room. Only when I hear their footsteps walking away do I finally breathe properly, then crawl out from my hiding place.

I have to get out of here. I brush down the dust from my dress, then my hand is on the doorknob when I catch sight of Melinda's upturned notebook.

I look; of course I do. I grab it quickly, scan over the double-page spread.

Lola Charles. Twenty-two, Australian. Fourth Stewardess, recently promoted from Junior role. Who was close to her? Need information on family.

She's making a record, no matter what the captain wants. I put the notebook back how it was originally placed and hurriedly exit the room.

I can't believe I make it out okay.

Hallie didn't have a proper investigation, just like I thought. Are the newspaper articles because Melinda wants to do things right? Find out the truth? No wonder she wants to be captain, with one as incompetent as Howard Asteridge. Thinking back to that terrible morning when we discovered Hallie was gone, Melinda was the only other person who ran around all the floors with me, checking every room.

What else have I found out? Axel was hired to work for *Ophelia* right after last season, so he's been here longer than everyone thinks. And for some reason he's not allowed on watch anymore. The captain *really* wants everyone to think this was an accident. And most of all: the footage from the party. Lola's fight with Sasha. And that scarf she was wearing, the one a deckhand hid in a storage box on the side of the sky deck.

I need to go and see if it's still there. Because that footage is all gone now. I'm the only one who knows it once existed.

Which could be what happened with Hallie. Was there footage of the entire night, but it revealed something incriminating and had to be deleted? Made to look like it hadn't recorded, when someone actually got rid of it?

I glance toward the bridge before taking off in the opposite direction, only letting out a breath when I'm down the stairs and back in familiar territory. I'm so focused on getting away that it takes me a second to realize I'm not alone on this corridor. Even though he has his back to me, I'd recognize the bosun's tall physique anywhere. He's kissing someone on the neck. She's hidden at first, only the side of her arm and leg visible, but when she steps away, shushing him, it's one of the stewardesses, with big doe eyes and high cheekbones.

She looks upset. Axel puts his arms around her but she pushes him away, shaking her head. "Stop it. Not out here like this. What if Imogen caught us?"

"She's making the primary a stupidly large cocktail, the last I saw," Axel replies. "Nice to see he cares so much about Lola's death."

She nods, but still seems perturbed. "You haven't explained why you were late meeting up if you didn't have to deal with Imogen first."

"I lost track of time," he says. "I made up for it, didn't I?"

"You always give *her* the time of day, but never me. Something serious has happened, and you still don't understand—"

Their radios sound, a deckhand requesting Axel's assistance with something.

"I gotta go," Axel says, blowing her a kiss. "Relax, babe. It's awful with Lola, but things will get better." To my relief, he heads out the side door at the end of the corridor, rather than coming down here.

"That's not what I meant," the stewardess mutters, but he's already gone.

I head toward her, deciding on a whim that I might get some answers this way. It's only when I get closer that I realize she's the stewardess who was arguing with the chef at the memorial service. "I need to speak to you."

She's nervous, clearly worried I saw them kissing. "Jasmine, right?"

"Right. And you are?"

"Effie," she says. "Second stew."

How should I play this? "I'm terrified. Did you see anything last night?"

She hesitates, considering me. For a moment, I forget I'm the new and improved Jasmine. I'm back to a year ago, when the other stewardesses thought I wasn't worth bothering with and Hallie was the only one who gave me the time of day. But then Effie smiles, that fixed, plastic smile they all have, and I remember I'm not a deckhand anymore. I'm a guest, and she has to do as I say.

"Nothing, I'm afraid," she tells me, and I could kick myself, because now that I'm a guest, of course that means I'm not privy to crew knowledge. She's not going to give anything up easily. Her radio sounds again, this time Jade asking where she is.

Last year is fresh in my mind after watching that footage. "The chief stewardess isn't giving you all some breathing space even after today?"

Effie's professional veneer breaks, just a little, as she rolls her eyes. "She has high standards. Can I help you at all, or can I go and see what she wants?"

I have to let her go, but she pauses at the end of the hallway, turning back to me. "You were really upset about Lola, weren't you? Why?"

God, what can I say to that? That I saw my missing best friend lying there, that I see her everywhere in these stewardesses, including her? It was foolish of me, I know. I drew too much attention to myself.

"I've never seen something like that before," I say.

Effie looks around. The corridor is still empty. Her radio bursts to life again, Jade once more demanding she come to the main salon.

"Ask the chef where she was last night," Effie says. "That's all I'm saying."

She's gone before I can question her, but she's given me enough.

The chef. Runa, I think her name is. She was the one who took Lola away from the fight with Sasha. Was she the last person to see her alive?

She's at the sink in the galley, washing dishes, earphones in. It's the first time I've been in here since last year, and nothing has changed. Hallie and I would sneak in here sometimes when the chef had gone to bed and make jam sandwiches and catch each other up on our shifts. She'd sit on the counter even though we weren't supposed to, swinging her legs, and I'd lean against the fridge and laugh at almost every word she said. I notice the preference sheets, Benjamin's name highlighted in yellow to signify him as the primary. I move closer, because it's occurred to me that my allergies will be listed, Benjamin's and Digby's too.

Not that the chef would ever make such a mistake. But if the food was left unattended and no one could prove what happened . . .

Well, that would be another thing altogether.

Would I go that far?

Hallie's note is the only reminder I need.

Digby's allergies and intolerances section is blank. Benjamin's says: *I don't like crab.*

I suppose it would have been too easy if both of them were allergic to nuts.

And too tempting if I found out they were involved.

"What are you doing in here?"

I whip around, startled. Runa is staring at me.

She takes both her earphones out. "Did you want something to eat?"

"I was walking around, trying to clear my head," I say, thinking fast. "Today has been a lot. I heard you cleaning the dishes and wanted to talk to you, as we haven't had the chance, despite your amazing meals. I wanted to thank you."

"Mmm," she says, giving nothing. "You're welcome."

"Must be pretty annoying," I say, "having to serve food to the likes of Benjamin and Digby. Don't tell anyone, but between you and me, they're assholes."

She raises an eyebrow, then surprises me, taking out a packet of cigarettes. "Smoke?"

I haven't smoked in years, always tried to get Hallie to quit, but I'll do anything if it means Runa might talk. "Definitely."

We head out a side door. It takes several attempts to light our cigarettes because of the wind, but we soon stand together in companionable silence.

I'm the one to break it first. "How is the crew doing?" *Where were you last night? When did you last see Lola?*

"It has not been easy," she admits, taking a long drag. "The captain is eager to return to normal now that we have had the memorial, but it feels rushed. It makes Benjamin and Digby happy, though, which is all that matters apparently."

"Eat the rich, am I right?" I say, and watch her eyes light up with pleasure.

"You get it," she says.

It's always there, this divide between guests and crew. Hardly disguised when every facet of this vessel is designed with guest luxury in mind and crew comfort last. Being a guest now, it makes me cringe being served practically on bended knee.

"The other stewardesses must be upset, though, right?" I say. "I heard there was some kind of fight at the end of the party."

"Oh?" She frowns, and I worry I've gone too far too soon. "There are always fights on board a yacht. It was nothing new. Lola was not . . . perfect, shall we say."

"I'm not sure I can tell the stewardesses apart," I say. "All those similar-looking women . . . it must breed a sense of competition."

"Owner's preference, apparently," Runa says. "You and the other escort look the same. Do you two share this sense of competition you speak of?"

"I guess so. You always want to be the one on top, don't you?"

"Not me," Runa says. "I'm the odd one out, aren't I?"

It's true. Among all of us, she stands out. I wonder how she feels about that.

"You were close to Lola, though, weren't you?"

Something flickers in her expression. Have I rushed it? But she shrugs. "Not particularly. But the others were . . . they could be cruel."

Now that I can believe. "Someone said you helped her last night, after the argument."

Runa frowns. "A little. And then we went our separate ways and I went to bed early."

Why tell me this? Is she covering for herself, trying to build a story? Effie wanted me to talk to her for a reason. Does she suspect something?

Runa finishes her cigarette, flicking it into the sea. "I have to get back to work now."

I've lost her.

"And Jasmine? I would not ask too many people your questions. They are not as . . . accommodating as me."

She turns and leaves, and I watch through the window as she puts her earphones back in and returns to the dishes.

Was that an innocent comment?

Or a warning?

I finish my own cigarette, regretting the horrible, lingering taste.

Time to look in that storage container.

The walk up to the sky deck is without incident, though I can hear people talking over by the hot tub. I stick to the side terraces, until I find the storage box I saw in the video footage. It looks undisturbed, and I'm able to pull it open.

The scarf is still in here.

I lift it out, then almost collapse to my knees.

The material is a soft wool. It looks well-worn, well loved.

It's also covered in blood.

CHAPTER TWENTY-TWO

IMOGEN

My brother died in a car crash when I was thirteen. I was in the car too—have a scar on my forehead that I pretend came from chicken pox. Do you see me calling it a conspiracy? That the other driver must have done it deliberately? No. You get over it or never get up again.

Mouse was a dumb cow. I'm sorry, but she was. Her being dead doesn't change that fact. She was acting like a fool at the party, trying something with Axel. Her fight with Sasha was sensational, though. I never thought I'd see that side of her.

For the rest of us, life goes on. I've spent the morning after on my hands and knees scrubbing marble floors and fluffy carpets. Can't let even the smallest of scuffs remain, heaven forbid. My back aches. I reek of disinfectant. Funny how only yesterday I was standing next to Mouse's body and now I'm polishing Benjamin's sink like nothing happened. And if anyone wants to spread some shit like I was upset about it—that's patently false. If they must know, it brought me back to the day my brother died. For a second. Then I was fine.

Jade has put me on with Sasha of all people. Number one drama queen. Prattling about how she was a nurse so she'd know the bruises weren't accidental. Excuse me, hon, but weren't you fired? Even if you weren't, you're not a nurse anymore. Gagging to be the center of attention even when Mouse was lying dead between us.

"Who's doing the toilet?" I ask, holding up a pair of rubber gloves. "You or me?"

Sasha sighs. "I'll do it." She's already done all the others, but I'm not about to volunteer, and I think she's learned now it's easier to go along with me. I still haven't forgiven her for her behavior before all of this. If she'd been the one to fall overboard I wouldn't have blamed people for thinking I'd given her a shove.

"Perfect." I grin. "Then it's the bed and we're done."

Benjamin's toilet is particularly bad, even with regular cleaning. It's like the man expels demons from his ass every time he uses it. I can't help laughing when I overhear Sasha gagging as she reaches in with the toilet brush.

We put the cleaning products back, then return to do the bed. Even though I've done it for weeks now, it's still difficult because the mattresses are so heavy. Guest comfort over crew health, that's for sure. On his bedside table, he's left out a ludicrously expensive-looking watch, and I smirk.

"Shall we put that away?" I ask.

Sasha looks afraid to even touch it. "Let's leave it."

"You can see why things are disappearing," I say innocently. "Look how easy it is."

Sasha's mouth twists. "I think Benjamin would notice if his watch went missing."

She's so easy to wind up. "True. It would be easier with a female guest. All those earrings and bracelets and necklaces . . . how do they keep track? Poor Eva still hasn't found her missing things." Sasha looks horrified, so I roll my eyes to let her know I'm joking. "I forgot I can't have a laugh with you."

"There isn't much to laugh about right now," Sasha replies.

"Evidently not with your sour face a constant reminder."

"Don't you feel bad about what happened?"

"Why?" I shrug. "It's not my fault Mouse fell off the boat, is it?"

"But—"

"I'm not going to pretend me and Mouse were friends," I interrupt. "And neither should you. She was nursing her sore cheek from your slap last I saw."

"That's why I want to find out what happened!" she says. "I feel bad. You really didn't see anything while you were waiting for Axel in the, uh, pantry?"

That stumble. Judgmental bitch. And so *boring*. No wonder Mouse made up stories about her. She's definitely the kind of person at a party to remind you to use a coaster. Where does she get off, pretending she cares about Mouse? She barely knew her.

I pause for a second, an exaggerated display of tapping my finger against my chin. "Come to think of it, I did see something."

She looks so eager. "You did?"

"This figure, out on the side terrace, wearing a red-and-white-striped shirt, bobble hat, and glasses." I throw a hand to my face dramatically. "That's right . . . I found Wally!"

Excitement turns to disgust. "Imogen! This isn't a joking matter."

"You're right, it's not," I agree. "It could have been Odlaw, Wally's archnemesis. Then we'd have been in real trouble."

I burst out laughing.

She's too fun to mess with. It's not like she doesn't deserve it. She's putting on some mock-hurt face as if she genuinely expected me to be serious. No doubt she'll run off telling tales to Jade that Big Bad Imogen has been mean. Time to put her in her place.

"It was an *accident*, Detective Dunce," I say. "I'm aware that's a rather long word in the English language so it might be tricky for you, but it means Lola fell over because she was an idiot, not because someone decided to do her in."

"It wasn't an accident," Sasha hisses. "And I've got proof. Lola kept a diary, and she said she was meeting someone the night of the party."

What? The humor dies in my throat. Lola had a diary? Why didn't I know this?

Jade comes through on the radio, interrupting us. *"Can Sasha and Imogen come to the crew mess now, please? Stewardess meeting."*

She and Effie are sitting at the table when Sasha and I arrive, and we join them without comment. There doesn't seem to be anyone else down here, and the table is bare, only a folder and notepad in front of Jade. I can't help looking up at the pinboard, seeing that Jade has scratched out Lola's name on the shift patterns, just like she did Zara's. Except this time there's no one to replace her.

Jade follows my gaze. "Observant as always, Imogen. We will of course all be working to a new pattern, having to pick up where . . . where there are now gaps."

Jesus. She can't be serious. Even Effie looks stunned.

"I want to address the elephant in the room," Jade says. I can see from here she's written at the top of the notepad *MEETING* and underlined it several times. Typical Jade. "It is tragic that Lola lost her life, but that doesn't mean we let it interfere with work."

"I'm sorry?" I say. Is she for real?

"Mr. Edmondson looked like he wanted to complain last night at dinner, so it'll only be a matter of time. We must remain on form."

I know I'm the one who thinks all this has been blown out of proportion, but *really*? I look around the table, baffled that no one cares that there's an empty spot where Mouse should be. I'm meant to be the bitchy one, the one who doesn't give a shit. They should be bothered. A wave of nausea rushes over me, thankfully passing just as fast.

"Did you give Captain Howard Lola's diary?" Sasha asks.

"Lola had a diary?" Effie says.

Jade doesn't meet Sasha's gaze. "I dealt with it as I saw fit."

"What is that supposed to mean?"

"If you must know," she says, "I got rid of it."

"You . . . got rid of it?" Sasha echoes. "Where?"

"I threw it in the sea."

Holy shit. What?

Sasha is distraught. "You promised! You promised you would take it to the captain."

"That's crazy," I say. "You shouldn't have done that."

"Since when do you stick up for Sasha?" Effie asks. "What's got into you?"

"And what's it to you?" I snap. "Jade got rid of something of Mouse's. I can think that's wrong too."

"You've been acting ever so strange lately," Effie says. "Don't think I haven't noticed you sneaking off at night. And I know you're not seeing Axel."

Something about the way she says this makes my heart begin to pound. "How could you possibly know whether or not I'm seeing him?"

"Because I know where he is at night. That's how."

She's just trying to get a rise out of me. But I can't help it, my temper flares. "What are you implying? Because if you're suggesting he'd be interested in someone like you—"

"He likes the chase, Imogen. Have you ever heard of that concept? It's incredible. What you do is you pretty much keep your legs closed for longer than five seconds—"

No. *No!*

"That's enough!" Jade shouts. "Imogen, sit down! Effie, stop talking!"

I am defiant. "But she implied she was with Axel!"

"I implied nothing." Effie grins. "I'm outright stating it."

"I don't care. What I care about is us doing a stellar job. You two can sort that out in your own time, not waste mine."

What I want to sort out is how quickly I can drag Effie to the side of the yacht and throw her in. And trust me, no stern line is going to be making sure she's towed along with us. I will stand there and watch that bitch drown. Although right now I'd settle for taking a handful of her hair and smashing her face down on the table. I can bide my time, though. I'm good at that. So I shut my mouth.

Jade looks at her watch, then rises to her feet. "I'm only going to say this once. No matter what happens, I'm in charge of you all, and if I say jump, you say how high. I got rid of that diary to prevent stupid arguments like this one. I am your chief stewardess, and the rest of this charter is going to be sublime for the guests. Have you got that?"

You don't throw that notebook in the ocean to prevent an argument. You throw that notebook in the ocean to prevent secrets from getting out. She's hiding something.

Does she have one of the secrets Lola was going to tell us about?

"Have you got that?" she repeats, when we don't immediately answer.

"Yes, Jade," we say, all as reluctant as each other.

I stare daggers at Effie, who blows a kiss back at me. Yep. She's dead. And Axel too when I get my hands on him.

CHAPTER TWENTY-THREE

SASHA

She got rid of the diary. Dumped it into the sea, as if it were nothing. I can't believe it.

"It's lunch service soon," Jade says. "Imogen and Effie, you're going to have to work together whether you like it or not. Imogen, come help me lay the table. Effie, go and fetch the guests from the sky lounge. And Sasha, you're on laundry."

She marches upstairs without so much as a backward glance, Imogen following behind. Effie hesitates. Her energy against Imogen has vanished and she looks exhausted, dark circles under her eyes.

What happened to the group of stewardesses who sat down before the Silver Soirée together?

"Effie," I say. "What was all that about? You . . . and Axel? Is that for real?"

"Yes, it's real." She buries her face in her hands. "God, I can't believe I just told Imogen like that. It's Lola's death. It's got me all messed up."

"What do you mean?"

She looks behind us. Jade and Imogen are gone, but she lowers her voice anyway. "I think I heard something. Something I shouldn't have."

I wait for the punch line, the catty comment. This is Effie. "Is this about what happened with Noah?"

"No. God, forget it."

"You said we were friends," I tell her. "At the start. I want that to be true."

She laughs mirthlessly at that. "When I was two years old, people stopped my mom in the street and told her what a pretty child I was. That she should get me into modeling, so she did. And then I was in all these magazines and commercials as a kid. No, a *toddler*. With makeup and hair extensions and dresses. Weird as fuck, right?"

Where is she going with this?

"She entered me in these child beauty pageants, and I won them all. I missed so much school because she was carting me across the country. I had my first national campaign when I was ten. And then when I was thirteen, she sent me to Paris. Got me signed up to an elite agency, and then I lived in a model house with all these other models, who were horrible. They'd steal my shit and make fun of me and tell me I was ugly, that I was never going to amount to anything. They took the batteries out of my alarm clock so I missed photo shoots. And then Mom got sick."

I let her speak, even as she pauses to take a deep breath.

"I asked to come home. But she said no. And then she *died*. She died while I was in France. I was fifteen, and all I wanted was my family. But when I came back for the funeral it was like my dad and brothers were strangers. They didn't know how to act around me. Said it would be better for everyone if I went back to Paris. Said that's what Mom would have wanted. Yeah, Mom, who wanted the prestige of having a model daughter so badly she didn't even see her before she died. So that's what I did. And then the industry said you're getting too old now, you need to drop twenty pounds, you need to have Botox, so I said fuck it and quit and came here. And I haven't spoken to my dad or brothers in years. Everyone in my life has either used me, let me down, or abandoned me."

"Effie—"

"So no, Sasha, I'm not your friend," she interrupts. "I don't do friends, I just look out for myself. Which is why when I first heard what I did, I just treated it as a bit of salacious gossip, a bit of fun to spread later. Now I'm not so sure."

"Tell me, then," I say. "What did you overhear?"

"I want to," she says. "I actually think you're the only person who wants to investigate Lola's death properly."

"What do you think about what Runa said?" I ask. "About Lola knowing everyone's secrets. Do you think that was true?"

Effie closes her eyes, considers this. "I think there are some secrets on this yacht which are dangerous to know."

A shiver passes through me.

She is done talking. "I need some air. Maybe I'll come find you later."

I don't argue with her. We have time. We're stuck together on this yacht and neither of us can leave. She stares at me for a long moment, then turns and heads up the stairs without another word.

I'm about to leave the crew mess myself when Drew comes out of his cabin, agog.

"I was taking a nap," he says, "and woke up to you all arguing. It was safer staying in there. Are you okay?"

The easy answer, *Yes*, is ready, my mouth opening to deliver it. But I stop myself, shaking my head. "No. No, I'm not."

"This has all gone so wrong," he says. "I'm so sorry, Sasha."

It's tempting to go to him, spend an hour forgetting. But I can't. Effie's words, *secrets which are dangerous to know*, are swimming in my brain. "What were you doing yesterday when I found Lola's body? You let me think you were on watch."

"Whoa, whoa." Drew backs off, hands up in surrender. "Where has this come from?"

"Answer the question."

"I couldn't sleep," he says. "I went for a walk."

He's lying. Another thought that comes unbidden.

He sees the disbelief in my face. "What's happened, Sasha? What's wrong?"

Noah told me to stay away from him. What if he knows something the rest of us don't? Something Lola found out about?

No. I can't think that of Drew of all people.

"I'm sorry," I say. "I can't do this right now."

"Sasha, wait—"

But I don't, and Drew is sensible enough not to try following me up the stairs.

Something isn't right.

But he waves away my concerns with a smile. "This is nothing, Sasha. You're worrying too much. It'll come with experience."

"I really think we should examine her. Recheck a few things—"

"And I said we're fine."

So I let it go. Big mistake.

The memory jolts me. I didn't speak up before and it cost me everything. I head outside, breathing in the fresh air, but it does little to help. My mind is on fire.

And then a high-pitched scream pierces my thoughts, coming from the deck above.

"Hey!" I shout. "Are you okay?"

I'm running toward the sound before I can even think about the fact I'm heading in the direction of danger, but instinct takes over.

A stewardess. Slumped on the deck. One wrong move and she'll be over the edge, into the sea like Lola. I'm there faster than I thought possible, rolling her around so she's face up and as far from the railing as I can manage alone. Her eyes are shut, and she's very still.

This time, I have my radio. I press down, speak into it with as much force as I can muster. *"Everyone, this is Sasha. All must come to the main deck aft. I need urgent assistance. I think it's happened again."*

Jade is first to respond. *"What do you mean, it's happened again?"*

"It's Effie," I reply. *"She's dead."*

PART THREE

CHAPTER TWENTY-FOUR

JASMINE

All I'm saying is they shouldn't let this affect their work," Benjamin declares.

We're sitting at the table outside, a gentle breeze helping keep me calm at Benjamin's infuriating words. The frankly ludicrous cocktails we just drank apparently don't qualify for his high standards.

The scarf is in my suitcase while I figure out what on earth I'm going to do. I can't confront the deckhand, not alone. He's dangerous. But I also can't trust anyone enough to tell them what's going on. I spent most of last night (after enduring Benjamin) lying in bed, staring up at the ceiling, terrified that at any moment the deckhand was going to come in, knowing somehow I had taken the scarf, and make me disappear.

"You're so right," Eva enthuses, even as a stewardess comes to clear the empty glasses away unprompted.

"It's a lot of money to charter a yacht," Benjamin says. "Accident or no accident."

Did he speak like this after Hallie disappeared? Was she one big inconvenience to him and his holiday?

"We wouldn't want you wasting your money, would we?" Digby says.

Benjamin looks at him strangely. "In any case, who manages to fall overboard? She was asking for it, really."

If Lola hadn't got caught up in that loose line, she'd have been gone forever. There'd be no proof either way of whether it was an accident or deliberate.

"Shall we ask one of the other stewardesses to go by her name?" he says. "Problem solved."

"Or Eva, in her stewardess costume." Digby grins. "We enjoyed that after the party."

Eva winks. "Let me go change into it again for you, sir."

"She was a *real person*," I snap, regretting the words the moment they're out of my mouth. The voice I've been putting on for them vanishes, and I have to quickly engage the disguise again. "Excuse me. I'm just upset about it. I'm sorry."

Digby narrows his eyes.

"Your time of the month or something?" Benjamin asks.

"She's sorry!" Eva blurts out. "I'll take her inside to freshen up and then why don't we get in the hot tub for some fun before lunch starts?"

Benjamin practically salivates. "Great idea."

Eva doesn't give me a chance to fret about it; she steers me toward our cabins, and as soon as we get inside hers she rounds on me, furious.

"What are you doing, Jasmine? Are you deliberately trying to annoy the primary?"

I shake my head. "I couldn't sit there and laugh like you—"

"Well, you're going to have to!" She starts pulling out bikinis and tossing them on the bed. "Do you think I found what he said funny? Of course not. Men like him don't care about the *staff*. And we're included in that category. If he and Mr. Johnson are pleased with us, we could share a tip of anywhere between ten and thirty thousand dollars. Do you understand how much that would mean for my family? For my little girl?"

I open my mouth to argue, then close it again. I want to tell her I do understand, that I too don't have much, don't have anything anymore. What savings I earned from yachting went straight on the clothes for this trip and the plane ticket to Gibraltar. I've spent the past year with barely enough to scrape by. That money would change my life too—but it's never been about that. It's been about justice.

"Mr. Johnson has already bought me a necklace that must be worth thousands," she says, going to her bedside table. "You could get things like that too, if you would only—"

She lets out a shriek, then takes the entire bedside drawer out, looking between the gaps before checking on the floor and under the bed.

"It's gone! The necklace is gone!"

That's not the first thing she's had go missing. There was that silver bracelet too, and an amethyst ring. Melinda's notebook instantly comes to mind, the sentence about a jewelry thief. This is bigger than just Eva, I'm sure. But I can't share it with her now, not when I'm not sure if I can trust her.

"I can't believe this," she says, and I think she's going to cry. "This is how I'm repaid. You have no idea what I've even been doing for you."

What is she talking about? "What do you mean?"

"That chief stewardess. Jade? She's onto you, whatever you're doing."

Shit. *Jade.* I need to be more careful. Eva throws me one of her bikinis. "Get this on. I'm taking a shower. Don't mess this up for me more than you already have."

I oblige, putting the bikini on in my own cabin and checking with relief that nothing has been disturbed in my suitcase. The bloody scarf is still in there, my passport, the photograph of Hallie and me together our first day on this boat.

What am I going to do about Jade?

Before I can think properly, two people start having an argument outside my room.

"Are you the reason why I've been taken off watch?" Male, aggressive, and with a distinctly American drawl; it's the bosun. I have to talk to him, find out why he was hired so soon after last season. "It doesn't make any sense."

"That's not me," a voice says, and I recognize it instantly as Melinda's. "That was the captain's decision."

"And why exactly? Because I try to follow procedure to the letter? And what about the missing life jackets? The missing life rings? The crew should know about them. For God's sake, the *guests* should know about them. You haven't even let me file a report or record it in the logbook."

Wait, the life jackets are missing? And the life rings? This is more than just a few pieces of jewelry.

"Captain Howard ordered me to make sure neither you nor I tell anyone about that," Melinda replies. "It's unusual, but what am I supposed to do? Defy his command?"

Holy shit. And Captain Howard is covering this up?

What is going on?

"If one of us had seen Lola fall in, there probably wouldn't have been any way to save her in time without a life ring. You realize that, don't you?"

"Yes!" Melinda snaps. "Trust me, Axel, things would be very different if I was captain. But that's the way things are on this boat."

Is this why Melinda was crying yesterday? She's been so busy trying to balance all of the different things the captain has ignored or let happen, and it's ended up in a stewardess dying? Maybe that's why Melinda wanted to talk to people, find out their statements for the night of the party. She *doesn't* want it to be an accident, because that then means she's partially to blame.

"It's whoever is wrecking things again," the bosun says. "We need to stop ignoring this. Something terrible is going to happen."

Again? How long has this been going on exactly?

"I have to go," Melinda says. "I'm sorry. There's nothing I can do."

Footsteps walk away, then someone punches the wall, making me jump.

"Fuck!" Axel yells. That punch was hard. He must have hurt himself.

Did Eva hear all that too? She must have, unless she was still in the shower. That would be just my luck. I can't count on her, not when her priority is her daughter. I have to figure this out alone.

I wait a few minutes, then poke my head out the door. Axel is gone. I guess which direction he went, and thankfully I'm right: he's out by the bow, hosing down the deck. He stops when he sees me approach, offering a wave, cool as a cucumber, as if nothing is awry at all.

"Jasmine, isn't it?" he says casually.

I beam. "Just the person!"

I'm at my most flirty, everything dialed up to ten. He glances up and down, taking in my bikini courtesy of Eva.

"What can I do for you?"

"I'm interested in what it's like being a deckhand," I say. I edge closer, and to my surprise he backs off.

"Well, I'm the bosun," he says. "The most senior deckhand. I'm responsible for a lot. No two days are the same."

"You seem well respected," I say. "I bet the captain is proud of you."

It's the perfect bait. His smile vanishes instantly, and he drops his guard. "He used to be, anyway."

"How long have you worked with him?"

"I was hired straight after last season."

So he's telling the truth at least.

"I heard last year was tricky," I say. "Are people normally hired off-season?"

"Well, you always need someone to maintain the boat," Axel says. "And there was a lot that needed sorting. You heard it was tricky? Where did you hear that?"

"Maybe I misheard," I say vaguely. "But you obviously did a great job, because look at the yacht now. What were the main things you were doing?"

"Changing equipment. General upkeep of the boat. And the owner requested everything was cleaned from top to bottom."

Does he know the owner, then? Did the owner request that because Captain Howard told them what happened with Hallie and they wanted to ensure nothing on the yacht could be linked to her? "Cleaning? That's odd for a bosun, isn't it?"

He shrugs. "I do as I'm asked. Unfortunately."

He's still sore about earlier. I want to question him about being taken off watch, about the missing life jackets and life rings, but I know I can't without giving away that I overheard. I need to keep my advantage.

"Still," I say. "Cleaning?"

"I've never known anything like it. Especially in the owner's suite, which wasn't even used that season, apparently. You'd think we were tidying up a crime scene." He finishes with the hose, wrapping it up. "Although saying that, the captain did apparently do some kind of inventory check and a statue was missing. Some mythology guy? I don't know, I'm not into that kind of stuff. I never found it, anyway." He gives me one of his megawatt smiles. "Right, I've got more to do. See you around, Jasmine. I'm free anytime."

A crime scene. He means it as a joke, but why else would you clean everything to that degree? If there was even the slightest risk a forensics team would come on board, you'd make sure the place was wiped. And why clean the owner's suite when it wasn't used? Does all this have something to do with Hallie?

I have to get up there.

For now, there are other cabins. Benjamin's and Digby's. No doubt Eva will be entertaining them in the hot tub right now. They won't miss me for a little while. And with the owner not on board, I can sneak into their suite at some point and look around. I'll make sure of it.

Digby's room first. Smaller than Benjamin's; a neon strip of purple light borders the massive bed, which is made up with a dozen pillows and a white fluffy throw. Across the way two doors open to a large walk-in wardrobe, and I start in here first, checking through the various expensive suit pockets and other clothes, hoping for a scrap of paper, a receipt, anything—but come up empty. His shoes yield no results, and I feel daft sticking my hand in them, but I do uncover a diamond Rolex (Jesus Christ), so I'm not totally dumb for thinking of that as a hiding place. More curious are the items on the desk, a series of documents relating to his several businesses, some marked in red, others with certain passages highlighted, but nothing to do with Hallie or Lola, so I keep searching. He has no laptop or other computer, which I find odd, but I guess you don't come on a yacht and work if you're a billionaire. The only thing of interest is what looks like a burner phone tucked within a box of tissues, but when I turn it on there's nothing: no contacts, no call history, no messages. He must delete his records as soon as he uses it. It's fully charged, though, ready at a moment's notice.

It could mean anything—maybe he's a drug lord and that's how he *really* makes his money. That would be the least surprising thing that's happened this trip. Honesty and wealth are certainly mutually exclusive.

Disappointed, I try Benjamin's much more lavish master suite with its adjoining lounge area and a king-size bed I've gotten to know well. His clothes are even more ostentatious, designer label after designer label, and I can't help wondering how a financial advisor is somehow able to keep up with his billionaire friend. And Benjamin is the primary! Benjamin must be the drug lord, not Digby. He certainly enjoys them; there's an entire drawer full. He also has some women's underwear, which, although unsettling, doesn't tell me anything. He could have a weird fetish for stealing them. Or maybe he likes to wear them. I can't hide my dismay. This was pointless.

I don't expect anyone to be in the corridor as I leave, so I jump out of my skin when I hear a voice call out, "Sorry! I didn't mean to startle you."

I turn around—and it's *him*. The deckhand from the footage. The one with the scarf.

"Leaving a surprise in Mr. Edmondson's room," I gabble, even though he didn't ask for an explanation. Now I look even more suspicious.

"Right." This flusters him, and if I hadn't seen that footage with my own eyes I'd swear it couldn't be this guy. He's shy, not meeting my gaze. His fingers flex, and I can't help wondering what else those hands have done.

"How are you feeling?" I ask pointedly. "It's awful what happened to Lola."

He nods. "I was devastated, couldn't believe it. Still can't, to be honest."

Except you're not being honest, are you?

"Were the two of you close?"

"Um." He pauses, a red flush creeping into his cheeks. I knew he was hiding something. "Not really. But we were colleagues, you know, so—I miss her."

"I loved the coat she was wearing," I say, then add, wildly, "and that scarf too."

He freezes.

And I'm very aware of the fact we're alone.

"Right," he says eventually. "I don't remember the scarf."

Liar.

"I have to go," I say, trying not to let my voice shake. "Oh—what's your name?"

"Noah," he answers. "And I know yours, of course. Jasmine."

I can't get back to my cabin fast enough. I hurry to the bathroom, splash my face with water, and only when I raise my head again to look in the mirror do I see the harsh, angry words written in lipstick staring back at me.

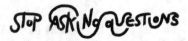

CHAPTER TWENTY-FIVE

EFFIE

My eyes fly open. I'm staring up at a deckhead, which means I must be lying on my back. To one side of me, the yacht interior. To the other, the drop-off into the ocean below. I try to lift my head, ever so slightly, and find Sasha staring down at me.

I scream, I can't help it. I scramble to sit up, woozy and weak, clutching my head. "What the fuck is going on?"

"Oh my God." Sasha sounds like she might cry. "You're *alive*."

What happened? My mind struggles to remember, confused. I was doing something for Jade, I'm sure, after the meeting disaster. Avoiding Imogen. Did I go and tell Axel what I'd done? Or was that what I was planning to do? I can't think. And then someone came up behind me . . .

My trembling fingers feel the back of my head, find something wet, and come away stained with blood. I stare, appalled, at Sasha. "You did this."

Sasha pales, shaking her head. "I *found* you. I heard you scream and came running."

I don't believe her. I had just told her I'd overheard something, that there were dangerous secrets on this yacht. Secrets that perhaps Lola heard about and are why she's now dead. Secrets that *I* know about and are why I've been attacked.

"What is going on? Effie, you're alive?"

Melinda's voice tears across the deck, and soon we're surrounded by the rest of the crew. Even Digby, Benjamin, and Eva are here, dripping wet in their bathing suits, and then Jasmine appears from inside, already looking anxious. Captain Howard arrives last, out of breath and red-faced. The only one missing is Noah, who must be on watch. I wonder what he's thinking right now.

"Thank goodness," Captain Howard says as soon as he's in front of me. "You're alive. When I heard that radio . . ."

"Radio?" I echo. My head hurts. My vision blurs for a second, everyone turning into amorphous shapes. As it regains focus, Sasha comes even closer. "Get away from me! You're the one who did this, I know it."

Sasha rises to her feet and backs off. "I'm sorry, I was just trying to check for a concussion. You have a head injury. I didn't do anything. I promise I didn't."

"What do you remember, Effie?" Captain Howard asks.

I try to recall the details, brow furrowing. "I was walking down here . . . someone hit me from behind. On the back of my head." I did scream, I remember. A horrible, anguished noise. "And then they hit me again, and everything went black, and the next thing I knew Sasha was leaning over making sure I was dead."

I could have died. Just like Lola. What would my dad have done? My brothers? Throw some ostentatious funeral like they did for my mother and then promptly forget about me, the black sheep of the family?

"Sasha told us you *were* dead," Runa says, frowning. "We all heard her loud and clear on the radio. Did you think you had got the job done, Sasha?"

"God, no!" Sasha protests. "I panicked. I saw Effie lying there and just—assumed."

"You were a nurse, weren't you?" Axel asks, and I want him to come to me, hold me close, make it all better. "You'd know how to tell if someone was dead. You'd know not to panic in these situations."

"Panic doesn't have logic," Sasha says. "This isn't like being in a hospital."

She's the new stewardess. The last crew member on board. All of this—it's been her. I won't let her get away with it. God, and I thought she was the one person I could confide in.

"You're the one who keeps trying to say Mouse's death wasn't an accident," Imogen says to her. "Is that because you killed her, and you're trying to throw the scent off now your attempt to dump her in the sea didn't work?"

"And Sasha found Lola and Effie first," Runa points out.

"That's a coincidence!" Sasha insists.

Jade folds her arms. "Also, Sasha was meant to be in the laundry room."

"I was having time to think, after our meeting."

"Sasha and I argued," I say, even though that's not true. "She's out to get me."

"That's not right," Sasha says. "We didn't argue."

"Just like Mouse," Imogen says. "You slapped her. We're all starting to see the common denominator now, aren't we? Prone to violence, are you, Sasha?"

Captain Howard orders us all to be quiet, and tells Melinda to begin administering first aid. She starts tending to my head. She's doing it too roughly, but I wince and try to bear it. Axel seems tense, gaze flicking between me and Sasha. Imogen has noticed too, narrowing her eyes at us both. If Sasha hadn't been leaning over me when I woke up, I'd have been sure it was Imogen after what I confessed. Benjamin is interested, though, and I can't help wondering if he's getting some kind of sadistic pleasure from this. By contrast, Digby is angry, and Eva rubs his arm until he shakes her off. Standing farther away, Drew seems especially bothered, focused on me and Melinda, but looks away when I try to catch his eye. That's when I spot Jasmine. She's pressing a finger to her lips, nodding at Sasha.

What is that supposed to mean? Is she on her side?

I look at her outfit: swimwear, but bone dry. Where has she been? Something about her gesture scares me, prevents me from speaking out.

Captain Howard clears his throat. "Let's establish a couple of things. Where was everyone when Effie was attacked?"

Eva speaks first. "I was in the hot tub with Mr. Edmondson and Mr. Johnson. Jasmine wasn't, though she was supposed to be."

This prompts everyone to turn and look at Jasmine. I don't like her. Jade seems just as displeased, fixing Jasmine with a quizzical glare.

"I was in my cabin," Jasmine explains. "Noah saw me not long before I heard the scream. He can confirm that's where I went."

"Noah did?" Captain Howard says. "He's on watch. Perhaps you meant Drew?"

"I agreed to take over briefly while Noah went to the toilet," Drew says. "Maybe that's when she saw him."

But why would Noah need to walk past the guest cabins to do that?

Sasha frowns at this, turning toward Drew with a puzzled look on her face, but she doesn't say anything.

"Where were you, Captain Howard?" Melinda asks. "It's best to lead by example."

This irritates him, I can see immediately, but he answers reasonably enough. "I was taking my break in my quarters, reading one of my books. But I kept my radio on, and that's why it's important to always have it on, even during your breaks."

"Well, Imogen and I were serving the guests," Jade says. "I told Euphemia to go and tidy the sky lounge after she'd brought the guests for lunch. And like I said, Sasha was meant to be doing laundry."

"You were inside for a while," Benjamin says to Jade, which makes her cheeks flush. "I was beginning to think you'd fallen off the boat yourself."

It doesn't matter where they all were. Sasha tried to kill me.

Axel frowns. "Effie was hit outside, right? We should go and check the cameras. We'll have our answer pretty fast."

Of course! Straight above us, with a perfect shot, is a CCTV camera. Melinda groans.

"Melinda?" Captain Howard says. "You can check the cameras, can't you?"

"I turned them off this morning," she admits. "I was trying to get the internet to work, and ran into further issues with the electrics . . . The cameras aren't working anymore either."

"What?" Captain Howard is beside himself. "I can't believe this. Who else knew the cameras weren't working?"

"No one!" Melinda says. "I mean, I don't think so. I might have mentioned it during our exterior briefing this morning . . ."

"For God's sake." Captain Howard closes his eyes. "Did anyone see anything at all that would back up Effie's assertion it was Sasha?"

No one says anything.

"It *was* her," I insist. "Why else would she be here when I woke up?"

"Because I heard you scream!" Sasha says. "I was here to *help* you."

"I don't know, Effie," Imogen says. "I wouldn't be surprised if you knocked yourself out to get attention. Can't have Mouse being more important than you, can we?"

"What about you?" Sasha says to her. "Effie told us in our stewardess meeting earlier that she and Axel were—"

"Rubbish!" Axel interjects, far too quickly.

"She already knows," I say, rising gingerly to my feet. "I told her earlier. Just before I got whacked."

Axel's face is a picture. He goes from shock to anger to furiously trying to fix a bewildered smile onto his face, but it's too late. "Imogen—"

She cuts him off sharply. "Don't worry, *darling*, we'll be having words. But not now. So you be a good boy and shut it, will you?"

His temper rises. "Don't talk to me like I'm dirt."

"No? Then don't act like it, there's a suggestion."

"Both of you are acting like children," Jade says. "It's unacceptable. We are in front of our guests and captain; you need to behave yourselves."

"Oh, I don't know," Benjamin says. "I'd quite like to see them fight. If things get physical, that's fine by me."

"One thing is for sure," Runa says. She has been quiet for so long I almost forgot she was here, standing with us, observing everything. "You were right, Sasha. Lola's death wasn't an accident. Not if whoever it was is now trying to hurt another stewardess."

Runa has said it. The fact everyone is trying to deny.

"You're not a big fan of the stewardesses, Runa," Axel says. "What about you?"

"What about *you*, Axel?" Runa claps back. "Or is fucking every woman that breathes not enough? You go in for hurting them too?"

"Not every woman," he retorts. "You're breathing, aren't you? Though maybe not for long with all this."

This is so typically us. Rather than stick together, which is more important than ever, we have split apart, drawn battle lines, refused to cooperate. No one trusts anyone, which means whoever the killer is could strike again and there's nothing we can do.

The *killer*. Lola's death was no accident.

There's a murderer on board.

CHAPTER TWENTY-SIX

JASMINE

STOP ASKING QUESTIONS

I t is written strangely, the *g* and *q* in lower case when the rest are in capitals, their tails an elaborate loop crossing under the rest of the letters. It shouldn't be what I'm focused on in this moment, but I am, the distinctive lettering easier to puzzle over because otherwise I have to think about what this means.

I'm being warned off, that much is clear. Someone knows what I'm doing and wants to make sure I stop.

Maybe I *should* stop. Show the police Hallie's note when we dock, tell them what I've learned. But will they take it seriously? Will they care when it happened a year ago and her case doesn't exist in the USA?

Hallie will get swept under the carpet, again, and I can't have that.

Threat or no threat, I need to carry on. Especially now Effie has been hurt too.

"You have my promise," Captain Howard says. "I will get to the bottom of what has happened, and you can be assured that your safety is our utmost priority."

He has gathered us into the main salon and delivered a rather pathetic speech. He's obviously floundering, not sure what to do in the face of all this. Eva is terrified, and even Benjamin looks concerned, ordering Jade to ply him with as many cocktails as possible. Digby requests a private word with Captain Howard, and the two of them leave the room after the captain tells us one more time that we are safe here.

Yeah, sure. We're real safe. Melinda has taken Effie off to examine her injury, and the other crew members have disappeared, probably having their own panicked debrief.

"Where were you when that stewardess was attacked?" Eva asks, voice low. We're sitting on the sofa together, but she still inches herself closer to prevent anyone else hearing. "You were meant to be in the hot tub with Mr. Edmondson and Mr. Johnson already by the time I got there."

"I bumped into the bosun," I say. Not strictly a lie. "I was speaking to him."

Eva doesn't believe me, and I'm not sure I can blame her. "What are you doing?"

I try to keep my face neutral. "What do you mean?"

"You don't seem . . . surprised by anything," she says. "This is an incredible yacht, better than any I've been on, and yet you walk around the place like you've done it every day. I still get lost going from the gym to breakfast. You weren't even seasick and I was terrible."

I can't trust her. She's made it quite clear her focus is on getting a big tip for her daughter. The moment she finds out I'm a fraud, she'll tell.

"And you seem keen to get to know the crew," she continues. "What's your fascination with them? Why do you keep disappearing off to do God knows what?"

Wait. She actually suspects I might have something to do with this.

I see it in her body language, hand gripping the armrest, turning her knuckles white. She's trying to hide it, but she's afraid. Of *me*.

"You can't think . . ." I have to give her something. Anything. "Someone left a threatening message in my cabin. That's why I didn't come. And then I heard Effie scream so went rushing there instead."

"A threatening message?"

"I'll show you."

She's reluctant. "I don't know."

"Eva," I say, exasperated, "if I was going to kill you, would I really do it when there are several witnesses that are watching us go off together?"

This convinces her. "Fine."

We make our excuses to Benjamin, say we'll be back in a few minutes, and I can't help but notice Jade frowning over at me.

Things are silent as we walk, only the whir of the engine. It's unsettling to think that, no matter how big this yacht is, in the end there's nowhere to hide.

My cabin is how I left it, but when my hand extends to turn the light on in the bathroom I freeze. When I heard the scream, I was standing in here staring at the mirror. The porthole to the outside was the next thing I looked at—watching Sasha run past, toward the noise. And then I ran too.

I didn't turn the bathroom light off.

Someone has been in here.

I turn on the light and stare at the mirror. There's not even a forgotten smudge of lipstick, nor any fingerprints. It's practically as clean as the day it was installed.

A professional job.

One of the other stewardesses? Jade, who brought us into the main salon then left Imogen to make the cocktails while she "dealt with something" and took fifteen minutes? Or Axel, the bosun, apparently great at cleaning considering he scrubbed this place from top to bottom like he was washing away a crime scene?

"It was here," I tell Eva. "Written on the mirror in lipstick."

"In lipstick?" Eva says. "What is this, a bad teen movie? You have to be joking."

"I'm telling the truth. Someone has wiped it."

Someone who must have known I'd seen it already. Because why write a message and then get rid of it before you can guarantee the person it's intended for has read it? They knew, and they made sure the evidence of it was gone before I could mention it to anyone.

"What, pray tell, did this message say?" Eva crosses her arms.

"It said . . ." But if I answer that, she'll wonder what I was asking questions about.

"Shall I tell you what it said?" she interjects. "It said, *Do what you were asked on here to do and nothing more.* Stop disappearing. You know what I think? You want it all. A complimentary holiday courtesy of Benjamin, free rein all over the yacht, and now you even want in on what's happened to these poor stewardesses by making up some nonsense message in the mirror. This trip is ruined. And I'm done protecting you."

She turns sharply and marches away. There's no point calling after her. I have to focus on figuring out who the hell did this.

It's Noah. It has to be. He was the one who put the scarf in that storage box. He was lurking around this corridor. He could have written that message on my mirror while I was snooping around Digby's and Benjamin's cabins.

Does Noah know the scarf has gone missing? Has he gone back to check yet? He must have by now, must realize that someone else has it and suspects him. Or maybe he hopes no one saw him with it because he was the one who deleted that footage.

Well, bad news, buddy. I saw you.

I know he's on watch, and that's where I find him: looking out at the horizon, hands clasped behind his head. There's no one else around, but even he must appreciate murdering me on the bridge would be far too public. In the corner, unoccupied, is the captain's desk, calling out to me.

"Hey, Noah," I say softly.

It's satisfying to watch him jump. He turns, wide-eyed, then laughs nervously.

"Hello," he says. "You're not supposed to be here. Are you okay after, uh, earlier? I heard what happened."

Oh, he's so convincing. The stammering, the uncertainty, the eager politeness. His gaze drifts down to my breasts, still prominent in the red bikini Eva loaned me, then snaps back up to my face, in that way men do that they somehow think is subtle. Did he kill Lola to satisfy some unrequited lust? Gets his kicks murdering beautiful women because they refuse to sleep with him?

Up close like this, I can see the acne dotting his chin and jawline, the way his hair hangs in greasy strands in front of his face. His nose is too narrow, with an upturned snub at the end, and his eyes are too small. But he has a nice smile, and a good body. Although when you're aiming for supermodels, it can be easy to feel slighted. Hard done by. Even though *he* wouldn't give average-looking women the time of day.

I should know. I lived the first twenty-two years of my life as one.

Well, I am what society deems attractive now. And I can use that to my advantage.

I ramp up my breathy, high-pitched voice, work up a few tears. "It's so scary!"

Immediately, his face softens.

I fling myself at him, wrapping my arms around his torso. "Do you think there's a murderer on board? What am I going to do? Will you protect me?"

His hands barely touch my back, clearly terrified of making the wrong move, but he doesn't push me away. "Of course I'll protect you. Try not to worry. We're figuring out how to handle this."

I lift my head, blinking my big eyes at him. "You were so nice, checking on me earlier, and I thought . . . I can trust you. You're not the one who hurt those poor women."

Hardly checking on me when we ran into each other, but let him think he's my hero. All men want is a damsel in distress.

He stiffens, just barely, but I can feel it. "No, I'm not. And yes, you can trust me."

"Poor Effie." I sigh.

He seems to be eating this shit up. If I can trick him into thinking I'm on his side, perhaps he'll start revealing some terrible truths. I wipe at my eyes, hoping my mascara is running prettily down my cheeks.

"Let me get you a tissue," he says, breaking from our embrace and looking around wildly. "There are some in the storage cupboard along the way—hold on."

I can't believe it. He's so wrapped up in this half-naked sobbing girl that he's abandoned the bridge to fetch me tissues.

The storage cupboard is only down the end of the corridor. He'll be two minutes at most.

Pouncing on the captain's desk, I tear open the drawers and ransack through what's inside. He has files on all the staff, and then letter after letter addressed to *Howard Asteridge* with big angry red words on the envelopes like *FINAL DEMAND* and *URGENT DO NOT IGNORE*. They've all been opened before, so I pick one at random and read.

It's from a credit card company. Demanding repayment of a staggering sum.

I check another. This one is from a county court, informing him he has thirty days to clear his debts or action will be taken. The date of the letter was two weeks ago, just before we started this charter.

They're unbelievable. Captain Howard is in *deep*.

Didn't he have loads of holiday brochures in his room? What is he playing at?

I shove the letters back in the drawer and check the small cupboard to the right of his desk. There's a mobile phone in here, tucked at the back underneath old accounts folders.

My fingers are trembling as I press its main button, and the screen comes to life. There's a crack across it, and the bottom is also damaged, like it's fallen hard. But those aren't the details I'm focusing on. Instead, I gape in horror at the background.

It's Lola, in sunglasses and a sarong, sunbathing on some beach. She's pursing her lips into a kiss and winking at the camera.

This is Lola's phone.

Why does Captain Howard have it? And why is the screen all cracked? Did she lose it during a struggle, and he pocketed it for himself? But why not chuck it overboard with her?

This doesn't make any sense. Noah hid the scarf. So how can the captain have the phone?

I try to swipe the screen to unlock it, but am prompted to input a passcode. Damn. There's no way I'll get in.

"What are you doing?"

"Oh!" I'm so startled I drop it, banging my head against the top of the cupboard. The phone clatters to the floor, but I'm able to scoop it up and shove it back inside before Noah comes hurrying over. I slam the cupboard shut and stand, rubbing my sore head and trying to stop my hands from shaking.

Noah is holding a box of tissues clutched to his chest, frowning. "That's private. Why were you looking in there?"

"I was looking for tissues!" I blurt out. "You were taking a little while so I thought that maybe there would be some in here . . . it's private? Oops! I'm so sorry."

I take some of the tissues from the box and dab at my face quickly, hoping to distract him, and to my relief he smiles.

"They were in a different place than I thought," he says. "I hope you're feeling better."

"Thanks to you." I beam. "I don't know what I'd do without you."

"Happy to help, ma'am."

"Please," I whisper, giving him a seductive smile of my own. "Call me Jasmine."

"Jasmine, then." This pleases him. "My break's in an hour if you wanted to . . . talk some more?"

"I would love that." Talk some more, maybe get you to confess that you're a psychopathic murderer and tell me whatever the fuck Captain Howard has to do with this.

He watches me as I leave, and I make sure to sway my hips and give him a show. Let him think I'm bowled over. Men will believe anything a pretty face tells them.

The wind is strong when I step outside, making my way up to the main deck, where Eva, Benjamin, and Digby will be, no doubt eager to begin lunch service after the delay with Effie. Too strong, in fact, my hair flying all over the place. Eva, Benjamin, and Digby are nowhere to be seen, so lunch must have been moved inside due to the weather.

Jade is here, though, stacking place mats from our abandoned original lunch with undisguised frustration, speaking to another stewardess. "Of course I read it. There was nothing of interest, which is why I got rid of it."

The other stewardess is scooping up the cutlery. "Sasha seemed convinced Mouse was meeting someone. Why couldn't you let us all read it?"

"I'm not in the business of giving you all a nosy peep into a dead woman's diary."

They must be talking about Lola. She had a diary?

"Stop asking questions," Jade says.

My body turns cold.

Stop asking questions.

Is *she* the one who left that message?

She spots me just as I'm thinking of leaving, her face breaking into that plastic smile she must believe looks genuine. She shoos Imogen away, then heads toward me, and there's nothing I can do. I have no sunglasses on, no added disguise. I have to tread very carefully.

"Jasmine," she says. She dials her grin down. I remember her last year ordering Hallie and the other stewardesses to always be smiling, but even she must realize beaming at me is inappropriate considering the circumstances. "I was just about to look for you. You do seem to love disappearing on us. Lunch service will begin soon. I'm so sorry for the delay."

Was that a jibe? "Thank you," I say. "It's understandable, considering what happened. Is Effie okay?"

Jade raises an eyebrow, and I realize my mistake. I shouldn't have used Effie's name, seemed so familiar with her. "Euphemia will make a full recovery, I am sure."

"I'm glad."

"I hope you know I am here for you, whatever you need," she tells me. "You do not need to walk around this yacht yourself. We are here to do your bidding."

"I have never been on a yacht before," I say, probably too quickly. "I like walking around it. And with everything going on it clears my head."

Her demeanor changes, instantly sympathetic. "Of course. I wanted to let you know personally that we are doing everything we can to resolve the situation. I apologize that it is disrupting your charter. Please let me repeat that if there is anything I can do to help, I will."

"I appreciate that."

"You know," she says, and my stomach drops, "I hope I am not overstepping the mark here, but have we met somewhere before?"

Shit. She recognizes me. I knew it would be Jade, out of anyone, that I would have to worry about. I can't stand here a second longer, not with her appraising eyes on me, not when she'll put two and two together and discover the truth.

"I—I don't think so," I say, cursing myself for stammering. "I think I just have one of those faces—"

And then—thank God. Her radio crackles, Melinda's voice coming through to say Effie is now recovering in the massage parlor, and why hasn't lunch service already begun? Digby and Benjamin are waiting.

"My apologies," Jade says. "I have to go. Please join the table inside and service will begin momentarily."

"I'm feeling a little unwell," I say, then hastily continue as she opens her mouth to offer me some solution. "I think I just need fresh air. Start without me."

"Of course." She fixes me with one last long, discerning look, then smiles again. "We'll continue our conversation another time."

I can't go in there and have lunch and pretend everything is normal, because it's *not*. I watch Jade go inside, then head in the opposite direction, toward the stern, and find one of the stewardesses. She is sitting on a deck chair, one of two left out from early this morning when Benjamin insisted we watch the sunrise together. I guess with everything that's gone on they've been forgotten about. Facing away from me like this, she could be any of them. She looks all alone; I know how that feels.

"Excuse me," I call.

She turns round, tears streaming down her cheeks; it's Sasha. The one Effie blamed for attacking her. The one who did slap Lola. Fortunately, I've accidentally come prepared for crying. I offer the tissues Noah gave me, then sit down next to her.

"I saw you running toward Effie when she screamed," I say. "I know it wasn't you."

"It doesn't matter," she murmurs. "They all think I'm a murderer."

"You're probably the only person I trust around here," I say, the words surprising me as soon as they're out, especially when I realize they might not just be a ruse to get her to talk. I might actually mean them.

"Trust?" she echoes. This seems to disappoint her. "You shouldn't trust me."

I ignore her. "You tried telling everyone Lola's death wasn't an accident and they didn't believe you. But I did. We're the only ones who want the truth."

I don't know why I didn't think of it before. Sasha can help me. If I have someone else, we can confront Noah about the bloody scarf together, find out what happened, and save anyone else from getting hurt.

Sasha bursts into a fresh set of tears, blackening her tissue with mascara, then looks at me hopelessly.

"But they're right," she says. "I *am* a murderer."

CHAPTER TWENTY-SEVEN

EFFIE

Melinda sits back with a frown. We're in the massage parlor, my head still pounding, but Melinda has flashed a torch in my eyes and insisted I'm fine, that there's no sign of concussion. The back of my hair is matted with blood. I'm desperate for a shower, but she tells me to take it easy for a while. And then she asks if I remember anything else about what happened.

I wish I did.

There's a knot of fear in my stomach that won't go away.

Melinda is disappointed when I shake my head. She leans forward, lowering her voice. "I'll be keeping an eye on Sasha, I promise you."

She believes me. The relief is palpable; I let out an exhale from deep within. "Thank you. She's been acting suspiciously ever since she got on this yacht. And she was the person who found Lola, who keeps trying to say her death wasn't an accident. Guilty conscience? Or trying to cover her back?"

"I want to assure you that you are being heard," she murmurs, "despite how it may seem. If I were captain, I'd be barring Sasha to only one room while we investigate, but—" She breaks off with a sigh. "We have to do what we can."

Sasha has been able to plead her case and go on her merry way.

When she *attacked* me. There's no getting around this one. She is targeting stewardesses. We're all in danger.

Captain Howard is just letting this happen. Either he's in denial or he's somehow culpable, because this isn't adding up anymore. Any other boat—hell, any other mode of transport *ever*—would be declaring some kind of emergency now. Contacting other vessels. Doing *something*. Not carrying on to New York like everything is fine.

"If you ever want to talk," Melinda says quietly, "I'm here. Any time."

"Why has Axel been taken off watch?"

The question surprises Melinda. She hesitates before answering. "I'm not sure if that's something I can talk about. Captain Howard wouldn't want me to."

"And you trust Captain Howard?"

She blinks. "Trust him? Effie—"

We're interrupted by a knock on the door, and Captain Howard enters the room.

"You're not filling her head with nonsense, are you, Melinda?" he says, trying to come across as lighthearted but accidentally sounding rather stern. He seems to realize too because he smiles awkwardly. "What I mean to say is, Effie should be resting. And Mr. Johnson wants a word with you."

"Sasha needs to be locked up somewhere on this yacht," I tell him. "She's a murderer and you're letting her walk around!"

Captain Howard flinches. "I cannot simply detain Sasha on hearsay. If you had *seen* her that would be different. But you have a head injury, however it was caused, meaning you might be unwell. Prone to misinterpreting or falsifying—"

"Are you saying I'm a liar?"

"Of course not. I'm merely suggesting that you need bed rest."

He's just trying to keep me quiet to suit him.

"Melinda?" Captain Howard says. "A guest has asked to see you."

She blinks, startled by his blunt tone. "On my way now, sir."

She pauses in the doorway and looks back at me, mouthing something that the captain can't see. She says it quickly, so fast I'm not sure if I've understood her.

Don't trust him.

As she disappears, I find myself, for the first time, unsettled to be alone with Captain Howard.

"When we dock, I promise there will be an investigation into your assault."

I thought I could wrap him around my little finger; now I'm not so sure.

"Keep what you know quiet, Effie," he murmurs. "If you know anything at all—keep it close to your chest until after we arrive."

I give a nod so he knows I've understood, but as soon as he leaves I let out a deep breath. What was that about? Keep what I know quiet? Is he protecting me? Warning me?

Threatening me?

"She's just in there," I hear Captain Howard say from out in the corridor.

"Effie?" Another voice. Axel's. Oh fuck.

He enters the room looking forlorn, but seems to physically pale at the sight of me, which is impressive with his never-endingly sun-kissed skin.

"How are you doing?" he asks, in a strange voice. "Is your head, um, doing better?"

"Melinda said I won't die," I say, trying to be as breezy as possible so he won't see how unnerved I am. "We can relax. You won't have to plan your funeral speech for me yet."

"About that . . ."

"About your eulogy?" I say. "Had it ready to go, did you?"

"Er, no." Why is Axel so flustered? "I meant about 'we.' I want to talk about us."

He can't be serious. I've had the "I want to talk about us" conversation many times—always started by me, because let's face it, men are lucky to even breathe in my presence—but never have I initiated it less than an hour after the person on the receiving end was nearly murdered.

"You're a really special girl," he starts, and I have to hold my hand up to stop him.

"Cut the crap," I say. "Are you seriously breaking up with me? When I was almost killed? Is that what's happening?"

Axel puts both his palms up in surrender. "I never wanted this to be, like, a complicated thing. And now Imogen knows, and it's just got messy. What did you go and tell her for? Let alone with everything else going on. I think we should just . . . call it quits."

This coming from a man who two days ago spent his break telling me I was sensational, that he was going to give me a tour of his favorite parts of California and I'd have to show him where I grew up someday. That as soon as we docked he was taking me to the fanciest restaurant in New York and treating me like the princess I deserve to be. That Imogen was history, he couldn't wait to get rid of her; the future was all about us.

What utter shit.

And I *believed* him. I'm as bad as Imogen is. He's used us both.

"Just go," I say. "I don't want to hear another word that comes out of your mouth. And don't think you've gotten away with whatever you were up to after the party. You were late seeing me, and you weren't with Imogen. I'm going to find out the truth."

"Effie—"

"I *especially* don't want to hear my name. You got what you wanted. We're done. Now leave me alone."

Coward that he is, he doesn't try to argue. Just takes off looking visibly relieved, which should make me want to throw something at him, but there's been enough head injuries for today. I'm so done with everyone.

I end up lying on the massage bed, angry at the tears that spill down my cheeks. I shouldn't be crying over that bastard. I don't even think I am. He's just the final straw, the last push I needed to completely break down.

I'm totally alone.

Can I really blame anyone? I've been a bitch. And now I'm reaping the consequences.

My hands automatically reach for my cell in my pocket, taking me to Dad's number. He's still in there. The house phone from my childhood, because he refuses to join the twenty-first century and get a cell phone of his own. We haven't spoken in so long, he'd ask who was on the other end if I called. Sometimes I think even if I said, "It's Effie!" he'd pause for a moment, then ask, "Who?"

I press the button to call him anyway, heart in my mouth, but it doesn't ring. There's still no signal, no way of contacting the outside world. I try again, even though I know it's pointless, and then I try sending messages to my brothers. The only reason I even have their numbers is because our grandmother passed away a couple of years ago, but I decided to skip the funeral to avoid an awkward reunion.

I regret that.

I regret a lot of things to do with my family.

We should talk when the charter season ends, I write to them. *I think I'm coming home. Maybe we can start again?*

The messages don't send, because there's still no Wi-Fi either, stuck in a permanent request to try again. In my frustration I throw my phone across the room, watching it hit the wall and fall to the floor. The screen cracks across the middle, damaged forever.

CHAPTER TWENTY-EIGHT

SASHA

'I've said it out loud and now I can't take it back.

Jasmine stares at me, appalled. "I'm sorry? You're . . . what?"

Dr. Martin's office is cold, but it's not why I stand here shivering.

"What are we going to do?" I whisper.

He takes me in his arms, and a gesture I once found so comforting becomes unbearable. I break free, pushing him away.

This changes things. His face turns hard, cold as the room.

"We aren't going to do anything," he tells me.

"But . . ." And I have to speak it out loud. "But we killed her."

"I'm a murderer," I repeat. "That's why I'm here."

Jasmine doesn't recoil. "You killed Lola?"

I shake my head. "Not her." Say her name out loud. *Say it!* "Janet Lesley."

"Who's Janet Lesley?"

Everything that has been bubbling up inside me, everything I've tried to squash down and ignore, is bursting to come out. I take a juddery breath, and begin.

"I was a nurse," I whisper. "Back in London. Had finished my training only three months before. Janet Lesley was a woman who came in with appendicitis. I was on that night with Dr. Martin."

Something about this makes Jasmine flinch. "Dr. Martin?" she repeats.

"He's one of the consultants," I explain. "When I first joined, he was very welcoming."

"Who have we here, then?" he says, all charm, offering me his hand. He has shiny white teeth, and the corners of his eyes crinkle when he smiles. He's older than me, but he's good-looking. Obscenely so. And as he glances up and down appreciatively I know he's thinking the same about me.

"New nurse," my line manager replies, halfway through giving me a tour of the wing I'll be attached to and less than enthused. "This is—"

"Sasha Quill," I breathe.

"Dr. Martin," he tells me. "It's a pleasure."

Jasmine bites her lip. "How old was Janet Lesley?"

"Twenty-six." I keep my eyes closed for a moment. I am the same age as she was now.

"What happened?" Jasmine asks. The perennial question.

Janet Lesley is sitting up in the hospital bed, drip attached and pale, but surgery done. There were complications, and she is made to stay under observation rather than go home.

"She says her stomach still hurts," her boyfriend insists. "And she feels hot to the touch."

"Perfectly normal," Dr. Martin tells him. "She'll be a bit sore for a few days."

In the corridor, I corner him. "Her white blood count is more elevated than expected. Maybe we should put her on some stronger antibiotics."

"She's fine," Dr. Martin says. "I'll keep an eye on her."

"She wasn't fine," I say to Jasmine. "She was showing early signs of peritonitis. I wasn't working the following day, and by the time I came back her immune system was so weak she had developed pneumonia and sepsis. We all tried to save her . . . but it was too late. She died."

One image that sticks with me is when we wheeled her away to surgery. She was barely conscious by that point. I knew then that she wasn't going to come back.

Later, Dr. Martin broke the news to her boyfriend, who raged and shouted and told us all we were to blame, and then, later, to her parents: to a mother stood frozen in shock, one hand on the wall to stop her from falling; to a father already collapsed on the floor, screaming, a terrible, animalistic keening pouring from his mouth.

"There was an internal investigation afterward," I whisper. "We were cleared of any wrongdoing, and that was that. We were expected to get back to normal, bar some reflection added in and extra supervisions for me. But I couldn't. I ran away. I knew about superyachts because Dr. Martin had told me about them, and it seemed like the perfect solution."

When Dr. Martin is called away for something and promises to be back in five minutes, I take the opportunity to rifle around his desk and am stunned when I find a photograph of a young woman. She's wearing some kind of uniform.

Why does he have this?

It's the first thing I ask when he returns.

"She's my daughter," he says. "Tessa."

"You have a daughter?" She looks around my age, only a few years younger. "You never mentioned her before."

He has a wife and two sons. They're eight and thirteen, and she's a teacher, but I don't want to talk about them so I don't know a lot. There's a family photo on his desk of the four of them on holiday at the Grand Canyon. The daughter is nowhere in sight.

"She has a different mother," he says.

He gives me the full story—how his first wife cheated on him, how he sees his daughter every other weekend when she isn't working but wants more time with her, how great of a bond they share.

"What's with her outfit?" I ask.

"She's a stewardess."

"Like a flight attendant?"

"No, no. On boats. Superyachts. They go off for months at a time all around the world. She's found an easy way to disappear."

He distracts me then; he doesn't want to talk about his daughter. Not at this moment. He wants to do something else.

"He said his daughter was a stewardess?" Jasmine asks, and I nod. *An easy way to disappear.* If only that turned out to be true.

"You were cleared of any wrongdoing," Jasmine says. "You're not a killer. It's awful, what happened, but it's not your fault."

I could let her carry on thinking that. I could give the usual excuses I've tried giving myself: I was new to the job, I put my trust in a far more senior person.

Or I could tell the truth. "The investigation didn't have all the details. I lied. Dr. Martin lied."

Now Jasmine looks concerned. "Lied about what?"

My heart is pounding. A panic attack threatens to arrive at any moment, and as soon as it does I'll be incapable of speaking. I have to get the full story out, get everything off my chest.

"Dr. Martin had a drinking problem. I knew and kept it quiet."

Above us, the clouds have parted, allowing the sun to peek through, making the sea glitter. I suck in the salty ocean air.

"Why would you keep it quiet for him?" Jasmine must read something in my expression, because she knows without my having to answer. "You were having an affair."

Shame hits, unforgiving. "Yes."

It felt so good at the time. Every nurse was in love with Dr. Martin, but he chose me. Called me beautiful. Made me the center of attention.

Which is why when I first noticed the half empty bottle of whiskey Dr. Martin tried to tuck away after I walked in unannounced, I pretended it was something else.

But then his behavior changed too. His hands shook in operations, making him clumsier, and sometimes he stumbled or had to redo something. His breath stank of booze.

"I did confront him before . . . before it happened. I told him it had to stop." Am I trying to appeal to her or myself?

Dr. Martin had shouted at an elderly patient when they refused an injection, and the senior nurse was fuming, ready to go to war. I volunteered to talk to him so he would come back and apologize, and when I walked in he was swigging straight from the bottle.

"Sasha!" he said, but there was no way he could explain his actions. "I'm . . ."

"You're drinking," I said. "You've been drinking for weeks. And I've been keeping quiet because—I don't know! Because of what we have. But now I have to tell someone."

"I'll stop. Don't say anything." He went to the sink in the corner of his office and poured the contents of the whiskey bottle down it.

"I still think someone should know."

He kissed me then, passionately, and told me he loved me.

"He'd never said that," I say to Jasmine. "I know now that was classic manipulation, but at the time—I don't know. He started promising things."

"Six months and I'll leave her," he said. "Then we can be together. I'm sorry. This ends today."

"I thought it was over," I say. "But during Janet's surgery, I saw his hands shaking, and he dropped a scalpel and another had to be fetched. And I wondered . . . but I thought maybe it was just lasting side effects. After her complications began, I checked the charts and he had changed them. Her results looked like the sepsis came out of nowhere, when that was never true. He was too busy thinking about his next drink to take the warning signs seriously, and then covered his ass afterward."

"Why didn't you report it at the time?" Jasmine says quietly.

The man is drunk in front of me, his breath stinks of alcohol, and it's his fault Janet has died. And my fault too. If I had told someone else what I saw, she could have been saved in time.

"We have to tell them immediately," I say. "You were under the influence during the surgery. You said you stopped! And then you changed her chart results."

"You're not going to say anything. Accidents happen, Sasha. They happen every day and you need to get that round your thick skull before you think about causing any problems."

"Dr. Martin—"

"I won't spend another second arguing with you. Accidents happen. Repeat after me."

He's so frightening I give in. "Accidents happen."

"Do you want to go to prison? Be barred from nursing? You're as much to blame."

"I didn't know you were still drinking!"

"Who's to say you didn't? The nurses aren't dumb. They know about our affair. Maybe I'll blame it on you. Who are they going to believe? A well-respected consultant with over twenty years' experience or a nurse known for sleeping around?"

"He threatened you," Jasmine says, and for a second I forget I've been telling her, the memories so vivid it's as though I've been reliving them.

I touch my face; it's wet with tears. "I didn't know what would happen if the truth came out. I lied when it was time to give my statement. I was a coward."

"And then you ran away."

Like all good cowards do.

"You see now," I say. "I deserve everyone thinking I'm the one that hurt Effie and murdered Lola."

"But you're not," Jasmine says. "And you didn't kill Janet Lesley either. You were a nurse just out of training. He was a consultant, for God's sake. He took advantage of you."

"You don't despise me?" I whisper.

"The worst thing you've done is prevent the truth from coming out for her poor family. You know you need to fix it."

Yes. This is why I've been plagued by nightmares, racked with anxiety, consumed by panic attacks. I've tried to run away and it hasn't worked, and my body is punishing me for it. And now, because life is just that ironic, I've stumbled into all this.

"You're not the only one hiding your past," Jasmine murmurs. "I'm not here as a guest. I'm here because I was a deckhand on *Ophelia* last year."

For a second I don't think I've heard her properly, but she returns my shocked gaze with a sincere one of her own. She was a *deckhand*? On this yacht?

"My best friend and I started yachting together," she says. "Her name was Hallie. We were both in care as teenagers and had the same foster parents. She was—" Her voice catches. It takes her a moment to recover. "She is *the* most important person to me. We ended up getting a flat together, making ends meet, and then she saw an episode of *Below Deck* and wanted to try it out. So we did. She was a stewardess, I was a deckhand. We had a whole season that went perfectly, and then we traveled around Europe with the money we had earned. But the following season, last year, we worked on *Ophelia*."

I can't believe this. "With Captain Howard?"

"With Captain Howard," Jasmine confirms. "Melinda and Jade too. And our guests toward the end of the season . . . Benjamin Edmondson and Digby Johnson."

She's repeating the same charter. The exact one she's already done, except this time she's a guest. "And no one has recognized you? Not even Jade?"

"I look very different to how I did last year," she says. "And I've changed my voice, put on a different walk. Digby and Benjamin wouldn't have looked twice at me before, so they're not a problem, but I've tried to keep as much distance as possible from the others."

"But why come back?"

"Hallie disappeared. She was working the late shift, and then she was gone."

It was her. The stewardess that went missing last year, the one Effie told me about at the restaurant. "I think I heard about it from one of the other stewardesses . . ."

"Yachting loves gossip." Jasmine lets out a short laugh. "The official line is that she fell overboard while out smoking a cigarette. Except the weather was fine that night. They didn't properly look for her in the morning. I was distraught, so Captain Howard dumped me at the harbor and said I'd be better off dealing with the trauma at home."

"Captain Howard did that?"

"Yeah." She shakes her head in disgust. "He did the same 'throwing the flowers over the side' trick too, in case you thought that was original. Only problem is this time we're in the Atlantic so he can't get rid of anyone asking questions."

"Didn't the police do anything?"

Jasmine laughs again. "Fuck all. It was a shoddy investigation, and that was that. No one is bothered about a girl who grew up in care. I tried getting local newspapers involved, but nothing came of it. The only option for finding out the truth was to come back."

She's jubilant, chin jutted high, and I can't help admiring her. She's the exact opposite of me. Where I ran away, eager to get as far from trouble as possible, she's done everything in her power to run straight toward it.

"And boy, have I uncovered some things." We're still alone, but she lowers her voice anyway. "Hallie left a note for me the night she disappeared. I wasn't able to get to it until now. It said: *We have to leave tomorrow*. And that's not all. The official report into her disappearance is missing loads of details. Axel started working for *Ophelia* straight after the season ended, and he said he had to do a lot of cleaning, like tidying up a crime scene."

My mind races. "Do you think Lola's death and Hallie's disappearance are linked? Effie's attack?"

"They have to be. It's too much of a coincidence otherwise."

"There are things going wrong on this yacht—missing champagne, Runa has lost one of her knives, and even guest jewelry is being stolen."

"Eva has lost a couple of things," Jasmine says. "Do you know about the life jackets?"

"The life jackets?"

"I overheard Melinda and Axel talking. They're missing too. All of them."

How can that be? Without them, if anything were to happen . . .

Who am I kidding? The worst has already happened.

"And the captain knows about this?"

Jasmine nods. "He's the one who told Melinda to keep it quiet, and to tell Axel to do the same. Axel has been taken off watch too. Something weird is going on around here and it's all got to be connected. The captain even has Lola's phone, hidden in one of his cupboards in the bridge."

He has her *phone*?

"What if they've exposed something they shouldn't?" Jasmine says. "That's got to be what Hallie's note is referring to. Maybe Lola found out the same."

Lola's secrets. What if she stumbled on one that got her killed?

"And Effie too?"

"We need to talk to her. But we have to be careful. I got a threatening message."

"You got *what*?"

"Written on the mirror in my cabin in lipstick. *Stop asking questions.*"

I can feel my pulse jumping in my throat, and for once a panic attack wouldn't be such an outlandish response.

"This is dangerous," I say. "People are getting hurt. *Killed.*"

"Which brings me to Noah," she says.

"Noah?"

"Let me show you."

By the time we reach her cabin I'm barely holding it together. She heaves her suitcase into the middle of the room and takes out a photograph. There are two women standing side by side, arms around each other, both grinning away at the camera. They're standing on the bow of this yacht. One is blonde, beautiful, another clone to add to the rest of us stewardesses. Her friend isn't as otherworldly; in fact she's distinctly back down to earth with her brown pigtails and toothy smile, but she's just as happy.

"That's Hallie on the left. I'm on the right. That's what I used to look like."

It's strange, but something about Jasmine in this image tugs at me, some trace of recognition. I glance across at her, but she's so different now. When I look at Hallie, an uncomfortable twist in my stomach arises, same as it did for the other stewardesses. She could be me. I could be her. I could disappear too.

"But it's this I wanted you to see," Jasmine says, bringing out the scarf Lola was wearing at the party.

It's covered in blood.

"Oh my God," I gasp. "Where did you find it?"

She explains then about sneaking into Captain Howard's and Melinda's cabins, about what she found in each of them. Her watching the footage, seeing Noah hide the scarf. How he lied to her about not remembering Lola wearing one. She asks about my fight with Lola, and I give her the full details, embarrassed.

"I hate that that was the last time I spoke to her," I say. "I was sensitive about my job because, well, you know."

But that's not important. The scarf is.

Lola's diary is screaming at me from my memory. "Lola said she was meeting someone after the party. What if it was Noah?"

"We have to confront him," Jasmine says. "He can't take on two of us at once. He's expecting me now that he's on his his break."

This is crazy. Surely Noah couldn't have done anything.

Jasmine senses my hesitation.

"You let someone get away with something terrible before," she says. "Don't do it again."

CHAPTER TWENTY-NINE

⌒

JASMINE

Noah is standing precariously on the edge of the swim platform when we find him, waves crashing against his ankles. I wonder if he is still expecting me after our conversation earlier. He seems distracted, not hearing our approach, and I'm scared we're going to startle him so much he'll topple over and fall into the sea.

Sasha filled me in on her own brushes with Noah along the way. His obsession with Effie and their altercation, his insistence she leave another deckhand alone. She seems to think he's relatively harmless, or at least she did before I showed her the scarf. We've brought it with us as evidence, though the closer we get the more I'm doubting our plan.

I'd be lying if I said I wasn't thrown by what Sasha told me about that poor woman in her hospital. Never in a million years did I expect she'd be here because of that. Not to mention . . . but no, that's a coincidence. A bizarre one for sure, but a coincidence all the same. I won't mention it to her as that would only complicate things.

I can't believe she was so stupid to let an *affair* cause such a tragedy. But no, I'm not being fair. I've observed the act men put on for younger women, all charm and facade and nothing of substance. I was a kid in care—anyone who so much as smiled at me was a god compared to how others had treated me. He would have used Sasha for his own interests and discarded her when he was bored even if something hadn't gone wrong. I bet he's done it with nurses time and time again. As if he was ever going to leave his wife. That's the oldest trick in the book.

Do I understand her actions? No. If I knew something was wrong, I'd have said so, as loudly and often as possible. But that tactic doesn't always work, as I have learned. Though as soon as we're off this boat, I'm going to make sure she does the right thing.

"Noah," I call.

He turns, smile wide, and then sees the two of us. I watch his face fall, confusion etched between his brows. "Oh. Hello, both of you. Is everything alright? You shouldn't come out here, it could be dangerous."

"Come back onto the terrace with us, then," I say in my best flirty voice.

But Noah seems to sense something isn't right here, because while he comes closer, he doesn't leave the swim platform, but stands with arms folded. "What is going on?"

Sasha doesn't have my patience. "We need to talk. What were you arguing about that day with Effie? You were grabbing hard on her wrist and didn't want to let go."

"Sasha," Noah says. "There is a guest here. We can discuss this later—"

"You don't have to worry about me being a guest," I say.

He frowns. "What do you mean?"

"Sasha's told me all about your behavior. And we want answers."

Understanding dawns on him then, that I wasn't really upset and seeking him for comfort earlier. An embarrassed flush creeps across his cheeks. "My behavior is perfectly fine."

"So grabbing Effie like that was perfectly fine?" Sasha presses.

"Not that again. I would never hurt Effie," Noah says. "I *love* her."

"Then what was that argument about?"

He takes a deep breath. "It wasn't an argument. I was asking her about something. I'd thought I'd got the wrong end of the stick. But actually I was right. I found out—I found out that she and . . ."

I'm lost, but Sasha seems to know what he's talking about. "You found out she was fucking Axel, didn't you?"

He hangs his head. "I was so mad. He gets *everything*. I wanted to— God, I don't know. I thought if I . . . if it was a moment of passion, I could convince her . . . I don't know. I grabbed her, I wanted to—"

This doesn't sound good. "You wanted to?"

"If I kissed her, she'd forget him. That we could . . . I know how stupid that seems. But she shrieked, pulled away."

Rejection. A classic excuse. I raise my eyebrows. "So you got angry, as men often do when they feel they're owed something—"

"No! That's not what happened!"

"And Lola?" Sasha asks. "Were you interested in her too? Did she reject you as well?"

"Wait," Noah says. "What does Lola have to do with this?"

"Lola is dead," I snap.

"You think I've forgotten that I helped pull her lifeless body back here myself?"

"It wasn't an accident," Sasha says. "I've been telling everyone that."

"You can't think—no. You can't seriously think I had *anything* to do with—"

"Lola was strangled," Sasha says. "There were bruises. Someone put them there."

"Someone good with using rope," I say, "or perhaps a scarf."

And then I take Lola's scarf out, and Noah's face pales.

"How did you . . ." He can't finish his sentence.

"How did I find this?" I say. "I hardly think that matters. What matters is what this means."

"I can explain!"

"So you're not going to deny this is Lola's scarf," I say. "Or that there's blood on it."

Noah talks fast. "The—the blood wasn't . . . it's not *hers*. She had given it to me as a joke, said I'd need her comfort scarf more than she did. I was wearing it and got a nosebleed. When I saw what a mess I'd made, I panicked. She was always going on about how it was some designer brand. But it started raining, and I knew Axel would go mad if I wasn't on deck, so I hid it in one of the storage boxes as there was no time. But then . . . the next morning she was dead, and I didn't know what to do."

A nosebleed? How *convenient*. Sasha clearly thinks the same. "You said she gave this to you as you needed it more. Why?"

"She said she knew I was crazy about Effie, that it was never going to happen. And then she told me what I already knew—that she and Axel were sleeping together. I cried about it, she said she'd get Effie back for me. I hate that man. You want to blame someone for all this, look at him."

Axel. Is this Noah's own jealousy talking, or is there something more? Axel could overpower Lola, could overpower pretty much anyone on this yacht.

"He gets away with everything." The sheer bitterness of his tone is evident. "He got Zara pregnant. He sleeps with Effie and treats her like shit. He messes Imogen around. It's not fair. When there are nice guys like me . . ."

"Did you see anything else at the party?" Sasha asks. "Did Lola tell you anything else when she gave you the scarf?"

His brow furrows. "She said she knew things about people. Secrets. That there was one in particular that was going to change her life."

Secrets again. What secret did Lola discover? How was it going to change her life? And why did it end up getting her killed?

"Were you able to get any information from her about it?"

"No. But after, I ended up speaking to Benjamin. He was giving me advice, saying it's better to be forceful—"

"What does this have to do with Lola?" I interrupt. I don't want to hear about Benjamin and his *forceful* advice, for God's sake.

"While I was talking to him, I saw her with Runa. Their conversation looked pretty serious. Whatever the secret is, I think it's to do with her."

"The chef?" I think of Runa, our conversation. She was the last person to see Lola alive after all. Is she hiding more than she's letting on?

"Can I have the scarf now?" Noah mumbles. "I promised Lola I would look after it, and I need to honor that. The blood is from my nosebleed, it has nothing to do with her."

What do we do? If we don't hand it over, we're admitting we don't believe his story. And where does that leave us? With him potentially knowing we're a risk if he really is a murderer. I exchange a glance with Sasha and she nods.

Reluctantly, I hold it out to him. But when I let go, he seems to as well, or maybe he never had it in his grasp at all. In any case, the wind seizes hold of it instead, whipping it up into the air before sending it catapulting down into the murky waters below.

"Shit!" I yell. The scarf is visible for a few seconds, floating on the surface, but then a wave crashes over it and it vanishes for good.

"I'm sorry!" Noah shouts. "I thought you were still holding it!"

Did he really lose it by accident? Or on purpose? I could scream. Sasha does, shouting in dismay even though it's long gone.

"You do believe me about all this," Noah says, "don't you?"

I open my mouth, but his radio interrupts us. "*Noah, Noah, this is the captain. Can you come to the bridge deck?*"

"I've gotta go," he says. "You're going to keep all of this quiet, right?"

We have to agree; what else is there to do? The two of us are left standing next to the swim platform, seeing the movement of the water underneath it, and we make our way upstairs to safer ground.

Sasha speaks first. "What do you reckon? About what he said?"

"I don't know what to think," I confess. "He seemed genuinely upset, but that doesn't mean anything. The scarf going overboard . . . I'm not sure if that was an accident."

"The nosebleed excuse?" Sasha's voice drips with disgust. "I can't buy that. Do you think Axel could do something like Noah is insinuating?"

"I have no idea."

"Lola definitely had some kind of secret. She had a diary, and Jade threw it overboard. Should we talk to Runa?"

"She's difficult to talk to," I tell her, informing her of my conversation with Runa. "I think we should focus on ruling other things out. Like the owner's suite. It's where Axel started cleaning after the charter last year. It's the only place I haven't checked."

"And if Axel was up there cleaning when no one is allowed . . ."

"Exactly."

"You're right. We need to go there."

"Together, then?" I say, holding my hand out. "Me and you?"

Sasha hesitates, so I lean over, take her hand in mine, and squeeze.

"We need each other," I say. "You on the crew side, me on the guest. We can find out who killed Lola, who attacked Effie, and what happened to Hallie."

I watch Sasha's face. Her mascara has smudged around her eyes from her tears earlier, and she looks pale and a little dazed at everything that has happened. She presses her lips together, and for a moment I think she's going to say no, that this is too much and she's choosing to run away again and pretend none of this is true.

"Yes," she says, surprising me with her conviction. She squeezes my hand back. "Let's do it."

Thank God for that. "We'll meet in the gym an hour before dinner, and then we'll head to the owner's suite. Let's make sure this yacht never fucking sails again."

CHAPTER THIRTY

IMOGEN

I'm not going to pretend I didn't have a shit-eating grin on my face seeing Effie on the floor with that nasty head wound. Bit of blood on the deck too that Drew has had to power wash away. Ouch. Very unpleasant. Very difficult for my mouth to stop aching from how much I'm smiling about it. It suits me that the blame is on Sasha. Anyone with half a brain would otherwise be looking in my direction, the injured party to Effie and Axel's sordid little affair.

I swallow down a rising tide of sickness, smile finally fading, hand clasped at my neck. How could he do this to me? Not her. I don't expect any loyalty from that bitch. She's been jealous of me from the day we met, making up that stupid nickname. But Axel—after *everything*. Tears prick at my eyes and I squeeze them shut, refusing to let them fall. I will not cry over that man. Even with . . .

Well. I go into my cabin to grab my toothbrush. As I'm brushing my teeth, I hear someone enter the crew mess, opening and closing the cupboards and sitting down on the bench with a thud. I'm hardly looking my best, but it can't be helped. I touch up my face with powder and dab on some lip gloss, then head out.

"Are you okay?" It's Noah, eating cereal straight from the box like some kind of animal. He's asking me the question, but he doesn't look particularly great himself. His hair is sticking to his forehead, slick with sweat even though it's not that hot outside.

I pause, wondering what to say. Noah and I barely speak; I've always just seen him as Effie's little cling-on, an awkward, unfunny man who isn't worth bothering with. He wasn't there when Effie was attacked, but he's surely been told all about it. "You know what happened with Effie?"

His hand stops mid-rummage in the cereal box, and I make a mental note to never eat from it again. "Captain Howard came to the bridge and explained. I'm glad she's okay."

"Mmm." I'm not going to agree with him.

"Everyone thinks it's Sasha," he says. "I'm inclined to agree. I think she's up to something. I don't trust her."

This surprises me; I'd always thought Noah had no critical thinking when it came to women. Since when has he had an issue with Sasha?

But it suits me just fine. "I don't trust her either."

"She hasn't said anything to you about me, has she?"

I frown, confused. "No? Like what?"

"Nothing," he says quickly. "I also know about . . . Effie and Axel." My body stiffens of its own accord, and I hate that he notices. "I know how you feel. Effie is . . . and you love Axel . . . we're the same."

"We're not the same," I snap. How dare he compare us? His unrequited crush on Effie is nothing like Axel and me. "And I don't *love* him."

Now he is the one who sounds uncertain, echoing my "Mmm" in a tone I'm not sure is mocking or just plain disbelief. The crew mess is silent for an awkwardly long time, only the hum of the engine making any sound. I don't have to stand here. Jade wasn't best pleased when I ran off during lunch service, but I pretended I must have eaten something bad that morning and had to go.

I'm about to make my excuses to leave when he speaks again. "I know you think I'm weird." Mind reader. "But Axel treats women badly. He did it to Zara as well."

Zara? I frown. Surely Axel didn't fuck her too? Surely he hasn't messed me around *that* much? "What do you mean?"

And then he tells me. "She was pregnant. Axel was the father."

I'm numb, my body freezing as if in an effort to protect itself from what it's hearing.

Zara. Pregnant.

"How do you know this?" I whisper.

"Lola told me," he says. "She found her pregnancy test. It's why she had to leave."

Her pregnancy test.

This is why Zara was asked to go? Why she couldn't even say good-bye to the rest of us? Why Sasha showed up two days later and has caused nothing but chaos ever since?

"Mouse spread vicious rumors," I say, surprising myself. "You shouldn't believe everything she said."

I don't listen to whatever else he's trying to say. I make my way up the stairs almost in a daze. The farther I get from his words the better. My body is on autopilot, so I realize too late I'm about to collide with Drew, who is also on his way up and doesn't see me, and then I crash into him and we both fall, me landing on top of him hard as he hits the ground. Whatever he's holding drops, clanging down and ending up about five steps down.

"Jesus!" he says. "Ouch!"

"Shit," I say, scrambling to my feet. "Where did you come from? Change your mind coming down or something and have to go back up?"

"I'm fine, thanks, Imogen," Drew mutters. "No need to apologize, you're alright. I was coming from the engine rooms if you must know."

The engine rooms? "What were you doing in there?"

"Checking something for Melinda." He rises to his feet gingerly, rubbing at his chin. "That's definitely going to hurt in the morning."

I move sideways so he can pass me to fetch whatever he dropped. "Sorry."

"Ah, there it is!" he declares, then offers me a small smile. "I get it. We've all got other things on our minds."

"And yet," I say, "duty calls. Can't leave the guests waiting too long."

But I still decide to take the long route back to them, my radio suspiciously silent to such an extent I even check if it's still on. When I first got on this yacht, the biggest I've ever worked on, I was sure I'd never be able to know my way around, but now I have these winding corridors down pat. Outside one window, I spy Sasha and one of the escorts deep in conversation. It's tempting to stay and figure out what's going on, but then I'm distracted by my own tear-inducing nightmare.

Axel is walking toward me from the opposite end of the corridor. Or Shithead, as I've affectionately decided to call him from now on. He's spotted me, stopping in his tracks, but it's too obvious for him to just straight up turn around and hurry away, even though that's exactly what I'm contemplating doing.

"Imogen," he says reluctantly.

"Oh, don't look so scared," I hiss, even as my heart squeezes at the sight of him. "I don't bite. Well, not anymore."

"Look, I'm not going to pretend I'm perfect—"

"Gosh, aren't you? That'd be a first."

He sighs. "If you're going to be childish, there's no point having a conversation."

The cheek. I march over to him, hands on hips. "How dare you. Do you realize how"—I stop short of saying how hurt I am, and quickly pivot—"how *pathetic* you are? Such low self-esteem you have to seek validation from two women instead of one?"

"I was going to apologize," he says. "But forget it."

And I was going to tell you something I thought would change everything, that night at the party, and now I don't know what to do about it.

"I wouldn't have accepted it anyway," I snap. "You're a waste of space, an absolute nothing of a—"

"I said *forget it*!" Axel shouts, slamming his fist into the wall and making me jump.

There's a mark from where his fist made its impact. Even he looks shocked but can't hide the fury still burning in his eyes.

Axel has always had temper issues but he's never been like this, especially not with me. My heart is thudding; I think I might actually be afraid of him.

He's instantly contrite, the calling card of any man who's done wrong. "Shit. That wasn't about you. It's all getting on top of me at the moment. I'm sorry."

My gaze flickers to the wall, to the chipped paint. *Could he . . .*

God, what am I thinking?

Shaken to my core, I don't call after him as he marches away. There's something terrifying about being a woman and knowing that if he wanted to, the man you are with could end your life and you'd be powerless to stop him.

CHAPTER THIRTY-ONE

JASMINE

The way to the owner's floor is through the interior staircase. The private terrace above has no exterior exit, to keep it as exclusive as possible. Once you're in, there's only one way out.

Unless you jump.

Sasha takes so long getting to the gym I'm worried she's been waylaid with work from Jade, but after an agonizing wait she arrives through the terrace doors, explaining she had to change the bedsheets and put a load of washing on, and then got made to vacuum every floor.

"I think Jade is punishing me," she says. "I'm not allowed near the guests until dinner, and I'm being kept as far from the rest of the crew as possible."

For my part, I have spent the afternoon with Benjamin in his cabin. Not an ideal way to pass the time, but when the alternative was board games in the main salon under Jade's watchful eye, it was almost tolerable. I can't have another conversation with her, can't finish what we started before. She'll catch on, I know she will.

We walk past the expensive gym equipment, dust-free from regular cleaning and lack of use—Eva does an hour on the treadmill and bike in here every morning but other than that I think it sits empty—and just as I'm about to open the door to the interior Sasha grabs me.

Then I hear them. Voices. I risk peering through the glass panel in the door and spot Captain Howard talking to Digby. Without exchanging a word Sasha and I understand that we're going to eavesdrop, pressing our bodies to the wall so we cannot be seen.

"You worry too much," Digby says.

"I worry just the right amount," Captain Howard replies.

"This is your last season before you retire. Concentrate on that. And you're joining us for dinner tonight, aren't you?"

"That's right."

"What were you doing up there, anyway?" Digby asks.

Captain Howard was in the owner's suite?

"Oh—just checking on a few things. But Lola . . ."

"Was unfortunate," Digby finishes for him. "All it has meant is speeding us along."

"Yes, I've told Melinda to stretch *Ophelia* as far as she'll go."

"Come on." Digby must be ushering him, as I hear footsteps. "We need to talk properly. That deckhand of yours . . ." His voice fades away down the corridor.

"Are they gone?" Sasha whispers after a few seconds.

I ease the door open and poke my head out, scanning the empty hallway. "I can't see anyone."

"Let's go," Sasha says.

She gives me a thumbs-up, and we start ascending the stairs, with their golden banisters and red-carpeted floors. When we reach the top a huge double door blocks our path, but thankfully it swings open without challenge, inviting us inside.

A small corridor with rosewood-veneer floorboards leads out to a wide-open living space on the right. From where we're standing, there are doors hidden within the wall, only the handles visible. The carpet is thick and white, but patterned grey rugs are dotted about too, allowing a sense of homeyness.

We open the first door before heading farther in and find a luxurious wet room. There are two sinks with stainless steel taps and a huge mirror above. Light-grey tiles cover the floor and walls, and at the back the shower controls the rest of the space. A large square window peers out onto the sky, allowing light to flood in. Beyond the spectacle, the sheer opulence, there's nothing to be found here. We shut the door and walk into the living area.

The whole room is shaped like an L, wrapping round to a dining area and more seats, as if the three sofas facing the biggest flat-screen television I have ever seen aren't enough. The walls are lined with books, all classic literature, travel guides, or language studies. There are sculptures too, white marble that must have cost thousands. The entire back of the room is glass paneled, allowing the full view of the sea and sky. Out on the terrace there are more seats, a hot tub, and gym equipment.

We return to the small corridor of doors. Another bathroom, with a bath large enough for six people. And the bedroom, complete with a walk-in wardrobe area that's bigger than all the crew cabins put together. The bed is unmade, sheets stripped. I falter when I see it, king-size and dominating the room. Something about that bed is screaming out to me: *terrible things have happened here.*

"What's that?" Sasha says. She walks across the plush carpet and bends down next to the corner of the bed, picking something up from the floor. "Look." She holds her palm out, revealing a gold hoop earring.

"That could be anyone's," I say. "What does it matter?"

"No," Sasha says. "I know this earring. It's Imogen's."

Imogen's? "But how? None of you are allowed in the owner's suite."

"She said she lost them," Sasha says.

"She could have been sneaking around with Axel," I say.

She nods. "That's definitely possible."

We glance around the rest of the bedroom. Sasha pockets the earring and starts pulling open the chest of drawers, then gasps. "Jasmine, come see this."

I don't need telling twice.

The bottom drawer is full of jewelry. Loads of it. Necklaces, earrings, rings, bracelets, even some cuff links and chokers.

It's the stolen guest items. They're all here.

I spot Eva's amethyst ring, put it in my own pocket with a quick explanation to Sasha.

"Captain Howard can't be the one stealing these," Sasha whispers. "He's a captain! He probably earns hundreds of thousands a year."

Oh shit. I haven't told her what else I know.

Her face falls when I tell her about the debts, the court wanting their money by the end of the month or else.

"But this?" Sasha doesn't want to believe it. "What—he's going to sell off a load of jewelry that fast and somehow recuperate his funds? That doesn't make sense."

"Some of this stuff must be worth way more."

"Even if he were able to sell it for the same kind of price, which I doubt, there's no way he'd be able to find a buyer in such a short amount of time."

"But what if it hasn't been a short amount of time? What if Hallie found this and called him out on it? What if he's been taking a year, maybe even longer, to put all this together? Maybe he's been selling it off regularly, maybe he has a buyer already."

"Surely not," Sasha says, but she looks more doubtful now.

"He has Lola's phone, Sasha. He's behind this."

"What do we do?"

"I'll give Eva back her ring," I say. "I'll tell her I found it at the bottom of the hot tub or on the floor somewhere and to keep it safe, not wear it again. But everything else needs to stay here. He can't know we've found it. No one can."

Sasha nods, biting her lip. "Would you really kill over this? Some stolen jewelry?"

"Debt makes people do crazy things. He's desperate."

"What if he's worried Effie knows too?"

"Didn't you tell me Effie was a notorious gossip?" I say. "She'll spread anything like wildfire. She mustn't know."

Sasha frowns. "She said to me, just before she was attacked . . . that she'd heard something. And she's keeping that quiet so far. But where does Noah fit into this?"

"He must be working with him," I say.

The last room is a small, more practical office space, painted black and without a window. It's artificial light that allows us to see anything in here. There's a big solid oak desk, and on top of it a laptop and dozens of documents. In the far corner is a half-drunk cup of tea, lukewarm.

"Oh my God," Sasha says. "This must have been where he was just now. There's a whole workspace!"

"What has he been doing?"

I grab at the documents, flicking through them, but to my disappointment they are nothing but reports from various businesses. Financial statements. Tax records.

"Does the captain own several businesses?" I ask, brow furrowing at them all. "Why wouldn't he just sell these off before getting into so much debt?"

Sasha goes to the laptop. "Jasmine!"

I whip around at Sasha's urgent cry. "What is it?"

She points at the laptop screen, face pale. "This is . . . I think . . ."

Her horrified reaction doesn't prepare me for what is on there.

It's a photograph of one of the stewardesses. I don't know which, because her back is turned. She is washing her hair in the shower, the rest of her body visible. I know this shower. The tiny space. I've been in there myself many times.

It's the one in the crew mess.

I click the arrow button at the bottom, and there are more images. Different stewardesses, all getting in or out of the shower. In some their faces are visible. They're all here: Jade, Effie, Imogen, Lola, Sasha, and, as we click back far enough, Zara.

"I'm going to be sick," Sasha says. "There must be a *camera* down there. This is too far now. We have to confront him. The others will be on our side if we show them this."

It occurs to me, with horrific clarity, that Sasha and the rest of the crew might not be aware of what I found in Captain Howard's bedroom.

"He has a gun," I say. "Captain Howard has a gun."

"*What?*" Sasha gasps.

"He keeps it in his bedside drawer."

This is dangerous, my brain screams. *Leave. Leave like Hallie wanted you to.*

Except I can't.

"You don't think he'd actually . . ." Sasha's words trail off.

"I don't know what he'd do. But we can't risk saying anything. You just need to find and destroy that camera."

"I will. That's the first thing I'm going to do."

I'm still clicking back through the images, noting their careful curation. Everyone uses this shower. There should be pictures of Axel and Drew and Noah and Runa too. But there aren't. Captain Howard is only interested in the stewardesses and has deleted the others. And then I have clicked back very far, landing on an image that isn't from this season. A stewardess who isn't on this charter.

"Sasha," I manage to choke out.

She's seen it too. Her face is full of terror.

Hallie.

CHAPTER THIRTY-TWO

EFFIE

When I wake up, it's difficult to know what time it is. The massage parlor doesn't have any windows, controlled by lights that can be dimmed to whatever setting the client desires. It's meant to be peaceful in here, with soft, soothing music playing, and there's a lingering smell of lavender from the oil selection. But it feels too closed in now, and the dark doesn't help. It could be noon. It could be midnight.

I sit up gingerly, feeling for my head wound, the gauze wrap already slipping slightly. Melinda clearly didn't do a good enough job. I wrench it off, feeling woozy at the sight of the dried blood, and toss it into the bin for someone else to take care of later. My phone is still on the ground, crack in the screen visible from here.

It's uncomfortable, bending down to reach it, but I manage, the time on the screen telling me it's just gone seven in the evening. Dinner service will be commencing. I have slept all afternoon, but I don't feel much better. My head is hurting not just from being attacked, but from trying to come to terms with everything. Why would Sasha hurt me? Why would she kill Lola? What is she hiding about her past?

I have to find out.

A shower is my first priority. Whoever was in here last has left it in a state, everything strewn about and the shower head half unscrewed, but I'm too preoccupied to care. The lukewarm water is a relief, to feel clean again incredible. After putting on a new uniform I make my way to the galley, which is a hive of chaotic activity, Runa barking orders, Jade shouting at Imogen to listen, Sasha gathering the side dishes together, but they all stop and stare when I walk in.

"Euphemia," Jade says. "What are you doing here? You are meant to be resting."

It's funny—any other time and I'd be relishing the opportunity to have a break. But something is going on around here, and I have to see who is on my side. Even if that means being near Sasha. I have to know what her game is.

She looks stunned to see me, a flush appearing on her cheeks that tells me just how guilty she is.

"I can't lie around doing nothing," I tell Jade. "I would rather keep busy. Be around people."

Imogen smirks. "Scared of being alone, Effie? That doesn't surprise me. You have a knack for making enemies."

Now, there is one woman who definitely *won't* be on my side. But I don't have time for her games, not after what's happened.

"Leave it, Imogen," I say, exhausted with her already. "This isn't about you and me—"

"No?" she says. "I suppose not. It's about you and that dickhead—"

"Not in my kitchen!" Runa snaps, clicking her fingers. She shakes her head at me, not Imogen! "It is better if you leave, Effie. It is not appropriate for you to be here."

"I can't believe this," I say. "I am the victim. I am the one who was *assaulted*, and yet I am the one made to stay away. Captain Howard and Melinda will be hearing about this. Perhaps when we get off this boat or the internet starts working I'll let the world know what's been going on this season."

Jade swoops in between us all, palms out, as if we're about to start physically fighting. Not that I wouldn't mind slapping that smirk right off Imogen's pinched face. But I resist. Sasha is the only violent one around here. "Euphemia, of course you can help with dinner service.

We need all hands on deck. Everyone, let's put what is going on to the side for now and serve the guests. That is our job."

Sasha nods, too eagerly.

"Pass the cooking wine to Runa, then, Sasha," Imogen says, handing her the bottle, but pulls back just as she's about to grab it. "Don't go poisoning it, now."

"Very funny," Sasha says, snatching it from her and spilling some across her arm.

"Oh dear!" Imogen shakes her head, delighted. "Still, you're used to getting a bit of red on you, aren't you?"

"Imogen," Jade says. "What have I just said?"

"I just find it amusing we're allowing a potential murderer to help us serve dinner." She shrugs. "Is that so wrong of me?"

"Quite frankly, I don't care if Sasha is Locusta herself as long as service goes well. We can't afford any more mishaps. So deal with it."

Mishaps. That's what she calls it.

But Jade's words do the trick, and we are able to get on with it, though Runa seems distracted, having to be told twice by Jade the accommodations to tonight's courses. This didn't please Runa at all, especially because she went to the extra effort of designing menu place cards for the table, handwritten in a gold gel pen that someone left-handed like me could only dream of using. But at least she's not shouting or screaming. If Benjamin and Digby can behave and not complain, we might just get through tonight without incident.

She plates up the starters, pushing them across the counter. "Truffled wild mushrooms with potato rösti, and a side of honey-glazed almonds for the primary. Quickly now!"

Jade goes first, Benjamin's side plate tucked in the crook of her elbow and his and Digby's starters in her hands. The weather is drizzling, a strong breeze ruining any opportunity of sitting outside under the awning, so the guests are just across the way, and as the doors open I can hear their grating laughter and the clinking of glasses.

Imogen does an elaborate bow to let Sasha go ahead of her, grinning when she hurries past avoiding any of our eyes. In fact, she's got her nose so far up in the air she doesn't see Imogen stick her foot out, taking full advantage, and it sends her flying.

The plate goes flying too, smashing to the floor and breaking into pieces, food splattered everywhere. The noise and chatter from next door comes to a sudden stop, so I know they've heard the chaos too, and Jade comes barging back within seconds, face like thunder that turns to horror at the scene. Sasha's on her knees, trying to salvage some of it, while Imogen cackles with laughter and Runa throws her hands up in defeat. I allow myself a small smile. It just feels good to see Sasha on the ground like that.

"Clumsy." Imogen grins. "Watch where you're going."

"What on earth is going on?" Jade hisses, trying to keep her voice down. "Can't I leave you alone for two seconds?"

"Dearie me," I say. "Sasha should be more careful. Wouldn't want her to get hurt when her back is turned."

"Imogen tripped me," Sasha says, gathering everything together into a pile. A shard of china pricks her thumb, blood rushing to the surface that she has to suck away.

Imogen gasps dramatically. "I did no such thing!"

"You're a liar—"

"And *you're* a killer," she pronounces. "I think I know which is worse."

"I don't care," Jade says. "Sasha, get the dustpan and brush and clear this up. Effie, take those plates to the other guests. Captain Howard will have to wait a second. Runa? You've got some spare, right?"

"Oh, of course." Runa rolls her eyes. "I am always prepared. Heaven forbid the captain does not get his truffled mushrooms."

Sasha rises to her feet, face flushed. "Jade, I'm telling the truth—"

She cuts her off sharply. "And I've just said I don't care. *I don't care.* All I want is a smooth service."

I take the side plates, enjoying hearing Sasha's pleas go unheard,

Jade full on ranting at her as the doors swing shut behind me. Benjamin gives a roar of approval when I walk into the room, telling me he knew I was made of stronger stuff, while Captain Howard gives me an approving nod. I'm always his favorite, however uncomfortable I feel about him now.

Benjamin pats me on the back as I serve the plates to Eva and Jasmine, letting his hand drift to my ass. I'd rather like to break his hand but Eva surprisingly catches my eye and gives me a sympathetic smile.

"An aperol spritz, stat," Benjamin barks.

"Of course."

I'm making his drink when Sasha of all people has the audacity to approach me at the bar.

"Effie," she says. "I didn't attack you."

"Stay away from me," I whisper, though I don't think the guests care to hear. Captain Howard is currently delighting them all with tales of his youth sailing around the world.

Sasha sighs. "I need to talk to you."

"Didn't you hear me?" I say. "I don't want anything to do with you."

I finish making Benjamin's drink and shove right past her, not caring when my elbow hits her arm. Benjamin is enraptured by Captain Howard's conversation at the table, but makes sure to thank me for bringing him his spritz by pinching my ass. When I flinch backward he doesn't even look at me, smug in the knowledge that if I challenged him it'd be his word against mine and I'd be causing a scene. Something about tonight, about everything that's happened, makes me *want* to cause that fucking scene. But I can't. I know I can't. He's going to get off lucky, as men like him always do.

"Did I ever tell you about the time we were nearly overrun by pirates?" Captain Howard says.

Benjamin rocks back with laughter in his chair. "No! You can't be serious!"

"About ten years ago. Fortunately for my crew and guests, I'm armed at all times."

He has a *gun*? What the actual fuck? Jasmine is about to swallow a mouthful of mushrooms when this makes her choke, coughing and spluttering.

I think of his comment to me in the massage parlor. Maybe it really was a threat.

Runa is in a state when we arrive with empty starter plates and expect the main course to be ready. The side dishes are laid out in neat rows: creamed sweet corn jalapeño and spring onion; hispi cabbage with anchovy butter; tenderstem broccoli and spinach; and two heaped bowls of butter leaf, avocado, and Dolcelatte salad with a champagne dressing. But the actual main course plates themselves are empty.

"Take these out," Runa shouts. "Has anyone seen the berries? I have some peppers, but it won't be the same. My menus have been changed enough, even though I took such care writing the cards . . ."

"They've gone missing?" Sasha asks.

Runa scowls at her. "Yes, they have gone missing. And I have yet to find my knife."

Someone is *still* taking things? After Lola died and I was attacked?

"Serve the fish with the peppers!" Jade cries. "Effie, take those salad bowls out."

The captain has finished his pirate story by the time I arrive.

"I'm very proud of this journey," he says, then clears his throat awkwardly. "It's been a difficult one for a number of reasons. But we won't let that spoil our dinner."

Can't let a little thing like a *stewardess being killed* and *another brutally assaulted* disrupt this lovely evening. I slam the bowls onto the table, definitely too hard.

The table display is particularly ridiculous tonight. It almost looks like a wedding. Candles are set in crystal glasses across the entire table, and around them are faux pearls and gold ribbon. In the very center is a large bouquet of fake flowers that drift down the rim of their gold vase. All the guests have matching place mats and cutlery. At the head of each setting is a carefully written menu card with the individual guest's name. Jade comes out with the main course, not a hair out of place. She looks tired. Bone-tired, the kind of exhaustion that settles into your body like a layer of cream. I should tell her she's getting old.

"You have such great stories," Jasmine says to Captain Howard. "What was last season like?"

But she's interrupted; Sasha comes with the last of the main course and Jade announces each dish.

"Where are the berries?" Benjamin asks, picking up one of Runa's menu cards and poking his finger at the swoopy handwriting that confirms their inclusion. "I was looking forward to them."

Jade forces a smile. "I'm so sorry, there was a mix-up in the kitchen."

"This is the trouble with female staff," Benjamin says. "You just can't rely on them. Can't even complain or they'll burst into tears."

He laughs, but even Digby can't seem to bring himself to laugh along with him. There's a moment where Digby stares at Benjamin with a look I would swear bordered on disgust.

Jasmine isn't done with the captain. "Did you do lots of Atlantic crossings?"

"For charters?" He shakes his head. "No. This is unusual."

"Why the change? Was something difficult about last year?"

What's with her? Has someone told her about the missing stewardess?

I hadn't even thought of her until now. That's got to be strange, hasn't it? One missing last year and now this?

I shiver when Captain Howard denies it, even though I know he's just protecting crew interests and shielding a guest from what she doesn't need to hear. "Not at all."

Main course done, I bring the plates back to the galley and start washing everything up while Sasha and Jade deliver the desserts—a

raspberry and white chocolate mille-feuille, served with a Mourvèdre—
and Runa adds the final touches to the after-dinner chocolates, mints,
and coffee, which Imogen is waiting to deliver. Runa has calmed down
somewhat, but still mutters under her breath, placing the chocolates
and dusting icing sugar on the plates in a careful fashion.

"You really care about this, don't you?" I say. "The amount of effort
you put into each dish . . ."

She shrugs. "I used to care. Now I just go through the motions.
These people do not deserve my food."

"Probably not," I say.

"This charter cannot end soon enough," Runa says. "I have plans."
There's a resignation to her expression. "Sorry, I am thinking of other
things."

"Is it Lola?" I ask. "You were the last person to see her alive."

She takes a spare raspberry and pops it in her mouth. "I have thought
of nothing else."

Should I talk to Runa about it all? She's different from us stewardesses. And she was Lola's friend, I think. More than we were, anyway.

"Runa," I say. "I'm scared."

She looks at me then, a strange look I don't quite understand, but
before she can say anything we're interrupted by Jade, letting Runa
know her dessert has gone down a treat.

"Frankly," Runa says, "those men can choke on it. But I'll pretend
I'm pleased."

But this doesn't deter Jade from her smug expression. I'm about to
ask her what she's so happy about when she tells us herself. "Captain
Howard just told the guests we should arrive in New York by the end
of the day tomorrow at the latest. We're almost there, ladies!"

Tomorrow.

We're going to arrive tomorrow.

I can do this. I just have to survive another night and day.

Easier said than done.

CHAPTER THIRTY-THREE

~

IMOGEN

Axel doesn't know I'm following him.

Jade let me off shift first, probably because she's sick of my snarky comments. Captain Howard made his excuses and left dinner early. No doubt he'll be tucked up in bed snoring away while the rest of his staff are still working. The guests are enjoying their after-dessert coffees and chocolates, the sound of them vanishing as I head outside and to the other end of the yacht. Axel has been out in the water-toy garage for some time. It's daft, standing out here in the dark, rain drizzling, but I need to know what he's up to. What he's doing.

If Captain Howard has taken him off watch, it's for a reason. He must know something the rest of us don't. And that punch in the wall . . .

Of course there's a part of me that thinks I'm being stupid. This is *Axel*. Yes, he's a man whore. But this is the man I have seen with clients' children, picking them up and throwing them in the air and making them scream with laughter. The man who secretly swots up on the areas he takes guests out to on the tender. The man who cares painstakingly about safety because he told me once in confidence that he saved a man from drowning and the experience has stayed with him forever.

However. It's always *however*.

He emerges, raking a hand through his hair, spotlighted on the deck. For a second he tilts his head back, eyes shut, letting the rain fall on him.

I consider calling out, telling him once and for all what I've been keeping from him.

"Noah told me Zara was pregnant," I say softly, to the wind and rain, knowing he'll never hear me. He doesn't even flicker. "He thinks you're the father."

The moment passes. Axel's eyes snap open, and he makes his way back up the terrace steps and inside. So instead I choose to follow him again, keeping my distance down the snaking corridors, careful to stay quiet. But he's not bothered about turning around. His focus is absolute, even as we near the sounds of the guests dining and laughing, reaching the spiral staircase and moving down.

At first I think he is just going to the crew mess, calling it a night. But no—he carries on, meaning there's only one other place he can go.

The engine rooms.

No one goes down there without Melinda's permission, and she's nowhere to be seen.

I hesitate. I've never been to the engine rooms before. There's no need for us stewardesses. But I have to find out what he's doing.

I'm barely down ten steps when I hear voices, hushed and urgent, and freeze where I am, straining to listen.

Two voices. Axel—and Captain Howard.

"I'll tell everyone," Axel says. "I'll tell them what you're doing. I've been protecting you for far too long, but this? Taking me off watch? Among everything else?"

Axel and Captain Howard have always been two peas in a pod. The captain always backs Axel up, even when it drives Jade crazy. I remember Axel telling me once, nestled in some bar on a night out where it was too loud for anyone else to hear us, that his dad was a film producer. A highly respected one, apparently, which is clearly where all his money has come from. He used to go sailing with his dad every

Saturday when he was a boy and it was the highlight of his week. But then his dad's career took off and there was no more time for sailing. No more time for Axel in general. I don't know when he met Captain Howard, but I think he reminds him of his dad. He sees him as a father figure, rather than a boss. He's forever defending him. And Captain Howard sees Axel as a son.

What has happened between them for it to get like this?

And tell everyone what? What has Captain Howard done?

"Taking you off watch wasn't my decision," Captain Howard says. Does he sound scared? Is he *afraid* of Axel?

"How can it not have been your decision?" Axel asks, the disgust evident in his tone even though I can't see his face. "You're the *captain*. It's your job to make the decisions. Or have you completely absolved yourself of all responsibilities now? Should I just go and find Chief and call her 'Captain' instead? Get her to sort this mess?"

'Once we're in New York, I'll explain—"

"The life jackets and life rings are missing. Effie was attacked. Lola is *dead*. This yacht is falling apart, and it's your fault."

The life jackets are missing? Is there anything not going wrong on this boat?

There's a silence in response to Axel's biting words. I picture the captain's face, try to imagine him, but I have no idea what that man will be thinking.

I can't be found here. I have to go.

I have so many questions. I need to uncover exactly what Axel is up to.

I need to know if the father of my baby is a murderer.

CHAPTER THIRTY-FOUR

SASHA

Dinner finishes at midnight. Jasmine and I will meet in the morning, see if either of us has found out anything worthwhile. We've agreed to keep everything else we've discovered quiet for now. We're getting off this boat tomorrow. We can come up with a plan then.

But I did destroy that camera in the shower before dinner service began, a tiny piece of equipment expertly placed within the showerhead and hard to remove.

Not hard to smash to pieces once it was out, though.

My bedclothes are in a pile outside my cabin when I get to the crew mess, and the cabin door is closed. I don't need this. It's been a hell of a day.

"Effie?" I bang on the door, and when there's no response I open it impatiently. "Why are my pajamas out here?"

She's standing at the mirror, untying her hair. "Are you being serious?"

Our confrontation has drawn attention. Noah pokes his head out from his cabin, while Runa, Drew, and Jade (who were sitting around the table winding down with mugs of hot chocolate) come over to see what is going on. Imogen and Axel are missing. Have they patched things up? Surely not.

"I just want to go to bed," I say. "I'm not causing any problems."

"As if I'm letting you near me!" Effie says. "After what you did."

"Voices down," Jade hisses. "It's only one more night."

"You sleep with her, then, Your Majesty!" Effie snaps. "If you're so cool about it."

"Imogen will need consulting," Jade says.

And Imogen will not want to sleep with Effie or me. We all know it. Where *is* she?

Drew clears his throat. "I'd offer you my bed if I could, Sasha. But then you'd be in with Noah, and that wouldn't be appropriate."

Drew. He's been avoiding me. Avoiding everyone, really. Keeping to himself. He doesn't look okay, the bags under his eyes even more prominent than before.

"So," Jade says. "What are we going to do about Sasha?"

"Chuck her overboard?" Effie suggests. "See how she likes it?"

"Oh, for goodness' sake, she can come in my room," Runa says. "I do not care. Let us just all go to bed now, please."

"Thank you," I say.

"Your funeral," Effie mutters.

Jade claps her hands together. "Off to bed. All of you."

People don't need telling twice. Despite everything, we're all exhausted, and it only takes another fifteen minutes before almost everyone is in their cabin, lights off. Someone has even started snoring. I don't blame Effie, but it hurts all the same. She really does believe I've hurt her. And it's not like the others were defending me. But at least Runa has let me in, otherwise I'd be spending the night on the hard wooden bench in the crew mess, underneath the shift rota where Lola's name has been unceremoniously crossed out to match Zara's.

I finish getting changed and go to fetch a glass of water when I see Drew sitting at the table. We haven't spoken since our awkward conversation.

"Sorry about before," I say. "I was stressed. You caught me at the wrong time."

He shrugs. "Don't worry about it. We're all stressed at the moment."

"Are we . . . okay?" It feels so tense. I can't believe we kissed at the party.

He heaves himself up from the table and stands opposite me, and takes my hand. "We're okay. But you've got to be careful, especially after what happened to Effie."

His grip is tight. "What do you mean?"

"I just don't want you putting yourself at any risk," he says. "I care about you."

"What risk?" I say. "You mean you don't think it was me who hurt her?"

"You know I don't," he says. "You'd never do anything like that."

Warmth fills my body. Drew is on my side. How could I have ever doubted him? All my feelings for him come rushing back, and I'm tempted to repeat our kiss here and now.

But Drew withdraws his hand. He still seems unhappy. "We should get some sleep. You'll stop investigating things until we dock?"

He is set on this for some reason, so I feed him a lie. "I'll stop. Promise."

Runa mutters a good night to me when I come in and settle down. If we can get to New York without Captain Howard knowing we suspect him, without Noah doing anything else, we might just be okay. And so, despite myself, my eyes close and I try to sleep.

I remember his daughter, Tessa. Her work as a stewardess.

It's the perfect solution. I can run away and never look back.

I wake up to something rustling. It's pitch black, but then someone uses their phone to light the way.

Runa, I realize, my senses returning to me from the grip of sleep. She's getting up, trying to be as quiet as possible.

I keep silent as she exits our cabin, listening for the soft tread of her footsteps. I give her a minute, then get up and follow her.

She snakes her way up the stairs, and I have to keep my distance, stumbling in the dark. It's only when we reach the very top that I understand where she's going.

The owner's suite.

I watch as she heads up the steps to the private entrance and doesn't hesitate before going inside.

What on earth is she doing in there?

I have to tell Jasmine. We need to confront her now.

I don't waste time knocking on Jasmine's door when I get there, just in case it wakes someone else up, but open it and whisper her name. When she doesn't answer, I apologize and turn on the light. Expecting groans of confusion, I groan myself when I see her bed unslept in. She must be with Benjamin.

What do I do? I could confront Runa alone. But I don't want to go to the owner's suite by myself. Not when I know what's up there.

I bend over Jasmine's bed, bringing out the suitcase to take another look at the photograph of Hallie. The frame is one of those cheap plastic ones you can get in ASDA for a pound, but the photo inside is priceless. I frown again at the old Jasmine, that familiarity coming back to me. Where have I seen her before?

I start scrambling through the rest of the suitcase to find the note Jasmine mentioned Hallie wrote and unzip the inner lining. Jasmine's passport is in here. I open it more out of habit than anything else, and my heart sinks through my stomach to my feet.

This can't be possible.

No. Surely not.

I can't fight the panic attack that comes on. Where they normally build up slowly, insidiously, starting in my throat and sliding down to squeeze my heart, this one is instantaneous, gripping me in the chest and sending my vision into a chaotic, spinning blur. I'm going to be sick, but there's no time to run to the bathroom. I take great gulps of air to calm myself down, to no avail.

I have to get out of here. My knees are shaking, passport tight in my hand. And then the door starts to open.

Fuck. Oh fuck.

My body is screaming *run*, but it's frozen.

I know now where I've seen Jasmine before. In another photograph, in an office far, far away from here, and in my nightmares. The photograph that convinced me yachting was a good escape.

The name on Jasmine's passport reads: *Tessa Martin*.

Jasmine is Dr. Martin's daughter.

CHAPTER THIRTY-FIVE

JASMINE

I'm prepared for Benjamin tonight—he might not have anything to do with Hallie, but he knows something about what went on last year. If this is our last night before we dock, I'm pulling out all the stops.

And Digby won't be interrupting us either. Eva is donning a negligee of her own, black to my red, and a pair of stockings. She applies dark red lipstick and adds some rouge to her cheeks, then offers to do the same for me.

A peace offering? I accept, wondering if we'll talk about the message in the mirror again. She's being helpful, no doubt hoping this final night will secure her tip. I sit on the bed and let her do what she wants.

Next to me is one of the menu cards Runa prepared for dinner. "How come you brought this down?"

Eva turns pinker than her rouge. "Oh—it's silly. I just like to keep souvenirs."

A rather sweet admission. I smile, turning the menu over in my hands and studying the courses we just ate. Runa has written everything in a swoopy gold lettering, from the truffled mushrooms to the raspberry and white chocolate mille-feuille. It's beautiful, yet there's something about the card that's bothering me. Whatever it is remains out of reach. No matter. I put it down and stay still as Eva applies the lipstick, her bracelet jingling.

That reminds me. I dig into my pocket, bring out Eva's amethyst ring. "I just remembered. I found this out on the terrace before dinner. I meant to give it back to you."

"My ring!" She puts it straight on, emotional. "I can't believe you found it. This was my grandmother's. I never would have forgiven myself if I had lost it for good."

You didn't lose it, I want to tell her.

She finishes, giving me a tissue to dab my lips with, then folds her arms. "I want to say, for the record, that I still don't approve of your sneaking off and doing God knows what, but . . ." She pauses. "Well, I don't think you're involved in any of the—what's been going on."

Has finding the ring brought on this change of heart?

"I'm not apologizing." She sighs and joins me on the bed. "I'm not sure why you're here. I think you're crazy. But whatever the reason is . . . I hope you find what you're looking for. Just be careful, okay? That warning on your mirror—"

"So you believe me after all?"

Before she can answer, there's a knock at the door. "Eva, are you ready yet, darling?"

"That's Mr. Johnson," she says. "We'd better go. Behave yourself tonight."

Oh, I will.

Benjamin's grin is wider than the Cheshire Cat's when he opens his door to find me standing there in my negligee, armed with two champagne flutes and a bottle of prosecco.

My mission: make sure this man is as drunk as possible. We finish the prosecco within minutes (Benjamin not seeming to notice I've been nursing the same small glass while he polishes off the bottle), and once he's good and sloshed he lies across the bed and starts talking unprompted about all the charters he and Digby have been on. Time to start asking about the captain.

"You and Mr. Johnson are friends with Captain Howard, aren't you?"

"Digby and I go way back," Benjamin slurs. "Asteridge too, though we weren't always the nicest to him, I'll admit. He was a scholarship kid at Eton, so you know what that means."

I've never thought about it, but it must be weird to have gone to school with people and then serve them on a superyacht where they're the guests and you're the crew, even if you are the captain. Did he just get resentful of it all? Is that why he snapped, started doing things he wouldn't have dared before?

"Mr. Johnson must appreciate you paying for these charters," I say. "You've got to be a good financial advisor to afford this."

I thought I was being flattering, but this irks him for some reason. He undoes his tie and throws it on the floor, muttering something I can't catch.

"What was that?"

"Digby doesn't seem to appreciate me much on this trip," Benjamin says. "After all we've done . . . I shouldn't have said that, I'm pissed." He leans over, opening his bedside drawer and taking out a couple of pills. "Want any, darling?"

"No, thank you." Now that I think about it, last season Digby and Benjamin were much more of a united front. Digby was more jovial too, almost as brash and arrogant as Benjamin. This time is different. There have been moments—even when we first arrived, Digby's barely concealed irritation at Benjamin for bringing me along—where Digby has gone off by himself, more interested in engine room tours with Melinda than anything else.

"How are you feeling about what happened to the stewardesses?" I ask. "Especially with this second one getting hurt. It's so frightening."

What is it about men and seeing a woman scared? I guess it really does hark back to that old damsel in distress idea. Benjamin visibly glows at the sight of me, same as Noah did before.

"Come here, baby," he says. "I'll look after you. We only have one more night."

I oblige, letting him wrap me in an embrace. I've learned by now that Benjamin likes things a certain way. I have to keep him talking for as long as possible.

"Has anything like this ever happened before?" I whisper into his neck, making sure my breath tickles him. "You seem so brave."

"Oh, yeah," he says. "Crew members have loads of accidents. Nothing like this, though. Still, whoever it is, they're after the stewardesses, so we're fine, babe. Though you look a bit like one, don't you? Don't put on one of their uniforms."

He's so nonchalant about it. It doesn't affect him, therefore he isn't worried.

Definitely the rich man's mantra.

"How did Captain Howard react when things happened before?" I press. "Has anyone gone missing?"

"Gone missing?" he echoes. He pushes me away, and even though he's under the influence of a lot of different things, I've forgotten how high his tolerance must be. He looks me dead in the eye, his intensity making me gulp. "What's made you say that?"

"I just thought . . . I'd heard something about a stewardess going missing last year."

I've said it. If he recognizes me now, I'm screwed.

I remember Benjamin the morning we were all searching for Hallie. Well, I remember how conspicuously *absent* he was, this man who had come barging into the crew mess once because he'd woken up at four in the morning and was disgusted to find the chef wasn't immediately on hand to make him breakfast. Melinda was the one who searched the guest cabins for Hallie that day, said she reported seeing Benjamin snoring away in his room without a care in the world.

"You've got that wrong," he says. "No one's gone missing. Now come and wrap that tie around my neck."

He's *lying*.

I expected him to embellish, perhaps make up something that put him in the starring role, or complain about it messing up his holiday. But not outright lie. Why change his story?

"You said there was nonsense afterward," I say, hoping he doesn't remember it was Eva he mentioned this to, not me. "Maybe I got the wrong end of the stick."

Benjamin lies back on the bed, beckoning me to sit over him. I don't have much of a choice if I want him to carry on, so I grab the tie and place it around his neck. There's something sinister about it when Lola had bruises around her own. The idea that he can still get off to that while on the very boat she was murdered aboard.

"That was about the business," he says.

Business?

But his eyes are drifting shut. "Stay there, darling," he mumbles.

Yeah, I'm just going to hang around on your lap while you sleep off your stupor. He starts to snore, and I ease myself off to not disturb him.

He lied. He knows for a fact Hallie went missing. There's no way he's forgotten, not even someone as uncaring as him. He's hiding something.

Eva is better at this than I am. Maybe she'd be able to get it out of him.

God. What am I thinking? I can't just use Eva the same way they do, get her to perform for me so I can have information.

I almost feel bad for writing her off. She's in this for her daughter. I need to respect that. And it was cute, the way she kept Runa's menu card as a souvenir—

Wait.

That's it.

I know what was bothering me about those menu cards.

Benjamin lets out a loud snort, and I'm terrified he's going to wake up. I dart for the door. It's late; the portholes mix sea and sky into one black image. I need to get out of this stupid negligee and find Sasha, middle of the night be damned. This is too important to wait.

And if I'm right—no, I *am* right—this blows everything we thought to pieces.

I stop short when I reach my door. There's a strip of light running underneath it.

Someone is in my cabin.

My heart takes off like a rocket. Is it the killer, come to finish me off because I didn't stop asking questions? Should I get someone, run and grab Sasha, then confront whoever it is, shouting and waking up the whole corridor? But what if they're gone by the time I get back?

And if they wanted to kill me, they'd have seen I wasn't in there and left. Why would they turn the light on?

Who the hell is in my room?

I open the door with a shaking hand, eyes squinting in the sudden light, and vaguely make out blonde hair and a stewardess uniform.

"Who is it?" I say. "What are you doing in here?"

"Jasmine?"

Thank God. It's Sasha. I close the door. "You're never going to believe it. The menu cards, they're—"

"Actually," Sasha interrupts, and for the first time I see what she's doing. She's sitting on the floor, my suitcase open in front of her, and she's holding out my passport. "You're not Jasmine, are you?"

Fuck.

CHAPTER THIRTY-SIX

SASHA

I see it now: signs of the girl in Dr. Martin's photograph reflected in the Jasmine standing in front of me now. There are only so many things a person can change about themselves. The weight loss is significant, the makeup carefully disguises certain features of her face, the hair makes a far more startling difference than one might imagine. But she has the same upturn to her nose, the same ears. This is the woman whose photograph I saw, who I thought of when I resigned from the hospital, Dr. Martin threatening me to keep quiet when he got me alone on my last day or there would be consequences. Her face, her standing there in that uniform next to *Ophelia*, was what inspired me to become a stewardess and find out if *Ophelia* was hiring.

How could I not have recognized her straightaway?

It's incredible what you don't notice when you aren't searching for it.

"You're not Jasmine," I say, "are you? You've been lying to me. You're Tessa. You're Dr. Martin's daughter."

Jasmine hangs her head. "When you said Dr. Martin before . . . that he worked in a hospital in London . . . but it's a common surname. I thought it couldn't be true."

"I saw your photo," I say. "*You* inspired me to become a stewardess. That's what Dr. Martin said you were. Was you being a deckhand a lie too?" My anger quickly takes over, and soon I'm speaking too fast, the words firing out of me like bullets. "Has this all been a joke to you?

Making up a sob story about a missing best friend? Did Dr. Martin put you up to it? To follow me, make sure I didn't say anything about what happened?"

But now Jasmine is furious too. "Of course the Hallie stuff is true! As if I would ever make up anything like that. And I was a deckhand. I don't know why he told you I was a stewardess. He probably didn't remember the truth. I don't even talk to him, he'd never be able to put me up to this—"

Liar. "You saw each other every other weekend. He told me himself."

"That's utter rubbish! He didn't even know me until I was twenty."

"He told me all about your mother, how he wished he could do more for you. You've been hiding that you're his daughter this whole time."

"Sasha, I promise you he was lying. How can you believe a word that comes out of his mouth after what he did to you?"

I shake my head, panic taking over. "My God, I told you everything that happened with Janet Lesley. What was I *thinking*?"

I lose it then, my breath flying away from me. Jasmine grabs hold of me and I want to scream but I can't find any power in my throat.

"Sasha!" she says. "You need to sit down. Put your head between your legs."

"Get off me!" I manage to gasp, pushing her away, collapsing onto the bed.

"I'm sorry," Jasmine says. "I should have told you straightaway, the moment you started telling me about Dr. Martin, that there was a chance you were talking about my father. But I didn't want to risk you no longer trusting me, thinking I had some ulterior motive. I *don't*, Sasha. Everything I've told you is true."

I suck in big, juddering gasps, focusing on the floor between my knees.

"I had no one," Jasmine murmurs. "Even when Mum was alive, she was a shit parent. I found out about my dad later, that he was a doctor in some fancy hospital in London, and I used to make up all these excuses for why he couldn't come and whisk me away. After Hallie and I moved in together and we needed the money to train for yachting, I thought it was the perfect opportunity to meet him and finally get a real parent." She laughs bitterly. "He told me about his wife and kids, that I was a 'complication,' and if he gave me the money for training and a bit extra, would I leave him alone for good?"

My breathing slows. It sounds like something Dr. Martin would say.

That's what he called Janet, in the end, after we'd gone through our internal investigation and were cleared of any wrongdoing. *A complication that had been resolved.*

I quit the next day.

"I took the money," Jasmine says. "And I sent him that photo of me you saw because . . . well, I don't know why I sent it now. Probably to try and win him back, which is pathetic. I went to him after Hallie disappeared. Tried to get his help. To use some of his influence. He told me we had an agreement, that I couldn't keep coming to him when I needed something. I asked him what else I was meant to do with a father. And he said he wasn't my father, that I was an accident he shouldn't have to deal with."

Accidents happen, Sasha.

I raise my head.

Jasmine is trying her best not to cry, blinking her tears away. "From that point, I was on my own. That's when I put my plan together. I'm sorry I didn't tell you the full truth. I was . . . scared, I guess. Other than Hallie, I've never trusted someone before."

"You really have nothing to do with him?" I whisper.

"God, no. And never again, knowing what I know now." Her conviction is clear.

"I'm sorry about what he did to you," I say, surprising myself.

She takes one of my hands. "And I'm sorry about what he did to you. We've both been used by that waste of space in different ways."

It's oddly refreshing, knowing there is someone else who understands entirely who Dr. Martin is. I can't believe I doubted her, seeing that name and going right back to how I was. I can't believe I still trusted any of his stories.

We sit together, taking everything in with a beat of silence, and then I go to wash my face and have some water while Jasmine gets changed. Once she is dressed, I explain why I was here to begin with.

"I'm sharing a cabin with Runa," I say. "Effie didn't want to sleep with me for, well, obvious reasons. I woke up to Runa leaving in the middle of the night, and followed her to the owner's suite. I went to come and find you, but you weren't in here, so I wanted to look at Hallie's note and your photograph again, and that's when I found your passport."

"I was coming to look for you too," Jasmine says. "It's about the menu cards."

I frown. "The menu cards?"

"Eva kept one as a souvenir," Jasmine says. "One of the menu cards Runa wrote. I glanced at it—and I knew straightaway something about it was bothering me, but I was distracted, I didn't have time to think. Do you reckon Runa is still in the owner's suite?"

"I think so. But what about them? What is it?"

"Then we need to go right now. The message I got on the mirror . . . whoever wrote it had a strange way of writing their g and q letters. Everything else was in capitals apart from these, and the tails were oddly elaborate. It was the same on the menu card. Same style, same odd flourish. It's too much of a coincidence to be anyone else."

Hold on. She can't think . . .

"What are you saying?" I ask. My heart is thudding.

"Runa is the one who threatened me."

"Then that means . . ."

"That means one thing," she tells me. "We were wrong about Captain Howard. Wrong about Noah. It's Runa. Runa killed Lola."

CHAPTER THIRTY-SEVEN

JADE

I can't get to sleep. I'm tossing and turning for ages before I finally give up. Someone is snoring loudly from another cabin. Any other charter, I'd tell them a quick sinus fix, both to stop the irritating sound in the future and also to take them down a peg. This charter, the idea is comically minor. We've moved far beyond petty jibes at one another.

A flicker of light passes underneath the door. I don't think much of it at first, assuming someone is using the bathroom, when I realize someone is already in there, the extractor fan buzzing incessantly. A great retching sound can be heard. A minute later, another light flashes by. The same person coming back? Or someone else?

I heave myself up, taking care not to disturb Imogen, and softly tread to the door, easing it open and peering out. It's someone with their phone, vanishing up the stairs before the corridor and crew mess are darkness once more. I turn back to grab my own phone and find Imogen's bed empty, sheets still tucked in from this morning.

Where on earth is that girl? Was that her sneaking around?

It's tempting to take my radio and call for her, but I don't want to wake anyone else up unnecessarily. I leave the cabin, but I don't follow the mystery person. It would not do well to follow someone in the dark. People are becoming paranoid. Any kind of accusation might fly about, however unfounded. It is my job to keep the peace, and I will do that as best I can. Instead, I take myself to the mess table, grateful for the silence.

I bend down, reaching for the secret compartment underneath the bench I'm not sure anyone else even knows exists. There is no handle, only a push mechanism, triggered by my foot pressing up against it. There are spare washing-up liquids and tea towels in here (no one ever seems to wonder where they materialize from, but then again I am the only one who insists on keeping the crew mess as clean as the galley, so I am often the poor sap stuck doing the dishes) but behind them, I have a few treasures.

My emergency chocolate for when things get hectic. A huge bar, only a couple of squares left. Some guilty-pleasure magazines like *Take a Break*. My packet of cigarettes for when things get *really* stressful, because I haven't smoked regularly in years. Now that pack of twenty, which has lasted me three seasons, is down to two. Not that anyone else knows. Filthy habit. It stains your fingertips and your teeth. I brush and scrub like mad the second I'm done.

And tucked away at the back, Lola's diary.

It was the right thing to do, lie to Sasha and the others and tell them I had thrown it overboard. It would have become a problem. Captain Howard and Melinda weren't going to give it the proper consideration, so it's better that I keep it, read through it, check what Lola's inner thoughts truly were, and decide what to do from there.

I open it, turn to where I left off.

CHAPTER THIRTY-EIGHT

SASHA

The darkness hangs like a fog as we creep along the corridor. It's tempting to use Jasmine's phone as a light source, but instead we tread carefully in case anyone else is around. There is always someone awake on a boat, keeping an eye on things whether you like it or not. Every so often, the yacht shifts with the waves, and I pretend the nausea I'm experiencing is from this rather than dread.

Jasmine leads, hand outstretched to avoid stumbling.

Seeing that passport, her real name, brought me back to everything I've been avoiding. But I trust her. We need each other. It was her, after all, who brought me here in the first place. It makes sense we're going to figure this out together.

And yet, we hesitate outside the owner's suite.

Jasmine swallows. "Are you ready?"

I don't know.

"Let's go," I whisper.

At first, the suite seems empty, dark all round and no one in sight. But there's a strip of light under the bedroom door.

"She's still here," Jasmine murmurs. "Come on."

We push our way into the room, the sudden light blinding us.

When things come into focus, Runa is kneeling on the carpet by the chest of drawers, a suitcase open in front of her. Half of the jewelry has been transferred, the rest lying in wait. She has a necklace in her hands, a large silver choker with sapphires that looks like it's worth more than everything I own. I glance around, just in case, but there's no one else. She's stunned when she sees us, mouth falling open and cheeks burning red.

"You're the thief?" I say. "It was you all this time?"

She rises, silver choker in her grasp. "I can explain—"

"There is no explaining!" I cut across her. "Everything that has happened . . . it's been so you can take some necklaces?"

"Wait." She drops the choker and it lands with a clatter back in the drawer. "I admit, it was me who was stealing from the guests, but I did not do anything else."

She's lying. It must be her. She was the last one to see Lola alive. Lola wrote in her diary she was meeting someone. And Runa is able to sneak around. She's her own boss, not beholden to Jade or Axel like we are. When Runa spoke about Lola having secrets, she was just trying to make us all paranoid. It was her own secret she was determined to keep under wraps.

Maybe it's something about realizing who Jasmine truly is, the fact I've told her my shameful past, but I feel a rage within me like never before. I'm not going to let someone else get away with their terrible actions. That is not me anymore.

"The message on my mirror," Jasmine says. "It was *your* handwriting. I recognized it from the menu cards."

Now Runa is fearful. "Yes—that was me. I was only trying to warn you off. Scare you a little. I did not want you investigating, asking things of people. I was worried you would find out about me taking the jewelry."

"Liar!" I say. "Let's see what everyone else thinks, shall we?"

I don't wait for her or even Jasmine to follow, taking off back down to the crew mess. The portholes reveal a glimmer of light, the beginnings of the sunrise.

We're arriving in New York today.

Runa runs after me, shouting my name, begging me to listen. I don't turn around. I bang on the cabin doors, each one, until I hear movement.

"Get up!" I yell. "It's Runa! Runa killed Lola!"

Jade emerges from her cabin in her uniform. Was she awake already? Axel comes out also fully dressed. Everyone else is in their pajamas, bleary-eyed and confused. Drew isn't here, Noah exiting their room alone.

The only other people missing are Captain Howard and Melinda. I spot Jade's radio attached to her belt. "Call for the captain and Chief."

"What's she doing here?" Imogen asks, glaring at Jasmine, who blocks the way back up the stairs. "This is a crew space. And what the fuck is all the shouting about?"

"This is a big mistake," Runa says.

"Jade!" I snap, not caring that she's my superior. "Tell them to get down here."

Maybe Jade senses how serious this is, doing as I ask without argument. Melinda's reply is affirmative; she promises to relay the message to the captain, who doesn't respond.

Everyone then turns to me and Runa.

"Jasmine and I just caught Runa with the stolen guest jewelry," I start. "She had loads of it stashed in the owner's suite, in the chest of drawers in the bedroom."

This receives the appropriate surprised reaction from Effie, Noah, and Imogen, but I can see clearly that Axel and Jade are confused. They exchange a glance before Jade speaks.

"Zara was removed from *Ophelia* for stealing the jewelry," she says. "It was found stashed under her bed and was promptly returned to the correct owners between charters. Axel, Runa, and I were aware of this, as of course were Chief and Captain Howard, but it was decided to keep this quiet from the rest of the crew. After agreeing to leave with a good reference, Zara departed amicably enough and the matter was settled."

I know why Zara left, was told the reason by Noah ages ago. Is this all to protect Axel from his bad behavior? But Jade *hates* Axel. Why would she protect him?

I'm done with all the lies.

But Noah speaks before I do, his own outrage obvious in his face. "That's not true. Zara was told to leave because she was pregnant."

"*What?*" Jade turns to him, baffled. "What are you talking about?"

Noah points a finger at Axel. "And *he's* the father. I know all about it, however much you in management might want to hide stuff from us. Lola *showed me* the pregnancy test."

There's a gasp from Effie, but it's Imogen I'm watching; her response isn't the horror I'm expecting. Instead, she closes her eyes for a moment, seeming to decide something with a small nod to herself. Jade, to her credit, seems completely bewildered, and I'm starting to wonder if Noah has got this right.

"I don't know what you're going on about," Axel tells Noah, shaking his head in disgust, "but I'm not the father of Zara's baby. We were never together like that. I didn't even know Zara was pregnant!"

"Oh, for Christ's sake, you idiots," Imogen snaps. "Zara isn't pregnant. That was my pregnancy test."

Imogen?

Axel's mouth falls open.

Imogen sighs. "I thought I wrapped it up and hid it well enough in the bin, but Mouse was sneaky. She must have gone through it and found it and jumped to the wrong conclusion."

Lola thought it was Zara.

Or, more likely, Lola decided it would be Zara for her own amusement. Probably to upset Noah.

And it worked.

"Then—Zara wasn't . . . ?" Noah can barely speak. He flushes and turns to Axel. "I thought you had abandoned her . . . all this time and it was a lie . . ."

So that's why Noah has had such a problem with Axel. He thought Axel had left Zara to be a single mother, carried on with Imogen and even Effie and didn't care about her or the baby he had made. That, and probably some of his own jealousy stirring within him, the belief that Axel had had Zara and didn't care at all.

But Axel isn't bothered about Noah. His bottom lip is quivering. It's the first time I've seen him truly *nervous*.

"Why didn't you tell me?" he asks Imogen. "If I knew—"

"If you knew you wouldn't have fucked Effie behind my back?" Imogen finishes for him. She shrugs. "I doubt that somehow. We'll talk later, Axel. This isn't the time."

"But—"

"Not in front of everyone."

"I can't believe this," Effie says. "And then—so Runa *did* steal the jewelry or didn't she? What is going on?"

Runa sighs. "It was me, not Zara."

Jade is still in denial. "But that can't be. I *found* the jewelry under Zara's bed—"

"Let me explain," Runa says. "Lola had walked in on me with a particularly garish necklace our previous charter guest had reported missing, so I had to put on a great show of acting like I had just found it in Zara's things and to tell her we had to inform the captain in person. So while she went running off to get him, I moved some of my stash under her mattress. Later, the rest I hid in the one place no one would find it—the owner's suite."

"Why would Lola make up that Zara was fired for being pregnant if she knew the real reason?" Noah asks. The betrayal is painfully evident in his tone.

"Lola wasn't as stupid as she made out," Runa says. "She came to me after Zara was gone, said she knew I was the one who really stole the jewelry. But she was willing to cut a deal."

"A deal?"

"She wanted in. Half of whatever I made on the jewelry so she didn't have to work. Noah, you were crazy about Zara. Lola said it amused her to see you freaking out about it. That made you angry at Axel, obviously, and she enjoyed the drama. I stayed well out of that."

Noah hangs his head. "I'm sorry, Axel."

Axel frowns. "We have bigger problems than your stupidity. That bitch Lola. I can't believe we—" And then he stops abruptly.

"We what?" Effie says.

Imogen rolls her eyes. "Oh, Axel, please tell me you *didn't*."

His eyes flash with anger, but he's saved from answering. Melinda strides in, radio in hand and hair loose, and it's only seeing her look slightly less than perfect that reminds me of the early hour. I've been awake practically all night, my body too wired to feel sleepy.

"Get me up to speed," Melinda says. "What's going on? And what is a guest doing here?"

"Where's the captain?" I ask.

She waves her hand at me. "On watch. He told me to handle this and update him."

Update him? On something as serious as this?

But I can't think about him. I fill Melinda in, surprised at how well she can keep her expression neutral, simply nodding and asking the occasional clarifying question in places. She seems uncertain of Jasmine, peering at her with furrowed brows, and when I finish I see Jade giving Jasmine a similar quizzical stare.

"Runa?" Melinda says. "Do you have any kind of explanation for this?"

Runa scowls. "The guests will not even miss it. They report it stolen, but they do not care. They will just buy another. Whereas for me . . . it will change my life."

"So all of this was for money?" I confirm, appalled. "You're stealing the jewelry so you can sell it? Lola was working with you to do that?"

Her temper flares; she speaks in short bursts. "Oh, that is so easy for you to toss aside as a justification, is it? Does it not drive you insane, serving people who spend more than you earn in a year on a meal at a restaurant? More than you have ever owned on a coat they are only going to wear once?"

"Why would Lola even need to be in on this?" Effie asks. "She had money."

"You never would have made shit with that jewelry," Axel says. "Do you have any idea the markup on those things? Lola should have known."

"Mouse didn't even know what a mortgage was," Imogen says. "I told her it was a kind of French cake."

Lola wouldn't have known, I realize. The designer clothes I wasn't sure about, the admission in her diary . . . Lola was *poor*. She pretended to be rich to fit in with the likes of Axel and Effie and not get made fun of for her lack of wealth, like Imogen did. She cultivated an outward facade that was built on fakery and lies. And selling the jewelry was going to help her maintain that.

Lola did a lot to me, but she's dead. Revealing her secret isn't going to change that or help matters. So I keep quiet.

Runa flushes, embarrassed. "I needed an escape. From *this*. You do not hate them, Axel, because you are practically part of their club. Maybe I want to be part of that club too, as much as I despise them."

"Money doesn't matter," Axel says.

"Spoken from the mouth of one who has never had to do without it," Runa barks.

"You have no idea what I've been through," Axel says. "You don't get to judge me."

I think about my conversation with Drew, his struggles with his family's poverty, his own resentment at the rich people who charter these superyachts. I understand Runa's frustration. But to kill for it? I could never understand that. I know the damage death brings, what this will do not only to Lola's family but to all of us, permanently.

"Why mess up things around the yacht?" I ask. "The missing champagne, your knife, the ingredients . . ."

"The life jackets!" Axel cries. "And the life rings. That was you, wasn't it?"

There's a brief panic as the rest of the crew learn these are missing until Melinda calms them down, but even she glares at Runa, daring her to deny this.

"Why would I ruin my own meals?" Runa says, incredulous. "And take my own knife? That doesn't make any sense. I only stole the jewelry."

"To make people not suspect you!" Effie declares. "And then you killed Lola and attacked me!"

"This is a lie! I did not kill Lola! Or hurt you."

"You were the last to see Lola alive," Axel points out. "You never did explain where Lola went after."

"I do not know!"

"Lola had a diary," I say. "She wrote in there she was meeting someone after the party. That must have been meeting you about the jewelry plan. If only we had the diary, I could show everyone—" And then Jade astounds me. She brings out Lola's battered notebook. "You said you chucked it overboard!"

Jade sighs. "I did not want this to cause issues. So I lied. But I read through it entirely. Lola was meeting someone, and it is pretty clear that Lola meant Runa, because any mention of her disappears after she starts talking about her secret plan."

"Wait, so you suspected Runa?" I say. "Yet you let me sleep in the same cabin as her?"

"Oh, please," Jade snaps. "She would have hardly murdered you after we all knew you were in there with her. And I didn't *suspect* her. Just thought that she was who Lola was meeting that night, for whatever reason. I was convinced Lola's death was an accident until . . ."

Effie has backed away from Runa entirely, her contempt obvious. "You were always jealous of me. As soon as I said I was a model you had to bring up your own experiences. Which were *pathetic*, by the way. A bit of runway doesn't make you Linda Evangelista."

Despite everything, Runa bites out a harsh laugh. "You have to be joking."

"You were always the odd one out," Imogen says. "We should have known."

Things are getting heated. Voices are raised, accusations fly across the room.

"Noah . . ." Jade says. She's the only person not staring at Runa, but now we all look at him, at the blood that trickles down from his nose.

He's having a nosebleed. Jasmine and I glance at each other. He wasn't lying. His ludicrous scarf story was actually true. Noah wipes it away with his sleeve, then grabs the bridge of his nose and tilts his head back. He's doing it wrong.

"Sit down," I tell him. "Lean forward and pinch the soft part and spit out any blood. I'll get you a pack of frozen vegetables to put on your forehead and a bowl."

My nursing instinct is returning. The moment I'm done passing the frozen peas wrapped in a tea towel, my hands start to shake at the thought of me offering care again.

"Sasha," Effie says. "I'm sorry. I really thought it was you."

An apology from Effie? I try to hide my shock. "That's okay. You were scared."

"I guess it's easy to think anyone could have hit me when I'm such a bitch," she says. "Noah, I'm sorry too. I've been terrible to you."

Noah, clutching the frozen peas to his nose, blinks. "Uh—thanks, Effie. You know, if you ever want to—"

"Yeah, I'm definitely still not interested in you." She cuts him off quickly. "That hasn't changed. Just apologizing for being a cow about it."

"I did not attack you either," Runa insists. "It makes no sense that I would hurt you or Lola."

Effie clicks her fingers. "It must have been *you* I overheard that day. You and Lola. Talking about your plan. You made it sound like stealing this jewelry was going to change things forever. It's weird. I was so sure there had been a male voice, but the way you were whispering obviously distorted it."

"I have no idea what you are talking about," Runa says. "Okay, Lola and I were supposed to talk after the party at midnight. But there was that fight with Sasha, and Lola and I had our own disagreement. Before this, she had tried asking for more money, said it was an extra for keeping quiet. I didn't think she still wanted to meet and talk, so I went to sleep, missing the entire thing. I did not want to tell you that because it meant revealing I had stolen the jewelry, and also because we had an argument before she died."

"That's motive if you ask me," Imogen says.

"You have to believe me!"

But no one does. She has guilt written all over her face. I think about her spot-on impressions, the way she's able to play any character, and wonder if we know her at all.

Jasmine clears her throat. "You said it was just you and Lola involved. No one else?"

Runa is immediately defensive. "No! Why would there be anyone else?"

"Then what can you tell me about Hallie Attwood?" Jasmine asks.

She's mentioned Hallie.

"I knew it!" Jade shrieks, jabbing a finger at Jasmine. "I *knew* it. You're *Tessa*. That deckhand from last year—"

I see the confusion in Runa's expression. "Who is Hallie Attwood?"

Melinda steps forward, putting herself face-to-face with Jasmine. "I knew there was something about you, and Howard wouldn't listen, but I'm right. Tessa. Is that you?"

Jasmine gives a little wave. "Hi, Jade, Chief. Took you both long enough."

"Did you know Tessa worked here before?" Melinda swivels to me. "How?"

"Not until yesterday," I reply. "Until we decided to try and find out what happened to Lola and Hallie together."

"What does *Hallie* have to do with any of this?" Jade says. "That was last season!"

"Who the fuck is Hallie?" Imogen interjects. "And sorry, are you saying Jasmine—Tessa—whoever she is, was a crew member?"

"Hallie Attwood was the stewardess who went missing last year," Jasmine answers. "I was a deckhand. My real name is Tessa. And I think it's too much of a coincidence that the same superyacht—the same captain, same chief officer, same chief stewardess, same bloody *guests*—has now had another stewardess turn up dead and a further one attacked."

The crew mess falls silent. Noah has stopped holding the bag of frozen peas to his nose, so transfixed by Jasmine that he doesn't seem to notice he's leaving it to soak his lap. Even Imogen has shut up.

Jasmine begins pacing around the room, but there's not much space, and people have to back away to let her pass, before coming to a stop in front of Melinda. "I saw you had the newspaper articles. I saw how the footage had been deleted too."

"I knew someone had been in my quarters!" Melinda says. "Jasmine . . . Tessa . . . let me explain."

"Explain, then," Jasmine says. "Why have all that stuff?"

"Because I agree with you," she says. "It was a terrible investigation, and I wanted to try and put it right. If I were captain it would have been different, I promise you. I've been gathering everything together to see if what was missed can be made right."

"Then why not contact me?" Jasmine asks. "Why keep it a secret?"

"Because I didn't want to get your hopes up. I wanted to see if I could find anything first."

There's a pause as Jasmine processes this. I'm not sure if she's happy or angry with Melinda, but she knows there isn't much she can do about it now. She looks back at Runa. "You're really saying you have no idea who Hallie is?"

"I do not."

"She's a murderer," Imogen points out. "How can you believe her?"

That's true—but at the same time she was nowhere near *Ophelia* last year. She's not some criminal mastermind manipulating someone else to kill Hallie for reasons unknown. She's just someone who worked hard for a job and grew resentful. Bitter enough to steal. Desperate enough to kill.

"Maybe Hallie really is separate," I say quietly. "Maybe she was an accident."

Someone's wake-up alarm sounds. Noah runs to switch it off, leaving the bag of frozen peas on the table.

"What do we do with Runa?" Imogen asks.

"Please don't tell the police about the jewelry," Runa says. "I will return it all."

"We'll be telling the police about a lot more than that," Jade says.

"Let's put her in the massage parlor," Axel suggests. "There's an adjoining toilet. Noah and I can guard outside until we dock."

Despite Runa's protests, we settle on this. After changing into our uniforms, everyone moves together to the massage room, as if we're scared now to be alone. There's even a cheer from Imogen after the door closes on Runa. Axel and Noah stand on either side like bouncers.

"What will we tell the other guests?" Effie asks. "There won't be any breakfast for them beyond a continental."

"I'll figure something out," Jade says. "I always do."

As she says this, light begins to filter through the portholes. Outside, dawn is breaking, the sunrise an orange glow between thick, dark clouds.

Our last day.

"I'm still in pain," Effie says. "I'm going to go sleep for another hour. But—thanks, guys." She sighs. "For finding out it was Runa. I appreciate it. Soon as we dock, I'm starting a new leaf. Be more honest about things. Hold nothing back. Watch out, world, Effie 2.0 is coming. Or should that be 3.0?"

Everyone else manages a smile as she leaves, looking better than she has for days, but I can't. This isn't over.

"Don't look so down, Detective Dunce," Imogen calls out to me. "You're not the killer after all! We'll be in New York soon."

CHAPTER THIRTY-NINE

JASMINE

Runa didn't know about Hallie. She's not involved with her disappearance.

So who the hell is?

Hallie's disappearance was not an accident. I refuse to believe that.

Sasha steers me to the galley, odd without Runa in it. A lone chopping board sits on the drying rack, and my eyes glance over at the magnetic strip that holds her knives, one still missing.

"We can still find out what happened to Hallie," Sasha says. She's trying to be strong for me, which should make me feel somewhat better but doesn't.

"Maybe," I murmur, my faith in finding out the truth beginning to fade.

I'm never going to get anywhere.

No. There are still loose ends here. What about the CCTV camera? That can't be Runa, surely. And why did Captain Howard have Lola's phone?

"We should still speak to Effie," I say. "Stay with her, just in case. I think we should *all* stick together until we reach New York."

"Speak to Effie?" Sasha says. "Jasmine, it was *Runa*. We'll be there in a few hours. Axel and Noah are going to guard the door now until we dock—"

"You can come with me or I'll do it by myself." I place my hands on her shoulders. "Please. If there's even the smallest chance she's still in danger . . . I won't be able to rest until we're all off this boat."

"Alright." It's clear Sasha doesn't agree, but she gives in. "Let's go."

The crew mess is empty when we head down, entirely opposite to when we confronted Runa all together. The portholes reveal only clouds now, the sun lost within them as the morning progresses. It feels strange down here, an energy I can't place. Maybe it's because there's no one around, but there's something off. I think Sasha can feel it too because she reaches out and grips my hand as we make our way to Effie's cabin.

The door is closed. We can't hear anything inside, so Sasha knocks three times.

No response.

"Effie?" Sasha calls. "It's Sasha and Jasmine. We want to talk."

There's still no answer, but I can't wait a second more, every bone in my body telling me that something is horribly wrong here, and I push open the door.

I think I'm seeing things at first. The light from the crew mess playing tricks in the dark cabin, making shadows where they shouldn't be. But then Sasha gasps, and I know it's not a hallucination. I flick the switch, flooding the room with light, and can do nothing but stare at the horror in front of us.

Effie lies on the floor, hair obscuring her face in thin strands. Her eyes are open, glazed. Her mouth is slightly open too, lips puckered as if preparing for a kiss. Blood has seeped from her stomach and one of her shoulders, leaving large stains. But most awful of all is the knife, Runa's knife, sticking into the center of her chest.

"She's dead," Sasha says. She kneels next to her, hand outreached as if to touch her but hovering hopelessly in the air.

We both know what this means.

"This isn't Runa, Sasha," I say. "We were wrong."

"It's her knife," Sasha says. "Maybe she got out of the massage parlor—"

"Jesus Christ, Sasha, she just got put in there! How would she somehow get out?"

But Sasha doesn't want to admit it. She takes her radio, speaking tentatively. *"Axel."* She holds the radio close to her face, breathing unsteady. *"It's Sasha. Has Runa escaped?"*

"Escaped?" he responds, somewhat muffled. *"What are you talking about? I'm outside the door."*

I can tell it takes everything in her to carry on talking. *"Can you check . . . can you just go inside and see if she's . . . still there?"*

"Of course she is." There's a crackle, a pause. *"Here. Listen for yourself."*

Runa's voice comes on, loud and clear. *"What is it? What is wrong? What have I done now?"*

"Nothing," Sasha whispers. Everyone will be listening in, about to hear the awful truth. *"It's Effie . . . you're not . . . we were wrong about you. Effie is dead."*

"You better not be messing about," Imogen cuts in. *"That would be a sick joke."*

"No joke," Sasha confirms. The sight of Effie lying like that, her open eyes, is too much to bear. *"This time I'm not wrong."*

Sasha must feel hot, because she starts pulling her uniform away from her neck and breathing rapidly. Is she going to have another panic attack?

For a second I think she might try to get away, but she's blocked by everyone else arriving, Runa in tow. There's still no sign of Captain Howard or Drew, but Melinda pushes her way to the front, hair now tied up in a bun, sinking to her knees in front of Effie, and pulls the knife out.

"Wait!" I cry. "There will be DNA on that!"

It's too late, though. The knife lands on the floor with a clang and Melinda leans over Effie, attempting CPR to no avail.

"I told you it was not me!" Runa says. "Now look at what has happened."

"I'm sorry," Sasha says. "I thought . . . with the jewelry . . ."

"The *jewelry*," she hisses. "Not a dead body! You all locked me up over nothing."

She is furious, rightfully so.

"Why kill Effie?" Noah asks. "I don't get it. If you're not the killer, why would the real one do that? Make it obvious we had the wrong culprit?"

"Because they want to pick off the stewardesses one by one," Imogen shrieks. "Well, you're not murdering me! Back away, all of you!"

"I think we need to get the guests now," Jade says. "Melinda? We need to tell the primary what's going on, get them all somewhere safe."

"They *are* safe, away from all this." Melinda closes Effie's eyes. "We are almost at New York. We stick together until then, and leave it to the police to figure out. Keep Mr. Edmondson and Mr. Johnson out of this."

"Fuck Benjamin and Digby, what about our *captain*? Where the hell is Captain Howard?" Imogen shouts. "*Why isn't he here?*"

"Wait!" Axel says. "Does anyone else feel that?"

Feel what? I freeze, expecting something dramatic, some shaking or tremor, but there's nothing.

"What is it?" Runa asks. "I can't feel anything!"

"That's the point," Axel says. "It's the engines. They've stopped."

PART FOUR

CHAPTER FORTY

JADE

Where before there was always a thrum, a vibration of movement across the water, now there is nothing.

There is no logical explanation for this. Euphemia only exacerbates matters. This can't be a coincidence—her killed and the engines failing.

I have to take some kind of lead. People are talking over one another, scared. I raise my voice to be heard above them and address our engineer. "Why have the engines stopped?"

Everyone turns to Melinda as if she's going to say something that will make it all better. But she shakes her head. "That shouldn't have happened."

"We need to see the captain," I say. "First Euphemia, now this. It is—" I want to say *ludicrous* that the captain of our vessel is not already down here, but I hold my tongue.

"Of course," Melinda says. "And I need to go to the engine rooms and assess the situation."

"We stick together," Jasmine says.

No, not Jasmine. *Tessa.* I cannot believe I did not recognize her straightaway. I knew she was up to something, that she was behaving oddly, but there was so much going on I never got the chance to truly confront her. I told Captain Howard last year that she wouldn't accept Hallie had fallen overboard, but he refused to listen, as always, and now here we are. Stewardesses are dead, Tessa is back, and the engines no longer work.

I'm just about to speak when the entire yacht plunges into darkness. Imogen and Runa scream. Even the emergency power is gone. Our only source of light is the window in the crew mess, a long horizontal strip, half seawater lapping against the glass and half moody sky. Perhaps it is the dark playing tricks, but the rocking of the boat is suddenly far more prominent. Everyone freezes, unsure of what to do, so I grab my phone and turn on the torch, shining a harsh light into the middle of the room. We use this to gather next to the window in the crew mess, leaving Euphemia behind in her dark cabin.

"The power's gone," Noah whispers, though I think that's obvious.

"Even the backup," I say. "What's happening?"

"That's what I want to know!"

Imogen screams again; Drew has come downstairs and placed his hand on her shoulder. He's holding a real torch, the strong beam rendering my phone useless.

"Where the hell have you been?" Axel demands.

Drew switches off his torch, the room now dim and dependent on the meager sunlight. "I was doing some work for Captain Howard when I felt the engines power off. I decided to come here and ask what was happening."

Some work for Captain Howard? That has taken all night? I look at the radio attached to his hip, noting its off position. Completely against the rules. What has he been doing?

"You really have no clue what's been happening?" Noah asks him.

"No. Why? What's wrong?"

"God. Where do we even start?" Imogen says.

"Euphemia is dead," I tell him.

"And people thought I did it," Runa says bitterly. "But that isn't the case."

Drew looks as though we've told him his family has been killed. I never knew he cared about Euphemia so much. "Effie is *dead*? You're lying."

"She was stabbed to death in her cabin," Runa says.

Drew runs to Effie's cabin and lets out a wail. He hurries to the toilet next, his retching the only sound we hear.

The boat shifts, tipping like a rocking horse.

When Drew returns, white and trembling, visibly traumatized, I take action. "First, we have to go to the bridge. Speak to the captain. Have him declare a Mayday."

"Melinda," Drew says. "This is—"

"Agreed," Melinda cuts across him, addressing us all. "I'm second-in-command here, and while the captain is not around, you all defer to me. Drew, you're going to come with me to the engine rooms and we'll see whether this can be fixed. Jade, you go to the guests and explain the situation and gather them in the main salon. Axel, you're in charge of the rest of the crew. Go to the bridge and get Captain Howard."

"No," Axel says. "We all move together, like Jasmine said. We all go to the bridge and get the captain."

"As much as I don't want to agree with the bastard," Imogen says, "there's still a killer among us."

Melinda shakes her head. "I really think—"

"We should stick together, Melinda," Drew says. "Okay?"

Surprisingly, she backs down at Drew's words. "Fine. The bridge it is."

And so we move.

It is eerily silent up the steps and along the corridor.

We go as one, Drew leading the way with his torch, shining our way forward. We keep our footsteps soft. The path of light makes the yacht seem smaller, the shadows creeping in at the edges, desperate to consume us. I stick beside him, which is why when we head up the stairs and round the corner I'm right there with him as the torch finds a figure in the darkness and we both scream.

Drew drops the torch and it lands with a thud, switching off. This corridor is deep into the interior and has no windows, so we're suddenly without a light source. I have to scramble for my phone again, shine out a tiny strip of light.

"Who's there?" Axel shouts. "Who is it?"

"We're going to die!" Imogen shrieks.

"Hello?" the figure in the distance cries, and to my relief I realize it's Eva.

"Eva, my God." Jasmine—it is hard not to think of her as that, looking like she does—gasps.

Eva is in casual clothes—black leggings and an oversized jumper, her hair pulled into a messy high ponytail. She's not wearing makeup and looks about ten years younger.

"What is going on?" she says, marching forward and clinging to Jasmine's arms as if she can't quite believe she's real. She looks back at everyone else, at Drew standing to the side staring at her, at the rest of us relieved she isn't some axe murderer. "I woke up and it was too quiet. Is the engine—have we arrived? We've stopped, haven't we? And the power . . . is it gone everywhere?"

She is a guest, and my first instinct is to protect her. Tell her to go back to her room, that someone will be through with a cup of tea and whatever breakfast she desires shortly. But even I have to concede that the time for my rules is over. I get her up to speed, not pulling any punches and laying out the hard truth.

She shakes her head in disbelief. "So now you're all heading to the bridge? I'm coming with you."

"You were with Mr. Johnson, right?" Jasmine asks.

"He kicked me out of his room at about three in the morning. I've been in mine ever since. What about Mr. Edmondson?"

Jasmine shrugs. "Asleep still as far as I'm concerned."

Melinda clears her throat. "I would recommend we leave Mr. John-

son and Mr. Edmondson in their cabins until we know precisely what
we are dealing with."

"She's right," I say, even though I was the one who wanted to gather
them before. "It's enough that Jasmine and Eva are unfortunately involved. If we can fix this without them knowing, that's better for their
experience."

"Better for their experience," Imogen repeats with a scoff. "Jesus
Christ, Jade."

"We take care of this ourselves," Melinda says firmly, and she nods
at me in acknowledgment; finally, the faintest glimmer of respect.

My stomach buzzes. At last I'm getting somewhere with her.

It's only taken two bodies and the engines failing.

We carry on, Eva in tow, reaching the corridor leading to the
bridge. The portholes along the left, a decorative element more than
of any use but now our only natural light source, show spatters of rain
hitting the reinforced glass. Bad weather.

That's all we need.

"Fuck," Imogen says. She's spotted it too, and her comment makes
everyone turn and watch the sky outside grow even greyer.

We reach the closed door of the bridge, and Axel knocks three
times. "Captain?" he calls, to no response. "Are you in there?"

Still no answer. It's at this point that I finally allow myself to feel a
little scared.

"I'm going first," Axel says. "Stay behind me."

"How noble," Runa murmurs, and how she has the time for her sar-
castic comments is beyond me.

Before anyone can say anything more, the boat leans violently to the
left, sending Eva tumbling into the wall and causing even the rest of us
to stumble. It lasts so long I think we're not going to right ourselves,
that the yacht is going to tip over entirely, when we get pulled in the
other direction and straighten.

"We need to hurry," Axel says.

He leads us into the bridge, which is brighter by virtue of the large glass windows, but shadows still cast across the room. The full view of the sky and sea across the horizon is clear, the water thick and black and churning, the sky its airborne twin. We're in trouble if we don't get things back under control. Another storm is brewing at the worst possible time.

But there's no one here. The captain is nowhere to be seen.

Noah checks all around the room, even bending down and peering underneath the captain's desk. "The captain was on watch. *Someone* has to be on watch."

"There's no one," Axel murmurs, barely able to believe it himself.

Beneath the windows all six screens are black. The leather seats sit empty, Axel and Melinda hurrying across to fill them and try and figure out what's wrong. Across the way, the captain's desk has had all drawers opened, documents spilling out onto the floor. It looks like someone has ransacked the place. Jasmine runs to a cupboard and searches through it but yells out in disappointment when she can't find what she's looking for.

The bun I tied this morning gives up, flopping against the back of my scalp. I reach up and pull it loose, letting my hair tumble around my shoulders, stiff and limp from hair spray until I tear my fingers through it. I take the pen from behind my ear and slide it into my front pocket. I've never let my hair loose before; it falls to my waist in a long blonde sweep, the ends practically white.

Ever since I was little, I've loved routine. Nothing thrilled me more than organizing tea parties at nursery school with full-on schedules and menus and rules on how each girl and boy should sit and sip their pretend drinks and eat their air food. When I started school, my supplies were always the neatest, and I won house points for tidiness if not for intellectual aptitude, and I became deputy head girl more from sheer administrative skill than true popularity. The head girl passed

on all of the "boring stuff" to me with no idea how much I relished
it. Even now I have three different diaries: work, personal, leisure. I
wake up at the same time every day and I live and breathe by the shift
patterns I've designed. If it's not in my calendar, I don't know about
it. Every impulse in me isn't so much screaming but *itching*, begging
to be scratched, for me to make all this somehow okay. I don't even
realize I'm clenching down hard on my jaw until releasing it brings a
warm taste of iron in my mouth. This is not how yachts are run. All my
training, all the things I have done to maintain stability in the past,
and this is going to be my legacy. I can see the headline now: MURDER
ON A SUPERYACHT.

"All systems are down." Axel tries to work the various levers and
buttons. Nothing happens. "Fuck. Chief, help me here."

Melinda tries to switch them back on too, but to no avail. "It's a
total systems failure."

"This has to be deliberate," Axel says.

"Not necessarily," Melinda says. "It could be—"

"Oh, come on, Chief! The person wrecking things before? The
missing life jackets and life rings? It's them."

Noah starts searching around the captain's desk, picking up various papers. "Why has everything been taken out? What was Captain
Howard looking for?"

"Where *is* the captain?" Imogen shouts.

We try our radios, calling out to him, but there is no answer. Only
our own voices echoing back to us, a cacophony that grows increasingly desperate.

"The only way to fix this, if there's any hope, would be manually,"
Melinda says.

"Manually?" I repeat.

"Going to the source," Melinda tells me. "The engine rooms."

"Why all this now?" I say. "The same time Effie was found murdered."

"And Captain Howard has left the bridge." Axel frowns. "After he banned me from being on watch shifts! To leave things unattended at a time like this . . ."

"Chief, what did Captain Howard say when you told him about Effie?" I ask.

"Just that I needed to handle it," Melinda says. "Nothing seemed out of the ordinary."

"He told Mr. Johnson when Lola died," Jasmine says, and we all turn to her, surprised. "He went to see him first before anyone else. Eva was there, she heard the whole thing."

Eva nods. "She's right."

Axel frowns. "Didn't Mr. Johnson pretend not to know what was going on?"

"Maybe he's gone to tell Mr. Johnson about this too," I suggest, though why he would consider that as a feasible action to take right now, I don't know.

"What is happening?" Noah moans, his nose bleeding again. He wipes it with his arm, but blood has already got on one of the documents he's holding. "What even is all this stuff? Minterne Limited? It's not doing well."

"What do you mean?"

"It's been a while since I was an accountant, but these figures speak for themselves." Noah flicks through a few more pages. "Minterne has been having to sell off assets for months. If I was in charge of their finances I'd expect to be fired for letting them get in such a state."

"Why would such documents be here on the bridge?" I ask.

"Those are personal," Melinda says, snatching the file from Noah and scanning it herself, not seeing the irony in her actions.

"Enough about that. It's not important. Maybe we can still report a Mayday somehow." Axel taps the screens impatiently.

"What about your radios?" Eva asks desperately. "Won't they be able to call for help?"

"Not our everyday ones, but—" Axel turns around. "Where's the ditch bag?" He bends down underneath the desk, then rises, shaking his head. "The ditch bag isn't here. Shit." His eyes flick to the hooks where all the keys are kept. "The tender keys are gone too."

No. That can't be right.

"What's a ditch bag?" Eva says, voice breaking with fear.

"An abandon-ship bag," Axel informs her. "It's filled with everything important needed to survive in emergency conditions. The EPIRB—that's an emergency locator beacon—and handheld VHF radios and GPS. Plus the satellite phone." He puts a hand to his forehead. "Even simple things like extra batteries. Torches. Flares. First aid."

Solutions, Jade. Be logical. It has saved you before. *Think!*

"Melinda," Drew says. "Shouldn't we . . ."

Eva is barely audible, her words a frightened whisper. "What does it mean that it's gone?"

"Taking the ditch bag means someone plans to get off this yacht," Axel tells her simply. "Along with the tender keys missing . . . I have a bad feeling about this. Taking those and the ditch bag would leave us stranded. Captain Howard wouldn't do that. He wouldn't leave us all on here."

"Wouldn't he?" Jasmine says. "How well do you all know your precious captain?"

Axel opens his mouth to respond, but nothing comes out. He looks again at the empty key hook and the space where the ditch bag should be, and finally swears under his breath. "Fuck. Drew, come with me. We need to check the tender."

Drew's eyes widen. "But what about sticking together—"

"For Christ's sake, Drew!" Axel snaps. "Come on. Everyone else, we'll meet you in the engine rooms. If the tender isn't there—"

"If the tender isn't there we're screwed," Jasmine says.

"Do we tell Benjamin and Digby now?" Eva whispers. She has dropped their titles, maybe without even realizing.

Axel hesitates in the doorway at Eva's words. He turns back, the stress visible on his face. "Just—hold on. Everything might still be fine."

"Famous last words," Imogen mutters.

They hurry out of the room, their footsteps pounding down the corridor, taking Drew's torch with them. We are left with our phones again, which do little to illuminate the space around us. Without the engines, the yacht continues to rock, challenging even my sea legs. Imogen is circling her phone around, shifting the light so incessantly I tell her to stop.

"It's Sasha," she says. "She isn't here. She didn't go with Axel and Drew; we would have seen her. Did she even come to the bridge with us? Where the fuck is she?"

What?

"She's . . ." I look around, meeting only the panicked faces of the rest of the crew.

Imogen is right. Sasha is gone.

CHAPTER FORTY-ONE

SASHA

No one has followed me.

The moment the power cut I saw my chance for escape, and with everyone distracted by Drew I made my exit. I don't have my phone on me, so I'm stumbling in the dark, feeling my way along the walls.

I tear down the corridor, feel the door to the spare office, burst through and slam it shut behind me. There's a large window that looks straight out to the endless ocean, letting in enough light to see, but the clouds outside leave shadows across the room. I grab one of the cabinets and push it against the door to block the way, not caring when it topples over and spills out dozens of old magazines with names like *BOAT International* and *SuperYacht World*.

Collapsing onto a chair, I put my head between my legs and breathe.

I didn't always have anxiety. I've been anxious, but that's different. Forever a perfectionist, wanting people to like me. It was this incessant need to be acknowledged that got me mixed up with Dr. Martin in the first place. I thought I was so special, so unique—God, what an idiot. But *anxiety*, this shadow of doom that sweeps me up and takes my breath away, that has only been present since Janet Lesley.

I thought I was getting better. What a joke. What good is telling Jasmine if I don't do anything about it? If I remain hiding, unwilling to go back home and fix things?

And now look. I've gone back to my first instinct when things get tough: run away.

Focus on distractions. That's the advice, right?

Five things you can see. The closed door. The upturned cabinet. The magazines. The grey carpet. A small white stain in the corner, years old.

Four things you can touch. My feet on the ground. My fingers gripping the hard plastic arms of the chair. The tears on my cheeks. What else? The rough fabric of my stewardess uniform.

Effie's was covered with her blood.

No. Stop. Concentrate.

Three things you can hear. My juddering breath. The whoosh of the ocean. The creak of the chair as I start to sit up. Not the engines, though. They're gone.

Seeing Effie—the blood—all I could think about was Janet. I didn't save her. And I didn't save Effie.

Two things you can smell. My own sweat. And a musty, heavy scent, the kind from a room forgotten and unloved.

One thing you can taste. My salty tears.

My breathing steadies. My heart rate begins to return to normal.

Gingerly, I move to sit down by the magazines, keen to tidy them away. It sounds daft, but if I can restore order to them, maybe I can restore order to my frazzled mind too. I'm not paying attention, adding them to a neat pile, when I see that Digby Johnson is on the front cover of one of them.

JOHNSON FAMILY EMPIRE MARKS NEW INVESTMENT, the headline reads.

What is it with rich people and calling their relatives an "empire"? Do they want that image of a colonial conqueror?

That's where these wealthy families originally made their money, after all.

It's a much younger-looking Digby flanked by two older people I assume are his parents. The son is a clone of his father but without the warm smile. He's easily in his eighties. Digby's mother is far younger, sixty at most, and extremely pretty, with long blonde hair.

I open the article to another spread of them all, and confirmation that they are indeed Digby's parents. Digby's father is sitting on a chair while Digby and his mother stand behind him. The caption underneath reads: *Alistair Johnson, owner of Minterne Ltd., seated center. Above left, his son and heir to the family fortune, Digby Johnson, and above right, his third wife, Ophelia Johnson, née Minterne.*

Ophelia. Like the name of this boat.

Didn't Jade tell me it was the owner's mother's name?

I flip back to the front cover. The magazine is called *SuperYacht World*. This is a story about the Johnson family's new investment.

Which means . . .

Digby is the owner of this yacht.

Not a guest. He's the *owner*. And he's been hiding that fact.

Captain Howard must have known. Benjamin too. And yet all three have pretended otherwise this entire trip. Digby wasn't even the primary. Why would they go to the effort of pretending he isn't the owner? He would get even better treatment if we knew. He'd be able to stay in his suite rather than one of the guest cabins.

Does anyone else know? Melinda? Jade? Axel?

I should tell someone. Jasmine. She's the only person I can trust. But that means leaving here. Leaving this room.

I'm a coward. There is no changing, not when I did something so terrible. Where Jasmine heads straight for danger, I back off in the opposite direction.

"Sasha?" Someone starts hammering on the door. "Are you in there?"

As if I have conjured her from my mind, it's Jasmine. She's come looking for me.

I could keep quiet. Let her move on, search the rest of the yacht. Remain a coward.

No. I stand shakily.

My arms are tired as I push the cabinet out of the way, the rest of the magazines forgotten, and open the door.

Jasmine doesn't hesitate; she wraps me in a hug, holding me tight. "Are you okay? I was so worried something had happened to you."

I didn't even think about that. I just wanted to get away. No wonder she's so relieved to see me.

"I'm sorry," I tell her. "I had a panic attack. It was all too much down there. Effie's body . . . it brought everything with Janet back. I'm sorry."

"I get it," she says, though how can she? Jasmine has never run from anything. "But you can't escape this one, I'm afraid. And we have an even bigger problem now."

"An even bigger problem than Effie being dead, the engines not working, and the power being out?"

"Let's call it an *equivalent* problem. But it could be a bigger one if it means what I think. The ditch bag is gone and so are the tender keys."

"What? That would mean . . ."

"That someone is planning on leaving the superyacht. Namely, Captain Howard. He wasn't on watch. He's disappeared."

"Then—" I can't believe this. "If the tender is being launched—"

"If the tender has been launched we're already too late," Jasmine says. "Axel and Drew have gone to find out if it's still there. They're meeting us in the engine rooms, because what we need to do is try and get the engines working again. But we need you too."

"You don't need me."

"Sasha, are you kidding? I can't do this without you."

"You're so much braver than I am. You charge headfirst into any situation—"

"Yeah, and I'm surprised it hasn't gotten me killed," she says. "Seriously, Sasha. I know you hate yourself, but you're not a monster."

"But—"

"You ran away from what happened with Janet Lesley," Jasmine says, "and all that's done is bring you trauma. It's hard. I get it. But don't choose to run away again. Don't give in to your fear. Besides, it's not just me. *We* need you."

She gives a wave with her arm, and soon the rest of the crew appear at the door, springing from the shadows. They've been waiting this whole time for me.

"We're in this together," Jasmine says.

"Look, Detective Dun—Sasha," Imogen says. "You've had some good instincts, alright? Maybe if we listened to you earlier things wouldn't have got so out of hand. Maybe Effie wouldn't have died."

Even Jade is contrite. "I'm sorry I didn't take you seriously when it came to the diary. You were right. I just wanted to focus on the charter, despite everything. It was all just—"

"It's okay, Jade," I say, and she blinks at me in surprise. "I'm scared too."

"I'm not scared," she says, unconvincingly.

"Oh, come on, Jade," Imogen scoffs. "We're all fucking terrified. You're allowed to be human, you know. You're not just our chief stewardess anymore, not after everything that's happened."

"All I wanted was to be the best chief stewardess," Jade murmurs. "My life is—well. We don't need to go into that. But this is everything to me. This season was going to be . . . I was so sure it would be perfect. And what have I accomplished? One stewardess was fired, two were killed, and the other two are stuck in whatever dire situation this is."

"None of that is your fault!" I protest.

"No. But I was so focused on doing my job how I thought it should be done that I missed things. Like Lola agreeing to that stupid jewelry scheme with Runa, and me thinking it was Zara. Not listening to Euphem—to *Effie* when she tried telling me what she heard. Not taking Lola's diary seriously. Your hidden *pregnancy*, Imogen. Not stopping your petty little arguments."

"Petty little arguments are half the fun of being a stewardess," Imogen says. "Don't take it personally. You did as good as you could have."

Jade's eyes widen.

"Oh, don't act so shocked." Imogen rolls her eyes. "I can actually be a nice person!"

I don't know why, but this makes me laugh, despite everything.

Imogen looks like she might be annoyed for a moment, but then she giggles too. Even Jade joins in, and the three of us stewardesses are suddenly laughing our heads off.

Maybe because it's easier than crying. The others look at us as if we're mad.

"Sasha," Imogen says when we calm down. "You're alright, actually."

"What?" I say, grinning. "I didn't quite catch that."

Imogen gives me a shove. "Well, I'm not repeating it, so you'll never know now."

Noah and Eva nod at me. Melinda hangs back, chewing her lip. Only Runa remains somewhat hostile. I don't blame her.

I inhale deeply, ignoring how this makes my heart pound faster, then let out a long, slow breath. It's the longest one of my life.

Bad things happen everywhere. There is no running away from that fact.

So I'm not going to run anymore.

"I'm coming with you all," I say. Something shifts, like a switch long forgotten and now turned on. I'm still terrified. But I'm not going anywhere. I'm really doing this.

Then, I promise silently, I'm going home and facing up to what I did to Janet Lesley. Her family deserves the truth.

I wait for that old voice in me to scream: *Run away, run away!*

It doesn't come.

I'm ready.

"But first, there's something I need to show you all."

CHAPTER FORTY-TWO

IMOGEN

Sasha shows us the magazine cover. "Someone has been hiding in plain sight."

I frown at the image. It takes a second to realize what she's getting at, and then I'm even more confused.

Eva has the same baffled expression I do. "That's Mr. Johnson."

Sasha juts the magazine forward, as if that will make a difference. "*SuperYacht World*. It's about his family investing in the superyacht industry. It features his mother, Ophelia."

"Ophelia," Eva says slowly, "as in the name of this yacht?"

"Oh God," I say, understanding now with horrific clarity. "You can't be serious."

Sasha nods. "He's the owner."

"Wait," Jasmine says. "Could the computer we found in the owner's suite . . . could that be his instead of Captain Howard's?"

What computer?

I want to throw up when Sasha explains what they found, the camera that she smashed to pieces in the shower.

We've been *spied* on. Gawked at when we didn't know.

The thought makes me prickly, like I want to tear my skin right off and never show it again.

"Why didn't you tell us?" I say. "We should have known! It's disgusting, it's—"

"The moment I found out I got rid of it," Sasha says. "We were wait-ing until later today when we docked. To be safe. Then we were going to explain everything to you all."

"And you thought it was Captain Howard?" For all his faults, the captain has never once ogled us. I've never caught him looking where he shouldn't, or letting his hand linger anywhere too long. Noah's eyes practically pop out on stalks if we're in a tight dress, Axel speaks for himself, and even Drew can't help a sneaky glance. It doesn't feel right. Yet Digby makes perfect sense. He might not be as directly touchy as Benjamin but he gives the impression it wouldn't do well to be alone with him.

But then Captain Howard has disappeared, taking the ditch bag with him. So what do I know? I have the worst judgment in the world, as is evident from Axel.

My chest aches and my mouth is dry. I've tried staying strong on the surface. It's easier to let them think I'm typical Imogen. People like me have to act a certain way. I don't have the luxury of running like Sasha and having everyone come looking for me. When my brother died I had to get back to normality and work hard at my GCSEs, or I'd be stuck in my council flat for the rest of my life, even though I spent every night crying my eyes out. I can't be overwhelmed or I'll be swept away with the tide.

I'm terrified. That's the truth. Seeing Effie like that . . . undeniable confirmation there truly is a killer on board, targeting stewardesses . . . and now this too? Being spied on, looked at in our most vulnerable moment for some kind of perverse pleasure?

"Surely not," Noah whispers, horrified.

"It's true," Jasmine says. "Whether you like it or not."

Runa shakes her head. "I promise I never saw this when I went into the owner's—er, Mr. Johnson's suite. I just hid the jewelry."

"We're going to get him for this," Noah says. "He has all that evi-dence on his computer. He won't be able to walk away."

"Rich men like him always do," Jasmine whispers.

Eva touches her neck. For the first time, I notice the line of bruises, some purple, some green. From Digby?

That does it. "This piece of shit is going to pay."

I look at the magazine cover again, focused on Digby's smug grin. All of his wealth and privilege and position, inherited from his parents. The man has never had to do a real day's work in his life.

"Minterne Limited," Jasmine says, reading the tagline. "Wasn't that the business Noah was just looking at in the captain's things?"

"Do you think Mr. Johnson is the one who . . ." Jade can't finish her sentence.

"I bet he and Captain Howard are in on this together," Jasmine says. "Old buddies getting their kicks murdering stewardesses."

"That sick son of a bitch," I say. "I was hardly Mouse's biggest fan, nor Effie's, for that matter . . . but to do that to them?"

"And to Hallie," Jasmine says, then falters. "I mean, or maybe she got away . . ."

She's kidding herself if she thinks her friend isn't as dead as those two. But I can understand that kind of denial. After my brother died I still saw him everywhere: waiting by the gates after school, among endless boys in backpacks and oversized blazers; in the four-leaf clovers he'd leave for me; in fog on the mirror; and every night in my dreams. I used to talk to him. Haven't in a while. He'd hate who I've become, probably wouldn't even recognize me.

Melinda is in denial. "We don't even know if that was Mr. Johnson's computer, from what you're saying. As for him being the owner . . ."

"Did you know?" I ask her.

"Of course not!"

I don't know whether to believe her.

Jasmine is as doubtful as I am. "Why would you not know? You've been on this yacht for how many years?"

"Five," Melinda says. "I only ever wanted to help and be the best possible. And that meant not asking questions. I had my doubts on occasion. But Howard was *captain*."

"You know about the debt problems, don't you?" Jasmine says.

What debt problems? Jade is as in the dark as I am, head whipping around at Jasmine's words and some kind of realization dawning on her face.

Melinda hangs her head. "I was hoping he would sort it out . . . you know he is getting a one-hundred-thousand-dollar tip if we make it to New York today? He told me about it, swore me to secrecy."

That's why he's been rushing. That's why he didn't want to turn around or divert when Mouse's body turned up.

For money. Of course. Is anything not about money on this godforsaken superyacht?

When our own tips have been taken off us to pay for replacement jewelry. And he was getting that.

"Whatever the truth is," Jade says, "we have bigger issues to deal with. We need to get to the engine rooms."

"And Mr. Edmondson?" Eva asks. "Where does he fit into all this?"

"I don't know," Jade replies. "And that's why it's best we don't get him involved right now."

Nerves squeeze my stomach into knots as we walk back along the corridor and start heading down the main stairs, a spiral journey to the very bottom, to the same place Axel and Captain Howard had their meeting and I hovered on the steps above to listen in. We're below sea level and it feels heavier, more claustrophobic than I was expecting.

It's an industrial level, not designed for guest exploration. Behind us, stored in the stern's bulkhead, are the tender and water toys, inaccessible from here. I can't help wondering if the tender is already gone. Beyond the first room we enter, with the generators and airconditioning system, are the engines themselves, as well as the various pumps, motors, and valves that make everything work that I wouldn't have a clue about. There's a loud whooshing sound from that direction, almost like running water, and it's only when I'm off the stairs that I realize that's because it *is* water.

We're ankle deep in it.

"What the fuck?" I shriek.

People start panicking, shouting and screaming and heading back to the stairs, and I'm right there with them.

"Have the water tanks burst?" Noah says. "Is that what's causing all these problems? Everyone, get out of here. This could be dangerous."

"It's not the water tanks."

The voice comes from up ahead.

It's Digby, walking toward us.

And Captain Howard is right behind him.

"Captain!" Jade yells. "Haven't you been getting any of our radio calls? What's happening?"

"We know you're the owner!" Jasmine shouts at Digby. "We know you lied."

Digby is surprised but recovers, glaring at Captain Howard. "You told them, did you?"

Captain Howard, though, is just as stunned. "How did you know that?"

"An old magazine with Mr. Johnson—Digby—on the cover," Sasha says. "And his family. We saw his mother, Ophelia. Like the name of this yacht."

Digby narrows his eyes. "What else do you know, exactly?"

About your creepy spy camera, and your murdering-bastard ways.

The engine rooms are unexpectedly cold, and goose bumps appear across my arms. I imagined down here would be hot and chaotic, but with everything not working it's chillingly silent.

Captain Howard addresses us firmly. "You all need to prepare to evacuate the vessel. It's no longer safe. Leave dealing with Digby to me. Melinda, take command."

Leave him to deal with Digby? *Evacuate?*

"Captain, what is going on?" Jade demands. "We've been left quite literally in the dark. Effie was *murdered*, the engines have stopped, water is gathering, and you're ordering us to evacuate?"

I am just as furious. "She's right. We need answers."

"Effie was murdered?" Captain Howard whispers, and from the look on his face, the whiteness engulfing his skin, it's obvious this is news to him.

"But—Melinda told you," Sasha says, frowning. "Didn't she?"

"You were on watch!" Noah says. "How could you leave your post?"

"He was busy with me," Digby says. "Sorry about that, folks."

"Why don't you tell us *all* what's going on, Digby?" I say, deliberately using his first name. The time for looking pretty and simpering at every word he says is over. "So that everyone is on the same page. You seem to be the one in the know."

He smiles. "That's part of the reason why I'm down here. I wanted one last look around, one final hurrah with my ship."

"One final hurrah?"

"Yes," he says. "Because it won't be around much longer. This superyacht is sinking."

CHAPTER FORTY-THREE

—

JASMINE

This superyacht is sinking.

It seems almost silly that we're all as shocked by this information as we are, when the engines have stopped, the power has gone, and we're standing in water that's one foot deep and steadily increasing. Yet my mouth falls open like a cartoon character's as gasps echo around me, bouncing off the steel walls. Here in the half light, half shadow created by our phones and the torches in Digby's and Captain Howard's hands, I can't see everyone's reactions, but I can hear them, *feel* them, the sudden shift in the air as we all take in that yes, unbelievably, things can get worse.

Captain Howard is the first to take action. "I told you all to prepare for evacuation. Melinda! Get them moving."

But Melinda stays where she is. The rest of us don't budge either.

"What do you mean, it's sinking?" Sasha asks. She's holding together quite well considering she almost gave up on us back there. For a moment I thought she would. But there's a confidence to her posture now, chin lifted and shoulders back, as if she can take on anyone. She reminds me of—well, Hallie.

Digby shrugs. "I'm not sure what's difficult to understand. We're getting our feet wet as we speak. If Howard hadn't delayed things—"

Digby seems ready for it, as if this whole thing was planned.

God. I could laugh. Of course it was.

His final hurrah, like he said. This hasn't happened by accident.

"You're scuttling it," I say, "aren't you?"

"Scuttling it?" Eva echoes. "What does that mean?"

"He's deliberately sinking it, Eva."

"But it's his yacht!" Eva says. "Why would he sink it?"

Why indeed? "Whatever the reason, this yacht is going down because of him."

"Well, indirectly," Digby says. "I never get my hands dirty. I had some help."

"No," I say. "You get your honorable captain to do the dirty work for you."

Captain Howard turns to me, dumbfounded. "What are you talking about? I'm the one that's been trying to stop him!"

"The jig is up," I say. "There's no point pretending anymore."

"Is this why Axel wasn't allowed on watch?" Imogen asks. "Because he'd reveal your plan?"

"Where is Axel?" Captain Howard asks. "And Drew? And is Benjamin—"

"Axel and Drew are checking to see if the tender was launched," Imogen says. "They should be here any second. They had to check because, you know, the ditch bag and tender keys are gone and so were you? So we thought you'd left us all here, apparently to drown!"

"No!" The captain is appalled, or at the very least putting on a good show of it. "I had nothing to do with that. The ditch bag and tender keys are *gone*? What do you mean?"

"Stop avoiding the question! You kept Axel off watch to suit yourself, didn't you?"

"I did that because Digby requested it," the captain replies. "I realize now he saw Axel as a threat if he caught wind of what he was planning. Apparently I was too foolish to see the obvious. Too trusting of my old friend. I had nothing to do with any of this."

"You're scuttling this yacht to cover up your murders," I shout, losing my patience with him. "Both of you. Lola was meant to be an easy one. Simply chuck her overboard after you've had your way with her and let the ocean do the rest. But you couldn't even give Effie that, you had to do it quickly, because you knew you'd be sinking the yacht today. Why today, by the way? I know Digby is giving you a big fat tip for it, Captain Howard, so don't try and pretend there isn't a reason."

"You've got this wrong—"

"You had Lola's phone!" I snap. "And now it's missing. Where is it?"

"It's missing?" Captain Howard repeats. "I found it that morning on deck. I kept it in my cabinet for safekeeping so I could deliver it to her parents when we docked."

"Liar!"

"And what about the photos and videos?" Imogen calls. "Was it you, Digby? Or was it you after all, Captain? I always thought you were respectful, but now . . ."

"What photos and videos?" Captain Howard says. "What are you talking about?"

"The ones of us stewardesses in the shower!" she shouts. "Taken without our knowledge with a hidden spy camera. It's disgusting."

And then Digby *laughs.* "You have Benjamin to thank for that one. That was his idea."

"It was your laptop," I say.

"That's not my laptop," Digby says. "That was Benjamin's. I let him use my suite because—well, previously it was because we were friends, but this charter it was just so he thought there were no hard feelings."

"You don't care, do you?" I say. "That their privacy has been invaded, that any of this has happened . . ."

"I knew you were trouble," Digby says to me. "I told Benjamin to let me handle the escorts, but no, he had to stumble upon you. Only he didn't stumble upon you, did he, *Tessa*? I have to say, you've considerably improved since last year. I had to be shown a photograph of you to remember who you were. Quite a forgettable entity before, weren't you? Looks like your friend disappearing did you a favor."

He knows who I am.

He wasn't there when I told everyone I was Tessa. Neither was Captain Howard.

So how does he know?

"And for what it's worth," Digby says, "I chose today because it is my mother's birthday. It feels fitting that the yacht named after her goes down in tribute to her too."

Captain Howard steps closer. "Tessa? Is that really you?"

"It's me," I say. "So don't try pulling your I'm-a-good-captain crap with me. I saw you for what you really were last year when you abandoned me in Greece, threw flowers over the side, and considered your job done. I should have known then you were involved."

Hallie wanted us to leave. But she sent that message too late.

I've always thought of Hallie as a missing person. A disappearance. I've not accepted the logic: if you're missing for a year, your odds of coming back are slim to none.

I can't acknowledge it. Can't admit that she might be . . .

No. I can't give up hope.

"Tessa." Captain Howard's voice is low. "Hallie's death was an accident. A tragic one, but an accident. We followed procedure. I know it appears callous to you, but . . . we moved on quickly because that was what Digby wanted. I removed you from the staff as I thought it was in your best interest. You were distraught."

"You didn't follow procedure!" I snap. "I've seen the incident report. Even your lapdog Melinda thought so."

"Melinda?" Captain Howard says.

"It was a poor report," she admits.

He opens his mouth to argue, then deflates. "You're right. I wasn't— I'm not in a good place. That's not an excuse, but it's the truth. I get paid a lot to be a captain," he says. "But I've been struggling. Financially. Last year I had to sell my house to pay off my debts, and since then they've only got worse."

"We know," I tell him. "I found your letters."

"I'm sorry," Captain Howard says. "I have a gambling problem. This charter—my retirement—it was my last chance to sort my life out. Digby promised me a one-hundred-thousand-dollar bonus, yes, if I made it to New York today."

"You were one of the best in the industry," Melinda says. "What happened, Howard?"

"I've done terrible things," Captain Howard says. "Looked the other way. Enabled certain behavior. But I do not have anything to do with Lola or Effie or *Ophelia* sinking. I suspected something—I looked into Digby's businesses, tried to figure out why I had a bad feeling. And then early this morning, Digby told me why he had made me maneuver the yacht into this position."

I won't back down easily. "Why keep his identity secret? What's the point? Why keep up a facade of Benjamin being the primary and Digby just one of his guests? I don't get it."

"It was always how Digby wanted it. A low profile."

"Why did you tell Digby about Lola's body being found before going down yourself that day?"

"It was my duty to inform the owner," Captain Howard says. "That's all that was. It was Digby who then pretended the conversation never happened, and I had to go along with it. I was spiraling, trying to live a lifestyle I couldn't afford. Trying to match the likes of Digby and Benjamin. I had a tricky childhood, mixing with people who had money I could only dream of and somehow being expected to match them."

A scholarship kid, I remember Benjamin saying.

Digby laughs. "Did you know we used to call him Have-Not How-ard? He would come in in a pre-owned uniform given to him by some charitable chap a couple of years above, and he never went on the school trips. He managed to scrape by through letting us copy his answers or writing our essays for us. I knew if I sold this as some grand retirement gift he'd fall hook, line, and sinker. He was as giddy as I was the day my father died and I took ownership of Minterne Limited. He had no idea."

Captain Howard didn't know.

The water is getting deeper. What was once ankle-deep is now up to our knees.

Minterne Ltd. is Digby's family business. His legacy. And it's been struggling. Almost about to go under, according to Noah. That's not to mention all the various documents I found in the captain's room. The ones I tossed aside because I was focusing on Hallie, ignoring the financial statements, the plans, the insurance schemes.

Insurance.

"You're doing this to claim on the insurance, aren't you?" I say to Digby.

He nods, and I can't breathe.

"You want the millions that will come out of that so you can rescue your business. The family business you managed to run into the ground. That's your plan, isn't it?"

Digby's eyes flash with anger. "*I* ran nothing into the ground. My financial advisor wasn't keeping an eye on the figures. It's *his* fault."

His financial advisor? Why am I getting a sudden feeling of dread, of recognition, that now all the pieces are coming together?

"Then take it out on your financial advisor!" Runa shouts. "Do not take it out on us. We are innocent in this."

"Oh, but I am taking it out on my financial advisor," Digby says. "You all know him quite well."

Benjamin.

Of *course*.

That's why he's been off with him this season. Why they've barely been together, why Digby can't seem to disguise his irritation around him.

"You won't get away with sinking a superyacht," I say. "There'll be an investigation."

"A cursory one," Digby agrees, "I'm sure. But we're actually positioned rather well—just over two hundred miles from the coast of New York. Close enough to get away on the tender. Far enough that we're still in international waters, and no one is going to want the responsibility of dredging this huge vessel back up to the surface. No, I think things will be fine, especially after a few convincing witness statements."

"And Lola and Effie's deaths?" Sasha whispers.

"Nothing to do with me." He waves his hand dismissively. "They can be recorded as victims. What's a real sinking without casualties?"

"You're heartless," I say. "Your business is going under. It's an embarrassment."

"How dare someone like you talk to me like that?" Digby rounds on me. "Your sort wouldn't understand. It's about building something. An *empire*. And I will not have it run into the ground by a buffoon who thinks fucking whores and getting high is the only lifestyle he deserves when he's done very little to earn it. He got too used to how I was treating him. I've been covering for him for far too long. That ends today."

"Why are you on here?" I say. "Kind of dumb, no? To be on board at the same time?"

"I had to be here," Digby says. "Like I said, it's my empire. My father's. I came on here with him over twenty years ago. I was on the maiden voyage. I had to be on the last."

"So Benjamin has no idea either that this is happening?" Eva says.

"Not a clue. I'm sure he's sitting waiting for his breakfast like the glutton he is."

My mind is still wrapping itself around the idea that Captain Howard isn't guilty. I think of everything we saw, and how it might not necessarily mean what we thought. Digby's previous words sit in my brain. "What did you mean when you said you've been covering for Benjamin for far too long?"

"Your friend Hallie must have been one of his girls," Digby says.

One of his girls?

My rage quickly evaporates into terror, and my mouth can no longer form words.

"What about Effie and Lola?" Imogen says. "Are you blaming Benjamin for them too? How do we know you're not just telling us a pack of lies?"

"Their deaths caused a headache for me," Digby says. "If I'm sinking a superyacht and claiming on the insurance, precisely what I don't need is a concurrent murder investigation."

The water is coming in thick and fast, reaching above our knees.

"We have to get out of here," Melinda says. "This area will fill within minutes."

There's a bit of a panicked rush for the stairs as the water rises, my legs becoming heavy and difficult to move. Each stair upward is like lifting two giant weights, but eventually I reach a dry step and break free of the ocean's terrifying grip. Most of us are soaked on our bottom halves, gathered in the crew mess, catching our breath. It's a relief to be out of the claustrophobic engine rooms, but we can still hear the water churning down there, making its way closer and closer to us once more.

"How do you expect to get away with this?" I ask Digby, surprised by how much I'm panting, how much energy I've wasted in just getting out. "When we arrive at New York we're going to tell the authorities."

"Originally, you were all meant to corroborate the incident genuinely, because you were never supposed to find out the plan, but like you said, you all know the truth now. So we'll have to come to some other arrangement."

"There is no other arrangement!" I snap.

"If the engine rooms are filling bow to stern there's still time to get the tender out," Jade says. "But we'll have to be fast. We need to act now."

"The tender is already set up and tethered," Digby says.

"So you took the keys for it!" Sasha shouts. "And the ditch bag!"

"Let's go, then," Runa says. "Let's go now."

"Of course you can come on the tender," Digby says. "But none of you will be telling the authorities what really went on here. We're going to tell them we had a total systems failure for reasons unknown and unfortunately lost two stewardesses and the primary in the evacuation."

He wants Benjamin to go down with the ship.

"You have this all figured out, don't you?" I say bitterly. "Except there's one flaw in your plan. There's no way in hell I'm going along with it."

Why would Captain Howard allow this to get so far? Why come down here to the engine rooms, abandon his post, not warn any of us on the radio?

And then Digby immediately answers me by bringing out Captain Howard's gun.

The reaction is instant: people back away, Imogen screams, Eva ducks her head, Noah gasps and lifts his hands in defense as if that will succeed in doing anything. The crew mess is crowded enough as it is, but now it's worse, with pushing and shoving as people try to get to the back of the group.

Digby is really holding a gun. And he's pointing it straight at us.

"Digby." To the captain's credit, he stands in front of us all. Only his trembling hands give away his nerves.

Digby addresses all of us. "Either you can come with me on the tender, get away from this sinking ship and agree to keep all of this quiet, safe in the knowledge I will compensate you enormously for your silence, or you can stay on the boat and die. The choice is yours."

CHAPTER FORTY-FOUR

SASHA

The engine rooms must be fully submerged, as the stairs leading down are now gushing water out toward us. We're tilting noticeably bow-first, the slant of the floor becoming more diagonal with each added wave. I'm amazed my seasickness hasn't returned, but I guess instead it's been replaced with fear and adrenaline.

Digby is holding the gun steady, waiting for our answer.

And it is at this moment Axel and Drew come barreling down the stairs into the crew mess.

"The tender is still here," Axel says, oblivious to what is in front of him, "but it's been taken from the garage, tethered to the—"

He stops, the sight of Digby and his gun now all too visible. Drew, behind him, pales with horror, casting a desperate glance at me, conveying something I can't work out.

"What is going on?" Axel asks. "Why is—"

"Perfect timing, both of you," Digby says. "I was just explaining to the others that they need to come with me to the tender."

Axel shakes his head. "Sorry, someone needs to tell me what the *fuck* is happening here."

"Axel," Imogen says. She's trying to sound casual, but her voice breaks and it's obvious how terrified she is. Despite everything, she is coming to his defense, saving him from a situation he doesn't even realize he's in. "I'll explain later. Mr. Johnson, we're coming with you."

Melinda nods. "I agree with Imogen. We need to be sensible here."

"I am definitely coming," Runa says. "You all locked me up like an animal. I have no loyalty to you."

"Me too," Noah says. He bites his lip. "I—I'm sorry. I don't want to die."

"To *die*?" Axel echoes, stunned. He whirls round to the captain. "Captain, can you tell me what's happening? This isn't you, is it? You're a good man."

The captain fixes Axel with a look that finally calms him down. "The ship is sinking, Axel," he says quietly. "Everyone needs to leave."

"I can't die either," Eva whispers. She steps forward too. "I'm coming with you. I have a daughter. She needs to see her mother again."

"This is crazy," Axel says.

"I have a baby too," Imogen replies, hands clutched at her stomach. "*You* have a baby, Axel."

"I'm coming," Drew says, shaking himself out of his terror. "We *all* are."

I can't do anything, not while Digby is holding that gun. Even if I explained the full situation to Axel and Drew, if they realized Digby was the owner of *Ophelia* and this was his whole plan, there would be no time. They'd be disorganized, confused, asking questions, and any attempt to rush at and overpower Digby would fail.

A small mercy is that the clouds seem to be breaking outside, the sun shining through the window. It's this that allows me to see Jasmine's face, to watch her mouth two words: *Play along.*

She's come to the same conclusion. It's too dangerous to do anything else. We have to follow Digby's plan, at least for now.

It's tempting to go along with him for real. To say yes, to get myself safely on board the tender and flee trouble once more. It's the easiest option, the one I'm used to taking. But I can't let another man get away with a crime.

"We're coming with you," I say.

"I'm glad you've all seen sense," Digby says. He lowers the gun but doesn't put it away. "Let's go."

"Captain Howard?" Axel asks.

"Do as Mr. Johnson says," Captain Howard replies.

Noah takes the steps first, Eva close behind, before Imogen, Axel, and Captain Howard follow. Runa takes one final look around the crew mess before she too takes the stairs. Jade is next, exchanging a glance with me. Jasmine is next.

"I need to get something from my room first," she says. "Is that okay?"

She must be talking about the photograph. I think of my own belongings. My passport is in my cabin, but other than that I have nothing of substance. Clothes, a couple of books, my phone. Quick to pack. Easy to disappear. That was my logic.

"Well, we won't be waiting for you," Digby says. "Once we're ready, we're gone."

Jasmine catches my eye again, mouths: *See you soon.*

Drew hangs back, and from the way he keeps staring he seems desperate to talk to me. Jasmine takes the stairs, and then Digby at last makes his move, Melinda right behind him.

I am farthest from the stairs, back toward the long bench we used to eat at that is now being submerged by the ocean. I think of my first day, seeing Effie, Imogen, and Lola eating their lunch all in a row, and my heart twists. The water has reached my knees, making it difficult to move, the swoosh of the water intent on keeping me pinned. It is cold, so cold and unpleasant, the waves lapping as more and more fills the area like being hit with icy knives.

"Are you alright?" Drew asks. He is by the stairs but waits for me, holding his hands out. "He didn't hurt you, did he?"

"Digby?" I shake my head. "He just got the gun out as a threat, I think. I don't think he'd actually *shoot* us. But this is insane. I don't know what we're going to do."

He grabs my hands, and I'm surprised by how warm his still are, comforted by the dry calluses on his palms. "We're getting out of here. If Digby wants to sink his own yacht, so be it. We just need to focus on getting to New York."

"You're right." I am about to walk forward, hurry up those stairs with him, when his words play back in my mind and I feel a sliver of dread across my spine, colder than the water around us.

If Digby wants to sink his own yacht, so be it.

"You weren't here when we found out Digby was the owner of *Ophelia*," I say slowly. "How did you know this was his yacht?"

Drew's grip on my hands tightens, ever so slightly. "What do you mean? He mentioned it when everyone was going upstairs—"

"No." I shake my head. "He didn't. And how did you—you said 'if he wants to sink his own yacht.' How did you know he was sinking it himself? That this isn't just some kind of accident? You weren't here when we found that out either."

"He said it," Drew says quickly. Too quickly.

He's lying.

"Forget it," I say, with what I hope is a cheerful laugh, a lackadaisical laugh, a laugh that has no place on a sinking yacht, in a room where the water is creeping to our thighs, where I am so cold I am shivering even in Drew's hot hands. "Come on, we need to get going. It's freezing here."

I try to remove my hands from his grasp, but it's no use.

He has me, he's far stronger than I am, and he's blocking the exit.

I had some help, Digby said.

"Drew," I whisper. "What have you done?"

Drew. Brilliant at getting along with everyone, always a nice guy, someone people can trust. So nice and trustworthy, in fact, that I went and kissed him.

Amazing how I have panic attacks at the drop of a hat, but now, in a real life-or-death situation, my body has abandoned me. I'm on autopilot, shaking and rooted to the spot, staring helplessly at the man who is blocking my way out.

His face crumples. "Sasha, you have to understand. This wasn't ever part of the plan."

The plan?

My heart finally remembers what to do when it is truly afraid: it begins to pound in my chest and throat.

"Oh my God. You're really working with him," I say. "You helped Digby do this."

"Yes," he admits, and my world might as well crumble at my feet. "Digby promised me more money than I could ever expect to get in a lifetime. So I blocked the bilge pumps, damaged the engines, forced open the sea cocks. I prepared the tender, I took the ditch bag."

He still has hold of my hands. Is still blocking the way.

"Drew," I say. "Can you let me go?"

He blinks at the way our hands are held, as if he has forgotten he's doing it, and immediately releases me. But when I try and move past him, he stops me.

"Wait," he says. "Just—hear me out. Please. This isn't—I don't know what you're thinking. The others can't—please."

I take a few steps backward. I have no choice but to humor him. "You knew Digby was the owner all along?"

"He approached me at the beginning of the charter. He knew my past."

"Your . . . past?"

"I told you before I had done things I was ashamed of, that you weren't the only one with history. I used to be in prison. I robbed houses. Anything to feed my family."

I feel as though I'm already underwater, my vision blurring, Drew turning into two people in front of me before snapping back into focus.

"Otherwise, only Noah knew I'd been in prison. I'd confessed on a drunken night out. I think he was always suspicious of me. He suspected me when the jewelry was stolen."

Noah's behavior becomes more understandable now. I should have listened.

"Did you murder them?" I ask bluntly. "Effie and Lola. Did Digby ask you to get rid of them? Did they find out about your plan?"

Lola, and all her secrets. Effie, and what she overheard.

"No!"

I take another step backward, hands out in front of me.

Again, he closes the gap. "Sasha, please. When Effie was attacked, we were down here. Just like we are now. Remember? How could I have had the time to find her and do that mere minutes after you left?"

My mind is whirling. I can't think straight. I try and piece together that moment. "You told the captain you covered for Noah on watch while he went to the toilet. That can't have been true either."

Drew's face falls. "I lied then. After feeling so guilty accusing me of stealing the jewelry, Noah promised to always back me up, and I did the same for him. I just wanted to protect him from getting into trouble. But I was still here, I swear."

"And us, our kiss . . . was that all a lie, to lull me into some false sense of security?"

"No!" Drew shakes his head vehemently. "Sasha, I promise you, that was real."

I don't believe him. He's desperate, he's dangerous, and I'm so cold I can barely feel my feet anymore. Soon enough I won't be able to get out of here, won't have the energy to drag myself up those stairs. Is that what he wants? Is that what he's doing? Keeping me talking, tiring me out? Letting me drown?

He comes forward and doesn't stop when I try to back away. "I promise you. This has all gone wrong and I want out of it."

He's getting closer, pinning me against the wall. He seems sad, but his eyes are scary, an intensity behind them that I haven't seen before.

The water is at my waist now, filling the room faster. He could push me down and get the job done.

There's nothing I can do but scream.

"What is going on in here?"

Like a miracle, like an angel, Melinda appears on the stairs, a thunderous expression on her face. She even has the gun, somehow wrested off Digby.

"Oh, Chief!" I gasp, my relief turning me into a sobbing mess. "It's Drew. He's the one helping Digby with his plan. He told me everything."

"Sasha, wait—" Drew appeals, but Melinda cuts him off.

"He told you *everything*?" she says.

"He's been working with Digby since day one and kept it all to himself. We have to get out of here and tell everyone!"

She points the gun at Drew. "What else did he tell you?"

"Sasha, stop!" Drew shouts. "You don't understand—"

"He's doing it for money. To help his family. I don't think he wanted this to happen. But it doesn't matter."

"You're right," Melinda says. "It doesn't."

And then she swings around, aiming the gun at me.

"Ch-Chief?" I stammer. "What are you doing?"

"You had to open your big mouth," Melinda says to Drew. "We were so close. No one suspected. I can't risk this failing now. Not when we're about to leave."

Drew looks terrified, stumbling backward until he reaches the wall beside me. "None of this was meant to happen. Digby wanted—"

"*Digby* has no idea what I've done to ensure this whole scheme has run smoothly," Melinda says coldly. "And I'd like to keep it that way."

"Oh my God," Drew says. "It was you, wasn't it?"

"Chief?" I say. "What is Drew talking about?"

She raises an eyebrow, considering me, then shrugs. "Well, there's no harm in you knowing now. I killed Effie and Lola."

My brain takes longer to process this than my body. For my body, the reaction is instant, primal: I raise my hands in defense, my throat closes, and for at least five seconds I cannot breathe. But my mind is delayed. It looks at Melinda, chief officer and chief engineer of *Ophelia*, and fails to compute.

"Why?" It's the only word I can manage.

"When Mr. Johnson's business recovers and he buys another super-yacht, you can say hello to its new captain."

Captain.

"You're dying to be captain," I say. "Everyone told me. But I never thought you'd actually *kill* for it."

Melinda shakes her head with a fury I didn't know was in her. "You have no idea how many years I spent working my way up to the position I'm in now. Yet the position of captain has always eluded me. And went to worthless men like *Howard Asteridge*."

It all becomes clear. "You were the person sabotaging things, weren't you? You got rid of the life jackets. The champagne. You were responsible for all of it."

Melinda nods, enjoying herself. "Yes, that was me. I made sure lots of things got messed up in different areas so that there would be several witnesses to attest to the incompetence of Captain Howard, manning a vessel with huge safety issues and obvious problems and continuing to press ahead with the charter to the danger of guests' lives."

"Why kill Lola and Effie?" I say. "I don't understand."

"Well, Lola was a mistake," she says. "Effie was wearing that coat when I last saw her. It was stormy that night. I thought it was her. It's not my fault you all look so similar."

Lola was a mistake. Her meetings with Runa, the whole stolen jewelry scheme, her spreading malicious rumors, her diary, all those secrets she was going to tell. None of it was why she died. She died because we stewardesses look exactly the same.

On a night like that with all the rain—she was just another stewardess in uniform with blonde hair.

A mistake. She could have been any of us.

"Her phone—" I look around wildly, as if it will materialize. "Jasmine said it was missing. You took it from the captain's cabinet, didn't you?"

"It's in the sea now. Along with that damn diary Jade still had."

"And why Effie?"

"Digby and I were talking about the insurance plan," she explains. "Someone—a stewardess—overheard us. We heard a noise, saw the flash of the uniform and blonde hair disappearing down the terrace."

That was what Effie had overheard. Not Runa and Lola.

Effie was killed next not because someone was aiming for stewardesses, but because she was the real intended target all along.

Around us, the water has been steadily rising. Melinda is safe up on the stairs, gun pointed at me. She isn't shaking, she isn't in the freezing sea like we are.

But something tells me Melinda won't just let us leave.

Her hand is trembling as she holds the gun, and I'm alarmed that at any second it's going to go off not because she wants to shoot me, but because she's losing control.

I have to keep her talking. Try and figure something out.

"You didn't tell Captain Howard about Effie this morning, did you?" I ask. "The things you've told us Captain Howard was in control of . . . that's come from you, hasn't it?"

"Better it be that incompetent clown everyone suspects."

"What about researching Hallie? You deleted the CCTV footage, didn't you?"

"Keeping tabs," she says. "And I'm the chief engineer. I messed with a lot. How's the Wi-Fi?"

It seems so obvious now. That's why nothing was fixed. She wanted it that way.

"You killed Hallie too, then," I say.

"Oh no," she says. "I truly have no idea what happened there. Nothing to do with me. She really must have just fallen overboard."

I try to reason with her, keeping my voice calm. "I won't tell anyone. All of this? I'll keep it quiet. No one else will know. Please. I promise."

"You *promise*? Well, why didn't you say so before? That makes all the difference." She laughs then, a dreadful cackle. "At least it'll be quick. Count that as a blessing. Lola and Effie weren't so lucky."

"Melinda," I squeak, my nerves getting the better of me.

"Melinda! Don't shoot!" Drew shouts, and he's trying to get to her, trying to push in front, but he's too far away, he won't make a difference—

He sacrifices his torch, throwing it into the water, just as Melinda aims the gun at me. It's hard to see, only the faintest of light and shadows, and I hurl myself to the left. There's a yell again, from him or her or me, I'm not sure, and then she fires.

I scream. Out of shock, out of fear, and then I'm falling into the water, going under.

CHAPTER FORTY-FIVE

JASMINE

Melinda has her finger on the trigger when I tackle her from behind, sending us both flying forward off the stairs. We crash down, but I'm too late to stop her firing. The sound of the gun cracks through the air, and someone screams. By this point, Melinda and I are already landing face-first into the ever-invading sea.

My body is working off adrenaline after my return from the guest cabins. I got the photograph of me and Hallie and went to the swim platform expecting everyone to be ready. I was already in a state from what I had just done: panting, heart racing, trembling. Instead I found Digby sitting on the tender, barking orders at everyone else to get food and drink from the pantry and to bring him dry clothes, and no sign of Sasha. No sign of Drew or Melinda either. And Digby was no longer holding his gun, though he kept patting his suit as if to suggest he could bring it out at any moment.

Something in me knew then. I can't explain it. The relief I had that everything was almost over vanished in an instant. Something was wrong. And I was willing to risk the tender leaving without me to find out what.

Heading back to the crew mess made me all the more aware of how badly the yacht was sinking. The stern was practically sticking up in the air in comparison to the bow, and getting down the stairs was a weird balancing act, even for me, the angle throwing me off course. At one point I stumbled on a step and almost fell, saving myself by a lucky grab of the banister. Where before the yacht had been silent from the engines stopping, now there was a great creaking and groaning as the vessel struggled to remain above the surface, slowly succumbing to being dragged into the shadowy depths of the ocean. The closer I got to the crew mess, the louder the rushing water became.

I was going to shout out, make some kind of noise, but my instincts told me to be quiet. That was when I heard Melinda talking, Sasha trying desperately to appeal to her. Drew too. It was only when Drew yelled at Melinda not to shoot that I understood what was happening, that she was there with Captain Howard's gun, that she was there to make sure Sasha and Drew did not come back from the crew mess alive.

I had a split second to act, but that was all I needed.

Now, underwater, all my senses are heightened. My heart is screaming in my ears. It's fucking *freezing*, suffocating, a dark blur. I had no time to draw breath, so I'm already struggling, and the anxiety spiking in my chest isn't helping either. Melinda struggles beneath me, kicking at my legs, and I can't hold on to her anymore.

I'm bursting, my body desperate to escape, so I fling my head up, gasping for breath. I have no idea if what I just did worked. It's terrifying, barely being able to see ahead of myself, and for a second I panic because my feet aren't touching the ground. They can't. I'm treading water. The sea has almost reached the ceiling, leaving only a small gap above my head.

"Sasha?" I shout. My feet find some kind of ledge—it must be the table—to stand on and I hold my phone in the air, the screen hardly functioning from being under the water, but the torch somehow, miraculously, is still shining. It flickers a few times, then manages to hold steady. My teeth are chattering, but I can't stop them. The shock of the cold is enough to have me gasping for breath.

"*Jasmine?*" Sasha cries, and then I find her. She's treading water,

Drew next to her. They both look terrified, and pale with lips that are almost blue. "You came back for me?"

Thank God.

"Are you okay?" I ask, practically screaming. "Did she shoot you?"

"Me," Drew replies. His face is scrunched up in agony, and he's treading water weirdly, only one arm out in front, his body jerking up and down from the odd distribution of his weight. "My left arm. I can't move it."

Shit.

Then Melinda surfaces too, throwing her hair back, and she's furious. "Tessa! I should have dealt with you the moment I knew it was you. Where is it?"

She's dropped the gun.

It's probably getting pulled away by the water as we speak, but Melinda is determined to find it. She dives under, but it's too dark to see where she is.

"We can't let her get it!" Drew says. "I'll grab her—" He winces when he tries to swim, cursing. "I can't. I'm in too much pain."

What do we do? I shine my phone torch, scanning the water. It's murky, impossible to make anything out. Do I sacrifice the phone for a few seconds under there to try and find the gun?

Not just that. Do I sacrifice any semblance of warmth I have left and go fully under that icy water again?

I think I have to. We might not get out of here otherwise.

I inhale a deep breath and dive, the light shining my way for a precious four seconds before dying.

But it's enough. For me—and Melinda, under here too—to see the gun, drifting toward the stairs.

She has to swim up to take a breath, but I'm able to go straight for it, reaching out with my hands.

And then, mercifully, I grab it.

Resurfacing is my problem.

Melinda pounces on me from above, yanking my hair backward before feeling around for where my hands are. She pushes me down and I hit out at her, trying anything to get her to let go.

It's no good. She has me trapped, holding me so strongly my back crashes against the floor, and the surface is very far away. She releases my hair only to grip my neck, even as I kick at her with all my might. My hands are occupied with the gun. I can't let her have it, my fingers working on instinct as they wrap around the trigger.

Sasha screams from above, asking where I am.

I have to breathe. My lungs are bursting.

Melinda finds the gun and starts pulling it away from me.

It becomes a tug-of-war, like we're children: one moment she has it to her chest, the next I have it pinned to mine. But this is far more vicious.

Melinda jerks the gun hard, and I don't know what happens.

One second we're tooth and nail, she has me pinned down, the next the gun fires and I'm not being held anymore.

I rise to the surface, gasping, choking, sucking in as much air as possible, the gun gone from my hands.

"What happened?" Sasha cries. "I can't see a thing! Jasmine—are you okay? The gun went off again!"

Right in front of me, I can make out Melinda.

She's floating face down.

"I think I shot Melinda," I whisper, horrified.

Sasha wades closer, turns Melinda over. "Melinda? Melinda!" There's a silence, and then: "I can't feel a pulse. Oh my God."

"I killed her," I say.

"I'll say it was me," Drew says.

The water is lapping against our mouths. There isn't time to process this, to decide if I should feel guilty or glad that she's gone.

"We need to move," I say. "We can figure this out after."

"I don't think I'll be able to," Drew says. "It's too cold. I'm in too much pain. Just go without me."

"Don't be ridiculous," I snap. My breath is still coming out in gasps. "Besides, how are you going to take the rap for me if you're dead? Sasha and I will support you."

"You can't do that. It's hard enough as it is."

"It's not a suggestion. It's happening."

I am exhausted. I've never been this tired in my life. Physically, mentally, emotionally—everything is drained out of me. I don't know what I'm running on anymore.

But we have to do this.

"Lean on my shoulder," Sasha says to Drew. "Jasmine will take the other side."

He's heavy. Heavier than I expected.

All I can hear is the rushing of water, getting stronger by the minute, and the force of it helps us, trying to pull us as we swim for the exit, my hand feeling our way along the walls. Drew, between us, makes this all the harder, though he is trying his best, yelling out in pain as he swims forward.

The water washes over my mouth as I propel myself toward what I think are the stairs, and my hand grabs the banister, closing around it with a viselike grip. The stairs are both a blessing and a curse: upward is our escape, away from drowning; downward is our doom, a powerful current that seeks to pull us under. There's a scary moment where Drew falls backward and I lose hold of him, but Sasha manages to use the wall to lean back and take his weight, and he rights himself again. I don't let go of the banister, heaving myself up, straining with the effort, and then Drew steps up too, followed by Sasha. I don't know how they're feeling but for me everything aches. Finally, we emerge from the water, panting and coughing as the sudden shock of being free hits us. At last there is some proper light up here, making plain just what a state we're in. We are soaking, dripping all over the place, our clothes clinging to our bodies like wet suits. Drew's arm injury becomes evident, the blood falling from his fingertips like paint splotches, but there's nothing we can do about it for now.

We don't have time to catch our breath. Even on this first step free of water the reprieve doesn't last long, waves crashing against it. We have to get to the tender.

We leave through a side door, clinging to the boat as we make our way around to the swim platform. The yacht is lying low on the ocean now. One slip, one wrong move and we'll fall right in.

Drew, able to walk unaided out of the water, stops. He is shaking, but then we all are. My fingers are numb, the nails an alarming purple shade. "Thank you. For getting me out of there. I don't deserve it."

Sasha jumps up and down on the spot to try and warm herself up, her words coming out perhaps more irritably than she intends. "You just got mixed up in something that was way over your head. I understand that people can make bad decisions. Believe me."

He looks like he wants to say more. He stares at Sasha with a kind of yearning, then lets the moment pass.

"Come on," I say. "We have to keep moving."

I'm trying not to think about how cold I must be. Dangerously cold. My hands are shaking, teeth still chattering. But I press forward. Because I have to.

As we get closer I finally hear everyone else, and relief washes over me. We haven't been abandoned on a sinking ship. People are shouting, though, and it doesn't sound good. I reach the corner and I can see the tender, engine running, Digby aboard, and everyone else on the swim platform.

Captain Howard is trying to negotiate. "Digby, we can talk about this. This is my crew, I have a duty to keep them safe. Let us board the tender and we can sort this mess out along the way to New York."

"Oh my God!" Imogen says, spotting us. "What the hell happened? Why are you all so wet?"

They have all dried off since coming on deck. A pile of towels is cast off to the side and Axel grabs a few now and throws them our way.

It isn't enough, not nearly enough, especially when these have been used by the rest of the crew, but I wrap a towel around me gratefully as we hurry toward them.

I explain what happened, watching everyone's faces display their shock.

"Lola was mistaken identity?" Imogen whispers, no doubt realizing how easily it could have been her.

I nod.

"I always knew how creepy it was that we all looked the same," she continues. "I never thought it could cause a murder."

"But why?" Jade asks. "Why would Melinda do this?"

"Digby promised her she'd be captain on his next vessel," I tell everyone. "She was obsessed with that, and did everything possible to ensure it happened."

I think of her frustration, her years of effort to get something Captain Howard walked into. She snapped.

"I worked with her for five years," Captain Howard says quietly. "I didn't . . ." But whatever else is left unsaid.

Digby laughs. "You've been a terrible captain. Look what has happened under your supervision. In any case, we're done here. Goodbye, everyone."

"Wait," Eva says. "What do you mean? We're coming with you!"

"I don't think so," Digby says. "Far too complicated."

"I knew it," Runa says. "And you were never going to pay us off, were you? It's all lies. Look at how you treated Melinda."

"You just used us to stock up the tender," Noah says.

Digby grins. "Thank you very much."

"You'll need one of us to drive it," Axel says. "You can't do this on your own."

"I've been playing with boats since I was a boy," Digby replies. "I'm afraid I am quite capable."

There isn't time to charge him. One or two of us might be able to get on, but he'll speed the tender away, throw us off. The water is freezing, as I know all too well. We can't risk it.

"You can't do this!" Drew shouts. "You *promised*. You said no one would get hurt, that everyone would be able to evacuate safely. I helped you!"

"I sent Melinda down to deal with you," Digby says. "Trust a woman to fail at doing a man's job."

Drew closes his eyes. "You were never going to give me any money. I'm an idiot."

"You said it," Digby says, "not me."

"Digby!" One final, desperate attempt. "You can't let us all die."

He raises an eyebrow. "Can't I?"

And that's it. He turns the tender swiftly despite the growing waves, and powers away. He doesn't look around at us, or even at his superyacht, his mother's namesake. He disappears into the horizon with the only escape we have.

"He got away," Imogen whispers.

"What is going to happen to us?" Eva cries. "I have to see my daughter again. I can't die here."

"I sent a distress signal," Captain Howard says.

"What?" I can't believe this. "Why didn't you say anything before?"

"Because it might not have worked," he explains. "I used the spare VHF radio I keep with me at all times. The signal was patchy, but I think someone heard us."

"You didn't get an affirmative response?" Axel says.

Captain Howard shakes his head. "I said Mayday again and again.

And our rough location. I think the message got through. We'll have to wait and see."

"Wait and see? That's our best hope? Why don't you try again?"

"It's all we have. Digby smashed the radio the second he saw what I was doing."

"And no life jackets or life rings," Axel says. "I can't believe it." He scowls at Drew. "Don't think we've forgotten about your involvement in all this too."

Drew hangs his head. His hand is clutching at his wound, the blood still seeping out.

Sasha leaps into nursing mode, her instincts back in full force, and she hurries to stop the bleeding. She rips the bottom of her uniform and begins to tie a tourniquet, glancing around desperately.

"Here." Jade understands, taking her pen from her pocket and passing it to her.

Sasha smiles. "Thank you. There's not much I can do without a first-aid kit. But this will help at least."

"So what happens next?" Eva asks. "What do we do now?"

"There's nothing we can do," Axel says. "Either Captain Howard's distress signal worked or it didn't. We're in the Atlantic, hundreds of miles from the coast. This superyacht is going down. And we're going down with it."

CHAPTER FORTY-SIX

SASHA

Think, Sasha. There must be something. Anything.

The waves are starting to crash against the terrace, pouring over the expensive decking before receding back into the ocean. Swimming is out of the question. We don't know if help is even coming, but we have to get away from this yacht before it sinks, pulling us down with it.

My eyes take in the frantic scene ahead of me: Drew groaning in pain; Axel marching up and down; Eva staring into the horizon as if Digby might come back any minute; Imogen, Jade, and Runa crying out every time the water hits them, soaking their clothes; Noah talking urgently to Captain Howard, who looks like he's given up. Jasmine is exhausted but even she is thinking, seeking a solution.

Ten of us. That's a lot.

No—eleven. I've missed someone.

Where is Benjamin?

I say this out loud, drawing everyone's attention.

"He must still be in his cabin," Captain Howard says. "I'll go get him, explain what's happened. Digby didn't let us alert him before."

"What, and he's not woken up to the yacht half submerged in the sea?" Imogen says.

"There's something I need to tell you all," Jasmine says. "I couldn't find a good time to say it—not with everything going on."

She's nervous. One hand is playing with her hair, still dripping wet. "When I went to get some of my things, I decided to tell Benjamin what was happening. So that he could get to safety. But when I went inside . . ."

No. Surely not.

"He was dead," Jasmine says. "I think Melinda must have killed him."

Dead?

Captain Howard can't hide his shock. "You're sure? There's still time for us to check—"

"She stabbed him to death," Jasmine says. "There was blood everywhere. Just like Effie. She must have done it at the same time."

"God." Captain Howard rakes a hand through his hair. "We went to school together."

"He was an asshole," Imogen says, then pulls a face when Jade glares at her. "What? He was. I'm not going to miss him."

I can't believe it. Melinda was truly mad.

"You're absolutely sure?" Jade says. "There isn't any possibility he might still be alive?"

Jasmine shakes her head.

"Good," Imogen says. "He can rot in hell."

"He was . . ." Captain Howard hesitates. "Complicated."

Complicated is one way of putting it. That man spent far too much of his life enjoying himself. From drinks to food to the water toys, he had it too good.

Wait.

The water toys. Jade's haughty, irritated tone comes back to me from the tour on my first day. Two sets of inflatables, one that would be able to hold five people, and then one that could fit up to eight. They might just save us all.

"The inflatables," I say.

"The inflatables?" Jade echoes.

I nod. "We can sit on them. Push them out into the water, get them away from the suction, and wait for help."

Axel is concerned. "On the ocean?"

It's no longer stormy, though that doesn't mean much on the Atlantic. There's a chance the inflatables will capsize immediately. They're hardly meant for emergencies like this—more for strapping to a speedboat and lying across them as they power over the water, or bobbing about on calm waves.

But they're the only option we've got.

"Do you have a better idea?" I ask, more impatiently than I would like.

"No." He sighs. "But we can't set them up here. It will take too long, and we'll be in the water. We'll have to go to the sky terrace to have the best chance."

"But we don't have any electricity to inflate them!" Jade says.

Axel snaps his fingers. "There's a battery pack we can use with the external air inflator that should still be fully charged and not affected by the power cut. Noah?"

He blinks, surprised to be called upon. "Yes?"

"You're in charge of the smaller one."

Noah flushes. "Okay. And . . . I'm sorry. For how I've been."

Axel shrugs, but I can see him softening somewhat. "Just get on with it."

Everyone springs into action. We all head into the garage. It's dark, and water has got in here too, filling up from the back.

"Come on!" Noah says, no hesitation in sight. Leadership has transformed him. "No time to worry about the water. Let's get those inflatables."

We all work together. The inflatables are heavy, but we lift them above our heads to carry them up the stairs. Axel is in charge of the bigger one, raising it with Captain Howard, Runa, Eva, and Jasmine. Noah leads the rest of us, calling out instructions, and he's surprisingly good at it. Drew is the only one who can't help, but even he has his use, standing at the top and shouting directions for where we all need to step.

We reach the sky deck panting and sweating despite the rain and chill in the air. No one wastes any time catching their breath, though—we have to act fast. Jasmine, Drew, and I are no longer the only ones soaking wet; everyone's clothes from the waist down now leave trails of water behind them.

Axel has himself, Runa, Jasmine, Eva, and Captain Howard working on the larger inflatable, while Noah gets Imogen, Jade, and me to help him with the smaller one. They're almost completely inflated now. Off to the side, Drew is collapsed in a deck chair, eyes shut, moaning softly.

In what feels like another universe, we had the Silver Soirée here. Lola and Effie and Benjamin and Melinda were all still alive and I still believed I had escaped my problems. Drew and I kissed on the terrace below, before it all went wrong.

I shake my head, blot out the thoughts, and focus on the task at hand. Jade, despite herself, can't help ordering me and Imogen around, telling us where to stand and what to hold, even when Noah overrides her. In the chaos she has lost her position, and she's obviously struggling with not being in control.

"Thank you for this idea, crazy as it is," Imogen says.

"We won't know if it will work until we get on," I say. "Don't go thanking me yet."

We finish before the others, so Noah and I head over to help them while Jade and Imogen run and fetch blankets from the sky lounge, stored in the sofas. They grab bottles of water too, and Runa joins them, bringing out as much ready-to-eat food that's left in the bar as possible. The sea swallows more and more of the superyacht, the once gigantic, sleek vessel reduced to two upper levels above the water, the owner's suite the only part still untouched. All the riches down below, lost forever. All that jewelry Runa carefully stole, and it was all for nothing.

I look at Runa as she hands the food to Eva, who is splitting it between the inflatables. "I'm sorry about taking your ring. I'm glad you got it back, before . . ."

Eva pauses for a moment. "I forgive you." She exchanges a glance with Jasmine. "I think I am done judging people from now on."

"Both inflatables are ready," Axel calls. "We should wait on the yacht for as long as possible before we use them."

So we wait: what remains of us, huddled together under blankets on the upper terrace with two huge inflatables waiting to take us out to sea. At last I'm starting to feel the cold. The adrenaline is wearing off, and I'm all too aware that I'm sitting here in a uniform that is soaked completely through, so wet it sticks to my skin like an adhesive, and goose bumps are scattered across my arms and legs. The ocean continues to rise, continues to consume *Ophelia* and all of her treasures. The crew floor, with Melinda and Effie floating inside, is long gone, far below the surface now. Benjamin too must be fully submerged, another victim of Chief's twisted game with Digby.

Jasmine and I are sharing a blanket, too cold and exhausted to speak, but squeezing each other's hand tight, when Imogen passes me her own blanket.

"But this is yours," I say. "It's freezing."

"I'm not as wet as you two are," she replies. "You have it. And don't go all soppy on me, I'll be snatching it back the moment I feel a chill."

"But your condition—"

"Don't you dare start treating me like an invalid. You're drenched to the *bone*, Sasha. You're shivering and you don't even realize it."

"Well, thank you," I say, but she walks away without another word, embarrassed by her own kind gesture.

Ironically, with the warm, dry blanket around me I'm colder than ever, my body finally catching on just how icy it's been in comparison. I'm shaking just like Imogen said. I wish I could have a change of clothes, but they're long gone.

I'm not sure I can last like this.

Across the way, I see Axel give his blanket to Imogen. She is reluctant to accept, but he drapes it around her anyway, standing awkwardly beside her but not saying much. He can't keep his eyes off her stomach, as if at any second it's going to protrude outward like she's nine months gone.

"Help is not coming, is it?" Runa says, wrapped in a blanket with Jade. "We cannot go on those inflatables and just float about, can we? Waiting for a rescue?"

"Help should be coming if my signal got through," Captain Howard says, though he doesn't sound confident. "Otherwise, we hope another vessel crosses our path."

It's not a comforting thought.

Axel clears his throat. "It's time to move, everyone."

"Now?" Eva says. "Can't we hold on a little longer?"

"We have to make sure we're far enough away from the yacht before it sinks."

Eva and Imogen are with Axel and Captain Howard on the small inflatable; the rest of us join the other one.

"I'll try and look after your wound," I say to Drew, though there's not much I can do other than apply pressure.

"You've done a lot already," Drew says, trying to be cheerful. He has been very quiet since we set up the inflatables. He's looking pale, and I'm worried about his blood loss.

Our larger one goes first, Axel and Captain Howard pushing us with all their might, and then we're off, into the sea, carried by the waves.

The smaller inflatable follows, and Eva screams as the sea splashes over her. I can't blame her. None of us are ever going to want to repeat this.

We all paddle for a while, though we're mainly at the whim of the wind and tide, and then once we are a few hundred meters away there is nothing to do but float at the mercy of the churning waves. We could tip over at any moment, but we try to counterbalance the weight as much as possible with Drew in the center.

Ophelia, white against the backdrop of grey and mist, sinks farther into the ocean, and we watch her disappear. The other inflatable is far enough away that we don't collide, but close enough that we can shout to one another if we need to.

"Sasha," Drew says. "Can we talk?"

"You need to focus on staying awake and conserving your energy," I tell him. His head is close to my lap, and I can't help but glance down at his tired face, his long eyelashes wet with either tears or rain. His lips are trembling, lips I kissed only days ago. A whole other lifetime.

"No. I have to say this. I'm sorry. For how I treated you. For what I've done."

"You've already apologized."

"I want to make sure you know I mean it."

"You're in a lot of pain," I whisper, aware that everyone else can hear us. "This isn't the right time."

"I just wanted you to know my feelings were real."

Mine were too, I say silently, only after he has closed his eyes.

Axel shouts something from the other inflatable and Jasmine and I turn. He's pointing behind us, to *Ophelia*.

She is disappearing into the water. The last thing above the surface is the flagpole. It takes another few minutes, but slowly, gradually, the superyacht sinks.

Ophelia is no more.

Down into nothingness she goes, and Lola, Effie, Melinda, and Benjamin with her.

And maybe all of us will be joining them sooner than we think.

There is nothing to do but watch the rolling waves, seek out shapes desperately on the horizon that never appear.

Time passes. How long has it been? Hours? Two, perhaps three? Maybe more. It's impossible to tell the time, all of our phones long drained of battery or underwater with *Ophelia*. The waves remain higher than I would like. We are tossed about, but remain somehow upright. I'm freezing, parts of me turning blue, and I don't know how much more I can take. The areas of my body that aren't painful are numb, and that's far more frightening.

Drew has fallen asleep, or fallen unconscious. I should rouse him, but my own bones are heavy with exhaustion and I can't control my shakes. Jasmine is the only other person on our inflatable still sitting up, but she's hugging her knees to her chest and looking out at the horizon. The others are lying down too, some staring up at the sun, which has started to peek through the clouds again, some perhaps asleep themselves, so I give in even though I know I shouldn't and lie down too.

My eyelids are starting to drop, tempting me into oblivion.

CHAPTER FORTY-SEVEN

IMOGEN

If I make it out of this alive I'm not getting on another fucking yacht ever again.

Our inflatable group is the only one still actively searching the water for some kind of rescue. The other one seems to have given up, everyone on their backs apart from Jasmine. Eva is like me, eyes focused on scanning every possible area. She told me she's going home to her daughter, and I had to admire the ferocity in her tone, even as I placed a tentative hand on my stomach in response. Maybe the others think we're naive to carry on hoping, but what else can we do? Close our eyes and hope instead that it will all be over soon?

No. If one thing has been proven this charter, I'm a scrappy bitch who won't quit.

Nor am I going to let little things bother me so much anymore. Looking at you, Axel.

Kidding, unfortunately. God really said *give him everything* when it came to that man.

He must sense me looking at him because he turns to face me. He should be ashamed, ducking his head, but of course he's not. This is a man who has never been told no in his life, who has been handed everything on a golden plate.

"Why didn't you tell me?" he asks, that question again, as if his right to know is the most important thing in all of this, and not him fucking two other stewardesses.

Our beef isn't worth it. We could die tonight. Axel being with Effie *and* Lola when they've just sunk with *Ophelia* seems minor by comparison.

So I park my tongue and decide to be serious, because we might not have all the time in the world, and if we do, that can come later. "I was scared. I thought I loved you, and I thought you'd call things off the second you found out. You'd tell the captain, he'd make me leave, and I'd find you'd never answer any of my messages. And then a few weeks down the line I'd check your Instagram and you'd be posting some story with someone else on your arm. I wasn't really wrong on that last front, was I?"

Okay, maybe a bit of snark. I can't edit out my entire personality.

"I wouldn't have ghosted you," he says quickly.

"Axel," I say. "We're on an inflatable in the middle of the fucking Atlantic. If you can't be real now, when can you be?"

He opens his mouth to protest, and Captain Howard of all people intervenes.

"I've known you for years, Axel," he says. "And you know I think you're great, and that you've become a fantastic bosun. But maybe I indulged your attitude, because I saw a bit of my younger self in you, and I wanted you to gain some self-confidence."

"Gain some self-confidence?" I say. "If there's one thing Axel doesn't lack it's self-confidence."

"You'd be surprised at the boy I first met," Captain Howard says. "But Axel, now you need to get your act together. This is serious. Imogen deserves that."

And then he turns around, back to us, to put himself out of the conversation again. I can't believe it. Captain Howard, Axel's number one fan, sticking up for me.

A typical man, Axel starts to see sense now that another man has put him straight.

"Okay," he says at last. "I probably would have ghosted you."

Halle-fucking-lujah. If Axel had done this to me even a week ago, hell, two *days* ago, my heart would have shattered into pieces. I'd be wishing I could sit on my sofa in a quilt-cave with McDonald's and brownies and wine, crying at the second season of *Fleabag* like any normal woman. But now his admission rolls over me—a tiny wave of hurt, not a big one.

"I was going to tell you at the party," I say. "You didn't show, and, obviously, when M—Lola's body was found the next day, things changed. I thought . . ."

"You thought it was me?" Axel finishes, and I nod. "Christ, Imogen. I know I'm a fuckup, and I know I've hurt you, but that?"

"What were you threatening Captain Howard about?" I ask, keeping my voice low so the captain doesn't hear us.

"How do you know about that? Were you following me?"

"Don't act high and mighty now."

He sighs. "His gambling. It's worse than you all think. I wanted to protect him, but it was going too far. I gave him a chance to sort it out and he didn't. It just got worse. And after his incompetence with everything that happened on board—"

"What was worse than we all think?"

"All the tips for each charter. He didn't dock them to cover stolen jewelry costs. He was stealing the tip money to fund his debt."

Jesus. What a mess this whole season has been.

"Why protect him?" I ask. "I don't get it. I know you've always been a fan of him, but protecting him over this? When it affects all of us?"

"You want me to be real, yeah?" he says.

Where is he going with this? "Duh."

"Captain Howard used to give me sailing lessons when I was a teenager," Axel says. "My father used to do it when I was a kid, but he got too busy. Captain Howard helped keep me on the right path. Helped me apply to colleges while my dad just threw money at them. But I lost my way at college, didn't have Captain Howard there to guide me. Dropped out, acted up, started taking it out on my dad. Years of being out of control. Eventually, he kicked me out."

This is the same Axel who told me about the time he saved a man from drowning. Emotional, raw. It is taking everything in me not to fall under his spell again, not to reach out and stroke his cheek.

"That was a year ago. I was homeless. Captain Howard hired me to work on *Ophelia* during the offseason so I'd have somewhere to live and then kept me on."

I understand now. Behind Axel, it is clear Captain Howard has been listening after all. He nods at me, confirming what Axel is saying is true, but doesn't speak. His eyes are red and I think the reason he turns quickly is to hide the fact he's crying.

"I'm sorry," Axel says, and this time I know he means it. "If I could go back and change everything . . . I promise you, Imogen, I would. This baby might be a good opportunity for us to have a fresh start, if we make it through this. We could have a proper relationship."

It's all the things I wished he would have told me before. But now the words sound wrong, and I know they're not what I want.

My heart still hurts. But he wasn't good. He made fun of my background, didn't accept me for who I really am. He cheated and he would do it again, even if he didn't mean to. He's not a bad person, deep down, and he has been through more than I ever expected, but he is never going to be husband material.

"We're not getting back together, Axel," I say. "But we'll figure something out."

He nods, and I hate to admit it but all I can see in his eyes is relief.

Yeah. We're done.

You *know* I'm going to be suing his ass for child support if he dips.

The deep dread I've been carrying with me for weeks vanishes. I feel my body lightening, my shoulders visibly lifting.

Maybe I'll become someone my little brother can be proud of, wherever he is. Maybe this baby will be a boy and I can give him his name.

If we don't end up joining him soon.

CHAPTER FORTY-EIGHT

JADE

It's quiet now. I have time to think.

I could have done so much more. Maybe things wouldn't have turned out like they did if I'd had better awareness. Instead of hating Axel and Captain for their boys' club, I should have wondered if Melinda felt the same resentment. It unnerves me that the two of us have a lot in common. Both workaholics, striving for the best. Both willing to do whatever it takes.

Runa, next to me under our blanket, has her eyes shut, but I don't think she's sleeping. I'm trying not to be angry with her. But it's hard.

"Runa," I murmur, and sure enough, her eyes open. "What will you do now?"

"I do not know." She isn't angry, just resigned. "I just wanted to be someone else."

Someone else? What's waiting for me outside of yachts? When you're in this long, you don't have any kind of life beyond that. I go home and there's no one waiting for me. All I can think about is the next charter. This is what I live for. Being chief stewardess.

I want to tell Runa she'll figure it out. But I don't know that. I also want to tell her that I wish we'd never uncovered her jewelry theft, because those pieces are at the bottom of the sea anyway. It didn't matter in the end.

I sit up and turn to the edge of the inflatable. I'm not going to vomit. I'm close enough to dip my hand into the freezing water, which isn't sensible but I do it anyway. I press a damp hand to my cheek, and whisper a goodbye to the yacht I sacrificed everything for.

I will figure out what to do next, like I always do.

CHAPTER FORTY-NINE

SASHA

Just when I'm giving up hope, I hear it. Faintly. So faintly I'm half convinced it's my mind playing tricks on me. But then it grows louder.

Eva hears it too from the other inflatable. She tilts her head back, searching the skies desperately. And then she's scrambling to her feet, almost falling into the sea, gesturing with her hands. She has the most resolve, the most energy of us all.

"Hey!" she shouts. "Here! We're here!"

Everyone else starts sitting up, peering above them. Only Drew remains still, eyes closed, but I can't fret about him.

The noise keeps increasing, a gentle whisper to begin with, now a constant, rapid churn of blades.

Blades.

"There!" Jasmine yells. She grabs my hand and lifts it with her own, waving. "We're down here!"

At last, following her line of sight, I find it.

A helicopter. Coming for us. Captain Howard's distress call worked.

"Thank God," I whisper, and then I burst into tears.

PART FIVE

PART FIVE

The Sunday Times
Sunday, October 5, 2025
12:01 A.M. BST

"MURDER BOAT": SUPERYACHT INSURANCE FRAUD LEAVES FOUR DEAD

Minterne Ltd. business mogul Digby Johnson has vehemently denied accusations of insurance fraud in the sinking of his 200-foot superyacht "Ophelia" last week, hundreds of miles off the coast of New York City. Three crew members—stewardesses Euphemia Brentwood and Lola Charles, and Chief Officer Melinda Fall—plus Johnson's financial advisor, Benjamin Edmondson, lost their lives in suspicious circumstances either before or during the sinking. All four bodies are unrecovered from the vessel, with initial sources close to the investigation suggesting homicide. Police have yet to confirm this, but with growing media attention, the magnate has publicly denied all claims, arguing the allegations are based on a "traumatised crew seeking to blame the very top."

CHAPTER FIFTY

TESSA

I never wanted today to come.

The photograph of Hallie is one I took when we moved in together. She's dressed down, hair slung back in a low ponytail, baggy sweatshirt and jogging bottoms. But she looks so naturally radiant that it's the one I have tight in my hand, as I stand in the park outside our old block of flats.

They haven't changed: still an ugly grey building, still graffiti everywhere. But our kitchen window, five stories high and three across, is still painted green compared to the peeling white paint of the other windows. I remember Hallie leaning out, crouched on the counter, determined to do it to make our home stand out among the rest, even when I shrieked at her to be careful. We didn't have a garden, she said, so this could be our garden, even though painting anything was expressly forbidden by the council. The row of cacti and succulents along the windowsill are gone, of course, replaced by what looks like a pot of utensils and a discarded tea towel.

It's tempting to knock on the door of whoever lives there now, but what would be inside? Maybe the same furniture, definitely the same wallpaper and terrible tiles. It wouldn't be ours, though. Hallie's candles and throws and shoes and trinkets made the place not just bearable, but a true home.

No. This is enough. The green window. The park we walked through every day, carrying shopping bags and always stopping for a play on the swings, a moment of acting like the children we never got to be. I'm on the swings now, bum wet from the drizzling day, and they creak as I run my feet back and forth.

Time, at last, to say goodbye.

This has been a long time coming; I decided to go it alone. Eva sent flowers, huge white lilies, and I have placed them on the grassy patch by the front gate, somewhere Hallie always used to say as we went past would make a beautiful gardening spot if someone cared. Eva and I formed an unlikely friendship after everything. She's in Spain, back escorting, but thinking of training as a solicitor. Said she wants to try and do some good in the world. Sasha gave me a photo album titled *2026*, writing on the inside flap: *To your future.* At the back, loose rather than slotted into one of the sleeves, was a photo of us, taken after our brief stint in a New York hospital and between various police interviews.

It was crazy at first. Captain Howard's distress signal had worked, alerting another boat nearby that contacted the authorities for a faster rescue. The helicopter, when it arrived, seemed stunned to find us there floating along on the inflatables. And being airlifted to safety is an experience I never want to repeat. I was one of the stronger people, one of the last to get off, and even though it was completely irrational I was terrified they'd forget about me, leave me there in the ocean. Feeling the last of the sea air in my lungs before the helicopter door was pulled shut and we flew away gave me a mixture of relief and devastation. Relief we were alive. I was alive. Devastation that again, I was leaving Hallie behind.

The police had *plenty* of questions, of course. But we all went to hospital first. Drew and Sasha both had hypothermia, and it was touch and go with Drew for a while because of his injury. He was the last to leave the ward we were all put on, kept together because it was far easier that way to avoid the press barging in and hounding us. "Unexplained

Sinking," they called it, and then as they learned more details: "Corruption at the Core," "Devious Disaster," and "Murder Boat."

Not that the press were all bad. Digby, obviously hearing we'd survived, had tried to do a runner but was picked up by the police, and one savvy photographer had captured a brilliant image of his shocked face, both arms grabbed by police officers, mouth open in clear denial at what was happening to him as he was taken away.

Ha. Take that, asshole.

As we each got out of hospital one by one they put us up in a hotel, made us endure several interviews. It was not fun explaining to the police why everyone knew me as Jasmine, but eventually they promised to "look into" Hallie's disappearance, and I didn't have the heart to tell them it was too little, too late.

The photo of me and Sasha is from her last day in the hospital. I'd been out a week by that point. She's still in her hospital gown. My initial reaction was to hide it away, like I was betraying Hallie. But I know she wouldn't mind, so it's the first one in the album.

I'm back to my old look. The dyed hair is gone, I've gained twenty pounds already, and I am much happier for it. I left Jasmine behind on *Ophelia* and changed my name to Tessa Attwood. I don't want any lasting connection to my waste of space of a father, but I do want one to the best friend I ever had. And even in death, Hallie still rescues me. Changing my name has helped me avoid the constant hounding from the press about what happened.

"Hi, Hallie," I say now, and it doesn't feel weird speaking to a crumpled photograph. The wind picks up, scattering leaves around me. "I hope you'd still be proud, despite everything."

Hallie grins at me innocently. The girl in that picture had no idea what was coming.

"I did it all for you," I say. "And I'd do it all again."

Tears well up, and instead of trying to swallow them down, I let them flow freely. I'm not ashamed anymore. I'm not hiding anything.

Well, I'm hiding *one* thing. But I don't think she'll begrudge me that. The world isn't going to miss a man like Benjamin Edmondson.

Of course Melinda didn't do anything to him. It just made sense to pass the blame onto someone who had already admitted murder.

It was me.

I killed him.

I went to get the framed photograph from my cabin when I told Digby I wouldn't be long, and that was true, I grabbed it and a jacket to try and warm up.

The only difference was I grabbed those *after* I'd already been in Benjamin's room. I went there first.

Benjamin had shouted after I knocked on his door. "What do you want?"

"It's Jasmine," I called. "Your morning treat. Time to wake up."

"Oh!" God, the sheer joy in his voice. "Come on in, then."

Did he not notice the boat leaning heavily to one side, the feeling of us being dragged under? Maybe he was still sleepy. Maybe he thought it was his drugs fucking with him. Either way, he didn't care. I opened the door and went through, closing it quickly behind me. I knew I didn't have much time.

Benjamin was on the bed, covers rumpled around him. He was only in his underwear, gut hanging over his boxers. Seeing me standing there, hair falling about my shoulders, he sat up, rubbing his hands together in glee and smacking his lips.

"What does my morning treat entail?" Benjamin asked.

"Lie down and I'll show you," I said.

He obeyed me immediately.

I knew inside his bedside drawer was a pair of fluffy handcuffs and thick rope; we'd used them together before. The bed in here was not the old-fashioned four-poster kind, but it did have round knobs on each corner. There was enough rope in here to tie each limb, holding him captive with no risk of his getting away or turning the tables.

"Let's put you in the correct position, shall we?" I purred. "Raise your hands above your head."

"Yes, mistress," he whispered, making my skin crawl.

First I handcuffed his wrists, then tied them further with the rope around the bed, making sure the knots were good and tight. He seemed less keen about his ankles being bound, but I carried on regardless, and soon enough he was entirely at my bidding without a chance of escape. Not that this bothered him; I'd never seen him so excited.

"Now let's have some fun," he said.

"You bet," I replied, sitting astride him and trying not to wince as he grew hard beneath me. "I have a game for you."

"A game?"

"You have to guess who I'm talking about."

Benjamin went to touch me, then realized just how tightly I had bound him. "Loosen these a little, will you, darling?"

"Play my game first."

"Fine. Do I get a clue?"

"Of course. Clue number one: she worked on this superyacht last year."

"I'm going to need more than that, sweetheart."

"She was a stewardess. Pretty. Beautiful, even. You liked her very much."

"I like every beautiful woman." He smirked. "Guess you'll have to punish me for not coming up with an answer."

"Punishment comes later," I said, even as I dug my fingernails into his thighs. "Her name was Hallie. You remember her now, don't you? Hallie Attwood."

"Sorry, babe. Like I said, I like every beautiful woman. Doesn't ring a bell."

"She's the stewardess you *murdered* last year. Does that help jog your memory?"

"What?" He finally understood I wasn't here to entertain him.

"You get it now, don't you?" I said. "We didn't magically meet at that bar by chance. You didn't invite me out of your own volition. I purposefully went there, purposefully turned myself into someone you'd want, so I could get on here. Because I wanted to find out what happened to my friend. And how *obvious*, how pathetically obvious that the reason Hallie disappeared was because *you* killed her."

"Get me out of these," he said, shaking his wrists, the handcuffs holding him firmly in place.

"Patience," I told him. "Don't you want to know who I am?"

"I couldn't give a fuck who you are." The anger came easily, but it wasn't from genuine fury. He was *impatient*. He rolled his eyes, as if I was *boring* him. He didn't care. He just really, simply, didn't care. Who I was, who Hallie was, who any of the women who entered his life were. Every one of us was a beautiful, blonde object, to be discarded at will.

We didn't matter.

And it was this that finally solidified everything for me: my decision, what I was going to do, was made by looking at this man's dismissive face and knowing that he would continue treating women however he wanted because he could.

"My name is *Tessa*," I hissed, stressing my name, making sure he knew it. "I worked on here last year too, as a deckhand, not that you'd recognize me. I wasn't quite to your taste then. Those photos of all the stewardesses on that computer—they were yours, weren't they? When did you set that up? How many years has that been there?"

"So what if I had some photos of them all? They weren't shared around. What they don't know can't hurt them."

The first admission. But I wanted more than that.

"What happened to Hallie?"

"I'm not telling you anything, you bitch. Untie me right now."

"You're going to tell me, or I won't."

"Then I can wait."

"You can't. The superyacht is sinking. We haven't got long and then you'll drown with it."

"Ridiculous," he said.

"I assure you it's not. Listen." I watched him strain to hear the engines, enjoying seeing his face pale when he realized he couldn't. "We're going under. Slowly. We're a big vessel, after all. It'll take time."

"Digby will come for me," Benjamin said, but he sounded uncertain.

"Digby doesn't seem to be very pleased with his financial advisor," I said lightly. "He's lost a lot of money. To recoup that, he's sinking *Ophelia* to claim on the insurance."

"What?" He was scared then.

"He's making his escape as we speak. He's not coming for you. He doesn't know you're tied up, and frankly, I don't think he'd care even if he did."

"That's not true!"

"Hey, if that's what you want to gamble on, fine by me." I made to leave, hitching myself up, and he finally broke.

"Wait! I'll tell you what you want to know. Happy now?"

"Delirious. What did you do? Where is she?"

He sighed, as if this was still all one big inconvenience. Forget his anger. *Mine* was raging, ready to explode. "Somewhere in the Mediterranean Sea, I'd wager. Fish food."

And there it was.

Everything I'd been looking for, summarized in the two most horrifying sentences imaginable.

It was as if he'd shot me dead in the chest. I even leaned forward, clutching my heart, a gasp escaping my throat. And Benjamin liked it. I could feel him stirring beneath me, and it was this that made me sit up straight, swallow down my emotions, and get ready for what I was going to do.

"I invited her up to Digby's suite—he let me use it whenever I wanted—under the pretense there was something wrong with the bedding."

I had to breathe like someone who was learning the action for the first time.

"The slut bit me," Benjamin said. "I was in agony. If she didn't want me, why did she lead me on? She was playing hard to get all of a sudden and I wasn't having that."

"She was working," I said. "It was her *job* to be nice to you."

"She was a cocktease," Benjamin replied. "I smacked her round the side of her head to teach her a lesson and she ended up hitting it against the corner of the bedside table. Blood everywhere. Absolute mess. Those sheets were Egyptian cotton, you know. Worth a fortune."

Hallie was really, truly dead. I had my confirmation.

"You *killed* her," I whispered.

"It wasn't my fault." His face was impassive. None of this mattered to him. "If she had just enjoyed herself, it wouldn't have happened. I went off to have a cocktail and a pick-me-up, and when I came back she was gone. Found out the following morning she'd been 'disappeared.' Sometimes these things need to be swept under the carpet. I didn't bother asking how it had been done."

By Melinda and Digby, no doubt. And he didn't even care enough to find out anything more. About this woman he had murdered.

"Had you been harassing her?" I said. "She wrote a note, saying she wanted to leave."

"No, that's the only time I went for her."

Then what was that note about? But I had the end result: Benjamin killed Hallie. That was what I had ultimately come here for.

"What do you want in return, then?" he asked. "It's money, isn't it? I can give you twenty grand. I know that's a lot for people like you. Have a nice holiday and keep quiet."

"You think I want *money*?"

"What else is there?"

What else was there indeed? This was a man who always had money to fall back on. It had never let him down.

"Fuck you," I said.

"Are you going to let me go now?" he said.

"Did Hallie want to be let go too?" I asked him, watching his hope die for good.

Before he could reply, I shoved one of his socks into his mouth so he couldn't shout for help.

"Tessa and Hallie," I said, as I opened the door to leave. I took one last look at him, his pathetic, begging eyes. "You'll remember us now."

And then I left him, ignoring his muffled screams. The ocean would do the rest.

Benjamin was a bad man. I couldn't let him get off that yacht alive. Hallie was *one of his girls*. That meant she wasn't the first, and she wouldn't have been the last. Women like Hallie exist and die because men like Benjamin decide it can happen. I'm not going to pretend what I did was noble, some grand deed that wiped out the wrong he did. Hallie still died. But I sleep better knowing he's at the bottom of the ocean too, that he suffered until his last breath.

She saved my life, and I wish I could have saved hers.

I don't know all the details. I don't know why she left that note. I don't know if things could have been different if I had been on watch that night, if the investigation had been done properly. There was no great conspiracy, no deep dark secret as to why she went missing. No miraculous return either, Hallie disguised as one of the other, looka-like stewardesses all along. That kind of thing only happens in films. She lived; she died. I could hold a lot of resentment for Captain Howard, for his incompetence, but he's getting punished for it. I could go after Digby too, but he's going to prison for sure. I can't let revenge consume me. From now on, I'm choosing to focus on the part where Hallie lived.

"Thank you for everything," I say to her photograph, tears falling on her cheerful face. "Goodbye, Hallie."

When I say this I feel her presence at my side, squeezing my hand.

She's always been there, I realize. With me.

I squeeze back.

And then I allow her to leave, letting her go at last.

CHAPTER FIFTY-ONE

―

SASHA

I t is overcast in London.

Around me, people stride down the street in coats. It's just gone half five, which means it's packed, but I stay where I am, gaze intent on the main entrance of the hospital.

It hasn't changed. Tall blue glass towers casting a shadow across the road, it is as busy as ever. A couple of nurses I recognize leave the building, one of them already reaching in her pocket for her vape as they hurry to the other end of the street. They're chatting and laughing and don't look around, but I still hold my breath and turn my face away.

Droplets of rain begin to fall, and as if in unison everyone opens their umbrellas. I'm grateful for the added disguise.

A message buzzes through on my phone.

Jasmine. Or Tessa, as I should call her now. It's hard not to think of her as Jasmine after all we went through together.

You're doing the right thing, it reads.

Eight weeks on from *Ophelia*, she and I have become real friends. Even when she left hospital before me, she visited every evening, filling me in on the developments with the police. The yacht won't be recovered, but our witness statements have meant Digby won't get away with claiming it was an accident.

We flew back to England last week, though we'll be needed in New York for whenever Digby's trial is. He is facing prison, despite all of the fancy lawyers he has. There's not much they can do against an entire crew all saying the same thing, though he has tried to offer us bribes to drop or change our statements. We've all held firm, even Runa. He won't be buying his way out of this one.

It definitely felt strange, coming home. I went to my parents, curled up in my childhood bed, and didn't leave it for three days straight. Finally started talking to them, and told them everything. Not just about *Ophelia*, but why I ran away in the first place. And Tessa has been constantly supportive. She knows what I am doing today.

The others have stayed in contact too, though I'm not sure how long that'll last. Imogen is training to be a teacher and seeing a therapist to deal with everything (past and present, she said, though I'm not sure what she meant by that), while Axel is back in California working with his father. He said he has a lot of making up to do with him, and I'm not sure what he meant by that either. But he'll be helping support the baby when it's born. Noah is returning to accountancy. Runa has a job as a chef in a Michelin restaurant, and we collectively decided to forget about the theft, given that all the evidence is at the bottom of the Atlantic. She's promised she's learned her lesson, and we're going to give her a second chance. Captain Howard, declared bankrupt, is looking at criminal negligence charges. It's not a happy ending for him, but perhaps it shouldn't be. He let things slide for too long.

Drew hasn't tried contacting me, or anyone else for that matter. He's facing time again. It must be hard, knowing that what connects us is something so horrible that it's easier to break away. I know the temptation of hiding; I've lived it. I don't judge him. But I need to sort my own mess out before I bring him back into my life.

I will, though. I won't let him become as lost as I was.

Jade is the only one of us willing to go back to yachting. She lives and breathes it, I suppose. She's also writing a memoir about everything that happened and has been doing several interviews and appearances, completely in her element, happy to talk to the press. *Below*

Deck have cast her in their next season as chief stewardess and it finally seems like she's got the recognition she's always wanted.

Now, I type a reply to Tessa: *Thank you.*

I'm so lost in my thoughts I almost don't notice the hospital doors sliding open to reveal him in his scrubs, raking a hand through his hair.

Dr. Martin.

I was sure I would revert to my old, panicked self at the sight of him—heart pounding, hands sweating. Or worse, further back, pangs of desire and longing. He is still devastatingly handsome, even in the rain with his face scrunched up. But nothing swells within me. The anxiety will never fully disappear. There is no off switch, no magic spell. Yet I'm not afraid of it anymore. I'm not going to try and swallow it down and pretend it isn't happening. I'll ride through it. I am observing him with a calmness I never thought possible.

He's heading for the car park down the road, and as he goes, I take note of the slight sway of his posture. He can't keep a straight line. He's still drinking.

An exhale escapes me from deep within; this is all the confirmation I need.

The nearest police station is about a twenty-minute walk away, but I manage it in half that time, hurrying through the front door and to the main desk, where a bored-looking young officer is waiting.

"How can I help you?" she asks.

It's now or never. But it doesn't feel daunting. I don't want to run away anymore. I have to face it. Whatever the consequences are, I will take them gladly. I'm only sorry it's taken me this long, and everything I've been through on *Ophelia*, to make things right.

"I need to report a case of medical negligence," I say, "about a patient called Janet Lesley."

EPILOGUE

H allie is bleeding.

I happen to be walking past when I see her, stumbling down the stairs that lead to the owner's suite. She's holding the side of her head, and that's when I see the blood.

The relief in her eyes is immediate. "Thank God you're here. It's Benjamin. He told me to come upstairs, said he wasn't happy with something, so I stupidly followed him, and—"

"Slow down. Take deep breaths. Let me look at that. Come with me." I guide her to one of the empty guest rooms, the only place I can take her where I'm sure no one else will barge in. She sits patiently while I take a flannel and wipe her face clean, then check her injury. She has a nasty cut to her head, the blood reluctant to stop even when I press the flannel against it, making her cry out in pain. It is going to need stitches for certain, as well as a head scan to check she hasn't got a concussion.

She is crying, choking breaths. "I would never . . . I thought he was getting me to clean something. But then he told me he saw how I'd been looking at him, that he knew I was interested. I told him I was leaving. He pushed me on the bed . . . tried to . . . and then he hit me. So hard I fell back and whacked my head on the bedside table. When I came to he was gone."

I understand. Men like Benjamin, it's not a surprise. Of course he would try it on.

Her body shakes. I shrug off my coat, even though it's my favorite, particularly for keeping warm on the open water, and wrap it around her. "You did nothing wrong. We'll clean you up a bit more, and then I'll go and tell Captain Howard you had a fall and we'll go back to Athinios, get you to the hospital."

"A fall?" she echoes, head whipping toward me and making me drop the flannel. "Did you not hear me? This was Benjamin. We need to report it."

"Now, now, we don't need to go to all that fuss. You'll be fine."

"All that fuss? This was assault at the very least. He deserves to be punished!"

"This is a superyacht!" I snap. "We don't divulge guest business. What happened is a private matter and I'm sure Benjamin will compensate you if you feel troubled enough—"

"Jesus Christ," Hallie says. "I don't want his money. You're crazy. I'm going to report him, and I'm going to report you for trying to cover this up."

Report *me*? She wouldn't dare.

"Hallie, it would not do well to cross me," I tell her. "Let's get you to the hospital and you keep your mouth shut."

"You can try and hide the truth all you want," she continues, "but the second I'm off this yacht I'm going to the police. I'll post about this online. I'll bring you all down if I have to."

"Alright!" I say. "I shouldn't have said that. I'm sorry. I wasn't think-ing. Let me go and get the captain. Wait here. Don't move in case you injure yourself further."

"And Tessa," she says, arrogantly smug, thinking she's got me cor-nered. "Please find Tessa. I need her."

"Of course." It's amazing how easily the lie slips off my tongue.

I step out and head toward the bridge, as if I really am going to tell the captain, but the moment I'm on the same floor I stop, listening to the raucous laughter of the guests and the sound of glasses clinking. No one else knows what's happened. I can even hear Benjamin, who has obviously decided someone else will clean up the mess he left behind, as always.

And here I am. What do I do? I can't have Hallie expose what he did, nor tell everyone that I tried to shut her up. I can't have everything I've worked for turn to nothing.

This is my life. Being on yachts—this is me. Before this, I was lost. Offseason, I don't have anyone. No family, no friends, no partner. I don't do anything, don't go anywhere. I prepare for the next season. Here, I am someone. I can't go back to being a nobody. Can't have Hallie ruin my prospects, or have her destroy me with this. I'll be lost. Desperate. On the streets, telling people that once upon a time I rubbed shoulders with billionaires, that long ago I was someone worthwhile.

No. I won't let her take it all away from me.

So what, then?

By the time I come back, plan fully formed, Hallie isn't in the guest room anymore. She's standing in the hallway near one of the fire extinguisher displays, and jumps when she hears me coming.

"Where's Tessa?" she asks. "And the captain?"

"I couldn't find Tessa," I lie. "And the captain has asked to meet us in the owner's suite so he can see what happened and you can explain it to him."

It takes Hallie so long to walk back I'm terrified someone will see us, but thankfully there is no reason for anyone to be near here. As we head through the owner's suite and into the bedroom I can see the evidence for myself.

A lamp knocked over, smashed to the floor. Covers rumpled, expensive sheets stained with Hallie's blood. It's a wonder she's still standing.

As if she can hear my thoughts, Hallie sways, woozy. She's definitely got some kind of concussion. She won't be thinking straight. I have to take my chance.

"Come and get some fresh air," I say, indicating the double doors that lead out to the terrace. "The captain will arrive soon."

She doesn't question how on earth we beat the captain here. This is encouraging.

Quick as a flash, I take the rope from the bedside drawer. I stocked this suite with its goodies myself.

Outside is cold, a dark sky full of clouds. No one will be on deck.

Hallie is leaning against the railing, back to me, when I take the rope and reach over her head and wrap her neck in it. She struggles against it instantly, sending us careering backward. I grip harder, pulling her toward me. She's a fighter, though, even with her head injury. She kicks and kicks. I think she might be trying to scream, or maybe gasp for air. She reaches up and hits me in the face, surprising me, making me release my grasp. She staggers forward onto all fours, trying to wrench the rope from her neck but failing. I can't let her get away, darting forward and grabbing it again, tightening and tightening until she falls limp.

I glance over the top of the rail at the waves below, then look around to see if anyone has heard anything. It's paranoia. Other than the bridge, there are no lights on, and it's impossible for anyone sitting there to see us.

The ocean can do the rest. Carefully, I slide the rope over her head. I must be sensible: I dart into the suite and take a small statue, a tiny but incredibly heavy bust of Odysseus, use the rope to tie it to her ankle and ensure she won't create a nasty surprise later. I brace myself, then push her body off the deck into the black waters below. She's heavier than she looks, but there isn't anywhere else for her to go. I watch as her body falls down into the sea, landing with a loud splash, Odysseus following behind her.

For a moment, she stays on the surface.

The body lies face down in the water, blonde hair fanning outward.

The backs of her arms and legs are visible. Barely, I can make out the glittering silver of her nail varnish.

She's still wearing the coat. Once red and fluffy, it is now sodden and limp, the collar stained dark with blood. The back of her head must have been sticky and wet with it, because a large area has now dried and become encrusted with the stuff.

Was death instant, or a slow suffering? A struggle to breathe as water gathered in her lungs and drowned her?

It is better this way, no matter how much I wanted to see the life leave her eyes.

Well. We have our confirmation now, don't we? The bitch is definitely dead.

I did warn her.

And then she is pulled under with Odysseus, sinking into the murky depths and vanishing forever.

Will anyone notice the coat? Notice that I'm not wearing it anymore, question where it's gone?

I know exactly where I bought it. I can get another before anyone notices.

Time to clean up the rest of this mess.

I'm the chief stewardess; I've been through lines and lines of these bitches and I always come out on top.

ACKNOWLEDGMENTS

First, readers: THANK YOU for buying this book. It is such a privilege to be able to write for you, and I hope you enjoy *I Did Warn Her*.

The second book is infamous for being difficult to write, and my experience was no exception. I got there in the end, but not without the help of some amazing people.

This book wouldn't exist without my agent, Helen Heller, whose insightful feedback reshaped this novel into something I am proud of. We spent many hours discussing plot points and characters at length, and you really brought the best out of me. Thank you so much.

Jemma McDonagh, thank you for your hard work with translation rights. Seeing my books succeed internationally is wonderful. Thank you to all the foreign publishers too.

To Mary Pender and the William Morris Endeavor team, thank you for your representation.

Thank you to my editor, Rachel Kahan, and everyone at William Morrow. To the marketing, publicity, and sales teams, who got this novel in front of readers. To everyone who helped transform this from words in a document to a real book—the copyeditor, proofreader, typesetter, designer, and more—you have my deepest appreciation.

It has been wonderful to join Viking, Penguin. I am very grateful to Rosa Schierenberg, Ellie Hudson, Laura Dermody, and everyone who is part of this great team for the work you have done bringing my books to the UK.

Much love to the booksellers and librarians, whose recommendations make all the difference. Also, to all the book influencers out there on X, Instagram, TikTok, or their own blogs: I couldn't be more thankful. Your posts are so creative and generous, and help spread the word far and wide.

To E. A. Aymar, for always being there. The writing community is so much richer with you in it.

For helping with early drafts, my amazing beta readers and friends: Lally Hunter-Innis, Victoria Vazquez, Sul Hati, and Kelly Mancaruso. All of your comments were absolutely integral to this book being written.

And to all my fellow author friends: thank you. I know I can turn to you for advice whenever I need it.

To my whole family, who are cheering me on and supporting my career every step of the way. Thank you for everything.

My magnificent partner, Joe, who constantly shows me how lucky I am. My earliest reader, my "rubber duck," my source of endless love and encouragement. Thank you, thank you, thank you.

Mum and Dad, my biggest cheerleaders, and there from the very beginning. It is with immense pride that I dedicate this book to you, because I wouldn't be a writer without your support. You instilled in me the belief that I could do anything and achieve any dream—and here I am. You're always the first phone call whenever there is news! Thank you for your unending excitement when each new copy arrives, and to Dad, especially, for sending me positive reviews that make me smile. Both of you truly are the best parents in the world.

Finally, to Toby. My gorgeous cat, who passed away while this book was being written. You lived all nine of your lives to the fullest. Thank you for being a companion on my lap for twenty-one beautiful years.

Sian Gilbert is the author of *She Started It*, a Book of the Month main selection and Amazon Editors' pick. After teaching for almost five years, she now lives in Cambridge with her partner. *I Did Warn Her* is her second novel.

Follow Sian Gilbert on Instagram and X @sianmgilbert.